TRIFLES AND FOLLY 3

A DEADLY CURIOSITIES COLLECTION

GAIL Z. MARTIN

SOL

CONTENTS

TRIFLES & FOLLY 3

A DEADLY CURIOSITIES COLLECTION

by Gail Z. Martin

eBook ISBN: 978-1-64795-025-5
Print ISBN: 978-1-64795-026-2

Cover art by Lou Harper
SOL Publishing is an imprint of DreamSpinner Communications, LLC

Thank you to all my wonderful readers, and everyone who contributes to the book creation process, and to my husband Larry and our family. These books would not exist without you.

INTRODUCTION

Welcome to my world. This is the third collection of short stories and novellas from the Deadly Curiosities' universe, and as odd as it sounds, it began with real life. Authors take inspiration from many places, and for me, life events took me down a dark and mysterious road. It all began with *Buttons.* (Included in *Trifles & Folly,* Volume 1) I was asked to participate in the Solaris anthology *Magic: The Esoteric and Arcane* and had to come up with a new story. I'd written several involving Sorren set in earlier times, but I wanted a fresh take and a modern setting, and Cassidy was born.

At the time, I was dealing with the recent death of my father, and my husband and I were settling his estate, dealing with auctions and appraisers, and sorting through a life-long collection of stuff. Not ordinary stuff, but the kinds of things that provided fodder for ghost stories. Though obviously, I took some creative liberties, some everyday items do have unusual providence, and oh, the things they've seen!

Over the course of the short stories and novels, the characters grow and change, as you'd expect if they were real people. When we first meet Cassidy in *Buttons* and in *Deadly Curiosities,* she is very new in using her gift of psychometry, and the visions often throw her for a loop. As time goes on, she gains more skill—both in controlling her magic and in using it defensively. Teag also grows in his magical abilities, and Sorren proves that continued growth and change are part of a successful long existence. By the time the stories in this collection happen, Cassidy and Teag have gained much greater mastery over their abilities.

This collection includes seven stories set in the Deadly Curiosities universe.

NOTE: One story—Crewel Fate—is an MM paranormal romance with adult content. (The other stories do not have adult content.) It is a direct follow-up to events that take place in *Inheritance* at Teag's birthday party.

I hope you enjoy these stories, and if so, there are more available and more to come, including the full-length novels: *Deadly Curiosities, Vendetta, Tangled Web, Inheritance,* and *Legacy*.

CATSPAW

First appeared in the anthology:
In a Cat's Eye

CATSPAW

"THAT'S THE LAST OF IT," I CALLED BACK TOWARD THE OPEN BACK door of the shop. I heaved the cut-down cardboard boxes into the dumpster. Teag Logan waited in the doorway, scanning the dark, empty alley. A cat yowled in the distance.

"Come back inside, Cassidy," he urged. "I don't know why, but I don't like the vibes I'm getting out here tonight."

Teag's intuition is fueled by strong magic, so I take his "vibes" seriously. I'm pretty good with both intuition and magic myself, and I felt a shiver go down my back. "There's something out here," I murmured, looking down the alley toward the streetlight at the end and seeing a dark shape in the roadway I had not noticed before.

"That's what I'm trying to tell you," Teag said. "Come back where it's safe."

Wardings protected the old antique shop against dark magic. Salt and iron lay beneath the sill of every door and window to repel evil, and as an added protection, sometimes we had a nearly six-hundred-year-old vampire staying in the secret room in the shop basement. Teag and I both wore protective amulets, and when it came to defending ourselves, we were no slouches. So when I lingered a moment longer, I took a calculated risk.

"We need to see what that is," I said, jerking my head toward the lump that lay near the far end of the alley. I let my athame slide down beneath my sleeve into my hand and jangled the old dog collar on my left wrist, smiling as the ghost of a large dog appeared at my side. Teag muttered something under his breath and joined me a moment later, carrying a wooden martial arts staff and a wicked knife.

Together, we advanced on the shape, which lay still in the dim glow of the distant street light. A mangy cat paced near the body, staying just out of reach as we approached, even though Bo's ghost growled and stepped toward it. If the cat could see Bo, the ghost dog didn't intimidate him. I paid attention to what my senses were telling me, shivering at the resonance something evil left in its wake. Yet the closer we got to the thing in the road, the more certain I became that the threat itself had come and gone.

"So much blood." I hadn't realized that I spoke aloud until Teag glanced at me, eyes wide with the same horror that thrummed through my gut. A woman's body lay at our feet, clothing soaked red, wreathed in a pool of crimson. Then Bo growled, and I followed his gaze to the necklace around the dead woman's throat. For all the mess, the body appeared intact, no claw or bite marks, nothing to explain why she bled out on the cobblestones.

"I don't think this was a mugging," Teag murmured, bending down beside the corpse, careful to stay out of the blood. He brushed the back of his fingers against the cuff of the woman's jacket, one of the few places not saturated with gore. At the same time, I crouched down on the other side of the body, letting my hand hover above the necklace.

Teag's hand jerked back. "Seriously bad juju. She never knew what hit her," he muttered, having picked up that much from the brief contact. He's got Weaver magic, the ability to weave spells into cloth —or recognize magic woven into fabric. I recoiled an instant later, without ever having to touch the piece of jewelry.

"It's the necklace," I said, breathless from the dark power I sensed. "I'm certain it's what killed her—and it's too dangerous to let it out of our sight."

"Then we'd better get it off her before the cops come," Teag

4

replied matter-of-factly. "And there's no way in hell you're touching it, so don't even try."

I'm Cassidy Kincaide, owner of Trifles and Folly, a 350-year-old antique and curio shop in historic, haunted Charleston, South Carolina. Nothing about us is what it appears. For one thing, I'm a psychometric —able to read the history and magic of objects by touching them. Teag is my assistant store manager, best friend, and sometimes bodyguard, and he's got his own powerful magic.

My business partner, Sorren—the vampire who keeps a safe room in the store's basement—founded Trifles and Folly back when Charleston was new, always working with a member of my family throughout the years. Sure, we buy and sell antiques. But our real job is fighting off supernatural threats and getting haunted and cursed objects off the market. When we succeed, no one notices. When we fail, the aftermath gets chalked up as a natural disaster.

Which is why we were crouched over a dead body in a back alley, preparing not just to "tamper" with evidence, but to remove a key piece from the scene of a crime—because whoever worked the magic that killed this woman was out of the league of the Charleston PD.

Teag ran back to the shop and returned a moment later with a pair of pliers, a lead box, and a long strip of cloth. I recognized the fabric as a piece Teag created, with protective magic woven into the warp and woof. I kept a lookout while he wrapped the fabric around his hand so that no skin touched the pliers, then snipped through the chain that held the necklace in place and gingerly placed the jewelry inside the lead box. The mangy cat watched every move from a distance.

"We need to get out of here," I muttered as he snapped a picture of the necklace with his phone, then flipped the lid shut. Bo's ghost wagged once, satisfied that I was in no immediate danger, and winked out. The odd alley cat rose from where it sat and padded off into the shadows. Teag and I jogged back to the store, closed and locked the back door, and exchanged a look.

"The sooner we're gone from here tonight, the better," Teag warned, placing the lead box on a shelf in my office for safekeeping and locking the door, just in case. "The bar up the street has pay phones in the back; I'll call in a scuffle in the alley and let the cops take it from there. Nice and untraceable."

I nodded, still feeling shaky from the sight of all that blood. "I'll call Sorren and let him know, and then I'll see if Rowan or Lucinda have heard anything or picked up any bad mojo." Rowan is a witch who's worked on a few situations with us, while Lucinda is a good friend who also happens to be a powerful Voudon mambo. If someone was working powerful dark magic in Charleston, odds were good that one or both of them sensed it.

"Okay," Teag agreed. "I'll walk you to your car. And when I get home, I'll see if I can find out anything about that necklace—and monitor the police chatter and hack their system to see what they learn about the vic. I'll call you later, let you know what they said."

"Deal."

As it turned out, Lucinda was waiting for me on the piazza of my Charleston single house, what most people call a porch. I didn't have to ask how she got past the wardings since she's the one who put them in place. Lucinda's suit suggested she had come straight from her work at the university, and its sand and ochre colors offset the darker tone of her skin. "Child, there's trouble brewing," she greeted me.

I locked the door leading off the side of the piazza to the street and let us into the house. Baxter, my Maltese, yipped and bounced in greeting until I scooped him up in my arms as we entered. "Tell me what you know," I said to Lucinda as I led us into the kitchen.

I poured glasses of sweet tea for both of us, then fed Baxter his dinner, and motioned for Lucinda to have a seat at the table. She savored the ice-cold tea for a moment and let out a long sigh.

"Someone is messing around with very bad magic," Lucinda said, giving me a sharp glance that told me she suspected I already had an inkling about that. I nodded, confirming her hunch. "Whoever's doing the magic is sloppy—which makes things even worse."

"You think he—or she—doesn't know what they're messing with?"

Lucinda shrugged. "Or maybe doesn't have the training to handle what they're attempting. Don't know. There's no mistaking that it's dark magic, so I don't think it's something someone blundered into by accident."

"Can you locate who's doing it?" I toyed with my glass of tea, reaching down to lift Baxter onto my lap, where he settled down, content to be in his rightful place.

Lucinda concentrated, then shook her head. "No. At least, nothing I've tried so far has worked. I've sensed the…ripples…of power, but it's too quick to get a lock on it. And there's something very odd about the way it feels. Not quite…human."

"What kind of 'not human?'" I asked.

Lucinda was quiet for a moment, sorting through her thoughts. "I'm sorry. That's all I can say right now. I wanted to warn you—but I get the feeling you already knew."

I told Lucinda about the woman in the alley. "I'll come by tomorrow and have a look at that necklace," she replied. "Don't you touch it. I'll look into it."

"Thank you," I said. "But we've got to hurry. Whoever's behind it —they've already killed once." I paused. "Maybe that's all there'll be. Maybe it was something personal. Still bad, still murder—but it might not be a crime spree."

She shook her head. "I don't think so. The ripples—I've felt them before, not long ago. I think there's been at least one more. We just don't know who it was." Lucinda finished her tea and stood.

"If anyone can figure that part out, it's Teag," I replied. "Let me see what I can find out from my sources, and I'll see you tomorrow at the shop."

I walked Lucinda to the door. "Cassidy—you and Teag need to watch your backs," she warned. "What's Sorren have to say about all this?"

I sighed. "He and Archibald Donnelly went to Philadelphia yesterday. I've left a voicemail, but he can't always reply when he's handling a problem." Donnelly was another ally, a powerful necromancer. He and Sorren went north to help my Philadelphia counterparts deal with something nasty and undead. "No idea when they're planning to get back."

7

"Then you and Teag take extra care," Lucinda said in a no-nonsense voice, the one I'm sure she used in her day job as a professor to chastise errant college students. "Someone finds out you two are looking into this; you might draw the wrong kind of attention."

"Will do," I promised as I saw her out. I locked the door and leaned against it. Baxter trotted out of the kitchen and sat down in front of me, blinking his black button eyes. "Not sure what to do, Bax," I said, running a hand back through my hair. "We've got a dead body, a cursed necklace, and a rogue witch—who might not be human. Even for us, that's a lousy way to start the week."

The next morning, I found a witch waiting for me as I opened the door to the shop.

"We need to talk," Rowan said. Anyone watching might have thought she was a tourist jumping the gun on a day of shopping, but I heard the serious note in her voice. I unlocked the door and gestured for her to enter first. The blast from the air conditioner made me tilt my face back in bliss since outside was already broiling and heavy with humidity.

"Teag called you?" I locked the door behind us and headed toward the office, knowing what Rowan came to see.

"Was he supposed to?" She looked honestly surprised. I slid her a sidelong look. Tall and slender, blonde hair up in a twist and wearing a loose green summer dress, Rowan didn't look like anyone's idea of a "witch"—unless you knew enough to recognize the protective runes on her bracelets and the sigils carefully stitched along the hem of her dress. "I felt a pulse of dark magic last night and came to warn you— except that the closer I got to the store, the stronger it felt."

"I might know why." I led the way into the office and pointed at the lead box on the shelf.

Rowan's eyes narrowed, and I could have sworn she let out a soft hiss. "Oh, that is *not* good." She glanced at me. "What's in there?"

"A necklace we took off the body of a lady who bled to death in the alley with no visible wounds." I fixed her with a look. "And no, I'm not touching that box."

Rowan smirked. She knew about my magic. She said a warding against evil under her breath and pulled a cloth down from a peg on the wall, a piece of fabric the size of a bath towel that Teag wove with protective magic running through its fibers. Then she took a deep breath, centered her power, and wrapped the cloth around the lead box, lifting it down carefully. I moved ahead of her into the break room and drew a thick circle of salt on the table. Rowan placed the box in the middle of the circle and withdrew the fabric.

"Even through the lead, something is making my skin crawl," Rowan said, eyeing the box as if it might attack.

"Do you need to open it, if you can sense it from here?"

Rowan frowned. "Unfortunately, yes. The lead dampens too much for me to get a good read.

I heard a key in the front door lock, heard the chimes as the door opened, and then Teag's voice rang out. "Cassidy? I've got Lucinda with me."

"We're back here," I replied. "And Rowan's already on it."

Teag clicked the lock, and a moment later, he and Lucinda came into the break room. Lucinda's gaze fell to the box immediately, and she fell back a step as if something pushed her. "Uh, uh, uh," she murmured, shaking her head.

Teag took the warded fabric from Rowan and carefully lifted the lid of the lead box. Even though I was several feet away, I could feel the resonance of the blood-soaked necklace like dirty oil on my skin.

Lucinda clucked her tongue. "Looks like dirty deeds done dirt cheap—and dead wrong."

I caught a glance between Lucinda and Rowan. "Meaning?"

Lucinda cocked her head as if waiting for Rowan to speak first. "Whoever did the spell has power but no finesse," Rowan said. Lucinda gave a nod in agreement. "A talented amateur maybe, or a fledgling witch attempting something out of their league."

"The necklace is cursed—and there's a whiff of death magic as well," Lucinda said, frowning like a chef trying to suss out the subtle flavors of a recipe.

"If it's cursed to kill, isn't that death magic?" Teag asked.

"Necromancy," Lucinda clarified. "Remember—I told you last night something about the power wasn't human."

Teag and I exchanged a glance. "I thought Donnelly was the only necromancer in Charleston," I said.

"And that's as it should be," Rowan replied. "But there's nothing to say someone new hasn't come to town—maybe even since Sorren and Donnelly went to Philadelphia."

"Necromancy isn't beginner magic." Teag eyed the box warily but did not move closer.

"No, it isn't—and it's dangerous power, even when it's used by a seasoned witch," Rowan agreed.

"But isn't necromancy about bringing someone back from the dead?" I asked. "How does that factor into a necklace that killed the wearer?"

Lucinda shrugged. "That's what we need to find out."

"Is there anything special about the necklace itself?" Rowan moved close enough to peer into the box, as did Lucinda.

"Unless you see modifications that I didn't, I found the same necklace online—just costume jewelry, nothing special," Teag said. When Lucinda and Rowan stepped back, Teag used the spelled cloth to carefully latch the lid and replace the box in the office.

"You said you'd felt ripples of power before last night," I said, looking to Lucinda. "Do you remember when?"

"A week ago. On Thursday."

Rowan glanced up. "I felt something then too—I just wasn't sure what. Nothing good."

"Anything else?"

Lucinda frowned, thinking. "Last Saturday, I felt a surge of something, and then it was gone. It felt...farther away than the other times." She managed a wan smile. "I remember because I was at the market, and I thought I might be getting a sinus headache from rain coming in."

Teag had already pulled his laptop from his messenger bag and set it up on the table, carefully dispelling the salt circle. "Thanks. That might narrow things down."

I glanced toward the front room. "I need to open the shop. Thanks for coming by," I said, walking with Rowan and Lucinda toward the door. "Can you keep your radar tuned in and let us know if you sense anything else?"

Rowan rolled her eyes at the idea of magic being like radar, but Lucinda chuckled. "Hailing frequencies open," she deadpanned. "We'll do some digging of our own." She frowned. "Don't you and Teag go busting in on anyone without us, you hear? Necromancy's nothing to fool with, and even an amateur witch can be dangerous."

If I doubted her, the memory of a blood-soaked corpse in the alley was enough to prove her point.

For a mid-week morning, the shop was busy with tourists, and then a soon-to-be bride and her mother came in to look at vintage silver-ware. I glimpsed Teag hunched over his laptop in the break room, but it was almost lunchtime before I had the chance to see what he had found.

"Lucinda and Rowan's 'ripples' helped a lot," Teag said, turning his laptop so I could see what he found. "The lady in the alley wasn't the only vic. Two other dead men, on the days Lucinda and Rowan felt something in the magic, both covered in blood without any visible wounds."

"Show me."

Teag's Weaver magic gave him the ability to weave disparate strands of data into information, making him one hell of a hacker. Normal firewalls didn't even slow him down. "Charleston police found a guy in a locked, parked car near the airport last Thursday. Soaked in blood, not a mark on his body." He brought up the police file on the screen, and I glanced at the details.

"What's that?" I pointed at a gray blur on the dead man's pant leg. Teag enlarged the image.

"Looks like he got against something—maybe pet fur?" Teag replied, leaning closer to make out the image. "Police file said they had to send Animal Control after a cat that wouldn't leave the crime scene."

"And then Saturday, another death, same thing. This time, a guy dies in a locked bathroom at a coffee shop. Security cameras show no one went in or out except the vic. No windows in the room, no other exit—nada." We watched the security footage from multiple cameras, saw the victim go into the bathroom as no one else showed up on any of the other feeds, nothing except an alley cat pacing in front of the bathroom door.

I sighed. "That looks like the mangy cat we saw out back. Can't be a coincidence. It's got to mean something. What next?"

Teag sat back in his chair and tilted his head to loosen his shoulders, then stretched his arms, laced his fingers together, and cracked his knuckles. "Now I really start hacking, looking for anything the vics had in common—besides dying bloody and that damned cat. There's got to be a connection—but it's going to take some digging." He raised an eyebrow. "On the other hand, with three victims, I've got a better chance of narrowing down matches than I would with just two."

"I'll run the store; you dig. I'm sure you'll find the connections."

By five o'clock when I closed the store, Teag was still at his spot at the breakroom table. I ordered pizza, figuring we had a few more hours ahead of us. "I think I know the why and the where, but not who or how," Teag announced as I walked into the room.

I sat down next to him. "Do tell."

Teag turned the laptop to show me his screen. "None of them owned a cat. But all of them died wearing or holding a piece of jewelry. And all of them went to the same jewelry repair kiosk the day before they died."

I frowned. "I get the 'where' but what's the 'why?'"

Teag met my gaze. "They all testified against a teenager named Ben Calvert six years ago when he went to trial for manslaughter."

"So that means Calvert's either the witch or the person who hired the witch—right?"

Teag shook his head. "Not that easy. Calvert was underage. I only got his name by hacking into the private files of a reporter who covered the trial. The media didn't release the name, and the records were sealed."

"So he changed his name and disappeared," I mused. "He could be anywhere."

"He could be—but let's start looking at that jewelry repair kiosk."

"So he goes by Brian Cade now," Rowan murmured from her seat in the back of the car, staring out the window at the night. "Same initials."

"Yeah," Teag replied. "The man at the kiosk said he started four months ago—a month before the murders began."

"He must have been targeting the victims all along," I mused. "And it's too much to think coincidence sent all three of them to the same kiosk right after he started working there."

Teag shook his head. "I'm betting he sent them all a special discount or coupon to lure them in. I don't think he left any of it to chance."

Teag, Lucinda, Rowan, and I parked on a dark suburban side street, watching the house at the edge of town where we'd tracked Calvert. "Can you tell anything more about his magic—or about the necromancy?" I asked. We were each fairly powerful with magic in our own ways, but none of us was a necromancer, and going up against that kind of power gave me good reason to be nervous.

"You know the plan," Teag said quietly. "Let's go."

Lucinda and I headed toward the front door while Teag and Rowan went around back. The small house had just one floor and what might be a loft or small attic above. Not much crawlspace and no basement. If Calvert was home, it wouldn't be hard to find him.

I laid down a salt line around the front of the house while Lucinda chalked *veves* to invoke the protection of Papa Legba and Baron Samedi, two of the most powerful Voudon Loas who held authority over life and death. Teag completed the salt line so that it went around the rest of the house, trapping the energies we released inside. We weren't taking any chances.

My phone vibrated silently in my pocket, the signal I'd been waiting for. I let the athame slip down into my hand and sent a cold blast of power toward the entrance, splintering the wood as it ripped from its hinges. I could hear Teag kicking in the back door, as Lucinda began to chant. With a shake of my left wrist, Bo's ghost materialized at my side, and before I could say a word, he let out a low growl and lunged inside, chasing after that same mangy cat from the crime scenes.

Lucinda and I charged in the front while Teag and Rowan barged into the back. The living room looked like the set to a horror movie, with candles burning on every flat surface and sigils drawn in blood on every wall. The carpet lay in a heap to one side, and more markings covered the floorboards, along with an obsidian knife and a bowl of blood. Calvert stood in the middle of the room, looking more like a junkie than a killer. Eyes sunken, cheeks hollow, and unshaven, brown hair lank and dirty, he stared at us like he was coming off a bad trip.

"You shouldn't be here," he said in a wrecked voice. "I'll kill you like I killed them. Aren't you scared? I'm a witch."

Rowan snorted. She raised one hand and clenched her fist. Calvert dropped to his knees as if he'd been sucker-punched. "I'm the witch. You're a poser with a good spell."

I kept my athame pointed at Calvert, backing Rowan up. I'd put bigger bad guys through walls with the blast of power my athame harnessed, and after seeing what Calvert did to his victims, I wouldn't lose sleep about roughing him up a little.

Teag and Lucinda each made a slow walk around the room's perimeter. "What I don't get is why he needed necromancy to kill those people with cursed objects," I said.

"He didn't." We all turned to look at Lucinda. "He needed a familiar to work the curse. Didn't you?" she added, fixing Calvert with a glare that made him tremble. Rowan held him with her power, forcing him to stay kneeling, hands at his side as if bound.

"You're so smart, you figure it out," he snarled.

"That's why that damned cat's been everywhere," I said. "He's the familiar." That's when I realized that Bo and the cat were sitting side by side like besties.

For the first time, I got a good look at the cat itself. Mangy didn't begin to cover it. I couldn't tell what color the cat's matted, dirty fur might have been originally. Chunks of fur were missing, the tail seemed abnormally short, and one ear had rotted away. The cat fixed me with a stare, desperate but too proud to beg. "He brought the cat—the familiar—back from the dead," I murmured. "Against its will."

"Where did you find the curse, boy?" Lucinda's voice held an undercurrent of power, and from the look on Calvert's face, that magic compelled him to speak the truth.

"I found an old book in a second-hand store," Calvert spat. "It wasn't hard to get everything I needed, but I've only got a little bit of magic, and that was a problem." The look on his face made it clear that we would all be next on his list if he had a choice in the matter. "Then I read that the familiar of a powerful witch can share its power with a novice. There was a guy a few towns over that everyone said was a witch with a freaky cat. I thought maybe I could buy the cat—or steal it. But when I got there, they were both dead."

Calvert licked his lips nervously. "But the old book—it had a bunch of spells on all kinds of things. And there was this ritual to bring something back from the dead. I didn't need the old guy, just the cat."

"So you used necromancy to bring the cat back to life and used the cat to work the curses," Rowan supplied, contempt clear in her voice.

The unhinged look in Calvert's eyes said more than any confession. "They testified against me. Sent me to jail. They had it coming."

We ignored him. "So what now?" I asked. "Release the spell on the cat, and he loses his mojo?"

Rowan frowned. "A bit more than that, I'm afraid. Problem with dabbling in magic that's out of your league," she added with a withering look at Calvert. "Necromancy comes at a cost—blood, life force...souls. A trained necromancer figures out what he's going to owe before he does the spell. Our boy here didn't read the fine print, and now he has a balance due."

For the first time, Calvert's eyes glinted in fear. "What do you mean?"

"Gotta pay the power bill," Lucinda replied, an unpleasant smile touching her lips. "And it's time to pull the plug."

"Found it." We all looked to Teag as he held up a small wooden box. "Cat bones. Vertebra—bits of its tail. Am I right?"

"Go to hell," Calvert snapped.

Teag set the box on the floor and poured a stream of salt on it from a container in his pocket, then used one of the candles to kindle the old wood into flame. Rowan began to chant in a language I didn't understand, but I felt chills down my back just the same. Lucinda sang strange words in a quiet voice while I kept my athame trained on Calvert.

I smelled pipe smoke and heard a dog bark from the front porch. I glimpsed a tall, thin man in a tuxedo and a top hat, dark glasses hiding the empty eye sockets of his skull, standing in the doorway. The mangy cat stood up with an air of threadbare dignity and walked straight toward the apparition, pausing only to fix Calvert with a baleful glare before it sauntered to the door.

Outside, two powerful Voudon Loa, Papa Legba and Baron Samedi, guardians of the underworld, waited to claim what belonged to them. The necromancer's cat went willingly.

Calvert did not.

Payback's a bitch.

THE ADVENTURE OF THE MELTED SAINT

First appeared in the anthology:
Baker Street Irregulars

THE ADVENTURE OF THE MELTED SAINT

"Don't take this the wrong way, Alistair, but if you're here, it means trouble."

Alistair McKinnon, Curator of the Lowcountry Museum of Charleston, jokingly preened. "Why, Cassidy! At my age, that's one of the nicest things anyone has said to me in a while. Do I look suitably dangerous?"

Alistair stooped, though the doorway was still an inch above his thinning brown hair. Today he wore a blue seersucker suit with a red bowtie, the natural apparel of the sartorially-inclined, old-school Charlestonian blue-blood. He held a cardboard box, and despite our banter, his brow furrowed with worry.

"You don't usually bring me your mail for show and tell. What's up?"

"For starters," Alistair replied, "I think this package arrived with its own ghost."

I figured that something supernatural lay behind his visit. That's normal for me. I'm Cassidy Kincaide, owner of Trifles and Folly, an antique and curios store in historic, haunted Charleston, South Carolina, and I've got a couple of big secrets. First, I'm a psychometric, which means I can read the history—or magic—of objects by touching them. That comes in handy with my second secret, which is that Teag, my assistant store manager, has his own magical ability to weave spells into fabric or weave data and hack computers with supernatural ease.

And those two secrets roll up to our biggest one—Trifles and Folly really exists to get dangerous magical items off the market and out of the wrong hands. We're part of a covert Alliance of mortals and immortals dedicated to shutting down dangerous supernatural threats with extreme prejudice and have been since our founding over three hundred years ago. When we do our job right, no one notices. When we screw up, the death and destruction usually gets chalked up to a natural disaster.

"Maggie can cover the front of the store for a while," I said. Maggie gave me a nod. She knows a little bit about what we do, though not quite everything, for her own safety. Alistair knows about my magic, but not about Teag's abilities and the Alliance. It's complicated.

Teag and I showed Alistair into the small break room kitchen, and Alistair put the box onto the table. He declined Teag's offer of tea or coffee. Teag went ahead and poured a big glass of sweet tea for me, figuring I'd need it to recover after I read whatever objects were causing Alistair fits.

"We received this box in the mail last week from the Adirondack Museum in New York State," Alistair said. "Apparently, it had been in their basement for nearly a hundred years. They sent it here because they felt the people connected to these objects had a stronger history with Charleston than they did with upstate New York." He shrugged. "I'd agree with them on that part, but they didn't mention that a ghost came along for the ride."

I eyed the box without touching it. If an object had really strong magic, I could often get an impression before I made physical contact. That was helpful because then I could brace myself for what was coming. "I'm not getting any really bad vibes," I said, letting my hand hover a few inches above the box. "What kind of problems has it been causing you?"

"The poor woman who works in shipping and receiving broke down sobbing when she handled the box. She was so distraught we had to send her home. No idea why—except the box was in her office all day," Alistair said. "Everyone who comes in contact with it mentions feeling down or sad, having a sudden change of mood. It's wreaking havoc with the museum staff."

Alistair's gaze slid away, embarrassed. "I have to tell you, I had a terrible time on the way over struggling with an overwhelming sadness that just came on me out of nowhere, for no good reason," he admitted. "I'm really hoping you can help. We can't put this on display. We'd have to offer free counseling with every admission ticket."

Now that Alistair mentioned it, I felt a strong downward tug on my mood, which had been pretty good until he showed up. Teag nodded, letting me know he was feeling it too. I closed my eyes and tried to get a bead on what I was feeling. Sadness. Regret. Those were strong. There was something else…a sense of something hidden, something secret.

"I'm not picking up anything dangerous." I opened my eyes. "But there are some strong emotions attached. Why don't you lay out the contents, and I'll see what I can find out for you." I gave Alistair an encouraging smile. "Once we know what we're dealing with, we can figure out better how to neutralize the supernatural heebie-jeebies."

Teag opened the box and set the items out on the table. The contents were an interesting jumble: An old journal, a stack of yellowed envelopes tied with twine, a man's ring, and a melted gold coin. There was part of a burned piece of stationary as well.

"What do you know about the previous owner or owners of the pieces?" I asked, still not ready to commit myself by touching anything.

"Not much," Alistair said with a sigh. "They came from the estate of a Mr. Jacob Whitley, of the New York Whitleys," he added. If that was supposed to mean something to me, I didn't get the reference. I raised an eyebrow quizzically, and he continued. "A very prominent and wealthy family around the turn of the last century. Made their money in a line of retail stores."

"The journal belonged to Marie de Brise Chastain," he went on. "You recognize those names?"

"The de Brise family and the Chastain family have been Charlestonian movers and shakers since the Huguenot days."

"The letters are between Rebecca Dumont and Mr. Whitley," Alistair continued. "Everything dates to around 1920."

I moved my hand closer to the objects and caught a flash of sorrow, a glimpse of flames, and the shadowy figure of a man. "There's some kind of tragedy involved," I said.

Alistair nodded. "Marie Chastain was killed in a fire in 1920. Jacob Whitley, a suitor, escaped with his life but was badly scarred. Rebecca Dumont was a friend of Marie."

"How did all of these pieces end up in the mountains of New York?" Teag asked.

"I have no idea," Alistair replied. "We hadn't started to research the pieces yet. I did put a call in to the Chastain family for information, but no one has called back."

"All right," I mustered my courage. "Let's see what I can find out."

I sat down at the table and reached for the diary. Later, Teag could read the journal entries, but for now, I wanted to pick up on the resonance of strong emotions left behind. The image of a woman's face came to mind. Not conventionally pretty, but with regular features.

"It's not magical," I said. "Mostly...not quite sad, but wistful? I'm guessing Marie might have had a lot of dreams she didn't get the chance to fulfill," I parsed through the images that came to mind. A shadow flickered in my inner sight. Not dangerous, but furtive. A man's silhouette, there and gone. Odd.

This time, I picked up the letters. The handwriting on the top envelope was faded, in the type of ink that told me it had been written with a fountain pen. The old-style script was a woman's writing, neat and compact. This time, I got a mental image of two people. One was a petite woman who wore her red hair in a bob. She must have been Rebecca. The other was of a dark-haired man whose face I couldn't quite make out, whom I guessed was Jacob. *Was he the shadow I glimpsed before?* I wondered. I picked up a sense of uneasiness, of something being out of place, and a hint of something secretive.

"You haven't read the letters?"

Alistair shook his head. "We really haven't had the box long enough to do more than catalog the contents."

"Interesting," I said, wondering what the letters and journal would reveal when Teag read them.

The sheet of stationery was partly burned. It looked like someone had snatched it out of the flames. After all this time, it radiated anger and disapproval. "You have pushed my patience to the breaking point," I read aloud. "There will be consequences." The man's handwriting was strong and sweeping. The note was unsigned.

"Any idea who wrote this?" I asked.

Alistair shook his head. "None. Sounds rather ominous, doesn't it?"

"Did they ever figure out what caused the fire?" Teag questioned. "Was it an accident?"

"From what I could find, it was blamed on a gas leak," Alistair replied. "Of course, forensics back then weren't what they are today."

I knew the coin and the man's ring would be the worst of the items, which is why I saved them for last. The ring gave me a jolt when I touched it. I sensed Jacob's energy and Marie's as well. *Was the ring a gift from her?* The energy was off, discordant, jumbled. I couldn't get a clear read on it, but it made me jumpy.

"Had the three of them been in any kind of trouble?" I asked. "It might even have been a scandal rather than something illegal. I think the three of them had a secret, but they aren't giving it up easily."

"Nothing comes to mind, other than the fire that claimed Marie's life," Alistair said. "I can have a look through the archives when I go back to the museum."

"I'll do some digging online," Teag added, "and Mrs. Morrissey from the Archive might know something too."

"When we hear back from the Chastain family, I'll make some discrete inquiries," Alistair added. Alistair was the soul of discretion, a necessity for fundraising and keeping well-heeled donors happy.

History could be messy, and a city like Charleston not only had ghosts in every old house but plenty of skeletons in closets as well.

I steeled myself and picked up the melted gold coin. Suddenly, I was propelled into a vision. *I saw the scene through someone else's eyes. The room was a well-appointed parlor, decorated in the style common at the turn of the nineteenth century. I smelled smoke and felt panic course through me as flames engulfed the heavy draperies that framed the windows.*

It was hard to breathe. The fire was spreading fast. Someone screamed. I ran for the door, only to find it blocked by more flames. Marie was trying to knock the burning draperies away from the window with a chair. A couple of the panes in the window were broken. Rebecca ran to the other door. It opened to safety. She beckoned for us to follow her.

Some of the burning draperies had caught the couch on fire, and the horsehair stuffing made thick, black smoke. The carpet was burning too. I could see Marie, but I couldn't get to her, and then a wall of fire cut us off...

I came back to myself with a gasp. Teag shoved a glass of strong, sweet iced tea into my hand, and I gulped it, trying to recover. I let go of the gold coin, and it gave a metallic ring as it hit the table.

"I saw the fire," I said. "I was seeing through Jacob's eyes. The room went up in flames so fast. He couldn't get to Marie in time."

Alistair picked up the twisted coin. "It's a twenty-dollar gold piece," he remarked. "A Saint Gaudens, named for the engraver who designed it." He held it up to the light. "Hard to read the date with all the damage, but the gold alone is worth a lot more than twenty dollars in today's market." He set it back down. "Pity it's partly melted. A coin like that goes for a lot of money in good condition, although of course, the gold itself is still valuable in spite of the damage."

We didn't deal in a lot of old coins, but I was familiar with the "Saints" as collectors called them. The engraving was a work of art, and the luster of the gold made it amazing to me that people actually spent the coins back in the day. They seemed too beautiful for mere currency. I looked at the twisted gold coin and felt a stab of sadness for the young people whose lives had taken a terrible turn because of that fire.

"What about the ghost?" Alistair asked.

I could sense a presence hovering just beyond my Sight, but unlike some of the revenants I've run into, this spirit kept its distance. I couldn't make out a face, just a faint shadowy form. Mostly, I felt disappointment and longing, as well as deep sorrow.

"You don't have any idea who gave the box to the Adirondack Museum?" I asked.

Alistair shook his head. "I've already asked them for any records they have about the acquisition. But they did a major renovation a while back, and some old records have been misplaced. Or it just might be that the 'gift' wasn't significant enough to do more than log it." He shrugged. "We'll have to wait and see."

"I can sense a spirit connected to the items," I said. "But since all three of the people involved are dead now, it could be any of them. It might be Marie, or it could be either Rebecca or Jacob if they held onto the items all those years. I can't tell from what I can see of the ghost right now." I shook my head.

"Will you look into it for me, please?" Alistair asked. "And see if there's a way to get rid of the ghost so we can store the items without giving everyone a breakdown?"

I chuckled. "I think we can handle that. But first, I'd like to figure out just why this ghost is hanging around—and what secret it's been keeping all these years."

"It's not really a job for the Alliance," Teag observed after Alistair left. He put the pieces in our store safe. Nothing like a lead box several inches thick to temper supernatural bad mojo. Locked up in there, the package shouldn't affect our moods the way it had caused mayhem at the museum. I hoped.

"No it isn't," I agreed. "I'm not getting the sense that the ghost is any danger, and there doesn't seem to be a supernatural threat to the rest of the world. But I'm intrigued," I admitted. "And I think that there's a story here that hasn't been told. Maybe if we find out what the secret is, the ghost will go away on its own."

"Alistair's already contacted the family," Teag said. "Let me do some digging into my sources."

"The Chastain family is still prominent in Charleston, and it's been around a long time," I replied.

"Are you going to head over to the Archive?"

I nodded. "Yes. But I've got a stop to make on the way. I think this is tailor-made for Charleston's most famous private detective."

"Cassidy! So good to see you. Come on in." Shelley Holmes welcomed me as I arrived at her home at two twenty-one Baker Street, out near the airport. She wore a satin purple bathrobe—more of a long smoking jacket—over what appeared to be loose silk pants and top.

Shelley cleaned away piles of papers and magazines to make room. "Please, have a seat," she motioned to the couch while she took up the one armchair that wasn't piled high with odds and ends.

"You said on the phone that you've got a case for me. How very exciting. Do tell."

Shelley Holmes was a prodigy. She studied chemistry and martial arts, became first violin with the Charleston Symphony, and filled her home with an homage of books and collectibles to literatures' greatest shamuses, private eyes, gumshoes, and detectives.

After she transitioned, Shelly Holmes invited her best friends for dinner to share the news and remained just as focused and indefatigable as ever.

I laid out what we knew about the objects Alistair had brought in, as well as poor doomed Marie Chastain and her friends. Shelley listened intently, puffing on a vape version of a clay pipe.

"What a lovely mystery. I am happy to take the case."

"How much is your fee?" I couldn't help glancing around the room. On one wall were framed posters from Sherlock Holmes's many silver screen and TV incarnations. On another wall, a Weber pistol hung in a shadow box next to a deerstalker cap that had been a movie prop. Several different sets of the collected tales of the "hound of Baker Street" graced the bookshelves along with a pipe stand holding a variety of tobacco pipes and other oddments.

Shelley was eccentric, and here in the South, we value eccentricity. I had never known anyone to so fully take on every attribute of a literary character to become a literal embodiment. Fortunately, a brief stint in rehab years ago got Shelley over her recreational use of cocaine, and she had promised her friends she would make sure that element of authenticity remained in the past.

"Store credit and a list of items I'd like to acquire if they come on the market?" She suggested a dollar amount, and I nodded.

"Sounds fair. What do you make of what I've told you?"

Shelley stood and began to pace. Tall and thin with angular features, she looked like a brooding hawk. Her dark hair was cut short in a feminine but practical style to accommodate her mixed martial arts workouts. I had gone to the gym once with her and limped for the next two days, unable to keep up. She made it look easy, just like in school, when she had been smarter than everyone else in the class and knew it. But her closest friends found her endearing in spite of her well-earned pride.

"I'll want to see the items for myself, of course," she said, puffing away at her vape pipe. "In case they speak to me, if you know what I mean."

I did. Shelley has flashes of clairvoyance, glimpses into the future. I wasn't entirely sure how her gift might help solve a mystery from the past, but I've learned never to discount anything when Shelley is on the case.

"Teag and Alistair are going to find out some of the missing pieces," Shelley said. "The answer is right in front of us, but we can't see it." She frowned, deciphering the glimpse of foreknowledge. "You're in danger," she turned to meet my gaze.

"Me?" I yelped. "Why on earth would an heiress's death from nearly a century ago put me in danger?"

Shelley shook her head as if clearing the ethereal fog from her thoughts. "No clue, girlfriend. But I've learned to take my psychic glimpses as seriously as I do my powers of deduction. So take the warning at face value."

Casting off her robe, Shelley put on a pair of shoes and grabbed a jacket from a peg near the door. She settled the jacket over her shoulders without slipping her arms into the sleeves, so it flapped like a cape, her gray eyes alight with the thrill of the chase.

"Come along, Watson!" she shouted. A disgruntled snuffle came from the direction of the kitchen, and then the click of nails on hardwood floors as Watson, Shelley's sad-eyed bloodhound, roused himself from his comfortable bed. She clipped his leash onto him and headed for the door.

"Let's go, Cassidy," she said. "The game's afoot!"

Every good investigator knows the price for an informant's help. In this case, it was a large vanilla latte from Honeysuckle Café.

"Cassidy! Shelley! What a wonderful surprise." Mrs. Benjamin Morrissey, Charleston doyenne and head of the Historical Archive, came out to meet us from her office at the historic home that housed the Archive. "And you've brought Watson!" She bent to pat Watson's head, and Watson gave her a lugubrious look in return.

"Go ahead and take him onto the back porch," Mrs. Morrissey said. "You can put down a bowl of water for him, and the doors are locked, so no one will bother him." Shelley took Watson to get settled and returned a moment later.

"And is that a vanilla latte?" Mrs. Morrissey asked, with a smile that told me she knew it was. "So let me guess—you need information?"

We all laughed, and she motioned for us to follow her. We walked through a partially installed exhibit in the house's large formal foyer, and I heard the sound of workmen upstairs.

"What's your new exhibit?" I asked. I've got to be careful with museums because the kinds of pieces that are important enough to save for historical reasons often have significant emotional resonance—and occasionally, a taint of dark magic. I'd had a couple of run-ins with some bad juju with prior Archive displays, but to my relief, whatever the new installation was going to be wasn't setting off my magical alarms.

Mrs. Morrissey grinned. "I thought you'd never ask!" she exclaimed. She's a real Charleston blue-blood, and when her husband passed on, leaving her with a wealth of money and social connections, she stepped into her role with the Archive as if she had been born to it.

"It's on 'Great Escapes—Grand Country Manors and Seaside Palaces.' Nowadays, tourists come for vacation to Charleston. But all throughout our history, Charlestonians went elsewhere to go on holiday. We've pulled together a display of photographs, diaries, and items from our collection all about the hunting lodges, beach homes, and getaway residences of some of Charleston's most famous residents over the years. It's going to be a fun exhibit!"

Given the enormous wealth of some of the old Charleston families —and some of its more recent celebrity sons and daughters, I didn't doubt the display would be a big hit with donors and paying guests alike.

"What do you know about Marie de Brise Chastain, Jacob Whitley, and Rebecca Dumont?" Shelley asked, leaning forward and staring intently at Mrs. Morrissey.

Mrs. Morrissey had a mind like a steel trap. She was the Archive's best "search engine," and she knew the collection like no one else. "She's the heiress who died in that fire, back in the Roaring Twenties, isn't she?" Mrs. Morrissey asked. "Terribly sad situation. Drove her father to suicide, or so they say."

"Really?" I raised an eyebrow.

Mrs. Morrissey nodded. "Of course, no one talks about it because the Chastain family is still quite well connected, but history is what it is," she said. We both knew that meant that history was the original and best "reality" show ever. Whether you were looking for murder, mayhem, scandal, oddities, or just plain weird stuff, Hollywood at its best couldn't out-do the exploits of real people. And historians—like antique dealers—knew all the old gossip.

"I might have to look up a date or two," Mrs. Morrissey admitted, looking as if that were a major fault, "but to my recollection, Jacob Whitley was courting Marie with the whole-hearted endorsement of both families. It would have been as much of a business merger as a marriage had everything gone as planned."

"But something went wrong," Shelley prompted.

Mrs. Morrissey nodded. "Marie didn't want to go through with the marriage. There are a couple of versions of the story. One story says that Marie just didn't care for Jacob and didn't want to marry without love. The other version holds that Rebecca and Jacob might have had eyes for each other." She paused.

"Rebecca Dumont was Marie's best friend and confidant. The two were inseparable. So it wasn't a surprise that Rebecca was there visiting even though Jacob had come to town to see Marie. He split his time between his family's interests in the Carolinas and their New York business."

She tapped on her keyboard, then turned the monitor of her computer around to face us. "Photos, from the archives," she said.

Shelley and I leaned forward for a better look. Rebecca was petite, and although the photo was black and white, I was certain she was the red-head I had glimpsed when I read the objects from the box. Marie was taller, with shoulder-length dark hair, and while she was striking, she wasn't as conventionally pretty as Rebecca, who smiled and laughed in every picture.

Jacob Whitley was a little older than the two women. They appeared to be in their twenties, while he was in his early thirties. Slightly built and nattily dressed, he had the sober, shrewd look of a man who was going to do very well in business. But I couldn't imagine him being an exciting date.

"Were Jacob and Marie really in love?" I asked.

Mrs. Morrissey leaned back in her chair. "That's been debated," she replied. "Most people think Marie's father brokered the proposal without asking her. It's hard to imagine the two of them together, isn't it?"

"Unless they shared some secret passion, they don't look like they would have even met otherwise," Shelley said, studying the photos.

"There's an old rumor that the night of the fire, Marie meant to break off the engagement with Jacob," Mrs. Morrissey said. "Of course, circumstances went tragically wrong. Marie died. Rebecca escaped unharmed, and Jacob survived, but badly injured and scarred."

"What happened?" I paged through the photos on the screen of Marie and Rebecca together in a graduation picture from a Swiss boarding school, and of them in a group of girls at a debutante party, and then another when they were young women, at a Christmas ball. There weren't a lot of public pictures, and I remembered what my grandmother used to say, that in her day, a woman with a good reputation only had her picture in the paper for her wedding and her obituary.

A number of photos accompanied newspaper articles announcing Jacob's membership in various business organizations or community groups.

"It's funny that you're asking about Marie and Jacob." Mrs. Morrissey had a few more sips of her latte. "Their story is so fresh in my memory because I had just pulled some photos of their family's vacation homes for the exhibition."

"Would one of those homes happen to be in upstate New York?" Shelley asked.

"Why yes," Mrs. Morrissey replied. "Come with me. The photos aren't mounted yet, but I can show you what I've got."

My cell phone buzzed. I glanced down and saw that the call was from Alistair. "Go on ahead," I said. "I'll be with you in a minute."

Alistair picked up immediately. "Cassidy—I've got to warn you. I might have accidentally put you in danger with that box."

I remembered Shelley's warning. "What happened?"

"Someone broke into the museum last night," Alistair said. "I didn't mention it when I visited because I didn't think it was related. The door was open into our acquisitions room, where we store new items before they're cataloged. Nothing was missing, so we changed the code on the door and filed a report with the police. Then today when I drove over to see you, I caught a glimpse of a white Toyota minivan that seemed to be following me. I thought I was imagining things. But after I saw you, I stopped for lunch. Someone broke into my car." He paused. "I think they were looking for something that wasn't there."

A chill went down my spine. "Thanks for the warning," I said. "I'll make sure Teag knows. The store is pretty well protected." In addition to a good alarm system, the store was warded by a Voudon mambo friend of mine.

"Don't take any chances, Cassidy," Alistair warned. "I don't know what's going on, but old secrets are the most dangerous ones."

I called Teag to pass along the warning. Then I went to join Shelley and Mrs. Morrissey in the boardroom, where photos lay in rows along the huge wooden table.

"It really puts things in perspective to realize that these 'cottages' were only used for a few weeks out of the year," I said, looking at the pictures. "Cottage" and "cabin" were a gross understatement. These grand vacation homes of Charleston's rich and famous were mansions.

"Amazing, aren't they?" Shelley admired the photos, then pulled out a magnifying glass and peered intently at two of the pictures.

"Find something?" I asked.

Shelley shrugged, warning me not to interrupt her train of thought. I looked over her shoulder at a picture of a sprawling log home the size of a modern hotel set against sharp mountain peaks. Two indistinct figures stood on the porch. "Maybe," she grunted. She took pictures of the photos with her cell phone to examine later.

"That's the Whitley 'grand camp' in the Adirondacks," Mrs. Morrissey said. "All the prestigious families had mountain retreats back at the turn of the last century. Vanderbilt, Morgan, Rockefeller—it was quite the thing to bring all your society friends up by train to 'rough it' in the wilderness," she added with a laugh. From the look of the log mansion, "roughing it" might mean limited amounts of caviar.

"And the beachfront homes are gorgeous," I said. "Is that Marie and Rebecca? Bathing caps hid their hair, but I was certain that they were the two laughing girls posing arm in arm in the surf.

"Yes," Mrs. Morrissey said. "That's the beach property on Sullivan

Island. It's long gone. It would have been built by Marie's grandfather. Those Victorians knew how to live large!"

"Do you have any other items from Jacob Whitley or Marie Chastain?" Shelley asked.

"Marie was so young when she died, just in her early twenties. She hadn't really had a chance to make her mark. But I think we do have a letter she wrote in favor of women getting the vote. Let me see if we can find it." Mrs. Morrissey signaled one of her interns and sent the young man off with instructions. "Jacob Whitley was a little older, but unfortunately, his life ended with the fire as well—in a manner of speaking."

"How so?" Shelley's gaze narrowed.

"While Rebecca escaped the fire unhurt except for minor cuts and superficial burns, Jacob wasn't as lucky," Mrs. Morrissey recounted. "He was badly injured—something to do with his leg—and he suffered disfiguring burns. Together with the death of his fiancée, it seemed to be too much for him. He moved up to his family's Adirondack home and became a recluse for the rest of his life."

"What drove Marie's father to suicide?" I asked. "Were they particularly close?"

Mrs. Morrissey shrugged. "Who can tell how someone will handle grief like that? I've heard that they argued about the arranged marriage. Both Marie and her father could be stubborn. Maybe he regretted that later." She gave me a sad smile. "For all his wealth and power, he couldn't save his daughter. People don't react rationally to loss."

Shelley sorted through the photos on the table. She peered closely at one and snapped another picture with her phone. "It's a formal photograph of the Whitley family," she pointed out Jacob, seated in the front row with his hands clasped on his lap. "It looks like he's wearing a ring. Is that the one you found in the box?"

I squinted and looked more closely, then shook my head. "I can't tell. The photo isn't sharp enough."

"Here's another one of Jacob with Marie and Rebecca," Mrs. Morrissey said. "That's odd—I don't remember seeing it before." I took the picture from her and glimpsed a man's silhouette out of the corner of my eye. The ghost was there and gone in a heartbeat. *Could there have been more to Marie's death than a tragic accident? I wondered. And after all this time, why would anyone try to steal back a box of things that have been sitting in a museum basement for years?*

The photograph showed three young adults in formal wear laughing and standing arm in arm. Marie and Rebecca were having the time of their lives. Jacob looked uncomfortable in his tuxedo, his smile forced.

"It's an odd pose for a photograph, don't you think?" Shelley said, staring at the picture. "They're not lined up by height." Jacob, the tallest of the three, was on the left. Rebecca was in the middle. She was the shortest one, coming just up to Jacob's shoulder and a little below Marie's chin. Marie was on the right.

"Probably one of those random red carpet photos," I said. The picture made me sad, and I could sense a depth to the melancholy that was not my own. *Something hidden in plain sight,* Shelley had said. *After nearly a century, why had the ghosts picked now to end their silence? And what secret had they guarded all this time?*

"Here's the letter you wanted," the intern said, returning with a yellowed envelope and a pair of archival gloves.

Mrs. Morrissey slipped on the gloves and carefully unfolded the letter. Shelley and I crowded around her to read a passionate letter in favor of women's right to vote written by a well-educated, outspoken young woman.

"Quite bold, wasn't she?" Shelley mused. "And unconventional."

Mrs. Morrissey chuckled. "The Twenties were a time when women with Marie's education and privilege began bucking convention in all sorts of ways, from wearing pants—scandalous!—to going to college to trying to enter male-only vocations."

"I wonder how Marie and Jacob would have gotten on if the marriage had happened," I said, as Shelley snapped a picture of the letter. "They don't seem to be temperamentally suited for each other."

"Opposites attract, or so they say," Mrs. Morrissey replied. "Although personally, I've found that birds of a feather flock together."

Shelley and I thanked Mrs. Morrissey, then we retrieved Watson from the porch and headed back to Shelley's house.

"Don't look now, but there's a white van following us," Shelley said. "Hold on. I'm going to make a detour."

I thought Shelley might speed up and start taking corners on two wheels, the way people do in the movies. Instead, she kept her speed constant and made a few extra turns that took us in a different direction. To my surprise, she turned down an alley next to a convenience store to emerge on the main road a few blocks later. The white van followed us most of the way, but must have realized that we spotted them, because it turned off not long after we had passed the store.

"What was that all about?"

"Samir, the guy who owns that convenience store, owes me a couple of favors," Shelley replied. "I helped him bust a shoplifting ring. He's got surveillance cameras all around the store, and he can get me copies of the tapes. With luck, they picked up a license plate on that van."

"Hey lady!" a neighbor called when Shelley and I parked at her house. He pointed at my Mini Cooper. "Is that your car?"

"Yes."

"Some guy was hanging around, looking in all the windows. I thought he might try to break in, so I yelled at him, and he got in his car and drove away."

"Thank you," I replied. Nothing looked damaged. "Did you see what he was driving?"

"Yeah. A white minivan."

I headed back for Trifles and Folly, constantly glancing in my rear view mirror. I even took a more roundabout route, just in case. I quickly discovered it was almost impossible to be on the highway or in a parking lot without spotting dozens of white minivans. Talk about hiding in plain sight. My stalker vanished by being everywhere.

"Everything go okay?" Maggie asked when I came in.

"Shelley agreed to take the case, no one got hurt, we found out some good information, and there's a white van stalking us."

"Hey, you got back here safely, boss. That's what counts," she said and shot me a thumbs-up.

"If that's Cassidy, tell her I've got stuff she wants to hear," Teag called from the office.

"It's me, and I'm heading your way."

Maggie jerked her head toward the office. "I'll handle the customers; you go save the world."

Something about Marie Chastain's death bothered me. There were too many loose ends and far too much interest in something long out of recent memory.

And then there was the silhouette. *Is he a ghost, or a lost spirit, or just a psychic impression that's a little more tangible than usual?*

"What did you find?" I asked, swinging through the break room for a glass of sweet tea.

"I love projects that scan archival documents," Teag said, cracking his knuckles and wiggling his fingers above the keyboard. Passwords don't stop Teag, and neither do firewalls—not even Federal level security, although we try to keep that kind of snooping for dire cases. "You scored?"

Teag grinned. "Oh yeah. A reporter named Peter Studebaker covered the fire that killed Marie Chastain when it happened. He was a bit of a muck-raker. A rogue investigative journalist. He had unanswered questions, but no one would listen to him, and he believed the Chastain family leaned on the newspaper editor to kill the story."

I sipped my sweet tea. "That's certainly possible. Money buys silence. Or, he might have just been nuts."

"I don't think he was nuts," Teag said. "Someone scanned his notes about the case and put them online."

"And?"

Teag sat back in his chair. "Studebaker thought it was odd that the initial firefighter's report said arson but was quickly changed to gas leak. He apparently was early on the scene, and says one of the first responders found evidence to suggest that someone set the house on fire with a homemade firebomb."

"Yikes."

"It gets better," Teag said. "Studebaker quoted witnesses who saw Marie Chastain and her father arguing not long before the fire. Studebaker suspected that Marie was in love with someone else and was balking at the arranged marriage."

"Let me guess. Whoever she was in love with didn't meet her father's standards."

"Studebaker's vague on that point," Teag replied. "If he had any idea of who the rival suitor was, he didn't say so. But he suggested Jacob Whitley might have been more interested in Rebecca than in Marie."

"Oh?"

"According to Studebaker, Jacob was injured in the fire, but he was vain enough to refuse treatment in Charleston, saying he would see his own doctor back in New York. Rebecca was studying to be a nurse, and she patched him up enough to make the trip. Observers say he walked with a limp, and his face was badly burned, covered in bandages."

"What about the letters?" I asked, remembering the bundle Alistair had given me.

Teag nodded. "Somehow, Studebaker found out that Jacob and Rebecca began corresponding after Marie's death, with Rebecca in Charleston and Jacob in self-imposed exile in the Adirondacks. Then a year later, Rebecca moved up to be his nurse. She never came back to Charleston."

"Interesting," I said. "But why would anyone care about this now? After a hundred years, why is someone following people around and breaking into cars?"

"Studebaker thought there was more to the story, but the police and the newspaper told him to drop it, especially after Marie's father committed suicide."

"Shelley's coming over to take a look at the items in the box," I added. "I think she's onto something, but she won't tell until she can make the big reveal."

"Dramatic, isn't she?" Teag laughed.

"Always."

My phone rang. It was Alistair. "What's up?"

"I've just heard back from Oliver Chastain." Alistair sounded upset. "Not only have they refused to provide any information about Marie's death, but they're demanding the box back—and he says they'll sue if we don't comply."

That was going to put Alistair in a bad situation, because the museum couldn't afford to get on the wrong side of the Chastains, major patrons to just about every charity in the city. "I understand," I said as I signaled to Teag that I would explain everything later. "Can we stall him for just a little while? I think Shelley's close to having a solution—and I suspect it's going to be worth our while to get to the bottom of this."

"I'll try," Alistair said. "But when push comes to shove, I'm going to have to give him what he wants."

I hung up and relayed what Alistair said. "Damn. Oliver Chastain has a reputation as a real son of a bitch, like his father and grandfather. I wouldn't be surprised if he hired Anthony's law firm for the suit on purpose, just to put pressure on us as well as the museum," Teag said. Anthony was Teag's partner. If Teag's fears proved true, that would put everyone in an extremely awkward position.

"But why?" I mused. "Surely no one would care if a hundred years ago, Marie wanted to break off an arranged marriage, even if she had another suitor in mind."

Teag rolled his eyes. "Even if she were pregnant—which would have been a big thing at the time—no one would bat an eye today. I agree. The reaction is over the top."

"It only seems over the top to us because we don't know something that Oliver Chastain knows. That's the missing piece—and Shelley believes the answer is hidden in plain sight."

A rap at the door signaled Shelley's arrival. Maggie watched the store so we could stay in the back. Teag took the box out of the safe. Immediately, I felt the effect on my mood. From the looks on Teag's face and Shelley's expression, I knew they sensed it too.

"What just happened?" Shelley asked.

"That's the supernatural effect that made Alistair bring us the box in the first place," I said. "There's an emotional resonance that makes everyone sad." Out of the corner of my eye, I caught the man's silhouette once more. I felt no threat; instead, the shadow seemed to be trying to watch. It was almost as if the spirit was rooting for us to figure something out.

"I have the oddest feeling that the ghosts connected to these items are trying to send a message," I told Teag and Shelley. "Maybe once we learn what that is, they'll be able to rest."

"Let's get started," Shelley said. A glint in those gray eyes told me she was fully invested in the case. Shelley gently loosened the twine that tied up the letters. As they fell apart, I could see that about half were to Jacob and half to Rebecca. "If you haven't read the letters or the journal, I think now is a good time," Shelley said. "Cassidy—can you handle one of those objects better than another?"

I held my palm above the letters and then over the journal. Neither one gave off dangerous vibes, but the emotions linked to the journal were stronger and more negative. "How about if I take Rebecca's letters, Teag takes Jacob's letters, and you read the journal?"

"That works for me," Shelley said. We drew chairs up to the table and spread out the items among us.

There were twelve yellowed envelopes in Rebecca's handwriting and twelve more in Jacob's script. *Interesting. That means they traded two letters each month between Marie's death and when Rebecca moved to New York to nurse Jacob back to health. That's a lot of conversation.*

I settled back in my chair to read. Rebecca's handwriting was compact but clear, in an old-fashioned script. The letters chronicled day-to-day life, the kind of things we'd say in a phone call or on Facebook, like what they ate for dinner or who they saw at a party—personal news about a circle of mutual friends.

39

I found myself caught up in the accounts. The letters implied a conversation between two people who knew each other very well. Rebecca and Jacob were very much in love and missed each other badly.

Did guilt over Marie's death keep them apart? Were they worried about being openly involved with each other so soon after Marie and her father died?

The letter that must have followed shortly after the suicide of Marie's father caught my attention. *I know you chide me for speaking my mind openly on this matter, and I do not wish to show disrespect for your feelings,* Rebecca had written. *But knowing him as I did, over so many years, never have I been acquainted with such a hard-hearted and close-minded man, who managed—despite his considerable business success—to make an utter ruin of his family. I know how much unhappiness he brought to Marie, and while you may fault me for saying it, I hope the Almighty requires recompense for the suffering he has caused.*

"Rebecca wasn't a fan of Marie's father," I said.

"Jacob seemed to have some lingering bad will there too," Teag replied. "Maybe he felt pressured to go through with the marriage to Marie even though she didn't love him because of Mr. Chastain's influence."

"I'd say it's unanimous that no one cared much for Marie's father, not even Marie." Shelley looked up. "And the journal removes all doubt that Marie was in love with someone else, although she never names names."

Shelley pulled out her phone and photographed a page of the journal, then one of each of the letters. "I'd like to look at the other items," Shelley said, getting up abruptly and circling the table. She lifted the melted St. Gaudens gold coin and examined it thoroughly, peering at it with her magnifying glass and jotting notes to herself on her phone. Then she regarded the partly-burned stationery with its ominous pronouncement and took another photo.

Shelley stood up, adjusted her necklace, squared her shoulders, and favored us with a triumphant, self-satisfied expression. "I've solved the case," she announced, holding up a hand to forestall questions.

"All will be explained in due time. There's not a moment to waste. We must call Alistair right away to arrange a meeting tonight with Oliver Chastain. I have a presentation to make that he'll never forget."

The museum was closed when we gathered in the board room. Alistair looked nervous, with good cause. Shelley would only say that she had solved the case and knew why Oliver Chastain was so eager to recover the items—and why the shadow figure was anxious for resolution. But she would not elaborate until Chastain joined us.

We had not been allowed in the board room as Shelley prepared her display of evidence, laid out on easel boards on stands that were dramatically draped to obscure them until Shelley made her big reveal.

Our small group waited quietly for the sound of the outside door opening. Oliver Chastain bustled in. "I don't know why I had to come down here at a certain time to pick up objects that belong to my family," he snapped when he saw Alistair. "You can be certain I'll mention this to the Board of Directors."

Oliver Chastain was the picture of a successful Charleston scion. He was in his sixties, and his bespoke suit was tailored to accommodate a portly figure from too much fine food and wine.

"We know why you're in such a hurry to retrieve the items," Shelley said, and her voice startled Chastain, as if he had not noticed the rest of us sitting in the shadows of the room's perimeter until she spoke. "We've uncovered the truth about what really happened in that fire back in 1920."

Shelley might be eccentric, but when the chips are down, she has a gravitas and a sense of self-assurance sufficient to silence even the bluster of a man like Chastain. "Sit down, Mr. Chastain. You must be tired from following Alistair and Cassidy and me around in that white van of yours."

"I don't know what you're—" Chastain protested.

41

Shelley whipped the cover from the first easel with a theatrical flourish. On the board were several grainy photos from a security camera of a white minivan, clearly showing the license plate.

"I've already run the plates," Shelley said emotionlessly. "The car is registered as your wife's personal vehicle. Note the timestamp on the photos. This was taken as you pursued Cassidy and me after our meeting at the Archive."

"That proves nothing," Chastain blustered, but I noticed he was sweating a little.

"Since you're a board member, you knew the museum door code, so you didn't have to pick the lock when you tried to find the box in the acquisition room," Shelley continued, with a gaze that gave no quarter. "I was able to pick up a partial fingerprint from Alistair's car door that wasn't his. It wasn't in the police database, but then again, I don't imagine you've ever been arrested, so it wouldn't be on file —yet."

Chastain was growing red in the face. "I've had enough," he said and started to rise.

Shelley's gaze stopped him. "Your family was able to silence Peter Studebaker, but with the internet, it's not quite as easy anymore. Sit down." Chastain glowered, but he sat.

"Your great grandfather didn't approve of Marie's choice of suitors," Shelley went on. "He wasn't used to being disobeyed. So after a particularly vicious argument, he decided to throw a scare into her," Shelley said. "He tossed a small bottle of alcohol with a burning wick through the window, expecting it to frighten her into listening to him, maybe even push her into Jacob's arms as her rescuing hero."

Shelley unveiled a photograph of the threatening note with a snap of the wrist. Next to it was a second photo of an old ledger page. "I'm a trained expert in handwriting analysis. But just to be sure, I sent these two examples to a friend of mine who specializes in such things for the FBI. We are both one hundred percent certain that these two specimens were written by the same person."

She turned to Oliver Chastain. "The ledger was undeniably written by your great-grandfather. And the evidence shows that the letter threatening Marie Chastain was written by the same person—her own father."

"This is ridiculous," Oliver Chastain fumed.

"Your great-grandfather was appalled that his little trick to frighten Marie went so badly wrong. We'll give him the benefit of the doubt about being heartsick over starting a fire that killed one person and injured another. I'm sure he also feared prosecution for the murder, should the truth come out. And that, ladies and gentlemen, is the real reason why Marie's father committed suicide."

"You can't prove that," Oliver Chastain snapped.

"I just have," Shelley replied with a smug smile. "I think the family knew—or strongly suspected—the reason for your family patriarch's suicide. But after examining the evidence, there's another story that you don't know—one that will be disclosed tonight for the first time."

Shelley whipped the cover from the third easel. "Marie Chastain did not die in the fire that night. The remains recovered belonged to Jacob Whitley."

Everyone stared at Shelley. "That's impossible," Oliver Chastain said. "Jacob Whitley lived to be an old man up in the New York mountains."

Shelley gave him a confident smile. "Someone using Jacob's name did indeed live several more decades in seclusion. But it was not Jacob Whitley. Observe," Shelley said, pointing to the display.

"Here is a sample of Marie Chastain's writing from her diary. And here is a sample of a letter ostensibly written by Jacob Whitley to Rebecca after the fire."

"They don't look anything alike," Oliver Chastain protested.

Shelley looked at the samples. "No, they don't. Nor does that letter supposedly by Jacob Whitley look remotely like the large number of documents historically confirmed to have been written by him before the fire." She wheeled on Chastain like the prosecutor in a courtroom drama.

"That's because Jacob Whitley never made it out of that burning room," Shelley said. "It was the melted Saint Gaudens that gave it away. The temperature at which gold melts is the same temperature at which a human body is cremated. Jacob Whitley had just completed a lucrative business deal the morning of the fatal fire. The record shows he was paid in twenty-dollar gold pieces—Saint Gaudens, the ledger specifies. He had one of those gold pieces in his pocket when the room around him went up in flames."

Shelley strode back and forth, smacking the poster boards with a wooden pointer for emphasis as she passed. "It all comes back to why Marie and her father argued so violently, why her refusal of an arranged marriage would have moved a solid community leader to extreme measures. It wasn't mere stubbornness. Marie had done something her father found unforgivable."

She stopped in front of the final exhibit and pulled the cover free. "Marie and Rebecca were lovers." Chastain looked like he was going to argue, but Shelley steamrollered over him.

"Look at this photograph, taken after the fire, when Rebecca was in New York with 'Jacob,'" she said. "Now look at the heights of the people in this photograph, taken here in Charleston before the fire." The photo of the three laughing friends made the contrast clear. "Marie Chastain was shorter than Jacob but taller than Rebecca. Now note the height differences in the New York photo."

Once Shelley pointed it out, I could see it immediately. Rebecca was closer in height to the man in the later photograph than the real Jacob. "And Exhibit B, the letters," Shelley said, wheeling to point toward the prior board.

"It is possible to disguise one's writing by using the non-dominant hand," Shelley said. "But computer analysis is nearly impossible to fool. Both the computer and my FBI expert agree—the letters after the fire written to Rebecca were, in fact, penned by Marie Chastain."

It all made sense. That was why "Jacob" had refused local treatment except from Rebecca before returning to New York. Why Marie —as Jacob—walked with a limp to hide the height difference and bandaged her face, claiming disfigurement. As Jacob Whitley, Marie Chastain laid claim to a fortune that made her independently wealthy, with no close family to gainsay her. The Adirondack home and her reclusiveness ensured her privacy. No doubt the handful of loyal servants were well-compensated for their silence. Playing the roles of dutiful nurse and longsuffering cripple, Marie and Rebecca could live out the rest of their lives together without interference.

The man's silhouette, the one I keep seeing. Is it Jacob, wanting the true story of his fate acknowledged, or Marie in her disguise, demanding that her family recognize her chosen partner after all these years? Maybe both.

Oliver Chastain sat still and silent. The color had drained from his face, and his hands gripped the chair arms, white-knuckled. "Now that you know, what do you intend to do about it."

Shelley regarded him coldly, like a hanging judge. "That all depends on you, Mr. Chastain. If you intend to make trouble for Alistair with the museum directors or endanger his employment, then I imagine the internet would find Marie's story deliciously juicy and relevant."

She paused. "On the other hand, if you stop stalking people and breaking into cars and buildings and swear to make no trouble—now or later—for Alistair and the museum, or for Cassidy and Teag, we can all agree to leave the matter in the past."

"That's blackmail," Chastain grated.

Shelley shrugged. "No, that's business. What'll it be, Mr. Chastain?"

Oliver Chastain swore under his breath. "All right. I promise I will not retaliate against Alistair or the museum or against Cassidy or Teag."

"Or me," Shelley added.

Chastain glared. "Or you. Or anyone. Just give me the damn box of junk and your word that the story doesn't leave this room."

We all made our promises. Shelley reached behind the podium and withdrew the old box. This time, I felt no sadness from its presence, only a sense of justice and satisfaction, long delayed. "Pleasure doing business with you, Mr. Chastain."

Shelley Holmes always had the last word.

KEEPSAKES

First appeared in the anthology:
Haven Harbor Halloween

This story was written as part of an anthology where we all got the chance to borrow a little from Jeanne Adams's world, which is about a town settled by descendants of the witches who fled the Salem Witch Trials back in the 1600s. Cassidy and Teag get drawn into a situation in Charleston that has its roots in old grudges and Haven Harbor.

The fictional town of Haven Harbor, Massachusetts, was created by Jeanne Adams. All references to Haven Harbor, Massachusetts, its locations and descriptions, the townspeople, place names, and business names are the intellectual property of Author Jeanne Adams, www.-JeanneAdams.com, and are used with her permission.

CHAPTER 1

"WHAT A WONDERFUL ILLUSION! TELL ME, HOW DID YOU MAKE IT look so real?"

I glanced up from where I was filling champagne flutes as quickly as possible and blew an errant strand of strawberry-blonde hair out of my eyes. "I'm sorry. What did you say?"

The woman in front of me was totally channeling the look of a perfect Hitchcock heroine: beautiful in an icy sort of way. Her not-a-hair-out-of-place chignon set off diamond earrings that each probably cost as much as my car, and her understated but obviously designer cocktail dress suggested old money. A donor, then. "The ghost of the sea captain on the stairs. You must tell me who does your special effects. I didn't know the Archive had those kind of connections!"

"I'll have to look that up," I said, trying not to look as freaked out as I felt. I glanced up at the massive, cantilevered staircase that was a key architectural feature of the restored historic home, but saw no one. "Um, what did you see?" I asked and then realized she probably expected me to know the inside scoop. "I mean, there are several different vignettes—which one did you see?"

Ice queen took one of the flutes and patted her perfect updo. "Oh," she gushed, "you mean the show changes throughout the evening? How utterly marvelous!" She leaned over to whisper to me. "I hope the tech work was donated and didn't come out of gala proceeds."

That, I could answer truthfully. "I can promise you that no Archive money was spent on those effects."

Museums and historic homes could prevent a lot of nasty hauntings if they'd skip the original furnishings and family heirlooms and settle for classy reproductions.

I scanned the room for Teag Logan, my best friend and partner in crime. For tonight, he put aside his usual scruffy grad student look and traded up to an elegant tux as one of the event docents taking tours through the newly restored historic home. Teag's wiry and slender, just over six feet tall, with dark hair in a skater-boy cut. He usually looks like a geeky graduate student, which is exactly what he used to be before he took a job at Trifles and Folly and discovered his own brand of magic.

At his elbow was Anthony Benton, Teag's long-time partner and a prominent lawyer from an established South of Broad family. Teag and Anthony couldn't have looked more different. Anthony was just a bit shorter, and his blond rich-boy-next-door good looks might have been right out of a soap opera. I always enjoyed the contrast in their styles when I saw them together, but no one could ever question how much they cared for each other.

I caught Teag's eye and gave a jerk of my head toward the stairs. He frowned and shrugged, letting me know he had no idea what I meant.

I finished filling the crystal glasses with bubbly and slipped from behind the table, glancing over my shoulder to make sure Mrs. Morrissey wouldn't notice. She was chatting up a couple I recognized as a state senator and his wife, both big givers to cultural and historical causes, so I figured she'd be a while. I whispered to one of the servers to take my place, then headed up the stairs to see if I could figure out what the hell was going on.

I knew for a fact the Archive hadn't sponsored any special effects.

That meant the ghost was real.

Halfway up the stairs, I felt a chill descend on me as if I'd entered a walk-in freezer. I had made sure not to put my hand on the burnished wooden balustrade since my touch magic lets me read the history—and sometimes magic—of objects through contact. That meant my own magic wasn't conjuring up the image of a stiff-backed older gentleman with mutton-chop sideburns who materialized two steps up from me and looked out over the party in the foyer and parlor with an expression of utter desolation.

I thought about saying something to find out why he looked so sad, but he started down the steps and went right through me as if I weren't there. I gasped at the intrusion as his freezing-cold spirit sliced through my living body and continued on his way. It felt as if I'd swallowed dry ice and Pop Rocks with a Coke chaser, and the sensation overwhelmed me, making me lose my balance.

I started to fall and grabbed for the railing, holding on tight enough to catch myself but wrenching my arm painfully. I cried out and hung on, even as the psychometric magic assailed me with hundreds of images, like a rapid-fire slideshow, taking in the life and times of the two-hundred-year-old house as the vision assaulted my brain and strained my control.

"Cassidy!" Teag and Anthony both sprinted for the stairs, guests be damned. The ghost continued his nonchalant descent, only to vanish once he reached the last step.

My arm and shoulder and my elbow might never be the same again, but at least I hadn't fallen to my death down the stairs. Teag helped me to my feet, and Anthony got under my shoulder on the other side, and together they helped me up the steps to one of the second-floor rooms where I could lie down and collect myself.

Below us, the gala patrons burst into enthusiastic clapping and cheers at our "performance." I was in too much pain and too unsettled to pay much attention, but I did catch the very concerned look on Mrs. Morrissey's face as she watched us go up the steps. She knew what we'd already figured out. We had a big problem.

The Kettinger House glowed with light from the fundraising reception in full swing that had a guest list of all the movers and shakers in Charleston society. Well, with a few exceptions, like Teag and me. Yes, we're on the Gala Committee, and we're here to help out Mrs. Benjamin Morrissey, Charleston doyenne and fearless leader of the Historical Archive, but we're more than that. Most people know me as the owner of Trifles and Folly, an antiques and curio store in historic, haunted Charleston, South Carolina that has been in my family since the city was founded, about three hundred and fifty years. Teag is my assistant store manager.

But the real truth—which is a pretty big secret—is that Trifles and Folly is a cover for a coalition of mortals and immortals who work together to save Charleston—and the world—from supernatural threats. We get haunted and cursed objects off the market and out of the wrong hands and wage a never-ending war against dangerous magical entities. My psychometry lets me read the dirty secrets of where objects have been. Teag's got Weaver magic, which enables him to weave spells into cloth and data into information, making him a hell of a supernaturally-enhanced hacker. We work with Sorren, a nearly six-hundred-year-old vampire, who's my business partner, to keep people safe from things that go bump in the night.

When we do our job right, no one notices. When we screw up, the damage and death toll is epic enough to be blamed on a natural disaster.

Right now, all I wanted was the chance to sit down before I passed out and an ice bag for my shoulder and elbow. Teag and Anthony half-carried, half-dragged me into the first bedroom and helped me lie down on the historic four-poster bed, ignoring the red satin cord and the signs that warned visitors not to sit on the furniture.

"What happened down there?" Anthony asked, taking a protective stance next to the bed as Teag went into the bathroom and wet down a hand towel to put across my forehead.

"It looks like the former owner never left," I said, biting back a cry of pain as I shifted and my shoulder protested.

"Let me get some ice," Teag said, rabbiting from the room before I could protest. Anthony bent over me.

"May I?" he asked, reaching for my shoulder. I nodded and bit my lip as he very gently probed the joint. I stifled a curse and a sob. My elbow proved to be just as tender.

"It's not dislocated, but not for lack of trying," he said, and I wondered when he added a medical degree to his Juris Doctorate.

Anthony gave a self-conscious shrug. "I have two older brothers. We used to roughhouse and tore each other up something awful just horsing around. Can't tell you how many times I've had to go into the ER to get a dislocated shoulder popped back in or had to do PT for a hyper-extended elbow."

"So I'll live?"

Anthony chuckled and smoothed the hair out of my eyes. "You'll live, but your arm is going to hurt like blazes for a while."

I sighed and shut my eyes. "I'll get Teag to drive me over to the urgent care tomorrow morning. I've got some ice packs at home and some pills left over from the last time I strained my knee, so I think I can make it through the night." I tried to sit up, but Anthony pressed gently on my good shoulder.

"Nuh-uh," he said, shaking his head. "Lie down before you fall down and add a concussion to the list. Teag'll be back in a minute with ice."

Teag returned not only with two bags of ice but a very worried Mrs. Morrissey.

"Cassidy, dear—are you all right?" Mrs. Morrissey inherited a fortune and a platinum-plated social circle when her husband passed away. She's leveraged that into becoming the go-to matriarch for Charleston's historic and cultural society, making her a force to be reckoned with when it comes to historic preservation. She's also a good friend and one of the relatively few who know the truth about what Teag and I really do. Mrs. Morrissey was a confidant of my Uncle Evan, who willed Trifles and Folly to me, and I wonder sometimes just how far their "friendship" went.

"Stupid ghost nearly knocked me down the steps," I muttered and sighed in relief as Teag positioned the ice bags over my shoulder and elbow, after first carefully tucking towels beneath both so as not to damage the reproduction bedspread fabrics.

"Since when does Kettinger House have a ghost?" Teag demanded. "We did the walk-through with you months ago to make sure this kind of thing didn't happen."

Mrs. Morrissey could be a true force of nature when she was in high dudgeon. Now, she looked perplexed and nervous, unconsciously twisting the expensive, diamond-inlaid watch on her wrist. "I don't know. That's why I have you and Cassidy come and tour early, so we can prevent this kind of thing. I'm so sorry you're hurt."

I waved my good hand in dismissal. "I'll mend. But I don't want anyone else to get hurt, and we know squat about the ghost, except that if I had to pick someone to look like a pre-Civil War sea captain, he'd be right out of central casting."

Teag frowned and looked back at Mrs. Morrissey. "Did you get in any furnishings or heirlooms that we haven't vetted?"

Antiques, heirlooms, and old stuff carry psychic residue. Most of the time, it's nothing serious, just enough good juju to make you feel happy when you handle a nostalgic piece or have a sense of something being wrong when the mojo is negative. Some items; however, are seriously effed up, poisoned with bad memories, depressing resonance, or plain old malice. Trifles and Folly tries to intercept those items and either neutralize the danger or find a way to destroy or store them so they won't cause further harm.

Mrs. Morrissey nodded. "Yes. I'm sorry I didn't think to mention it earlier. We got in two boxes of items from people I have scouting for family heirlooms or period-appropriate pieces. Just came in yesterday, and we only had time to put a few items out on display. The rest are in crates locked in one of the upstairs bedrooms."

Teag and I exchanged a glance. "Well, that solves one mystery," I said, closing my eyes and willing the ice to take away the throbbing pain in my arm. "Something must have come in with those crates that juiced up the old man and gave him enough power to be seen. The lady

I talked to when I was pouring the champagne had already seen him once and thought we had amazing special effects," I added.

Teag rubbed his eyes, staving off a headache. "All right. So at least some of the guests can see the ghost, but they think it's part of the show. As long as he doesn't attack anyone, and we keep people off the steps, maybe we can get through the reception without a problem."

I swallowed a couple of ibuprofen and insisted on getting back up. "I'm not going to be much use pouring," I said ruefully, grimacing as I moved my strained arm, "but I want to be able to observe—and maybe head off Moby Dick if he shows up again."

"Ishmael," Teag said.

"Gesundheit," I replied.

He shook his head. "No, Ishmael was the name of the sea captain. Moby Dick was the whale."

I rolled my eyes. "Figures you'd know that," I sighed. Teag let me use his arm to steady myself as I got to my feet, and Anthony had just turned to open the door when we heard a yelp of surprise and a crash.

"Crap," Mrs. Morrissey murmured, and the mild oath seemed so out of character I had to chuckle. I'd had several words run through my mind, none of them "mild."

"Go on down," she said. "I'll join you in a minute. I want to go check on the boxes."

"Do you want me to come with you?" I offered.

She shook her head. "No. Go see what's happened. I promise I won't be long."

When we reached the foyer, we found a server hurrying to clean up a dropped tray of goblets and the attendees abuzz about Captain Kettinger's latest appearance. The wife of one of the Archive's big donors was blushing and grinning as she recounted her surprise at having the Captain appear at her side.

Mrs. Morrissey found us a few minutes later. "It looked like someone opened one of the boxes," she murmured. "According to the packing list, we're missing a lady's fan. That doesn't make any sense. It was one of the least valuable items in the shipment."

I didn't have time to think much about it because right then,

Kettinger showed up beside the front window, doing his best Captain Morgan pose, and I realized that at the time the house was built, that window would have looked out onto the water. Charleston's harbor filled in quite a bit since the early days—largely from old ships leaving behind their stone ballast—and there are now two more streets between us and the ocean. I suspected the ghost's view remained as it had been, since he showed no indication of anything being amiss.

The crowd gasped, then clapped, and some people pulled out their phones and began taking pictures. I doubted they'd have anything to show for it except some glowing orbs, but no one was freaking out, and they all were unreasonably happy about the "entertainment," so Teag took my place pouring drinks while I filled in as docent for him.

"I really wish you could tell me you hired a special effects crew," Anthony murmured, stepping up beside me but never taking his eyes off the Captain's ghost until it wavered and vanished—to thunderous applause.

"Nope. Sorry. He's the real deal."

"Do you think he's dangerous?" Anthony asked.

I was just about to offer tentative reassurance when I heard an odd sound from outside. Anthony looked like he'd picked up on the noise as well, and he followed me to the front windows.

"What the hell?" he muttered under his breath.

A calm fall evening had suddenly turned into a stormy night, which hadn't been on any weather predictions. Outside, high winds whipped the trees along the street and in the neighbor's garden as if a hurricane had rolled into town. Anthony glanced at his phone for a storm warning text but shook his head.

Papers and debris hurtled down the narrow street, past the cars parked on either side. The wind picked up enough to whistle through the chimney and bang the shutters, catching the attention of the guests.

"Just the wind," I said, plastering on my best reassuring smile, even though everything about the freak squall felt wrong. "Everything's fine."

Right on cue, the string quartet began to play in the main parlor, and Mrs. Morrissey lured guests out of the foyer and into the next room with the whispered promise of hot hors d'oeuvres. Teag poured the last of the bottle in his hands and came over to join us.

"Holy hell," he muttered, standing beside me. "First a ghost, now weird weather?"

"It's not normal," I said, knowing the truth of that in my bones. Teag's eyes widened as he touched his magic, and he nodded. The air felt tainted, and the power I could feel stank of malice, a low, ominous rumble of discordant magic from which nothing good could come. And it was getting stronger.

I only had a glimpse of something dark and solid coming straight for the windows before Anthony shouted a warning and pushed me down, yanking Teag with us into a pile on the floor. The large glass window shattered, and the howling icy wind now swept through the foyer, cold and sharp, strong enough to knock glasses to the floor and bang paintings against the walls.

Screams from the other room only barely rose above the wind, and then I heard the squeal of wrenched metal and the sound of impact after impact in the street just outside. I was buried beneath Teag and Anthony's bodies, so I couldn't see anything, but the crash of metal and breaking glass sounded like a ten-car pile-up. A car alarm blared, and then another.

As quickly as it started, everything fell silent. After a moment or two without any new threat, Anthony and Teag sat up, shaking broken glass from their hair and tux coats, and I drew a deep breath, trying to collect my wits.

The foyer around us was trashed. Goblets and carafes lay smashed on the floor. Napkins draped where they had fallen after being caught in the wind. A spiderweb of cracks marred the glass over two of the large paintings on the walls, and the lovely printed guide sheets we had handed out to all the guests about the home's history had all been blown up against the far wall like so much garbage.

Teag helped me to my feet, and I glanced at both men, assuring myself they had escaped injury. Teag was bleeding from a cut along his temple, and Anthony's blond hair was matted in the back with blood where a piece of glass had stuck, but other than having been slightly squished beneath them, I was fine.

"Oh my God!"

I don't know who said it, but the comment echoed through the sobered crowd as they filed out of the parlor and looked at the devastated foyer. Several were taking pictures, while others were on the phone, perhaps to the police or their lawyers. Mrs. Morrissey caught my eye, and I nodded, indicating that we were all right, so she shifted into damage control mode, moving from one frightened guest to another.

We dared to step closer to the broken window and looked out into the street. The wind had tossed four cars out of their parking places, tumbling them down the cobblestones like toys and piling them all atop an unfortunate silver Porsche two-seater, crushing it flat.

"My car!" A woman stared out at the wreckage and balled her fist at the sight of the ruined cars. "Shit," she added quietly. Dark hair in a chin-length bob flattered high cheekbones and arched brows, and her slim, burgundy silk skirted suit still looked pristine, despite the storm. She strode for the door on her red-soled designer stiletto heels, with nary a wobble despite the broken glass.

The rest of the guests crowded toward the window, and three men quickly followed the woman in the red suit. Their voices carried, as did the curses that threatened to turn the storm-heavy air blue. In the distance, sirens blared.

"I think she owned the Porsche," Anthony murmured. "I can't tell you how glad I am that we walked."

We couldn't clean up before the police arrived, and possibly not until the insurance adjuster had a chance to document the damage. Teag, Anthony, and I headed back to help Mrs. Morrissey soothe upset guests. Someone had brought out the rest of the champagne, and while Teag and Anthony helped pour bubbly into the surviving crystal flutes, I alternated between consoling stressed-out donors and making my own assessment of the ruined foyer.

For the first time since the fundraiser began, I took a good look at the guests. I'd seen the guest list ahead of time and remembered Mrs.

Morrissey remarking on who hadn't been able to come. I'd want to look at that short list again. Most of the invitees showed up—Mrs. M. was hard to say no to, and Charleston's elite liked to see and be seen.

I recognized the majority of the guests from other soirées around the city. Trifles and Folly's true purpose might be getting rid of dangerous supernatural objects, but as far as the rest of the world knows, we're a damn fine place to buy antique silverware or to sell off great-granny's vintage jewelry. Teag and I often got called in to do appraisals, and it was good business to mingle with the upper crust at as many of these events as possible. That meant bumping into the same folks at multiple galas, so I could put names to faces even if we didn't actually know one another.

All except for five. The woman in the red suit whose car got pancaked was not someone I'd seen before, although her clothing, jewelry, and manner suggested she fit right in with this crowd. The Hitchcock blonde who commented on the "special effects" wasn't a regular. One of the other men who had dashed outside and now stood talking with a cop was also unfamiliar, and I did my best in the dim light to memorize his features. Another stranger button-holed Anthony, and they were talking as if they knew each other, so I figured I'd get the scoop on him later.

That left the fourth man. He stood about Teag's height, but with broader shoulders and a more solid build, with auburn hair and a close trimmed beard artfully manscaped into civilized scruff. I'd heard him talking with other guests, and his accent definitely wasn't Charleston or from anywhere south of the Mason-Dixon. New York, maybe, or New England. That alone wasn't too surprising: Mrs. Morrissey's invitations cast a wide net, and plenty of out-of-towners had business that brought them to Charleston. He could be someone with a historic preservation group or even the plus-one of another invitee.

Just then, the stranger turned as if he sensed he was being watched. He caught me looking at him and met my gaze. I saw a flash of something in his eyes before they narrowed, but it wasn't fear. A hint of a challenge, maybe? A dare to find out who he was and why he had crashed the party? Then I felt it, a flicker there and gone against my skin, and I saw triumph and wariness in his eyes.

Whoever he was, he had magic, and somehow he had just discovered that so did I.

The cops let the exhausted guests go home around eleven. The unlucky car owners gave their statements early, then left with the flatbed tow trucks that came to haul away what remained of their mangled luxury vehicles. Teag, Anthony, and I stuck around to help clean up. A couple of the catering staff quit on the spot and left as soon as the cops gave the okay, so having us pitch in squared things away before the wee hours.

Mrs. Morrissey made several calls in between giving her statement to the police and repeating herself to the insurance man. A workman pounded nails into place, securing sheets of plywood over the ruined front window. I'd made a thorough check of my own; nothing else had been damaged except the front foyer and of course, the squashed cars.

Through it all, Mrs. Morrissey never lost her cool. She had to be in her mid-seventies, but her slim St. John suit and coiffed hair looked as perfect as when she arrived. I knew her well enough to see the exhausted squint around her eyes and the worried set of her mouth, but whenever any of the donors approached her, she stood ramrod straight, shoulders back and chin high, assuring everyone this was a minor setback and all would be sorted quickly, posing no threat to the scheduled grand opening.

Except the part about the ghost.

We walked Mrs. Morrissey out to her car, parked on the street behind the Kettinger House. "I don't know what I would have done without you," she said, clasping my hand. "I imagine my morning will be hell dealing with the aftermath, but call me in the afternoon. We have to do something about the Captain's ghost, and I need your help to find out which of the new items in those boxes caused the haunting."

"Will do," I promised, although right then, all I wanted was a stiff drink, some ice for my shoulder, and a soft mattress. Teag and Anthony walked me back to the shop, where I had left my RAV4 parked, and I offered to give them a ride to their place, which they accepted. We said little on the walk, too tired and overwhelmed to tackle the topic right then, but when I pulled up in front of the house they shared, Teag turned to me and put a hand on my arm.

"Don't go back there without me, Cassidy," he said. "We don't know what the ghost can do or whether it threw those cars around, but something powerful made that happen. It's a miracle no one got badly hurt." He glanced at my sore arm. "It could have been a lot worse."

I shuddered, trying not to think about tumbling down that long staircase headfirst, and nodded. "I promise. Get some sleep. I'll see you at the shop in the morning."

By the time Mrs. Morrissey finally had time to meet with us, five o'clock had come and gone. All day, the customers who came into Trifles and Folly talked about the "happenings" at the Kettinger House, and the tales grew with the telling.

"I practically expected to hear about how a Yeti went bowling with the cars in the alley." I rolled my eyes and took a sip of coffee. I clutched the cup like it was the difference between life and death, and right then, it felt like that.

"Somehow, a Yeti is still better than terrorists, Chinese gangs, or Russian mobsters," Teag replied. "I heard all of those at least once, and one woman even wondered whether or not it might be UFOs."

I covered my face with my hand and shook my head. "How is it that a plain old haunting and some dark magic starts to look boring compared to all of that?"

"Hey, at least they still think the ghost is just high-tech sleight-of-hand," Teag reminded me as we locked up and went to meet Mrs. Morrissey.

"I know, be thankful for small favors," I said, happy to let Teag drive since my caffeine-to-blood ratio was still out of kilter.

We had managed to identify everyone at the event except for the lady in the red suit, the blond guy who had gone to deal with his squashed car, the Hitchcock blonde, and the guy with the scruff who had triggered my magic. He seemed the most likely to be involved somehow, but none of us had ever seen him before.

"Kell called last night," I said, leaning back against the seat and closing my eyes. "He saw it on the news and knew we'd be there. Wanted to make sure we were okay."

Kell and I had been seeing each other for about a year. He doesn't know the full scoop about my magic or about Trifles and Folly's true purpose, but since he heads up a local paranormal investigations group, SPOOK, he's pretty cool about the not-exactly-normal things he's seen first-hand with me.

Teag grinned. "If you'd have asked, I bet he would have come over with ice and hot pads for some physical therapy," he joked, managing to make it sound utterly lascivious.

"He offered," I said. "But by that point, I definitely wasn't good company. I took some pills, put a cold pack on my shoulder, and slept like a rock."

"Anthony took it all pretty much in stride," Teag said, keeping his eyes on traffic. Charleston doesn't have the kind of rush hour you'll find in Atlanta or L.A., but we get enough tourists who don't know where they're going that driving here requires careful attention—and patience.

"He's seen worse," I remarked. "And he knows we all got off lucky." Teag hadn't intended to tell his partner about the kind of magic and supernatural threats we deal with, to protect him and let him keep his illusions about the "normal" world. Anthony pieced a lot together on his own, combined with some first-hand experiences with things we couldn't explain away. Last year, when a particularly rough battle saved the world but almost cost Teag his life, Anthony swore he'd keep our secrets if we would just give him the whole, ugly, implausible truth.

"Did you hear from Sorren?" Teag asked.

"I left a message with the key points. Asked him to look into Kettinger's background and told him about the guy with the Northeastern accent." Yes, my business partner, the six-hundred-year-old vampire, has a cell phone and email. He says that immortals who can't adapt with the times don't last long. Sorren doesn't look much older than Teag and I—mid- to late twenties at most—but he was turned before Columbus sailed for the New World, and at one time, was the best jewel thief in Antwerp.

"Think he can get anything from the Boston shop?"

I shrugged. "After the bombing last year, I don't know if they're fully up and running again. He's still touchy about it."

"It wasn't his fault."

"I know. And so does he, but Sorren feels responsible for all of us. We break easily." An old enemy of Sorren's had pursued a vendetta against him last year, striking at the other shops like Trifles and Folly that Sorren had established throughout the world. Some of us were lucky and escaped being badly damaged. Boston's shop went up in flames.

"Do you think the Captain flipped those cars?" Teag asked, and I was pretty sure he kept the conversation going to keep me from falling asleep.

"We both felt the magic behind the storm, but I don't think the Captain had anything to do with it," I said, resigning myself to staying awake and shifting my position in the car to look at Teag. "Remember, the ghost went right through me. I'm not sure he was more than a repeater, a stone tape loop. He didn't shove me down the stairs; he caught me by surprise. And he didn't try to hurt any of the guests. He just blinked in and out, going about his business. We were the interlopers in his house."

"Still, he's got to go if they're opening it to the public," Teag said. "Knocking people down the steps attracts more lawsuits than donations."

We stopped to pick up tea for Teag and lattes for me and Mrs. Morrissey at Honeysuckle Café on our way and found her waiting at the door to the grand old restored mansion the Historical Archive uses as its offices.

"You brought me a latte, you amazing, wonderful people!" Mrs. Morrissey swooned, taking the cup and cradling it in her hands. "Come into my office, and we can add a dollop of scotch. It's been that kind of day."

She motioned us to the armchairs and high-backed formal sofa on one side of her office, where she usually meets with donors. I sank into the velvet cushion and tried not to get so comfortable that I'd doze off. We had a ghost to bust.

We let her drink her latte while Teag and I filled in what we had learned about the guest list. We'd been busy enough in the shop that Teag hadn't had a chance to research Kettinger himself, but I had the feeling the Captain wasn't at the heart of the incident.

"The woman in the red suit is Mona Ridenhaus," Mrs. Morrissey said when we finished. "She hasn't been to many of our galas, but she's a small donor with the potential to do more, hence the invitation. I see her more often on the garden club circuit. Her family's been around these parts for a long time, and she's got the resume to prove it: Swiss boarding school, Ivy League women's college, and a die-hard sorority member."

"How about the ice queen blonde?" I asked.

Mrs. Morrissey shook her head. "I saw her, but she must have been someone's 'plus one.'"

"How about the other guy?" Teag asked. "The one with the beard?"

"I don't know him," Mrs. Morrissey replied. "Spotted him right before everything went to hell, and then confronting a possible gate crasher no longer seemed like a priority. Media, perhaps? Except I didn't really see him chatting anyone up. When I noticed him, he was either just watching from the sidelines or examining the furnishings like there was going to be a quiz afterward."

"We'll have to see if he's in any of the pictures," Teag said. "The photographer was busy."

She chuckled. "Yes, but I've already heard back that none of his photos of the Captain turned out. Just blobs of light or a patch of mist."

"Par for the course. Ask Kell how much trouble SPOOK has trying to get pictures of any hauntings." The latte's warmth calmed me down, even as the coffee hit my bloodstream and woke me up.

"How about Kettinger?" Teag asked. "Any reason why he'd be a restless spirit, even if it was something in those boxes that gave him the mojo to manifest?"

Mrs. Morrissey sat back in her seat, holding the cup close, and shook her head. "Cornelius Kettinger owned a merchant ship called the *Lady of Storms* back in the mid-1800s, before the War. He was originally from Massachusetts, but he came down here to expand his Caribbean trade, and he had the bad timing to do it right as tempers started to flare between the North and the South. That meant both sides considered him suspect, and neither was willing to completely trust him. Even so, he did a good business until an accident at sea hurt his back so badly he had to give up his ship. He came home to his house here in Charleston, and everything I could find says he died of natural causes, still pining for the sea."

"Not exactly the kind of guy who starts tossing cars down an alley," Teag said. "So maybe the ghost and the storm aren't related." He finished his tea and set it aside. "How about you? Find out anything new?"

"This is the first I've come up for air all day," Mrs. Morrissey said, "as you can imagine. But I did have two of my staff go back to the house and catalog the items in those new boxes."

"Any sightings of the Captain?" I asked.

She shook her head. "I picked the two least imaginative people on my payroll. Maybe they didn't see him because they don't believe in ghosts, or maybe he was too tuckered out from last night's performance to make an appearance. But they did get through the boxes."

"And?" Teag asked.

Mrs. Morrissey pulled out a folded paper from a pocket of her jacket and smoothed it out on the coffee table in front of us. The color picture of an antique woman's fan probably didn't do the real thing justice, but it still took my breath away. The delicate ribs of the fan were an ivory color, with remarkable etching and carved symbols that were the work of a master.

"I didn't think it was legal to own ivory," Teag mused.

"It depends, and museums get some wiggle room, but that's not ivory," the Archive's director replied. "That's bone."

I felt a chill down my spine. "What kind of bone?" I asked, straining for a better look at the inscriptions. My spidey sense tingled a warning.

"No one's had it tested," she answered. "That's museum-speak for 'we don't want to know.'"

"Well, someone thought it was special," I said, glancing up at Teag. "Take a look at those etchings on the ribs. There's a lot of embellishment, but those are magical symbols. Witchcraft. If we can figure out who stole the fan, I bet we'll get a lead on who called the storm."

CHAPTER 2

As upscale art and antique auction houses went, Linzer's of Charleston was often mentioned in the same rarefied circles as Sotheby's and Christy's. Fine art, old silver, and furniture from makers like Chippendale or Hepplewhite graced the full-color pages of the catalog it sent out several times a year to entice well-heeled bidders.

"We aren't welcome here." Teag adjusted his tie for the third time in ten minutes and glanced around the room. Many of the notable items that would be featured in the afternoon auction were on display—under heavy guard—so that potential buyers could get an up-close view.

"That's not exactly true," I replied, although I had also felt the frosty glare of the auction house's owner when we walked in. "Art Linzer never told us not to attend. Hell, he'd love it if we bought something. He just didn't want me to 'preview' any of his items."

"God forbid he should lose a sale and protect someone from a cursed heirloom," Teag muttered. He glanced at me. "Speaking of which—you picking up any vibes?"

Through trial and error, and some spectacularly embarrassing incidents, I've learned how to shutter my psychometry so that I don't pick up resonance unless it's especially strong. Fortunately, most things—

even very old items—don't have the powerful memories or traces of magic that make my gift perk up and take notice.

Right now, the elite crowd milling around the preview room caught my attention more than the items for sale. I smiled and nodded or greeted many of the same people who were at the ill-fated Kettinger House event last week or that I recognized from other galas for the Archive or Lowcountry Museum. Some were regular customers at Trifles and Folly, using us to divest themselves of antiques or heirlooms that lacked the providence or price point to attract the attention of the Linzer auction. Teag and I weren't in the same financial strata as this crowd personally, but we served that clientele. And Sorren—well, immortality is good for acquiring wealth. Unfortunately, never appearing to age might be a dead giveaway that he was undead, so he left the socializing to us.

"I'm not getting much beyond the usual low hum old stuff usually gives off," I murmured. "A few images and whispers, a bit of an old song or two, but nothing strong or dangerous."

"This isn't everything," Teag replied, leaning toward me so he could speak almost directly into my ear. "There are a couple of very expensive pieces they didn't put on display. Not after what happened to that obsidian bowl."

I could only imagine how much Art Linzer hated having his organization's name appear in anything less than glowing terms, but the report of the theft of a polished obsidian bowl that had belonged to a notable Charleston family did make the news. I guessed the police released the information to put pressure on the thief, making it harder to unload a hot item to buyers who could not claim to be unaware. The theft also explained the presence of enough armed guards to protect the president, whom I was pretty sure wasn't likely to show up for the sale.

I hadn't counted on doing any magic here, beyond my psychometry, but I'd learned to be prepared. My athame—made from the handle of my grandmother's wooden spoon, a cherished keepsake—was in my purse, along with an old ratty dog collar that called my spirit protector, the ghost of my late golden retriever, Bo. I wore an agate necklace for its protective properties and had loose salt in my pockets, just in case. I knew Teag had several weapons—magical and mundane—hidden beneath his blazer as well. Just in case, I accessorize with an antique walking stick that had belonged to Sorren's maker, Alard. Like my athame, the walking stick enabled me to focus my magic for defense.

The crowd politely moved around the display room, studying the objects coming up for bid, and I took note of the overlap in guests between this event and the last one. Neither Mona Ridenhaus—the lady in the red suit with the pancaked Porsche—nor the other drivers of the totaled cars were among those sipping wine and checking off items on their bidding lists. Then again, they probably needed their spare cash to repair or replace their cars. Some of the familiar faces were such fixtures at the city's dinners and fundraisers that I wondered if it was the way the upper crust avoided ever having to eat at home. The Hitchcock blonde who first spotted the Captain's ghost was there, on the arm of a good-looking man whose body language suggested "friend" instead of "partner."

I caught a glimpse of auburn hair and turned, expecting to see the mystery man, but when I looked, he wasn't anywhere in sight. A few other people drew my gaze. One very thin, hawk-faced older man had stood staring at the same antique French clock since we arrived, with such a look of longing that I wanted to suggest he and the clock just get a room. A man and a woman whose wardrobe and attitude screamed "power couple" spoke in whispers to each other in front of a Nineteenth-century landscape painting that didn't hold any appeal to me at all but looked likely to go home with them when the bidding was done.

Another woman looked like a professional buyer, perhaps for an interior designer. She jotted down notes as she moved around the room, zeroing in on particular objects. Unlike the power couple or the red suit woman at the gala, the buyer's dress and jacket were expensive but low-key, suggesting secure enough status to no longer need to impress anyone.

The chime of a bell called us all to the main room, where the bidding was about to start. Teag and I took places in the back row so we could watch the crowd, and I clasped my hands in my lap, so I didn't scratch my nose and accidentally signal the auctioneer to register a bid. Teag looked equally nervous, and I knew we both wished we could change into the more comfortable clothing we usually wore at the shop.

Despite the high ticket items, the bidding was furious, and it was easy to get caught up in the drama as competitors one-upped each other, driving the prices higher and higher. I found myself rooting for total strangers, picking a "winner" in each round, like betting on a horse race. When "my" bidder won, I found myself grinning like I shared in the victory, and when my favorite lost, the stab of disappointment felt personal.

"That's three times now," Teag murmured.

I jolted out of my vicarious bidding war and frowned. "Three?"

He nodded toward the Buyer woman, whose scowl suggested deep frustration. "She's been outbid on every single item, always at the last minute."

I shrugged. "There's always a winner and usually multiple losers. Lots of people get shut down."

Teag shook his head. "It feels...wrong. There's enough money at stake here, do you think someone's resorted to heading off the competition?"

We had certainly seen people cursed for much less expensive reasons. "Could be. Or maybe she's just not good at bidding."

Teag gave me a guilty grin. "I snapped a picture of her and put it on Facebook—the facial recognition tag gave me her name. That's Maria Nevin, the interior designer and decorator. Does all the custom shopping for her very wealthy clients. She's such a regular at this auction I'm surprised she doesn't have her own parking space out front."

I started paying attention and quickly realized Teag was right. In every bid Nevin made, she and her rival would be neck-and-neck until the final seconds, when someone else put in such a large increase that she had to let it go. Maybe there was something to his hex idea.

"Hey, he's here." Teag followed my gaze and saw the guy with the beard from the gala. "Can you see if you can get his name too?"

Teag reached for his phone and maneuvered to be able to get a stealthy photo, but when we looked back again, the man was gone.

I lost my patience with the auction, wishing I could easily slip out to track the man from the gala but staying where I was to avoid making a scene. Nevin's bidding had grown more determined—nearly desperate—and I wondered if she had a major commission riding on her success in bringing back pieces a client coveted. Getting shut out might damage her business, and it certainly wouldn't do good things for her reputation. The idea of a hex seemed more and more likely.

I glanced at the time and then at the audition book that listed the items in order of their appearance. We only had a couple more pieces to go, and I was antsy.

Then they brought out the next object, and I felt my stomach drop. The oil painting of a staggering beautiful young man was completely at odds with the cold, dark malice I felt rolling off of it. The sense of evil hit me like a physical blow, and I couldn't believe that even the mundanes in the audience were oblivious. I glanced around. Clearly, some of the crowd had enough latent sensitivity or strong intuition to recoil. Beside me, Teag tensed as if ready to fight.

We had seen paintings like that before, portraits of fallen angels and Nephilim that served as a portal for the unholy creatures to step out of the portrait and into the real world.

"Silver frame," Teag murmured. "Think it's warded to keep him contained."

"That only lasts until the new owner decides to have it reframed," I replied. "We've got to either buy it or stop the sale."

"The next item is our surprise unveiling," Art Linzer announced. His tone tried for excited and jovial, but I picked up an undercurrent of uneasiness, even in the master showman. "The artist is unknown, and the work is unsigned, but paintings by this master have turned up now and again in galleries, even here in Charleston."

I remembered a larger, similar painting from an exhibit at the Archive that set several Nephilim loose on the city and almost brought about a real, literal Judgment Day with all the pissed-off heavenly host trimmings. That had been a bitch and a half to shut down, and it had taken all that Teag, Sorren, and I had to do it—plus the help of a bunch of friends with some considerable combined magic mojo.

We were not going to do that again.

"I'll bid on it," I hissed. "Figure out how to cause a distraction." Teag slipped out of the row as Linzer droned on for another few minutes about the painting's qualities. Then he opened the bidding, naming a steep minimum price.

Maria Nevin's hand went up immediately. I raised mine to counter, but Linzer glared at me. "I'm sorry, Ms. Kincaide, but sales are only open for registered bidders," he chided.

I called out a figure several thousand dollars higher than Nevin's bid, knowing Sorren would cover it. Linzer blanched. Much as he liked his rules and disliked Trifles and Folly, money was money.

Before he could speak, Nevin's upped the bid, and I saw in the set of her chin that after a day full of losing out, she was determined to win this one—come hell or high water.

I couldn't speak to the "high water," but the hell part was a definite possibility if the fallen angel with the sinfully sexy smirk got loose from his painted prison.

Crossing my fingers, I called out a higher number. Nevin looked daggers at me, and Linzer's expression suggested sudden stomach problems. Nevin topped my bid, and I went higher, trying not to let my voice shake. Sorren would understand. But I was still out on a limb and going farther with every minute.

Nevin jumped to her feet, waving her numbered plastic paddle like a badge of legitimacy, and instead of edging up a little at a time, she jumped the number up by half and gave me a defiant glare, daring me to best her.

I opened my mouth—and just then, the lights went out, plunging the windowless room into complete darkness. Gasps and curses filled the silence. The emergency lights did not kick on.

A few seconds later, the burglar alarm did.

Teag suddenly appeared in the doorway, framed by the only light. "This way!" he shouted, motioning urgently. I hung back in the shadows, watching as the others filed to the door, keeping an eye out for Art Linzer. I circled back around toward the dais where the cursed painting still sat on its easel. As the last few people moved toward the door, I shook the dog collar, calling to my ghostly protector.

"Fetch!" I murmured, pretending to throw a ball, and Bo went bounding in the direction of the doorway, causing the stragglers to cry out in alarm as a ninety-pound glowing translucent dog came galloping toward them. He was friendly to a fault, but they didn't know that as he bore down on them, with massive paws and a wide-open, toothy grin. They screamed, and while their attention was on Bo and scrambling out the door, I focused my magic, concentrated on my target, and sent a stream of blue fire from the walking stick that hit the Nephilim painting square on.

Flames wreathed the painting, but hell was always the natural habitat of the portrait's subject. I blocked out the alarms and the shouting from outside the room and kept my eyes on the fallen angel. He turned to face me, recognizing a threat. His gaze met mine, and his come-hither smile turned to a serial killer smirk. The Nephilim saw me, although the panicked patrons didn't since I still hid in the shadows. And I knew that if he and I ever met again, there would be hell to pay.

Playing his part to the hilt, Teag pushed Linzer and the other stragglers aside. "Cassidy!" he shouted, panic thick in his voice. "Oh God, where is she?"

That was my cue to rush back to the row where we'd been sitting and collapse on the floor before someone turned the lights back on.

Smoke filled the room, and fire alarms blared. The painting burned fast, though its silver frame remained intact, suggesting magical reinforcement. Faking it to the max, I leaned heavily on Teag, who wrapped an arm around my waist to support me as I staggered out, coughing and blinking as if I had been overcome.

"There's a fire in there," I croaked, "The painting just went up—whoosh—and then the smoke—" I coughed and gagged, trying to balance believable with overdone, and it must have been enough for the paramedics because one of them untangled me from Teag's grip and put an oxygen mask over my mouth and nose.

Teag hovered, playing the worried colleague. I didn't miss the fact that he positioned himself to watch the door to the auction suite, just in case the Nephilim survived the fire.

For the second time in as many weeks, Teag and I ended up giving our statements to the police at a high society soiree gone horribly wrong. At this rate, our social calendar was going to be nonexistent. The only saving grace was that many of the other guests had also been at both unlucky events, so the odds of being blackballed for our mere presence was slim.

After the paramedics cleared me, I watched the cops take statements from everyone else. The auburn-haired stranger and the Hitchcock blonde had vanished. Maria Nevin, however, looked ready to take someone apart with her perfectly manicured nails. Yet beneath her rage, I caught a glimpse of fear and desperation and decided there was more here than met the eye.

Teag and I stopped for coffee at the Honeysuckle Café on our way back to the shop, where our assistant, Maggie, had been in charge while we were gone. Maggie has a wardrobe from Woodstock and a head for business, and the retired schoolteacher is tough as nails despite her earth mother exterior. She looked up worriedly as we entered, smelling trouble—or probably, smoke.

"What happened to you?" she fussed, and I realized Teag and I both had streaks of ash on our faces and clothing, and we probably reeked from the fire.

"Do you remember those fallen angel paintings?" I asked, my voice a husky rasp despite the hot tea with honey.

Maggie's expression hardened to a no-nonsense glare. "Dear God, don't tell me they're back!"

"Not anymore," Teag replied. "A new painting came up for auction, and we took care of it."

Maggie gave a curt nod. "Good. We don't need more of that nonsense." She frowned as we moved to take up our usual places behind the counter.

"I've got the front," she said, making a scooting gesture for us to go into the back. "It's been slow all day. Nothing I can't handle. I'm betting you have things you need to do. So go do them." She grinned. "I'll holler if I need you."

"You're the best, Maggie," I said gratefully as I went into the small kitchen that served as our break room. Teag followed and joined me as we sat down at the worn Formica-topped table. As soon as he finished his drink, Teag went to the office and brought back his laptop.

"I want to look into our unlucky bidder and dig a little deeper on Mona with the smashed car," he said. Once Teag dives in, no records are safe, firewalls and security be damned. I'm just glad he's on our side.

"Let's look a little more closely at the fan that was stolen and the painting," I suggested, wondering how long it would take to get the tang of smoke out of my nostrils and throat. "I just wish we could get a fix on that stranger with the beard. It can't be a coincidence that he's been at both incidents—and vanished before anyone could talk to him."

While Teag dug around the dark corners of the internet, I texted Sorren with an update, assuring him we were both safe but filling him in on the incident. His prompt reply surprised me, and I stared at my phone for a moment until Teag looked up.

"What?"

"Sorren decided to stop by Boston on his way here," I reported. I knew he had a new team of associates and a new store in that city after last year's attack, but it would be hard to replace a location that had been open even longer than Trifles and Folly's nearly 350 years.

"He's probably worried that there will turn out to be a connection," Teag said, going back to his hacking. "You know he takes what happened personally, and he'd known that team for a long time. He's still grieving."

I did not envy Sorren his immortality. I remembered the pain of burying my grandparents and the friends I'd lost along the way. The thought of caring and then losing people whose mortal lifespans would seem so brief terrified me, yet Sorren continued to make himself vulnerable. He told me once that enduring the pain was worse than losing what remained of his humanity if he no longer risked caring. I'd seen the way he protected Teag and me—and our other mortal allies. Living forever wasn't for the faint of heart.

"Got something," Teag said after a few minutes of silence. "The fan originally came from Massachusetts. It's old enough to have a long provenance, but it was originally owned by people who lived in Haven Harbor—descendants of accused witches who fled the Salem trials back in the 1600s."

I let out a low whistle. "Seriously? So were the owners themselves witches?"

Teag shrugged. "Don't know. It's changed hands a lot—it's been a long time. The fan belonged to a merchant's wife, and it got passed down from mother to daughter to the wife of Captain Kettinger, who was a many-times great-granddaughter," Teag said, leaning back in his chair.

"Okay," I said slowly, thinking about the ramifications. "That picture of the fan definitely showed magical inscriptions on the bone ribs, and old magic is strong magic."

"So you're thinking whoever stole the fan knew what he or she was taking."

I nodded. "Absolutely. It's too much of a coincidence. If the thief wanted something valuable, there were other pieces in those boxes worth a lot more." I shook my head. "Someone took the fan deliberately. Now the question is—was it for the magic or the connection to Salem?"

"What about the painting? It didn't get stolen."

"Could you find anything out about it? Does it have a Salem connection?"

Teag's fingers moved so fast on the keyboard they nearly blurred. He shook his head. "Nope. Came from a private collection in Cleveland. No Massachusetts provenance at all." He frowned. "Hold up. What's this?"

I couldn't help leaning forward, although the back of the computer case hid the screen from me. "That piece that was stolen from Linzer's before it could go up for auction," Teag said, scanning his screen. "The obsidian bowl. They still have no idea how it vanished—all the doors were locked, and none of the alarms went off. But—hold onto your hula hoop—this is the important part, the bowl came to a Charleston family from the estate of a woman in Virginia, whose ancestors on her mother's side, came from Salem, via Haven Harbor."

"Shit. That's the connection. And we still don't have a clue as to why."

Teag cracked his knuckles and crossed his arms over his chest. "So at the first event, we get a freak storm, and some cars get knocked around. At the second one, the painting shows up, but it might not have anything to do with the fan and the bowl." He shook his head. "I don't get it. Nothing else weird happened."

"How about Mona and Maria?" I asked. "Any luck turning up something on them? Maybe that will show us the connection."

"Checking," he said, and his head dropped as he focused all his attention on the screen. I got up and poured myself a cup of coffee and washed down a couple of ibuprofen to get rid of the headache I hadn't been able to shake since the fire.

"Nothing. Nada. Bupkis," Teag finally said, pushing away from the table in frustration.

"You can't find anything?"

He shrugged. "No, I found plenty. But no connection. Mona is a successful real estate agent, who is beloved by her clients and not so much by her colleagues and competitors, who say she's abrasive and overly aggressive."

"That squares with the impression I got, and I didn't even tour a house with her."

"Maria Nevin is an interior designer. Divorced, well-regarded in her industry, even gives some talks at conferences. They don't live in the same neighborhood, didn't graduate from the same schools. The only thing they've got in common is that both are from old Charleston families, but then again, so are most folks who live or do business south of Broad Street."

Broad Street in Charleston had long been the demarcation line between the blue bloods and everyone else. Pat Conroy even wrote a novel about the area. Plenty of people lived there who had no connection to magic, witchcraft, or Salem. We had hit a wall.

"How about our bearded stranger," I asked.

Teag looked up. "You know, if you weren't dating Kell, I'd think you had a thing for this guy with how often you've mentioned him."

I gave him a withering look, which he totally deserved. "Not interested in that way. You've gotta admit, it's suspicious that he was at both events, and we've never seen him before."

Teag chewed on his lip as he thought. "Maybe. He could be someone's guest or plus-one. Or a gate-crasher who knows how to pull it off."

"I'm not buying it," I said, tilting my chair back on its rear legs. "If he were a guest or companion, he wouldn't have booked it out of there like the cops would find his mug shot. And I could believe a gate-crasher once, but twice so close together?" I shook my head. "Doesn't seem likely."

"I'm going over the security camera footage from the auction house," Teag said, stopping every few minutes to type something. "Okay, that's just wrong."

"What?"

Teag looked up. "I found him. Only every time he comes in range of the cameras, his face blurs. You'd almost think it was magic."

CHAPTER 3

"I HAVEN'T SEEN A RASH OF THEFTS LIKE THIS IN THIRTY YEARS." Alistair McKinnon generally was not a man given to venting his frustrations. But I could practically see his nostrils flare from the tone of his voice over the phone.

"I'm just giving you a heads-up so you know to protect yourselves," Alistair went on. "Someone might try to pass something off at Trifles and Folly. I know that you know your business, but be careful."

The director of the Lowcountry Museum of Charleston sounded like he had worked himself into a dither. Teag and I worked closely with Alistair on many occasions, and he was a good guy. I hated to see him so upset.

"Have there been thefts from the museum?" I asked, knowing it was a sensitive question. Museums hated to admit vulnerability, and directors could find themselves held personally accountable by donors and board members, although they had no control over the situation.

Alistair's sigh conveyed the weight of worry on his shoulders. "Yes. Several. Damned black market. Collectors will stop at nothing to get what they want, even if it robs the rest of humanity of being able to enjoy and study a significant piece of history."

This wasn't the first time I had heard Alistair inveigh against obsessive wealthy collectors, who thought nothing of paying shady characters to steal from exhibits or museum storerooms, defraud owners, or even rob historical sites for the joy of laying claim to a coveted treasure. Even if the purloined piece had to be hidden away to avoid prosecution. For some people, the thrill of ownership mattered more than the law, morality, or common sense.

"I'm sorry to hear that," I said, feeling for the tough position the thefts created for the museum and its director. "What will you do?"

"We're doing a security audit," Alistair said, and I could imagine him pacing and running his hands through his well-coiffed white hair. "I imagine that will recommend all kinds of new gadgets and gizmos, which will drive my staff crazy getting access to their own offices, and probably won't slow down a determined thief at all."

"Was there any connection among the pieces?" I probed. "Were they part of the same lot? Come from a single estate sale?"

Alistair doesn't know the full truth about Trifles and Folly being a cover for a cabal of mortals and immortals who get haunted and dangerous magical objects off the market and save the world. But he does know about my psychometry, and he's called on our assistance more than once with display pieces that came with a little unwanted "something extra."

"If you're looking for some kind of paranormal provenance, I'm sorry to disappoint you, but there's nothing in common except that they were here, supposedly safe."

"Can you give me a list of what the items were?" I asked. "In case something would show up at the shop," I hastened to add, although I figured Alistair read the fib for what it was.

"Sure. I had to give the cops a list, and I emailed it to the museum collective, so my colleagues can be on the lookout. Why not?"

We ended the call with a promise to meet for lunch, and I retrieved the list from my email. Teag came into the office as I finished reading.

"Something up with the museum?"

I filled Teag in, and he frowned. "I go back to the belief that there are no coincidences. First the fan, then the bowl, and now a bunch of unrelated stuff from the museum. Want to bet that one of those pieces isn't unrelated at all?"

"But why steal more than what you'd need?" I wondered aloud. "I'd think that would just increase the risk. It's not like they can be easily fenced for a quick buck."

"I don't think our thief is looking to pay off his gambling debts," Teag replied. "If so, he'd knock over a convenience store. Maybe the pieces were packed together in a crate, and someone just grabbed the box and ran instead of taking the time to fish out what he wanted. Or maybe we've got someone clever enough to grab a bunch of stuff just to cloud the issue."

"Doing a pretty good job of it," I groused.

"How long ago were the thefts?"

I thought back to the conversation with Alistair. "Pretty recent. He's still dealing with the fall-out."

"Poor guy. I hope the board and the donors don't rake him over the coals."

Alistair had that old money Charleston stiff upper lip that took bad luck and natural disasters in stride, but I knew how much he loved the museum and his work as a curator, and I didn't want him to come to any harm. "He's built up a lot of goodwill over the years, and he's got a rock-solid reputation. I'm sure he'll weather the storm," I replied, crossing my fingers to make it so.

Just then, my phone rang. I glanced down. "It's Kell."

Teag grinned. "I'll just leave you two lovebirds alone then," he said with a wink, grabbing his laptop and heading into the office.

"Hi! What's up?" Kell didn't usually call during the workday unless he had the kind of problem Teag and I were particularly suited to handle.

Kell Winston ran the Southern Paranormal Observation and Outreach Klub, better known as SPOOK. Charleston was one of the most haunted cities in the United States, and we seemed to have paranormal investigators and ghost tours on every corner, but Kell and his crew were the real deal, serious, respected parapsychologists who knew their stuff and did it right. Needless to say, our work and my touch magic meant that Kell and my paths crossed often and that eventually led to a relationship.

"Hey, Cassidy. Can you talk?" Kell sounded strained, and that told me immediately that this wasn't a social call.

"Sure," I said, getting up to toe my office door shut. "What's up?"

"I got a call from a lady about a haunting, but I've got to tell you, I think it sounds more like a curse."

"Oh?" Kell and I had both been around enough supernatural stuff to have pretty good instincts.

"She got a quirky present as a housewarming gift when she moved, and now she thinks it's sicced a ghost on her."

"Is she seeing filmy figures? Feeling cold spots? Are plates flying across the room?"

"Worse. Her 'lucky vase' was supposed to make all her dreams come true, and within two weeks, she's gone from on top of the world to the brink of ruin."

Which explains how I found myself getting out of Kell's car on a lovely side street in a good neighborhood less than an hour later. Amy Bedford waited inside, hoping we could put an end to her affliction.

"Are you sure she's going to be all right with you bringing me into this?" I asked, eyeing the stately home. The style was Charleston single-house, presenting the narrow side of the home to the street and blocking off the wide front porch with its own doorway for greater privacy. The rainbow-hued stucco home near The Battery was on one of the city's most sought-after and prestigious locations, and these homes usually remained in wealthy old families for generations or sold for millions to celebrities or internet billionaires.

"Right now, I think she'd welcome the Devil himself if she thought it could fix the damage—no offense intended," Kell added with a smile.

"None taken," I replied. "Although I really doubt the kind of 'damage' that's happened can just be rewound like an old videotape."

Within two weeks, since getting the questionable vase, Amy's husband had walked out on her, she'd received bad lab reports from her doctor, her stock portfolio had inexplicably tanked, and hackers had siphoned off most of her bank account. Her dog had come down with a mysterious ailment, her credit cards were stolen, someone side-swiped her new and expensive car, and the IRS contacted her accountant about a problem with back taxes. As if that wasn't enough, she had an acne flair-up, her hair started to fall out, and she'd gained ten pounds.

I pitied her, but I was also a little afraid to go inside in case the bad luck was contagious.

"Where's the rest of your team?" I asked, expecting to see Drew, Pete, and Calista waiting for us.

"I didn't figure this was their kind of gig," Kell replied. "Does it sound like a haunting to you?"

I shook my head. "No. If I had to guess, I'd guess a curse or hex."

"Yep. Which is more your kind of thing. I'm here for backup and to introduce you as my 'ghost-hunting colleague,'" he added with a grin and a look in his eyes that promised a different sort of collaboration later. "Figured we could catch dinner afterward if you're up for it."

"Definitely. Let's see if I can keep things from getting worse, even if I can't put things back to where they started."

Amy Bedford met us at the door. One look told me she was a woman at the end of her rope, and with the litany of bad luck Kell had reported, I understood why. Under other circumstances, I imagined she could look very professional and put together. Her haircut looked expensive, but I guessed she had done nothing to style it, perhaps not even blown it dry. Without makeup, the dark circles beneath her eyes looked like bruises, and her skin flaked around the angry acne as if she had overdone the drugstore cleansing wipes that promised salvation to pockmarked teenagers.

The baggy gray T-shirt and sweatpants she wore only heightened the sense that all of the life and color had been drained from her. "C'mon in," she said, as if she had given up hope that anyone could actually save her, but she was resigned to going through the motions because we were there. She waved us in with a hand, and I noticed her nails were bitten down until they bled.

A glance around the house as we followed Amy to the kitchen suggested that before everything went to hell, she had done well for herself. The place had a pulled-together look that made me think Amy either had exceptional taste or she had hired a decorator. The furnishings, paintings, and knick-knacks were good quality, well-made but not extravagant. Yet at the moment, the interior was as disheveled as its owner. Unopened mail lay on the counter. Dirty dishes piled in the sink. I could see into the living room, and from the bags of chips, wine glass, empty carton of ice cream on the coffee table, and the nest of pillows and blankets on the couch, it looked like Amy had given up and decided to escape into one long, Cabernet-fueled binge watching marathon.

"Thanks for coming, but I don't think anyone can help me," Amy said and motioned listlessly for us to sit down at the kitchen table. "Coffee?"

We both shook our heads, and she looked a little relieved. I got the feeling just putting one foot ahead of the other took all her energy.

The minute I set foot inside, I could feel magic hanging heavy over everything, like cloying incense. Two different types of power, warring with each other. The first kind of magic felt benign, middling in power. It sank into the furniture and carpet, the wood of the walls, and the fabric of the drapes like a signature floral perfume, clean and citrusy. Not dangerous. The other magic was of a different sort, and I guessed it came from the curse or hex that had caused all the problems. It gave a rank, putrid note, like a dead mouse in the heating vent. Definitely very, very dangerous.

"This is Cassidy Kincaide, a colleague of mine," Kell said in a voice that managed to be gentle without condescension. "She's got a knack for this kind of thing. I briefed her a bit, but can you tell her what was going on for you right before things started to happen. Don't leave out any details; sometimes little things make all the difference."

Amy reached for an electronic cigarette and puffed out a wisp of clove-scented steam. "I didn't smoke before everything fell apart. Now,

I figure with my luck, I'll probably get lung cancer and drop dead before they can foreclose." Her hand shook as she held the device, and the expression on her face suggested utter resignation.

"What was it like…before?" I asked quietly.

Amy barked a bitter laugh. "Before? I apparently had the world in the palm of my hand and didn't realize it, because let me tell you, the fall to where I am now has been pretty damn long." Another puff, and I saw her eyes flicker to the counter, where a half dozen bottles of wine and whiskey were well on their way to being empty.

"I was a senior manager for a big computer company," she continued. "Flew around the country managing development teams; hell, sometimes I flew all over the world, depending on the project. VIP suite at the big industry trade shows, everybody wanted to wine and dine me to get contracts. Married a guy I met in grad school. He had just as good a job for a management consulting company. We were, as they say, a 'power couple,'" she observed, her voice heavy on the irony as she mimed the air quotes.

"We just moved into the house six months ago, not long before the shit hit the fan," Amy said, and this time the pain in her eyes knotted my stomach. She drew on the e-cig and fell silent for so long that I didn't think she would continue.

"Lots of people knew about the move," Amy finally went on. "Everyone sent housewarming presents: family, friends, old neighbors, co-workers, even some of the vendors and suppliers we worked with a lot. That's why I didn't think it was strange when I couldn't find the tag."

My head jerked up. "What tag?"

"A gift came in the mail, and it looked like the return address had gotten wet, and the ink had smeared. Couldn't read it. Figured there would be a card but no tag, no card. So maybe an oversight, I thought. Inside was a beautiful antique vase. It looked expensive. I couldn't imagine who might have sent it. The only thing with the vase besides the packing paper was a little calligraphy card that said the vase was a 'wishing well.' I was supposed to write down things I wished for and put the slips of paper in the vase, and…my wishes would come true."

Kell and I traded another glance. "Did you sense anything about the vase when you handled it?" I asked. "A strange tingle, an odd feeling."

"I know what magic feels like!" Amy snapped. "That's the hell of it. You'd have thought I'd have picked up on bad mojo. I'm a witch."

I hadn't seen that coming.

Before I could say anything, Amy leveled a jaded look at me. "Go on. Say it. No such thing as witches, magic isn't real."

"I'm here with a ghost hunter," I replied. "I'm hardly going to throw stones at glass houses." I paused, then decided to just jump right in. "Tell me about your witchcraft."

Amy stared at me from slitted eyes for a moment as if working out whether I was playing her for a fool. "All right," she said, taking another puff. "All the women on my mother's side of the family have been witches. They've helped their families do well for themselves, financially and socially. It's an old South of Broad family. You can look it up in the Social Registry," she drawled in a voice like honeyed poison.

"I guess I was the runt of the litter, because my so-called magic never seemed good for much. Other people got a knack for beating the stock market or the horse races or even moving things with their minds. Me, I can make plants grow like nobody's business. Plants. You want to know what's really funny? I'm allergic to pollen. Yeah. What kind of useless magic is that when I can't be around the things I can grow without breaking out in hives?"

That explained how a cursed object had gotten by her. A poisoned floral arrangement, she might have noticed. I wasn't ready to touch Amy—I didn't know how the curse worked, and I wasn't going to take chances—but just sitting near her, I picked up a faint glimmer of power. I'd overlooked it in the overwhelming cluster of impressions that assaulted my senses before, but now that I knew what to look for, I could feel it.

Amy's power matched the floral-tinged magic I'd felt permeating the furnishings, and now that made sense. Even if her witchcraft wasn't strong, daily exposure would sink into everything around her like day-old cigar smoke. The magic that I sensed when I concentrated on Amy felt weak and flickering, and I wondered if the curse drained her power, making her increasingly vulnerable and unable to fight back.

"The wishes you wrote down, the things you put into the vase—"

"Gone," Amy said, and this time, she got up and poured whiskey into her empty coffee cup. "I wished for a long and happy marriage. He left me. I wished for a successful career. Fired. A happy home. Fore-closed. Good health." She didn't even bother countering that. "I wished for my best friend, Maria, to get more clients because her business was struggling. Instead, the clients she did have are jumping ship, and after that auction she got shut out of, she'll probably lose the rest. Every single effing thing I wanted to go right, it twisted and took away. Though, since I got my labs back from the doctor, maybe I don't have to worry about it for too much longer. Huntington's Disease—it's genetic and inherited. Want to know the kicker? No one in my family ever had it."

"Wait a second," I said. "Back up. Your best friend Maria is going to be ruined because of an auction?"

Amy nodded. "She's an interior designer, and her clients always loved how she could find them really different accent pieces. Maria's been a genius at picking gold out of trash at estate sales and auctions. But she had a big commission riding on that last sale at Linzer's, and she got shut out on every piece. It was like the universe conspired against her. And then she lost the commission, and several of that client's friends bailed. She's probably going to have to file for bankruptcy."

"Maria Nevin?" I asked. Amy nodded.

"You know her?" Amy asked.

"I happened to be at the sale. I saw the bidding, and I'll agree it seemed strange," I replied.

The longer we stayed in the house, the more I could sense the evil, the sheer malice of the curse. I couldn't imagine how Amy managed to live there, except that she had already given up hope. We were likely her last chance, and that firmed my resolve to find a way to ease her suffering even if we couldn't set things back to how they were before.

"Do you have any enemies? Anyone who would hate you enough to do this?" I asked. Of all the supernatural phenomena I run into, I hate dark magic the most because of the intentional cruelty.

"I didn't think so," Amy replied, toying with the e-cig. She took a sip of the whiskey in her mug. "I mean, you never know in a corporate job. Someone who wanted my job, someone who got passed over for a promotion and blamed me, someone I fired." She shrugged. "I tried not to be a bitch, you know? Didn't have a problem giving orders but tried not to be a dick about it. Got good 360-reviews from bosses, co-workers, subordinates. Outside vendors asked to work with me. Never gave the neighbors any reason to call the cops." She shook her head. "I don't get it."

"Your ex-husband?"

"Rob? He wasn't a vengeful kind of guy. Decided to go into the priesthood. Imagine that. Wasn't even Catholic. Kinda hard to argue that he shoulda picked me over God, you know?"

"Anyone who might have known about your magic?"

She gave me a hard stare, trying to figure out whether I was mocking her. "No. My mother was disappointed that I couldn't do more, but she died five years ago. No sisters. I mean, the plant magic I can't use without getting a rash isn't much of a threat to anyone."

"And you have no idea who sent it?"

Amy shook her head. "No. I went over the packaging to figure out where it came from so I could send a 'thank-you' note." She shrugged. "My mom was a real stickler for manners. Even took it to the post office and the UPS place, but they couldn't trace it back to anyone. Apparently, someone paid cash to mail it from a small town on the way to Myrtle Beach. There's no trail."

"All right," I said. "Let's take a look at the vase that ruined your life."

Even in the basement inside an old refrigerator, the vase still polluted the house with so much dark magic I could feel it like a coating on my tongue.

"I put it down here, trying to see if I could get away from it," Amy said. "Maybe I should have tried putting plants in it and getting them to grow over it, but I figured it would give me poison ivy."

Up close, the curse felt old and complex. "Whoever sent this to you didn't create the bad magic," I said, struggling not to recoil even from several feet away. "It's a very old vase, centuries maybe. It should be in a museum."

That triggered a thought. I excused myself and walked up the base-ment steps to get a signal on my phone, then speed-dialed Alistair. When I described the vase, he recognized it immediately as one of his stolen treasures.

"Um, I don't think you want it back," I said and told him briefly about its curse. "Since it's already 'missing,' how about we agree this conversation never happened, and I get some friends with special abili-ties to make it go away, so it never hurts anyone again?" Alistair agreed faster than I expected, so I could do what I intended to do anyhow with a clear conscience.

"One more thing," I said before Alistair could hang up. "Do you know who the collector was who owned the vase?" I listened and closed my eyes when I heard "Massachusetts." "All right. Thanks. We'll handle it."

"It's Etruscan. Even older than I thought," I told Amy. "Somebody stole it from a museum. I just spoke to the curator. Some temple cults had 'curse jars' they believed drew on the power of the gods. I can't say for sure where this thing gets its juju, but I can get rid of it for you."

"Will that fix anything?" Amy asked, although the look on her face told me she already knew the answer.

"Probably not," I replied reluctantly. "But it should stop more from going wrong. And maybe things will take a turn for the better."

The old refrigerator looked like it had been in the basement for a long time, because it was probably from the 1950s. I remembered a movie where a guy climbed in one to survive a nuclear bomb. And yet, it hadn't completely stopped the curse.

Kell and I went out to my car and returned with a lead box that was heavy as hell and a big canister of salt.

"I don't know whether this vase has some kind of evil spirit attached to it, but it might fight us getting rid of it until it's finished its mission."

Amy blanched, guessing that the "mission" had been to kill her. "All right. What do you need me to do?"

I smiled at the first sign of fighting spirit Amy had shown since we arrived. "For now, just stand out of the way—unless any killer plants sneak up on us," I added with a tight smile.

"Gotcha," Amy replied.

I took a deep breath and let my left hand rest on the protective stones of my agate necklace. I kept its energy charged up by placing it out in the light of the full moon each month and having the blessing of a Voudon mambo renewed every time I relied on its power to help me out of a tight spot. In my right hand, I gripped a big canister of salt.

Kell stood behind me with a pair of iron tongs coated in silver and blessed with holy water. The lead box had a protective coating of salt inside, and inscribed runes and sigils covered every surface, creating additional levels of protection. It was the supernatural equivalent of a hazmat container, and I was really glad we had brought it along.

Touching something with that kind of evil magic would be a big mistake, considering my psychometry. But I couldn't let Kell—a guy who believed in the paranormal but had zero magic of his own—take the first shot.

"Okay," I said, hoping I sounded braver than I felt, "I'm going to dump the salt into the vase. No idea how it will react, but I doubt it will go over well. Assuming we don't get a mushroom cloud, you grab it with the tongs and put it in the box. Try not to break it—if there's a spirit or demon trapped inside, we don't want to make things worse by setting it free."

Kell accepted my instructions like they were the most normal thing in the world. Amy stared at us, and I could tell she was wondering what kind of batshit crazy people were loose in her house.

"Trust me, I'm a professional," I said with a wry smirk. "This probably won't be the worst thing I'll see this month." True, but also depressing. I didn't have time to dwell on it.

I lunged forward, hoping the vase didn't have a sentient spirit possessing it and pulled the sliding refrigerator shelf forward, then dumped the salt out as fast as it would pour. An enraged shriek split the air, making the walls tremble, and I wondered if my ears were going to bleed. If I had laid my head on top of the most obnoxious and loud ambulance/police/fire siren in the world when it was going off full-tilt, it couldn't have been more deafening or painful. I gritted my teeth and kept the salt stream steady, vowing to make a bigger hole in the canister next time, because it was taking too damn long.

Thick black smoke began to pour from the vase. It smelled like a funeral pyre.

"Hold your breath!" I shouted to the others, ducking my face inside the collar of my shirt to try to keep the noxious, greasy smoke from getting in my nose and mouth. My head felt like it was going to crack open from the shrieking, and my lungs burned as I tried not to breathe. The canister grew lighter in my grip, but the thing inside the vase wasn't subdued.

"Water!" I shouted at Kell, who ran forward and sloshed a generous amount of holy water onto the vase and a fair amount of spillage onto me. The smoke turned to sizzle, like meat cooking on hot coals. I choked back the need to puke and decided right then I wasn't eating steak for a long time.

"Go!" I yelled as I poured out the last of the salt.

Kell's mouth was a grim line of determination as he grabbed the tongs in a relay from hell and clamped on to the lip of the vase, lifting it gingerly from the shelf and carrying it a few feet away to the lead box. When he snapped the lid shut and wound silver chains around it, just for good measure, the air cleared like the break in the clouds after a tornado.

"Is it...gone?" Amy asked.

I shook my head. "Contained. Still dangerous, but that's spell-worked, blessed lead with silver and salt. It'll hold just about everything except Lucifer himself." Maybe.

"Don't think I'm not grateful, but...what are you?" Amy asked hesitantly.

"An antique dealer and a ghost hunter," I replied truthfully.

She let that slide. "What are you going to do with it? Can something like that be destroyed?"

I intended to give the box and its problematic contents to Sorren to dispose of. My guess was we'd have Father Anne do an exorcism, just in case, and then Sorren would probably hand it off to the Briggs Society, an odd, secretive group that served as the supernatural equivalent of a bomb disposal unit.

"We'll make sure it never hurts anyone again," I promised her. "And if you like, I can have a priest or a mambo stop by to dispel any remaining bad energy." I paused. "Amy, you haven't seen a man with auburn hair and scruff of red beard—you know, the trimmed stubble style—have you?"

Amy thought hard. "That sounds familiar, but it's not anyone I know. I might have seen someone like that. Wait," she said, and I didn't blame her for being a little scrambled after all she had been through. "I did see him. I thought maybe he was new in the neighborhood. He's been around for the last week or so. Not stalkerish, just passing on the sidewalk, sitting on a bench in the park down the street, and I wondered if he'd just moved in."

"He didn't try to talk to you or get into the house?" I pressed.

Her eyes widened. "Hell, no! Why, do you think he will? Break in, I mean."

I knew Amy had been through a lot, and I didn't want to needlessly worry her, but I also knew that forewarned is forearmed. "I'm not sure," I replied truthfully. "He's turned up in some odd situations lately, and we don't know who he is. If he does approach you, don't tell him anything about the vase and get away quickly. You might want to stay in well-traveled areas. And if he comes to the house—"

"Don't worry. I won't let him in," she said with a tired smile. She took a deep breath and let it out again, willing herself to relax.

"It's over," she murmured, more to herself than for our benefit. "It's finally over." But it wasn't, not really. Whoever had hated her enough to ruin her life had done a damn fine job of it, with damage that couldn't be set right. What we could do was find the person behind the attack and make sure they paid for what they had done.

"Thank you," Amy said, walking us to the door as Kell and I carried the lead box between us. "And when you find out who did this —kick their asses for me."

Kell and I agreed to take a raincheck on dinner since neither of us wanted to leave the lead box and its toxic treasure in my trunk any longer than necessary. I called Sorren, and he was waiting at the back door of Trifles and Folly when I arrived, with Teag behind him, looking worried and curious.

"Got a new wrinkle," I reported as Sorren transferred the box to his car. "The victim is a witch."

Sorren and Teag listened intently as I told them what had happened at Amy's home. At my description of the vase—and Alistair's confirmation of its origin—Sorren actually winced.

"I'll give Archibald Donnelly a call," he said when I finished. "He's best prepared to deal with something like that. He can either find a way to dispose of it without bringing about an apocalypse or put it in that damned *wunderkammern* of his with the rest of the things that should never see the light of day."

Donnelly was a powerful necromancer and the guardian of the Briggs Society, an arcane organization that slipped through time and space, removing particularly dangerous objects and providing shelter for those explorers unfortunate enough to be caught in a time glitch. If anyone could deal with a murderous Etruscan curse pot, it would be Donnelly.

"It turns out Amy was friends with Maria and accidentally got her caught up in the curse. So now we know what was going on at the auction. And we've got a Massachusetts connection," I added, recounting what I'd learned. "Did you find out anything from your Boston people?"

"I have them working with contacts in the Haven Harbor community," Sorren replied. "That town was founded by the witches and their families lucky enough to flee Salem and escape the Trials. Among themselves, they're pretty open about their magic, but you can understand why they'd be hesitant to trust outsiders."

Sorren had told me all about what happened in Salem from a unique point of view, since he had been living in the Colonies at the time. He'd avoided the more religious settlements since they liked vampires as much as they liked witches, but members of the supernatural community took any persecution of other paranormals personally. Sorren recalled horrors the history books had long forgotten. I shivered.

"Do you think someone from there is behind the attacks?" I asked. Something about that theory struck me wrong, although the link provided strong circumstantial evidence.

Sorren frowned. "I doubt it, unless they've got a rogue. In which case, I would expect they'd be trying to stop the perpetrator themselves and contain the damage."

"That red-haired guy," Teag said, just as the same thought crossed my mind.

"I didn't see him, but Amy said he's been around in the neighborhood. She thought he was a new neighbor."

Teag went to fetch his laptop. "Let me see if there are any security cameras I can hack in that area," he said. "Of course, if it's like the last time, he gets lost in a lens flare," he muttered. "I'm still betting witch or shapeshifter."

"I'm betting perp or P.I.," I replied. "What do you think the odds are that he's either the one behind the attacks or he's been sent by the Haven Harbor people to get their items back or stop a witch who's gone off the rails?"

"Pretty high, actually," Sorren replied. "Let me give them his description and see what they come up with. You know I remember what happened in Salem—and some of the original settlers in Haven Harbor were friends of mine. I don't think there's a conspiracy, but there could be a bad apple. I promise you, I'll get to the bottom of this."

CHAPTER 4

"How do people figure this stuff is harmless?" Teag muttered under his breath as we made the rounds a special exhibit at one of Charleston's many galleries. As fellow merchants on King Street, showing face at neighboring shop's open houses and receptions was part of doing business, even if I sometimes just longed for an evening at home binge-watching old movies and snuggling my little Maltese dog, Baxter.

"Because they don't watch TV or read horror novels," I replied. "Or they think all that stuff is just pretend." As if.

Normally I adored the displays at the Glassworks shop. The Dale Chihuly exhibit had me swooning, and the Murano glass spectacular dazzled me with color and craftsmanship. I could only fault Halloween enthusiasm for the unfortunate theme of the current end of October event. "Lucifer-Morningstar: The Lightbringer."

"You'd think the church people would be picketing or something," Teag murmured. "After all, this is the 'Holy City.'" Charleston has a historic church on just about every corner, and it has its Old School adherents. Either the kinds of folks who took to picketing on a Saturday night thought they'd get more bang for their buck protesting a violent movie, or they didn't keep track of what the chi-chi art galleries were up to. Either way, to my relief, the street outside was empty of anything more than the usual traffic.

The tourist rush was over, but late October was a wonderful time to see the city when the heat and humidity hovered at more reasonable levels. Cool breezes tempered the remaining warmth, and I'd probably be able to turn off my air conditioning soon. Still, shoppers packed the gallery, and I hoped as we queued up to enter, that the provocative title was just a stroke of marketing genius.

"Uh-oh." Teag pointed, and I followed his direction to see arcane sigils etched into the glass of an elaborate set of hurricane lanterns, twining up and around the crystal chimneys in an intricate, magically significant pattern.

"Recognize them?" I asked quietly.

Teag frowned. "Nothing dark there, mostly protection runes. Handy in a hurricane, but you'd be better off with a good generator."

I greeted David and Ed, the shop owners, and complimented them on the beautiful exhibit. Despite my reservations from a magical perspective, the gallery looked wonderful, filled with candlelight reflecting and refracting through crystal lamps, candelabra, candle-sticks, and lanterns, made even more beautiful with silver knick-knacks and handmade mirrors.

David and Ed thanked us for coming and accepted my gushing remarks, but they both seemed edgy. I wanted to ask what possessed—no pun intended—them to go with a Lucifer theme, but I couldn't quite figure out the right way to bring it up. When Ed slipped outside to talk to someone, I followed discreetly, leaving Teag to work the room and scope out potentially dangerous baubles.

Tonight, the gallery had a wine bar set up just inside the big front windows, so I had an excuse to work my way up to where I could see the street. Ed was talking with a couple of cops, and from his expres-sion and gestures, he seemed pretty worked up about something.

Just then, three fire engines raced down the street, sirens blaring.

I took my glass of wine and one for Teag and turned back to the exhibit, having lost my pretense to hover by the window. When I rejoined Teag, he looked worried.

"Ed's talking to the cops. Something's wrong," I reported.

"Dave looks a little twitchy," Teag agreed. "He should be working the room like a boss, and he's not. That's unusual."

I nodded. "How about the display pieces? Anything likely to summon the Antichrist or open the gates of hell?"

He shook his head. "Fortunately, no. A lot of the items are etched with occult symbols, but it's all protective, if not just decorative."

"Seriously?" To me, that was like casually stenciling the nuclear bomb detonation codes as a living room border. I get that many people don't believe the supernatural is real but have some respect. Ancient warnings are there for a reason.

Then again, if more people stopped to consider that fooling around with powers they don't understand just might be like playing with gasoline, we'd have a lot less business at the shop.

"Have you seen Stubble Guy?" I asked, scanning the crowd as I sipped my wine.

"Nope. Not as much overlap as the last two events. I don't recognize most of these people."

Teag was right; this crowd was mostly downtown merchants and tourists, not the pâté and patronage crowd. The Hitchcock blonde wasn't among the admirers who wound their way through the breakable displays, and neither were Mona or Maria.

Just then, my phone buzzed. I glanced down and saw a text from Sorren. *Come now.*

"Gotta go," I said, nudging Teag's elbow. Ed was nowhere to be seen, so we set our empty goblets aside and said our goodbyes to David, then headed back to Trifles and Folly.

When we entered the back room at Trifles and Folly, Sorren stood guard over the red-haired man, who was tied to one of our break room chairs. I recognized the rope—a special blend of fibers soaked in a solution of spell-dampening plants, shot through with silver and iron. It looked like the guy had put up a good fight. He had a bruise starting on his cheek. His shirt was torn and dirt streaked his pants. The man hung against his bonds, unconscious, and I figured Sorren had glamored him. The chair sat inside a circle inscribed with protective runes and a circle of salt. Whatever juju the guy had wouldn't be helping him go anywhere.

"Where did you find him?" I asked.

"Skulking around the alley behind the glass exhibit," Sorren replied. "Right after the owners reported a theft, but before an old house south of Broad went up in flames in a mysterious fire."

Yikes. "You think it's related?"

Sorren nodded. "At this point, we can't afford not to, until proven otherwise. The real question is, do we have an ally here or an enemy?"

"You glamored him?" Teag said it with a chuckle, as if Sorren was a real bad-ass, which he totally was.

Sorren rolled his eyes. "Would you have preferred me to pummel him into submission? He's a witch. I'm a vampire. It would have gotten messy."

Teag pulled out his phone and tried to get some photos of the guy. Whatever he had done to keep from being recorded before must have been a conscious effort, because the pictures came up just fine. "I'm going to text them to Rowan and see if she knows him," he said. Rowan was a local witch of considerable power who had helped us out on more than one occasion.

"Can you wake him up without getting us all struck by lightning?" I asked, eyeing the bound witch warily.

Sorren chuckled. "He's powerful, but I'm old. Experience trumps talent every time." Hearing Sorren call himself "old" struck me funny, since he's got the look of a twenty-something European hipster, but he was already two hundred years old when he met Shakespeare.

"Go for it," I said, stepping back nonetheless.

Sorren moved forward, tipping the man's chin up and speaking a word to him I could not catch. The red-haired guy came awake struggling, shouting a powerful invocation that…did absolutely nothing. No one said anything as he railed and fought until he finally quieted and glared at Sorren with a baleful look that promised trouble once he got free.

"I don't have time for this," the man spat. "I've got important work to do, and you're getting in my way."

Sorren crossed his arms. "I found you behind a shop where a powerful magic item had just been stolen."

"And you didn't find said item on me, did you?" The red-head snarled. "Did you check in my pockets? Maybe it's in with my wallet. I was tracking the thief, you idiot!"

I rocked back on my heels, and Teag's eyes widened. Even when he's doing his best impersonation of a mortal, Sorren has something about him that makes assholes give him a wide berth. Our prisoner was a witch of some power, so he had to know Sorren was more than he appeared, and I'd be shocked if he didn't realize exactly what manner of being his captor was—or that Teag and I both had significant magic as well. And yet...

"Who are you?" Sorren continued as if he hadn't heard or didn't care.

"My name's Peter Hinson. I came here to stop a killer."

Sorren cocked his head regarding the man. "There's been mayhem and some cursed objects. But no one's died."

"Yet," Hinson snapped. "The longer you keep me here, the more likely it is that's gonna change."

"I've got a hit on the Darke Web," Teag reported, looking up from his laptop. The internet has its back alleys and red light districts. The Darke Web, hidden from prying eyes with ensorcelled encryption, is where the supernatural community trades secrets.

"Peter Hinson. Known witch. Has a reputation as a 'fixer' for supernatural problems. Comes from old Salem stock, via Haven Harbor." Teag looked up with a Cheshire Cat grin.

"Well?" Sorren asked, giving Hinson a glare that would have a mundane falling over himself to curry favor. Instead, the witch glared back.

"I'm on a mission that's no business of yours. Trying to avert a minor catastrophe. But I can't," he spat, "because I'm tied up in the backroom of a junk shop."

That made me see red. "Hey, watch your mouth." Trifles and Folly was plenty of things, but a junk shop wasn't one of them. I got my temper under control. "Ever heard of The Alliance?"

Hinson startled a bit at that.

"Well, you've found them," I drawled. "And maybe we're on the same side. We saw you at the Archive gala, right before Captain Kettinger showed up and the freak storm blew into town. You were at the auction too, but you left before the main event."

Hinson frowned, looking genuinely puzzled. "Main event?"

"The Nephilim painting? Complete with real Nephilim?" I prodded.

His eyes widened. "I don't know anything about a painting. That's not why I was there—"

"You were after the missing bowl or the person who took it," Teag supplied.

"What happened to the painting?" Hinson asked, ignoring Teag and focusing on me.

"I handled it," I replied evenly. "No thanks to you."

That seemed to make him reconsider. For a moment, he dropped his gaze to the floor and worried at his lip, and when he looked up again, his shoulders squared despite the bonds, and he seemed to have come to a decision.

"Maybe we should start over."

"Might not be a bad idea," I retorted, still smarting over his rude comment about the store.

"Three items are missing, and all had magical properties," Sorren recapped. "The damage each time has escalated, from wrecked cars to an auction buyer's career damaged to a woman's whole life destroyed."

"Four," Teag broke in. "Something went missing from the glass exhibit tonight. And those sirens—a house fire of undetermined origins broke out. One person—a woman—went to the hospital with third-degree burns."

We all looked at Hinson, waiting.

He let out a long breath. "All the items that have been stolen have a provenance from Haven Harbor," he said finally. "And all the victims have been witches, with no tie I can find to Salem or any of its families."

"Who sent you?"

"The governing coven," Hinson said. "The pieces that were stolen had family history. Back in the day—as I'm sure you remember," he added with a pointed look at Sorren, "Massachusetts and Charleston ruled the Triangle Trade. Ships called both ports home. It wasn't unusual for business partnerships or marriages to unite the two. So it shouldn't be a surprise that some of those brides who came down from the North had Salem blood."

"Mona, Maria, and Amy?" I asked.

Hinson shrugged. "I don't know who they are."

"The women who got the short end of the wand with the missing items of power," Teag supplied.

"Not ours," the prisoner said. "But the fan, the bowl, and the vase were all owned at one time by Haven Harbor residents, and the fan and bowl came down to Charleston as part of dowries when their owners married Southern boys."

"Not the vase?" Sorren watched Hinson carefully, watching for any hint that he withheld information.

Hinson shook his head. "The vase came to be owned by a collector in Haven Harbor, who purchased it because he recognized its potential for danger and wished to remove it from circulation. It was stolen from his collection and apparently made its way here to Charleston, where it was stolen again, from your museum."

I resented the whiff of judgment in his tone, as if Alistair didn't run a tight ship at the Lowcountry Museum. "Seems like it got nicked in your neck of the woods first," I replied.

Hinson rolled his eyes. "It's not a competition."

"Who's behind it?" Sorren asked. "The thefts. The attacks."

For all his bluster, Hinson deflated. "I don't know. The person who came out of the glass exhibit backroom wore a ski mask and had enough magic to cast a glamour that made it hard to get a fix on details. I tried to pick up a trail, and that's when I ran into you," he added, glowering at Sorren.

"You're here at the behest of your grand coven to find the person who's behind this and reclaim your stolen relics," Sorren said.

"And stop people from getting hurt," Hinson said forcefully. "I'm not the bad guy here."

"We—The Alliance—are guardians of Charleston and beyond," Sorren continued. Just in the time since I inherited the shop from Uncle Evann, we'd managed to save the city, the East Coast, and maybe the world from a variety of horrific attacks.

"Rowan vouches for him," Teag reported. "Says she knows him by reputation, and she will be most put out if he gives us any trouble."

Peter rolled his eyes and then turned to Sorren. "Could we continue the conversation without the ropes? It's been a long day."

"Can we trust you to finish the discussion without resorting to magic or bolting out of here?" Sorren asked. "Because either of those occurrences would make me reconsider whether or not you are the 'bad guy'—and you'd piss off Rowan, which wouldn't be wise."

"Yes, you can trust me. No, I won't bolt or mojo you. And I definitely don't want Rowan pissed at me," Peter replied.

Sorren smudged the warding circle and went to untie the ropes. I kept my athame handy and saw that Teag casually adjusted his position to be able to move quickly if Peter caused any trouble.

Peter rubbed his arms and wrists when the spelled ropes fell aside and stomped his feet a few times to get feeling back in his legs. He looked from one of us to the next. "See? This is me not causing trouble."

We brought his chair back to the table, and Teag handed Peter a cup of coffee, which he accepted gratefully. "I've told you how I got here chasing the missing items. What clued you in, and how did you find the connection?" he asked.

Peter listened carefully as Teag and I gave a somewhat sanitized recap of our involvement. I still didn't completely trust Peter, so I wasn't ready to completely tip our hand or name allies. "And then we came back from the gallery and found you here."

"What was stolen?" Teag asked.

"A glass candelabra, covered with sigils and spell work," Peter replied. "It's another legacy piece that found its way through dowries and inheritances from one of the old families down here, and they want it back."

"So you were supposed to steal it, and someone else stole it first?" I asked.

Peter shook his head. "Not steal it, buy it. Unlike the bowl, it hadn't been stolen originally. But when I got to the exhibit, I realized it wasn't there, and I poked around—in time to get a glimpse of the thief."

"What makes you think it had anything to do with the fire?" Sorren asked.

"Because it originally belonged to a fire starter, and its magic would enhance the use of fire."

Teag had turned his attention back to his laptop. "Getting some information in now on the fire. Woman's name is Katrina Voorhis. Old money pedigree, married to another old money scion, pricy South of Broad neighborhood. Odd thing from the fire and police reports is that it's just her house that went up. Fire didn't touch anything around it, and it appeared to combust at once but didn't explode."

Peter raised an eyebrow. "I'm betting you didn't get that from the six o'clock news."

Teag grinned. "Nope." He wiggled his fingers. "Skillz."

"The fan controlled air, and the scrying bowl used water," I mused. "The clay pot was made from something that came out of the ground. And the candelabra—"

"Fire," Peter finished.

"So the fan likely whipped up the storm that crushed the cars," I said, connecting the dots aloud. "The scrying bowl might have been how whoever's behind this shut Maria Nevin out of the auction, or that could have just been Amy's cursed pot at work—maybe both. And now the candelabra…"

"We got rid of the pot," Sorren mused, and Peter's head snapped up. Sorren shrugged. "Too dangerous to leave it lying around. It's been taken care of, permanently."

"It didn't belong to you—"

"And whoever it did belong to was careless," Sorren snapped, his eyes narrowing. "When it becomes our mess to clean up, I get to choose the method. It's done. Move on."

Peter's expression made it clear that he was not pleased with the outcome, but he let it go for now. "Assuming the same person is behind the attacks, we still don't know why," he said. "What's prompting the strikes? Why those victims? What's the endgame, or are we dealing with a supernatural serial killer?"

"Do you think there's some kind of link back to Haven Harbor?" Teag asked.

Peter shook his head. "Other than the provenance on the items? No. Remember, the witches who fled Salem and founded Haven Harbor had powerful magic, which passed down through the generations. So it stands to reason that arcane items they owned would also be more powerful than usual. They'd be like a beacon to someone who wanted to steal relics with enough mojo to give their own magic a boost."

"So we might be looking for someone who doesn't have a lot of magic personally but wants to 'power up' to strike at enemies?" I mused.

"That's a workable theory," Sorren replied.

"I asked Rowan if she knew any of the victims," Teag said after his email chimed with a new message. "She said she had only met two of them, and only briefly. But she confirmed that Amy and Mona are witches. Want to bet Katrina and Maria are too?"

"Does Rowan know why anyone would be targeting witches in Charleston?" Sorren looked worried. We knew from experience that whether it was human fanatics or a supernatural threat, anything that targeted a group within the paranormal community was likely to ultimately broaden its scope to others.

"No, but she's going to do some digging," Teag replied. "Not sure whether she meant that literally or not, knowing Rowan," he said, cringing at the thought. "She'll let us know if she hears anything."

Sorren leaned back against the break room wall. "I agree that it's not a coincidence about the items having once belonged to powerful witches. So someone did his or her homework to find pieces like that and trace them to Charleston. There's a plan behind this; we just aren't seeing the way it fits together."

"It's escalating," Peter warned. "Whoever is behind this is either learning to control the magic or figuring out how to draw more power out of the stolen items. The fire tonight nearly killed someone. The next one will."

CHAPTER 5

"THEY'RE ALL PART OF THE SAME COVEN." ROWAN FLICKED HER BLOND hair over her shoulder and crossed her arms. She was pretty in a witch-next-door way. Silver and onyx rings glinted on her fingers, and her agate bead bracelets and silver phases of the moon necklace all suggested protective talismans. "All four women came from old money Charleston families, and they had some kind of country club coven going." She shrugged. "You don't usually choose your coven members by their bank accounts, but to each her own."

Teag frowned. "I thought this last victim—Katrina—was married to a guy who made a killing in software."

Rowan nodded. "Yeah, but Katrina herself came from a family that's been in the city for more than a century, and her husband's family is also old money."

"Any idea who else might be in this coven?" I asked. "Because it looks like someone has it in for them."

Rowan walked over to pour herself a glass of sweet tea from the fridge in the break room and leaned against the counter. "Maybe. I'm still digging. Maria and Mona wouldn't talk to me. Katrina can't. Amy finally gave in and admitted it, because I'm figuring she doesn't think she has anything left to lose."

"How did we miss them all being witches?" I asked. "Teag and I were in the same room with Mona and Maria."

"If someone isn't actively using magic or wearing an amulet with some power behind it, nothing about them screams 'witch' unless they're crazy strong. Good thing too. That's how we've survived this long," Rowan replied, draining her glass.

"So why didn't Amy tell you the names of the others in the coven, if she gave up that information?"

"Because Amy didn't know the real names of the other two members," Rowan said. "That's why witches have 'use names'— aliases we go by in the craft. Knowing someone's true name gives you power over them."

"Hard to keep that kind of secret easily in a town like Charleston, in a coven that's hereditary," Teag observed.

"Not if someone wanted to hide it badly enough." Rowan began to pace. "Not too hard to figure out why. Being a witch wasn't any more popular here in Charleston in the 1600s than it was in Salem. Even now, we're in the Bible Belt. Lots of people still aren't comfortable with the idea, and these are powerful, wealthy families we're talking about. It wouldn't do to be ostracized or lose out on business opportunities because of scandal."

"And think of the advantage it could be to have a spouse who's a witch," Teag pointed out. "Especially if no one else knows it. Nudge with a little magic influence here, poke with a little magic interference there, and the family could come into significant business and political gains."

Rowan nodded. "Exactly. Plus, this isn't the kind of coven that doubles as a Bunko game and wine night get-together at someone's house. They meet four times a year on one of those little mostly uninhabited islands off the coast. It's set up in advance. Amy thought that the coven leader might know everyone's real identity and how to contact them—"

"But she doesn't know who the coven leader is in real life," Teag finished with a sigh of exasperation.

"If the coven leader knows the identities of the members, then she has to know what's happened to four of her sisters," I said. "It's been in the papers and on TV, and even Amy's fall from grace would have made prime gossip in those social circles."

Rowan's eyes narrowed, and her jaw clenched. "And that's a big problem because it tells me the coven leader is a bitch as well as a witch. Leading a coven isn't like leading a social club. It shouldn't be decided by popularity contest. A coven leader has *responsibilities*." She bit off that last word, and I could tell the situation really bothered her. "The coven leader isn't in charge of making sure there are cookies and tea sandwiches. She's supposed to see to the training of the coven members and their protection. At the risk of her own life, if need be. It's not a friggin' sorority!"

"Does magic always increase across generations? Can it stay the same, or even decrease?" I wondered aloud.

Rowan nodded. "Sure. Sometimes it even skips a generation. Most of the time, it 'breeds true' as we say, but it's not uncommon for someone to end up inheriting atrophied power the way a genetic abnormality can cause a damaged arm or leg. And sometimes, you get a prodigy out of the blue, the same way that happens to mundanes. Magic makes sense. Genetics is crazy."

"So maybe the coven leader knows what she should do but thinks she's outgunned," I suggested. "If she's inherited the position but lost the genetic lottery when it came to magic, she might have headed for the hills." I held up a hand to stay Rowan's protests. "Not saying it's right, but it would be a very human thing to do."

Rowan's expression made it clear she had already passed judgment. I did not intend to get pulled into witch politics.

"I might have found our fifth coven member," Teag said in a tone that filled me with foreboding. "This just came in across the police channel. Got a 911 call when a woman's housekeeper came home and found her employer dead in her bed—smothered by a quilt she'd never seen before and sewn into her sheets."

"Sewn in how?"

"I'm not sure I want to know," Teag said, sounding sick. "Her name was Andrea Hillings."

I pulled out my phone to call Sorren and realized I had missed a call from Alistair. I'd asked him to let me know if he heard of any other heirlooms or valuable items going missing. With a sinking feeling, I played the voice mail on speaker.

"Cassidy—I don't know if this is what you were looking for or not, but as you've probably guessed, those of us in the historical community in town talk to each other a lot. Word just went out in my circles that the Daughters of Charleston had an antique quilt stolen from the display they were getting ready for the textile conference at the college. I'm texting you a photo, just in case you come across it. Hope helps."

"Did the picture come through?" Teag asked. I nodded and pulled it up on my screen. Teag and Rowan gathered close and peered over my shoulder.

"Can you blow up the photo, zoom in on the stitching?" Teag asked, with an odd note in his voice. I closed in on the tiny, intricate patterns stitched into the quilt. The incredible detail and precise needlework amazed me, but the longer I looked at the quilt, the more uncomfortable I became and the more convinced I was that the patterns were moving.

Rowan caught her breath, and Teag swore. "It's textile magic," Teag confirmed. "Just think—every one of those tiny stitches made with intent, forming spells and runes and sigils."

"Why would someone make a quilt to curse someone?" I asked. "Surely it wouldn't stay an heirloom after it smothered the first person who used it!"

Teag blinked as if trying to clear what he had seen from his retinas. "I don't think the original intent would have been harmful. It was probably made for protection, a way to keep the sleeper safe without ever knowing about the magic. But if the person behind all this is getting more powerful, then maybe she figured out a way to subvert the original magic." He looked up. "We've got to let Sorren and Peter know about this."

I turned to Rowan. "There's only one person left now, and I'm betting it's the coven leader. Anything you can do to help us figure out her identity might help us catch the killer and save a life."

Rowan looked thoughtful. "Amy said the leader and her second-in-command not only hid their names but masked their faces when they convened for sabbath. Amy knew the names of the other members because they were all much less worried about people knowing they were witches. They didn't make it common knowledge outside the coven, but they weren't afraid of each other."

"Younger generation?" I mused.

"Maybe," Teag replied. "It's easier to be 'out' in a lot of ways now than it used to be. Although this whole situation kind of makes you think there was a reason for doing it old school."

"Could the coven leader be the killer?" I asked.

"Anything's possible," Rowan replied. "But...I don't think so. Gut feeling. Might be wrong, but I'm betting it's someone outside, someone with an axe to grind."

Teag got that look on his face that means he's had a flash of inspiration and ran back to his laptop. "Amy didn't know Andrea's name because Andrea kept her face covered and used an alias. But the coven leader would know who her second-in-command was, right?" he asked, looking up at Rowan.

"I'd be shocked if she didn't."

"And I bet Andrea knew who the coven leader was too," Teag said, fingers flying over the keyboard. "So it stands to reason they would have communicated with each other. Let's see what Andrea's phone records have to say."

Rowan gave me a skeptical look. "Can he do that?"

I nodded. "Oh, yeah. Compared to some of the sites he's gotten into, a cell phone provider is nothing."

Rowan looked like she was concentrating. "He's using magic."

"Yep. It's part of his Weaver gift. He can turn data threads into hard-to-find information, just like he can weave magic into cloth."

"That's...amazing." Rowan liked to come across as if she had seen everything, so the admission surprised me.

"I'm in," Teag mumbled. "All right, let me access her call records for the last year, and then we can slice and dice the data on our own time. Got it."

I texted Sorren while we waited. If he wanted to bring Peter in on the situation, I'd leave that up to him to decide. Peter rubbed me the wrong way, but I had to admit my hackles were still up over his sleight about the shop. But he'd be able to tell us whether the quilt, too, had Massachusetts links.

If we could get ahead of the murderer, we might be able to prevent the next incident and save the coven leader's life. So far, the killer hadn't seemed to notice us, but if we started to interfere with her plans, that was bound to change. Would she stop without killing the coven leader, or did she have something even bigger in mind? And if Peter did turn out to be a "good guy" like he said, what kind of magic could he bring to a fight?

"I've got a couple of possibilities," Teag said finally. "Andrea made a lot of phone calls," he added. "I've narrowed it down to four names she called the most. And if I sorted by time of year, two names stand out as having the most calls around the eight holidays witches celebrate."

Immediately, my mind ticked off the names: Yule, Imbolc, Ostera, Beltane, Litha, Lughnasadh, Mabon, and Samhain. Yule, Ostera, and Samhain imperfectly synched up with Christmas, Easter, and Halloween, but the old calendar predates the Christian holidays by centuries, if not millennia.

"So let's start with those two," I said.

"Elizabeth Rinehart and Lisa Monroe," he answered. He looked to Rowan. "Ring any bells?"

"It's not like witches all hang out at private club and have a secret handshake." Rowan made a note of the names. "I'll look into it." Rowan let herself out the back door, and I dropped into one of the chairs beside Teag.

"Why do I have the feeling everything's about to hit the fan?"

"Because it is," he replied, leaning back and lacing his hands behind his neck as he arched to stretch. "We're going to have to take this witch down, preferably before she kills again. It would be nice to figure out what she thought she was going to get out of all this, but it doesn't really matter as long as she's stopped."

"And Peter?"

Teag shrugged. "You know the saying. Lead, follow, or get the hell out of the way."

CHAPTER 6

ROWAN LOOKED INTO THE NAMES IN HER WAY, WHILE TEAG AND I decided to work the leads as well. If we were right, one of the two women was marked for death, and from the way the attacks had grown more vicious, I felt sure the killer wouldn't be merciful.

Nothing Teag turned up online narrowed our choice, so we left Maggie in charge of the store and decided to pay a visit to each of the candidates for murder. She promised to stop by my house to feed Baxter and let him out in case we ran late.

As we drove to Elizabeth's house, I replayed everything that had happened in my mind. Teag glanced at me when I sat up straight and swore under my breath. "Dammit. I forgot about the Hitchcock blonde."

"The what?"

Teag had once dabbled with the idea of a film minor in college, while I could only blame my knowledge of old movies on occasional bouts of insomnia. "Tippi Hedron, Grace Kelly, Janet Leigh—Alfred Hitchcock always used 'ice queen' blondes in his horror movies. And at the first couple of events—"

Teag nodded. "Yeah. I remember her. She caught my attention, and

I don't even bat for that team. Very elegant. I saw her at the Captain's house—"

"And then again, at the auction." We were used to finishing each other's sentences.

"But not at the glass gallery," Teag finished. "Then again, half of the who's who of Charleston was at those first two events, and they're not all suspects."

"Yeah, but we know who they are," I replied. "Peter gate-crashed both affairs. What if Blondie did too?"

"If I'd known it was that easy to get into parties with good champagne and hors d'oeuvres, I'd have bought a nice suit and taken up gate-crashing as a hobby when I was a starving college student," Teag said.

"Both events were invitation-only but hardly high security," I mused. "Invitations aren't difficult to forge, and honestly, if a woman like that came up and flirted with any of the single men on the way in and casually took his arm at the door, no one would even ask."

"I'm hardly an expert on feminine wiles," Teag said drily. "But yeah, that could work. And once she was inside, dressed appropriately, no one would question her. Do you think she's Elizabeth or Lisa?"

"Maybe," I said, chewing on my lip as I thought. "Or maybe she's the killer."

"That's a bit of a stretch, don't you think? She might have just been the plus-one for someone who came to both galas, and that's if she wasn't an invited guest herself."

I pulled out my phone. "Let's find out." I knew the owner of the auction house wouldn't talk to me, but Mrs. Morrissey would. I smiled when she picked up on the second ring.

"Cassidy! Do you have any news about the missing fan?"

"Um, not yet. But we've got some leads," I said, as Teag slid me a sidelong glance. The situation had escalated far beyond a missing accessory, however historical. "I've got a question about the guest list." I described our quarry, expecting that Mrs. Morrissey would need to go look at her guest list.

"No, I don't know her," she replied immediately. "I thought she must have been someone's guest. Why? Do you think she had anything to do with the fan?"

"I'm not sure," I answered. "Maybe. We've crossed paths a couple of times, and it's gotten suspicious. As soon as I know something, I'll fill you in. Thanks."

Teag glanced at me as we pulled up in front of Elizabeth's address. "I can try to access the security footage at the auction, but the Kettinger house didn't have theirs hooked up yet. I heard Mrs. M telling that to the police after the incident with the cars."

I nodded. "There's got to be a thread that pulls this all together, but I'm sure not seeing it yet," I said, getting out of the car. Elizabeth's home wasn't on one of the most expensive streets in the historic neighborhood, but the area was still desirable and very pricey, which put Elizabeth in the right income bracket for the exclusive coven.

Still, the vibe I got as we knocked at the door didn't put me on edge. I touched the doorknob, bracing myself in case I picked up the resonance of a homicidal witch, and got images of sugar cookies and apple juice instead.

A harried-looking woman in her thirties came to the door. She had a sleeping baby in a sling across her stained T-shirt, and behind her, a four-year-old played with a toy truck in the enclosed garden. "If you're selling something—"

"We're friends of Amy's," I said, giving Elizabeth my friendliest smile. "I'm sorry to bother you, but I just wanted to ask you how I can help her—she's been through so much, but she isn't good at asking for what she needs." I reached out to shake her hand and got nothing out of the contact except sticky residue that I guessed might be the apple juice.

Elizabeth pushed a stray lock of dark brown hair from her forehead, careful not to jar the sleeping baby. "Look, I can't invite you in right now—my two-year-old is taking a nap, and she was up all night with an earache. But you're right about Amy. She's a peach, and she really doesn't deserve what's been happening."

Elizabeth brushed a hand over the baby's head, an unconscious gesture of protection. "It's great that you're doing this. Count me in. As far as what she needs—wine, therapy, and maybe a one-way ticket to Maui?" She added with a frazzled chuckle. "Honestly, if you could give her leads on reasonably priced apartments and maybe a job for someone with a degree in fine arts, that would be the best help. And I wasn't kidding about the wine."

The child behind her started to howl, and the baby in the sling jerked. Elizabeth's eyes widened. "I've got to go. Thanks so much. Have a nice day." With that, the door closed in our faces.

Teag and I looked at each other. "I don't think she's our suspect," I said, feeling buzzed from the chaos that surrounded Elizabeth.

"I'm betting she's having trouble fitting in eating lunch, let alone plotting murder," Teag replied. "But seriously, I can connect Amy to my old landlord when this is all over. My apartment had 'character'—which meant it was old but not a dump—and I could afford the rent as a grad student." He had moved in with Anthony a while ago. I wouldn't be surprised to get a wedding invitation in the mail one of these days.

"And if we all survive this, Alistair or Mrs. Morrissey might need a docent or a staffer," I mused. "But the way we can help Amy the most is by getting rid of the killer—before she decides to come back around and finish off the ones she left alive."

Lisa Monroe's house had a stunning view of the harbor in a coveted neighborhood that wasn't quite Rainbow Row but close to it. It also looked uninhabited.

No one answered our knock or came when we rang the doorbell. Teag tried calling, but it went to voicemail. I looked at Teag. "Either she's on a conveniently-timed vacation, or she figures she's next and ran."

"My money's on running," he said.

My phone buzzed with texts from Sorren and Rowan. Rowan confirmed what we'd already figured out, that Lisa headed up the coven. Sorren said that he'd be by the shop with Peter just after dark. My boss avoids daylight for obvious reasons, but that doesn't always mean he's asleep.

"I'm going to see if I can turn up anything off that security footage and dig up possible places Lisa might have gone to ground," Teag said as we drove back. We picked up a pizza on the way since it looked like one of those nights.

"If Peter came all the way down here to retrieve those stolen heirlooms, then he's got to know more about what they can actually do than he's told us," I said. "It's time he spills the beans since psycho witch still has the fan, the bowl, and the candelabra, and that means she might be able to use them all together." Fortunately, the Charleston police had the killer quilt locked up for evidence.

"Aren't you just a ray of sunshine," Teag muttered.

Road repairs routed us back a different way, taking us past an old block of commercial buildings from the 1800s that were under renovation. That's a part of daily life here in Charleston, where you can't turn around without running into some kind of historical marker. Scaffolding towered against one wall, with piles of bricks stacked on the planking where workers had left for the evening. Plastic sheeting flapped in the breeze as we approached.

The street around us was empty, unusual for this time of night. As we got closer to the wall, a sudden gust of wind sent the plastic snapping in the breeze. The scaffold toppled toward us, and although Teag gunned the engine, I knew we couldn't get clear in time. I felt dark magic and cold malice on the strange wind and knew we weren't alone.

I had my athame in the sleeve of my shirt, and I shook it down into my hand as the metal piping, loose boards, and bricks started to rain down around us. Drawing on the memories connected with the handle of the old wooden spoon, I pulled hard on my magic and sent a blast of cold white force against the falling debris, doing my best to shield the passenger compartment of the car.

My magic deflected some of the falling objects, but I braced for the worst as a brick slammed into the windshield, shattering it and Teag shouted curses, trying and failing to evade the collapsing metal framework and everything it held.

I couldn't hold the steel skeleton up for long. Already, I felt sweat bead on my back with the strain. The scaffold was too large to merely toss out of the way and laden with tools, bricks, and planks of wood, I had to push away multiple targets.

Debris pelted Teag's old Volvo, slamming into the roof and hood, rocking the car with every hit. The wind howled down the street around us like the middle of a hurricane. I could hold off some of the avalanche, but more and more pieces rained down on us around the waning blast I used to protect us from being crushed.

I felt my control slipping, and when it did, the weight of the whole scaffold would land on us, smashing down on the roof and trapping us if it didn't kill us outright. I mustered all my power and tried to hold on as long as I could, although my head pounded and my heart thudded as if I'd run a mile.

I felt the pressure lift, and the scaffold shifted without me doing it.

Run, Peter's voice said from everywhere and nowhere. *Get out, now*.

Teag must have heard it too because we both scrambled for the least damaged door and crawled out, arms over our heads to protect ourselves. We only had to cover a few yards to get to the safety of an open parking deck, and a moment ago, I would have said that was like running through machine gun fire. Now, I could almost see a safe corridor open for us, deflecting the falling hazards to one side or the other.

Go! Peter's voice urged. We ran, and the corridor folded in behind us, hard on our heels, but despite a hail of brick shards, metal pipes, bolts, tools, and other impromptu shrapnel, nothing touched us.

We dove into the parking garage as the scaffold thundered down behind us. A cloud of dust and grit rose into the air, and in the distance, we could hear sirens wailing.

I crouched on my hands and knees, heaving for breath, trying to grasp the fact that we were both alive and unhurt. Teag rose to sit on his haunches, pale and shaken.

"What…the hell…was that?" he gasped.

"Are you okay?" Peter came around the corner of the entranceway, concerned but unruffled. "Hope you don't mind; Sorren asked me to keep an eye on you while he was indisposed. I had hoped there'd be no need for me to show up but…" He gestured toward the chaos in the street outside. "I'm glad I could help."

"Thanks," I said, trying to get my breathing under control. "Can't believe that was an accident."

"It wasn't," Peter confirmed. "But I could chase the perp or keep you from getting flattened."

"Good choice," Teag said, sounding just as shaken as I felt.

Peter offered a hand to both of us, pulling us onto our feet. "I've got a car about two blocks behind you, and we'd better get it if we want to leave before the cops come."

"What about my car?" Teag asked, staring at the crumpled Volvo beneath the heavy, twisted scaffold.

"Report it stolen," Peter said, hurrying us along. He bundled us into his rental sedan and made a sharp U-turn, then took a right, so we avoided looking like we were fleeing the scene. I felt a buzz of magic and wondered if he had added an attention deflection spell when two police cars passed us and never gave a second look.

"Yes, it's a spell. So long as we don't do anything loud or obnoxious to draw attention to ourselves, it makes people pay no attention as if we're terribly boring," Peter said, taking a twisting set of turns that wound around and back again enough that I figured he was trying to lose any pursuers rather than actually going somewhere.

"Are you lost, or are we making evasive maneuvers?" I asked, fighting the urge to throw up as the adrenaline crash hit my system. My head still pounded. I'd used more magic in outright fights that lasted longer, but going into a battle that you knew was coming felt different than getting attacked out of the blue.

Peter chuckled. "A little of both. I wanted to get well away from both the responders and whoever brought that down on you before we went back to the shop."

"If the witch knows who we are, she'll find the shop," Teag pointed out from the back seat.

"But your shop is heavily warded," Peter replied. "I could feel that the last time I…visited."

"That helps, but it's not a guarantee," I warned. "Still…we're probably safer there than anywhere else." I texted Maggie and asked her to take care of Baxter for a day or two. She's designated herself the "Doggy Aunt" and dotes on him something awful. Teag texted Anthony to tell him he was safe but tied up with a situation. I shuddered to think what Anthony might have thought if the cops called the house about Teag's ruined car.

Since the pizza was a casualty of war, we stopped for another one and headed to the store. I had grown used to the wardings that friends of ours had placed, but now I paused, checking to make sure the protections were in place. Voudon, Hoodoo, and Wiccan wards overlay one another, along with a blessing from an unorthodox Episcopalian priest and a Cherokee shaman, magic, belief, and arcane power strengthened by the bonds of friendship. Sensing that protective energy made me feel warm and loved.

It didn't hurt to know that my friends were also total bad-ass mofos in a fight.

I could tell that nothing had bothered the wards and felt a sense of relief at being in a safe space once we were inside. Teag, Peter, and I made short work of the pizza, with only a slice or two left over.

"I think the witch behind this attacked you because we're getting close," Peter said, wiping away a bit of pizza sauce. "She meant to scare you off—maybe kill you."

"Thanks again for the help," I said. "I'm not sure how that would have gone if you hadn't turned up."

Peter chuckled. "I keep telling you—I'm one of the good guys." He pushed back from the table. "And I'm even missing the Halloween Gala to handle this, which shows real dedication."

"Gala?" I asked, amused that a "fixer" like Peter minded missing a Halloween party.

"Oh, it's not just any Trick-or-Treat event," Peter assured us. "Haven Harbor is a whole town of the descendants of Salem witches. We know how to have fun on Halloween, but we take the sabbath seriously too. It's the event of the year."

"Do you think the date has something to do with the attacks?" I asked as Teag pushed his plate aside and wiped off his hands, then pulled out his laptop once more.

Peter nodded. "I'd hate to bet against it. It's a time when the natural power waxes strongest. The killer seems to be building up to something, with the pieces she's picked and the ferocity of the attacks. Halloween would be a way to go out with a helluva bang."

"Got something," Teag said, staring at his screen. "Lisa Monroe has a beach house, near that little island where Amy told us the coven met. She's probably holed up there unless she's skipped out entirely, but people usually go to ground someplace familiar, where they feel safe."

"It's a good bet. Near the water, which has its own energy, and near a place of power where the coven has invested a lot of magic over the years. That can help us. Get the address. I'd bet money that's where the showdown will be, tonight."

A text let me know Sorren and Rowan were on their way. I saved the last of the pizza for Rowan. Sorren always managed his own sustenance.

"It'll take about an hour to get there, give or take," Teag said. "That's without witchy interference. Hold that thought about going to war tonight. I want to see if I can hack that security cam and get a picture of that elusive blonde."

I turned back to Peter. "Once Sorren and Rowan are here, I think it's time we find out everything you know about the pieces the killer stole and how they work together. If we're going to fight her, I don't like surprises."

"I'm game," he replied. "And I'd like a better idea of exactly what your group can do. If I'm going to fight alongside you, it would be good to know what kind of magic you've got going for you."

"You'll show us yours, if we show you ours, is that it?" Teag asked with a wicked grin, not looking up from his keyboard.

"In a manner of speaking," Peter replied, but I heard the chuckle in his voice.

"Got it," Teag said a few minutes later. He turned the laptop so we could see a black and white frame from the auction house's footage, showing our Hitchcock blonde. "It's not the best picture in the world, but it's good enough to make out her face."

I heard a ping as he sent the photo to my phone. I sent it on to Amy, asking if she recognized the woman. She called me right back, and I put her on speaker.

"That's Elena Gregory. Oh my God, are you telling me she's the one doing this?" Amy sounded stunned and horrified.

"We're still investigating," I said cautiously. "She showed up at two events where incidents happened and items went missing."

Amy's quiet sobs carried. "Elena wanted to join the coven. She's new in town and rich enough to be used to getting what she wanted. We never found out how she even learned about the coven—we keep that pretty quiet—but she was determined to bull her way in. Our leader told her no."

"Why?" I asked, thinking that Lisa had pretty good people instincts if all of the destruction and anguish and death had been over a socialite's hurt feelings.

"I know it sounds snobby," Amy replied, her breath hitching as she tried to control her tears. I couldn't imagine how she must feel, discovering that she had lost everything and had her life destroyed over something as petty as someone wanting in a clique. "But the leader always told us there was a reason why the coven has been limited to the same families all down through the centuries. She said there was power in those bloodlines and that the magic we wove together overlaid what our ancestors did before us. I don't think she thought Elena actually had any real magic, either."

"If you're friends with Mona and Maria, maybe y'all should hunker down together tonight, put up the strongest wardings you can summon, and ride it out. We think Elena's going to make her big strike tonight."

"What about the coven leaders?"

I closed my eyes and swallowed. "The assistant leader is dead. We aren't sure where the leader is. She's vanished." That was true, and I certainly didn't want Amy or her other witch sisters stumbling in to the fight if we were right about the showdown at the beach.

"All right," Amy said. "I'll call them."

"Even if they don't come, you sit tight, gather everything you've got to protect yourself, and stay put," I warned.

"Yeah, don't worry. But if you catch her? Tell her I'm going to sue her ass," Amy said, and the anger strengthened her voice. "The only thing more dangerous than a pissed-off witch is a lawyer with a grudge."

I didn't think Elena would be around to deal with legal trouble, one way or the other, but if the thought gave Amy hope, I'd let her hang onto it. "Yeah, I'll tell her if I see her," I said. "Keep your head down."

I ended the call and looked up just as Sorren and Rowan came in the back door. I pointed to the pizza box, and Rowan grabbed the last slice. I knew from Sorren's expression he had bad news.

"I've heard back from Boston," he said. "A museum up there just noticed a missing relic. Someone's stolen a hand of glory, and it was taken from one of the Salem witches that was hanged back during the Trials."

Peter looked as if he were going to be sick. "Do you know whose hand—" He couldn't finish the sentence, and I knew that for him, those unfortunates in Salem weren't just historical figures, they were ancestors of his friends and neighbors.

"Aurinda Solart," Sorren replied, and Peter winced.

"I know someone who is a descendant," he said. "Are you certain the relic is authentic? If the Haven Harbor governing coven had known, I'm sure they would have tried to acquire it long ago."

Sorren grimaced. "It's authentic. But apparently it's been stuck in the back of the museum storage room for who knows how long. Some long-ago archivist might have wanted to avoid the salacious appeal of a hand of glory from a Salem witch and intentionally 'misplaced' it."

"We've got a name on the killer—and Peter thinks she's going to strike tonight."

Rowan looked up. "I agree. Her power would be at its strongest."

Teag and I exchanged a glance. Much as I'd love more of a chance to prepare for a supernatural battle, most of the time, we get thrown into the middle of it and have to sort things out the best we can.

"If we're going to do this, then we need everyone's cards on the table," I said, "starting with Peter."

Teag put on another pot of coffee. We moved the pizza box out of the way and sat down around the table. Two witches, a vampire, plus Teag and me with our own weird special magic—just another day at the office.

"The killer—Elena—is more powerful than I guess anyone gave her credit for being," Peter said. "From the way the attacks have ramped up, I'm betting that's not all natural talent. I think she's able to tap into the stored power of the pieces to do more damage than she could do on her own."

"A leech," Rowan said. We looked at her. "It's a term for someone who can 'steal' magic from others or from places or objects but doesn't possess the same level of power herself. They're usually dangerous because they can't control the stolen power well, and taking the magic —especially without permission—weakens the donor."

Peter nodded. "I've heard of them. Needless to say, they're usually not welcome among practitioners."

"Tell us about the relics," Sorren said. "It sounds like they were chosen for a purpose."

Peter rose to pour himself a cup of coffee and returned with the pot and several mugs for the rest of us. "The fan was passed down through Abigail Dawkins's family until she married your Captain Kettinger and brought it with her. She died without a daughter, but her daughter-in-law may have taken the fan; we lost the trail at that point. Abigail was a wind walker, a witch who could speak to and control the wind and weather. The kind of witch that started the legends about flying on broomsticks. Her fan was her athame, and the bone ribs were made from the willingly donated bones of her grandmother, who was a witch herself and wanted to be 'part' of her legacy."

I shivered. Willing donor or not, that was just plain creepy.

"The bowl belonged to Hepziba Reynolds, a seer and a water witch. It was made from obsidian, and the legend says that Hepziba foresaw her death and sent her magic into the bowl before she crossed the Veil to provide help to those who came after her. I suspect Elena used it to scry on you and Teag once she realized you were getting too close to answers, and that's how she knew where to bring down that scaffolding."

"And the candelabra?" Teag asked.

"Elspeth Harker, a fire starter. She used the runes and sigils carved into the glass to focus her magic. It's said she formed the glass into its shape herself, setting her intention into it in the furnace."

"I'm guessing that whoever made the killer quilt had Weaver magic, like Teag," I ventured.

Peter nodded. "Hagar Alexander," he said. "She could spin and weave magic into cloth, and her goods were sought after for protection and healing. Even the thread she spun could bind a spell into stitches. There's never been any hint of scandal about Hagar's gifts being used for ill, so Elena must have truly gained power to be able to twist the magic to murder someone."

"What about the curse pot?" Sorren asked. "That's hardly benign."

"It was never meant to be used," Peter replied with a sigh. "Much like your Alliance does with its network of shops like Trifles and Folly, we have elders among us who keep an eye out for magical relics that ought not be in circulation. They acquire them and either destroy them or hide them away. A piece like that pot has very old, very strong magic. Destroying it might unleash even more trouble, so it was secured. We still don't know how it was stolen."

"Elena must have been planning her revenge for a long time," I said, letting the coffee warm me.

"Or she just had enough money to buy henchmen," Teag said with a shrug. "That sounds more like her style."

"We've gotten rid of the pot—for good this time," Sorren assured us. Peter raised an eyebrow but didn't argue this time. Perhaps he figured it was safer not to know. "The police have the quilt. You said something before about the killer—Elena—being able to call on the four elements with the pieces she has and amplify their power. What will the hand of glory add to that?"

"Nothing good," Rowan replied. "I've been fortunate never to come across one, but a teacher of mine did. Nasty things. What they can do depends on the original purpose intended by the one who made them. It varies. They can be a perpetual light, or the ultimate lock pick, or—but this might just be legend—it can unlock a door into the Chasm."

"The Chasm?" I asked, unsettled at the expression of alarm on Sorren's face. When a centuries-old vampire looks unsettled, I consider that worrisome.

"It's the space Between," he replied. "The equivalent of being undead if you're a soul without a body."

"And not a ghost, wraith, or revenant?"

Sorren shook his head. "Not on our plane anymore at all. Not heaven, hell, limbo, or purgatory—assuming you believe in them or their equivalents. A bit like being an astronaut in a space suit drifting away from the ship—only you never stop having consciousness. Ever."

"Seriously?" I couldn't believe what I was hearing. "Over getting cut from witch sorority rush?"

Rowan chuckled. "I don't believe I've ever heard it put quite that way before, but then again, people kill for amazingly small reasons every day."

We parked the cars half a mile from Lisa's house, making sure to block the roadway. I had no idea whether she had set up any magical alarms, but if we got any closer, she would surely hear the engines. I glanced at the faces of my companions and saw determination and the grim awareness that we were heading into battle.

Along with my protective agate, silver, and onyx jewelry, I'd brought both my athame and the walking stick that had once belonged to Sorren's maker. In my pocket, I had a small agate spindle whorl that amplified my magic, a gift to Sorren from a Norse demigoddess. On my left wrist, I wore an old, frayed dog collar. I shook my wrist, and a large ghostly dog appeared at my side. Bo, my beloved golden retriever, had become my spectral protector. Just in case, I had a silver knife and a *chakram*, an oddly useful disc-knife.

I had no idea what weapons or charms Rowan and Peter carried. Sorren's speed, strength, and fangs were usually all the weapons he needed, but I assumed he carried his usual swords. Guns were a bad bet against witches since even a novice could make a firearm blow up in the user's face.

Teag wore his protective amulets, and he carried a thick fighting staff that stood as tall as he was. Woven strips of thin fabric around one end imbued the rod with Teag's Weaver magic, as did the runes carved into the wood itself. Several knotted strings hung from his belt, a form of stored magical energy. He wore his *espada y daga* fighting swords, and a long, thin silver whip hung coiled from a clip on his belt. His pack carried salt and holy water, a rope soaked in colloidal silver, and a throwing net also laced with silver. We were as ready as we were going to get.

Teag had gotten us a satellite picture of the house and its grounds, which let us make a plan of approach. Sorren circled around to get Lisa out of the house and hidden in a nearby cement block utility shed, the safest structure on the lot. Then he planned to come back and join the fight.

Battles never go according to plan.

The beach house sat on a slight rise above the ocean. Hardly a cozy cottage, it stood at least three stories tall, one level on stilts raised to accommodate the fickle sea. A few lights shone in the windows, but the house felt unnaturally still, and I wondered if Lisa had set her own protections and wardings, anticipating that her would-be killer might find her hiding place. Amy believed Lisa to be a powerful witch, but I had my doubts since she seemed to have had no inkling about Elena's potential. Whenever she had figured out the coven was under assault, I'd seen no evidence that she had bothered to warn her fellow members, which led me to my own conclusions.

Waves thundered at high tide, gleaming under the moonlight. We emerged from the palmetto-lined lane to find Elena waiting for us. Her pale blonde hair looked ethereal, and her flowing black top over inky leggings was more Rhiannon than Necronomicon. Then again, someone willing to maim, destroy, and kill over being invited to join a club would probably obsess over the right dramatic costume.

Elena waved a hand, and a gale-force wind made us stumble for our footing as it blew us nearly off our feet. Teag planted his staff in the sand to steady himself and grabbed my arm. I leveled my athame at Elena and loosed a blast of cold, white force, countering her wind and clearing a cone-shaped path in front of us.

I could feel our magics vying for dominance as her wind strained against the push of my channeled power. Bo's ghost barked angrily at the threat, hackles raised.

As suddenly as the wind rose, it fell, and in the seconds as we staggered for our footing, I felt power rise to the summons. A wave of flames roared toward us, and I cried out and shrank back, raising the walking stick, intending to see if I could, indeed, fight fire with fire. Before I could draw on my magic, in that heartbeat of decision, an unfamiliar power raced past me, slamming into the ground just ahead of us, sending a thick spray of sand into the air to quench the flames.

Elena's lips pulled back in a feral grimace, and a waterspout rose above the sea and wended toward us. Rowan made a sweeping gesture and deflected the spout so that it veered harmlessly to one side.

I wondered if Elena had used the scrying bowl to see our approach and whether she had timed her attack to rid herself of us as well as Lisa. Madness glinted in her eyes, and I wondered if it had always been there, or whether the hand of glory had brought it to the fore, strengthened its hold. Perhaps, I thought, it was a little of both.

"Give up," I shouted at Elena. "You can't win, and we're not the only ones who know about you."

"I've already won," she snarled. This time, she sent a sandstorm roaring our way, a fast-moving curtain of grit that could blind our eyes and strip away skin. Peter countered with an iridescent scrim of power that held off the brunt of the storm. He glanced at Rowan and me, and we caught his meaning. The instant his defensive barrier dropped, she and I both sent power flowing toward the menace, scattering it apart.

Sorren appeared at my side. "Where's Lisa?" I asked.

He shook his head. "She had the house heavily warded to keep

Elena out, and Elena overlaid those with her own spells to keep Lisa in. I couldn't get through." As Sorren often reminds me, he doesn't have magic; his vampiric gift *is* magic, of a very particular sort.

At the moment, Peter and Rowan were trading shots with Elena, but so far, we were at a stalemate. Our attacks weren't doing much to her, and we'd been able to stave off damage from what she threw at us. The hand of glory was the game changer, and I had the feeling things wouldn't stay equal for much longer.

"You've failed," Peter shouted as Elena dodged a blast that sent dirt flying.

"I'm just getting started," Elena yelled back. She cried out with a word of power, and fire engulfed the beach house, enveloping it in flames like a bomb had gone off.

"Lisa!" Teag gasped. No one could have survived the inferno that blazed on the rise above the ocean. Rowan reached out with her magic to pull sheets of water from the waves to put out the fire, but Elena's laughter rose above the crash of the waves and the roar of the flames, and a twitch of the bone fan dashed the water back into the ocean.

A growl behind us made me turn, athame raised. Two pairs of red eyes stared out from the darkness, with a low warning rumble that would have sent wolves running for cover.

"Shit," I muttered. "Hellhounds?"

The creatures moved into the moonlight, dark, shaggy canines with matted black fur and wide, strong jaws.

"Too small. More like heck-hounds," Teag quipped, but I could hear the nervousness in his voice as he reached for his silver whip.

"*Grims*," Peter yelled over his shoulder, still trying and failing to do something to put out the house fire. "Supernatural black dog. Nasty piece of work."

"I'll take care of them," Sorren said. "I can't do much against Elena. Stop her from using that hand of glory to open the doorway. I've got your back." With that, he squared off against the two *grims* with a sword in each hand, a fight between apex predators.

The two *grims* advanced slowly, spreading out to flank Sorren. He smiled, a terrible, cold smile I had seen in other fights.

"Let me teach you how to play dead," Sorren said and sprang into motion. He launched himself at the *grim* on his right, just as the hound to his left started forward. By the time the second black dog reached where Sorren had been standing, Sorren barreled into the first creature, going down in a flash of silver blades and yellowed teeth.

The second *grim* circled the fight, looking for an opening. Blood sprayed, and I hoped it wasn't Sorren's. The black dogs snarled and growled, swiping with their massive, clawed paws and snapping with fangs that could take off a limb.

Every instinct warned me not to turn my back on the creatures, but I knew Sorren could handle himself and amped up with the power of the stolen relics and the hand of glory, Elena was proving a tougher enemy than I expected.

The hand of glory was taking a toll on Elena. Her perfectly coiffed white-blonde hair hung in wild straggles around her face, which looked more pinched and gaunt than when we started. The winds tore at her clothing, and the rain soaked her to the skin, but it was the edge of madness in her voice that told me that her vengeance came at a terrible price that even she might not yet realize.

"You!"

The newcomer's voice startled all of us, and I dared to look away from Elena and Sorren as another figure strode up from the direction of the beach. Lisa Monroe's singed hair and blistered skin suggested a close call, as did her scorched clothing. She was definitely alive, and very, very pissed off.

"You burned my house!" Lisa screamed above the roar of the waves. "You slept with my husband! Killed my coven. And for what?"

Elena smiled a rictus grin. "I wanted to give you a taste of what it felt like, to lose. Look how far you've fallen."

Elena sent a blast of power toward Lisa. Lisa lashed out with magic of her own. Rowan and Peter tried to separate the two as I took aim with my athame, only to find that an iridescent barrier that hadn't been there a second before now kept us from interfering as their fight got personal.

Watching the two witches battle reminded me of a martial arts fight between two well-matched combatants. Lisa sent a blast of flame, only to have it deflected. Elena returned with a hail of rocks, which were swept harmlessly to the side. Strike and counterstrike seemed to put the duel arcane at a stalemate, yet as I watched closely through the shimmering curtain of power that kept us from interfering, I realized the fight really wasn't equal at all.

Lisa looked like she had dragged herself out of a war zone, but the magic she drew on was her own. Elena borrowed from the power of the hand of glory to stoke the strength of her stolen relics, to keep the barrier between us, to match Lisa's magic. If she noticed that the price was that she aged and withered in front of us, she did not seem to care so long as vengeance was satisfied.

"You humiliated me!" Elena shouted above the wind. "You didn't think I had enough power to be part of your little clique. Look who's winning now, bitch!"

The wind around us grew stronger, cold and damp with the sea air. Flames leaped high into the sky, giving the battle a hellish glow. Behind us, Sorren still battled the black dogs while the rest of us cast about for a way to stop the two witches from mutual assured destruction that might take all of Charleston with them.

I could feel the roiling, dark magic of the hand of glory like stench on the air. Whatever infernal power gave the abomination its energy glowed a phosphorescent green as Elena drew on its poisoned essence. It grew stronger as she faded, and I wondered if the price of her revenge would be her soul.

Teag caught my eye and nodded toward where the wind ripped at a tarp covering a boat on a trailer. One corner of the tarp had come loose, flapping and snapping in the gale. I nodded, following his thinking, and we waited for our chance.

Lisa cast a spell that lashed across Elena's face like invisible claws, opening bloody tracks. Elena returned with a thrust of power that caught Lisa in the shoulder like a bullet, making her stumble as crimson blossomed on her shirt.

The shimmering barrier fell as the hand of glory flared in a blinding, foxfire glow. Behind us, one of the *grims* let out an unholy shriek.

Elena screamed a word that seemed to burn the air and hit us all like a cudgel, and the night sky tore open, revealing the dark night of the damned souls.

Lisa rushed at Elena, arms outstretched and hands clawed just as Teag's magic shot silver rope over the flapping tarp, and it ripped loose from its bindings. I hit the tarp square on with a blast of cold force from my athame, propelling it like a sail toward Elena. In just a heart-beat, Lisa tackled her, and for a few desperate seconds, the ensorcelled tarp interrupted both witches' magic.

Peter dove for the stolen relics. Rowan started chanting, desperate to close the rip. Teag sent his spell-worked rope snaking after the tarp, trying to hold back Lisa and Elena from the portal that loomed dangerously close behind them. Sorren gave a shout of rage and pain, and I dared not look to see if he was losing his fight. I trained Alard's walking stick on the hand of glory and sank my magic into its memories, pulling on its power with everything I had in me.

Elena and Lisa, still locked in a fight to the death, tangled in the tarp, stumbled through the rip and vanished into the darkness even as Teag tried in vain to hold on to the silver-shot rope and pull them out. A stream of flame from the walking stick hit the hand of glory, and it exploded like a grenade.

The force of the blast ripped the rope from Teag's bloodied hands, and he landed on his face in the sand. The concussion sent Rowan and me flying backward. Peter clutched the rescued relics in his arms and rolled, tucking himself into a ball around the heirlooms he had come to rescue. Another hellish shriek came from behind us, nearly lost in the roar of the ocean, the howl of the wind, and the rush of flames as the beach house fire raged.

When I caught my breath and got to my feet, I saw the still bodies of the two *grims*, and my heart stuttered as I searched for Sorren. Then he rose like a blood-soaked god from between the corpses, swords gripped in each hand, blades crimson and dripping.

"Is the rip closed?" Teag rose to his knees, and I could see the cuts across his palms where he had tried and failed to hold onto the rope.

Rowan staggered from the shadows, one hand pressed to her temple if the battle had left her with a throbbing head.

"It's gone," Rowan replied, wincing as she sent a delicate tracery of glowing magic across the sky where the rip had been. The tendrils of power spread across the night like threads on a tapestry for a moment, then vanished. "Sealed," she confirmed. "Nothing got out."

"They're trapped in there," Teag said, sounding seriously rattled by what we had seen. "Forever?"

Rowan shrugged. "No idea. Not sure anyone knows. They might be dead. Or…somewhere. But they're not coming back."

Peter uncurled slowly as if awaiting another attack. He stood, still cradling the heirlooms against his chest. "The fan and bowl are still intact," he said, sounding sad and shaken. "The candelabra—whatever Elena did to cast her fire spell forced too much power through the glass, even with the sigils. It shattered."

"And the hand of glory is gone," I said, pointing to a stinking pile of ashes, all that remained of the horrific relic. Teag dug out the salt and holy water from his pack and just for good measure, dumped a liberal amount of both over the ashes and then set it aflame again with a squirt of lighter fluid for good measure.

Sorren walked past us into the surf, washing away the blood that soaked his clothing and hair, and returned soaked but no longer looking like a golden-haired serial killer. When he rejoined us, the light from the house fire lent a warm glow that softened his usual pallor.

"As remote as this island is, someone is going to see those flames and come to investigate," he said. "We'd best be gone by then."

I glanced back at the bodies of the *grims*. "What about them?"

"You can salt and burn them if you like, but they're unnatural creatures. They'll decompose too rapidly for the authorities to worry themselves about it."

"Did she call the monsters?" Teag asked.

Rowan shook her head. "Doubtful, although she might have enticed them more than controlled them. Dark magic attracts dark magic, and the hand of glory would have been like waving a raw steak in the air."

The bodies of the *grims* burned down quickly, with the corpses deteriorating faster than the flames could consume them. We had all been injured in the fight, and though Sorren fared the worst with gashes from the black dogs that would have killed a mortal, he healed the fastest. I suspected Rowan and Peter would have nasty bruises from how hard they hit when Elena tossed them aside. Teag's hands were badly rope burned, and I promised to take care of him once we got back to my house. I felt more drained than injured, but I had pushed hard at my limits, and I knew I would feel a bone-deep weariness until my system had a chance to recover.

"We didn't save her," Teag said as we limped back to the cars. "Lisa got pulled into the rip, just like Elena intended."

"Except that Elena didn't plan to go too," I pointed out. "And after hearing what Lisa said, I wonder if she came out here to trap Elena more than to hide from her. If she suspected who was behind the attacks, she didn't do anything to protect her coven. Maybe she intended all along to turn Elena's magic back on her and didn't figure on getting sucked in along with her."

"You won't be able to return all of the stolen pieces," Teag said, turning to Peter, who held the remaining heirlooms tight to his chest as if he feared they might be wrested away from him. "Will your grand coven be angry with you?"

Peter looked as exhausted as I felt, and a bruise on his cheek suggested he had hit hard when he fell. But he shook his head and managed a wan smile. "No. They'll be relieved to have any of the items returned, and I can report that the curse pot and the hand of glory were eliminated as threats. As for the quilt," he said, shrugging, "who knows? It might vanish from the evidence room under mysterious circumstances."

"Certainly wouldn't be the first time something like that happened," Rowan replied, trying and failing to look innocent.

"It's too bad you had to miss your Halloween Gala back in Haven Harbor," I said, thinking that even a root canal would have been more fun than the way we had spent the evening.

Peter's tired smile broadened. "Well, it was for a good cause. And there's always next year. I meant what I said—you're all very welcome to visit anytime, but the Gala is when the town really shines. Let me know if you come up, and I'll make sure you meet some of our more interesting residents who don't usually mingle with the tourists." He glanced at Sorren. "You might find that you have friends in common."

I might consider a trip north next Halloween, but once I got Teag's hands bandaged up, and I reclaimed Baxter from Maggie, I looked forward to calling Kell to wish him a Happy Halloween on his ghost hunt and spend the rest of my night with a glass of wine, a good book, and ice packs on the places I'd made a hard landing. We'd saved the city, maybe the whole East Coast, and as usual, almost no one was the wiser. Still, I had good reason to celebrate tomorrow.

Halloween chocolate would be half price.

INNOCENCE LOST

First appeared in the anthology:
Release the Virgins

INNOCENCE LOST

I NEVER SAW HIM COMING.

A relaxing walk on Hasell Street suddenly turned into a contact sport when the skinny guy in a hoodie slammed into me. I stumbled toward the street and caught myself on a parked car. He staggered into the low bushes next to a parking lot but never slowed down, turning the corner onto crowded Meeting Street before I could catch my breath.

"Are you all right?" The woman had a Midwestern accent, very noticeable here in Charleston, South Carolina. She might have been my mom's age, and she and her husband planted themselves on the side-walk, so everyone had to go around us, giving me a chance to catch my breath.

"Yeah, I'm fine. Thanks," I said, pushing a strand of strawberry-blonde hair out of my eyes, more shaken than hurt. I'd gripped my small purse on reflex but slung cross-body, nobody was going to get it without a fight. Funny, but the man who shoved me hadn't even tried to take it.

"Do you want us to call the police?" the man asked.

I shook my head. "No. Thank you. I didn't see his face, and he didn't take anything."

"You could have been hurt," the woman huffed.

She was right, but aside from perhaps a bruise where my hip hit the passenger door handle of the car I smacked into, neither the car nor I was actually damaged. "Lucky for me, it's a soft car," I joked. I thanked the couple again for their help and watched as they walked away toward the touristy parts of town. I stayed where I was, trying to get my bearings.

I felt the pull of magic, something old and strong that hadn't been present moments before. It took a moment before I collected my jangled nerves enough to focus. A few steps brought me to where the man had stumbled into the shrubbery when he bounced off me. The glint of gold caught my eye, lying beneath a short, slightly mangled boxwood.

When I bent down, I saw a small statue of the Virgin Mary, no larger than my hand. The gold leaf paint looked real, as did the small gems that glinted on her Queen-of-Heaven crown. I grabbed my scarf and used it to pick up the statue without making skin contact, then I slipped it into my purse.

What was a guy who looked rough around the edges doing with an old statue that gave off strong magic vibes? "Stealing it" was the obvious answer, but why? Maybe I'd end up calling the police after all, but before then, I needed to check into the magic piece of the puzzle and figure out what was going on.

I'm Cassidy Kincaide, owner of Trifles and Folly, an antiques and curio store in historic, haunted Charleston, South Carolina. Most people think of the store as a great place to find estate jewelry or the perfect vintage accent piece, but the store—and I—have some pretty big secrets. I'm a psychometric, which means I can read the history and magic of objects by touching them—hence the careful handling of the statue. And the store, which has been around since the city was founded 350 years ago, is part of a secret coalition of mortals and immortals who keep Charleston—and the world—safe from supernatural threats. So when I decided to have a closer look at the stolen statue, I wasn't just whistling Dixie.

Even wrapped in my scarf and tucked into my purse, I could feel the buzz of the statue's magic as I power-walked back to the store on King Street. Maggie, our part-time helper, was busy with a customer. Today, Maggie had a sari-silk broomstick skirt-of-many-colors with a matching strip of bright pink tied like a headband around her short, gray hair. Teag Logan, my best friend, assistant store manager, and sometimes bodyguard looked up when I walked in. With his chin-length, asymmetrically cut dark hair and whipcord build, Teag looks more like a skater boy than the Ph.D. drop-out he really is. Let's just say he found a higher calling in kicking supernatural ass than finishing his dissertation.

"Everything okay? It took you longer to get back than you expected." Teag automatically looked me over from head to toe, checking for injuries. I shook my head and walked to the break room. "You're limping," he pointed out.

"Someone ran into me pretty hard on the sidewalk," I said. "My hip slammed into a parked car. Could have been worse." I glanced over at the customer who was busy looking at beautiful old signet rings with Maggie, and Teag nodded, realizing there was more to the story.

"I'll be fine," I promised. "Let me put my purse in the office and grab some coffee, and I can come help up front." Mostly, I wanted to get away from the buzz of energy the statue put off, although I could use some java too.

The store got busy then, and I didn't have a chance to talk to Teag for a couple of hours as we matched shoppers to their ideal antiques. As I wrapped up a large, heavy silver tea set, I wondered how the purchaser—who told me excitedly about the bus tour she was on—intended to get it home. I mentioned shipping, but she said there was plenty of room under the bus. Hopefully, none of her fellow travelers decided to buy equally large souvenirs, or someone would be walking back to Toronto.

By mid-afternoon, the influx had slowed to a trickle. Maggie waved us off, promising to yell if she got swamped. Maggie knows what we really do at the store, and she's a godsend. Teag and I headed to the break room, and I sat down with a sigh.

"Spill," Teag ordered, giving me a worried glare.

"I was coming back from lunch, and a guy in a hoodie ran past and slammed me out of his way. When I got my bearings, I felt magic tug me from the parking lot—where he'd stumbled. And I found this." I pulled the scarf out of my purse and set it onto the table, where the small statue rolled free.

Teag leaned over for a closer look but kept his hands behind his back. We've learned the hard way not to touch without sizing up the danger first. "Looks old and authentic. Meaning I don't think it's a souvenir piece. Wanna bet it's stolen?"

"That's what I figured, but it seems like a weird thing for someone to steal," I said, shifting on my chair to ease the tender spot on my hip. "Easy to identify, hard to fence."

As an antique store owner, I have to be very conscious of where the items we buy for resale come from and make sure the owner actually owns them. That's aside from determining whether or not the pieces are cursed or haunted—which is true more often than people might think.

"Here." Teag went to the fridge and pulled out an ice pack, which he handed to me. Given the nature of what we really do—fighting off things that go bump in the night—the break room has an unusually robust first-aid kit. I pressed the cold compress against my sore hip and sighed in relief.

"How about you sit with that ice while I see what I can pull up online?" Teag grabbed his laptop and went to work. He's got Weaver magic, which means he can weave spells into cloth and hidden data into information, making him a hell of a hacker. Moments later, he looked up in triumph.

"Looks like there's been a rash of break-ins at churches all over the Lowcountry," Teag said. "All of them Catholic, which isn't as common down here as it is up North, so that's interesting right there."

Plenty of churches had valuable items if a thief just wanted a quick buck. Silver crosses, antiques, artwork, even loose change in the donation box could be fair game for a grab-and-run. But the thief—or thieves—had concentrated on Catholic churches, which had to mean something.

"Can you tell what was stolen?" I asked, trying to figure out the connection.

"Give me a sec," Teag's fingers flew across the keyboard. After a short while, he sat back, stared at the screen, and chewed his lower lip, a tell that he was trying to make sense of what he found.

"Anything?"

"Yeah. In every case, all that was taken were statues—mostly of the Virgin Mary, but also of some saints. Not just the regular image of Mary, but some of the special ones like the Virgin of Guadalupe, the Virgin of Lourdes, Virgin of Montserrat. Most were old, some were said to contain relics, and—get this—several had reputations for miraculous healing or warding off evil."

Well, that explained the "magic" I'd sensed. Power—regardless of its source—calls to power. Miracle or magic, puh-tay-toe, puh-tah-toe.

"Which brings us to the million-dollar question—why?" I mused, taking a sip of my coffee.

"Could be a collector with specialized tastes," Teag speculated, still glaring at his laptop like it could be intimidated into giving up the missing information.

I shook my head. "I didn't get a look at the guy's face, but when he bumped me, I got a glimpse of his emotions. He was terrified—and I don't think it was of the cops."

"So maybe it's like the kid in that movie who could see dead people? You know, where he made a blanket fort and stole all the crucifixes to keep the ghosts away?"

"Yeah," I said as I weighed the statement and felt my intuition respond. "I don't know what he was scared of, but that would make sense."

"It must be pretty big if he's the one knocking over all those churches," Teag replied. "Because there've been at least twenty break-ins according to the report I hacked into."

I pulled out my phone and hit a number on speed dial.

"This is Father Anne," came the greeting. "Hi, Cassidy!" Father Anne Burgett is an unorthodox Episcopalian priest who moonlights as a demon hunter. She's one of our allies when shit gets real, and she's also wicked with Cards Against Humanity.

"Hey there," I said, shifting again to keep the ice on my sore spot. "What do you know about the thefts of statues of the Virgin Mary and random saints?"

She was quiet for a moment. "Not much, other than the scuttlebutt I've picked up through the inter-faith meetings. Newsflash—clergy gossip. And when someone starts breaking into churches and stealing sacred objects, word travels fast."

"What are they saying?"

"Aside from telling everyone to lock their doors? Some people think it's an attack specifically on the Catholic faith because it's only been their churches targeted," Father Anne replied. "Others have pointed out that Catholic churches are more likely than others to have really old, really valuable objects. Protestants don't usually go for as much bling."

"Anyone talking about a supernatural cause?"

"Not out loud," she replied. "But I've heard some whispering inside the Society that the pattern could suggest the thief is either trying to summon something or ward it off—and neither of those options is good." "The Society" was the St. Expeditus Society, a secret organization of priests dedicated to eliminating supernatural threats.

"Thanks," I said. "Keep an ear to the ground for us, okay? We'll let you know what we find out because I've got a feeling that whatever's up ties in to your area of expertise."

I ended the call and turned back to Teag, who was hunched over his laptop. "You look like a hound dog on a trail," I said with a chuckle. "Next thing, you'll be sniffing the computer."

Teag barely looked up. "None of the churches that were robbed had security cameras. But the corner where he ran into you did. I'm piecing together splices from the cameras along his route to see where he went."

"You're awesome. A little scary, but amazing," I replied. I went back up front to make sure Maggie didn't need help, but the afternoon tourist bump had already started to trickle off. By the time I came back to the break room, Teag greeted me with a Cheshire cat grin.

"I think I've got him," Teag said. I stood behind him and looked at the grainy footage of Hoodie Guy getting into an old, beat-up Toyota. The license plate was clearly visible, even though I still hadn't gotten a good look at his face.

"Let me hack the DMV, and we'll have an address," Teag said, making it sound like business as usual. Which it kinda was, for us.

A few more minutes at the keyboard turned up a name—Jason Durant—and an address. "Now all we have to do is figure out why he wants all the statues and what to do about it," Teag said, sitting back and stretching.

"Once we close up, I thought I'd take a look at the figurine and see what I can read from it. Maybe it'll shed some light on why Jason was so afraid."

Maggie rang up our last sale of the day, checked in to see if we needed anything, then headed out, locking up the front as she went. Teag poured me a glass of sweet tea from the pitcher we always kept in the refrigerator and sat beside me at the table.

He held out one end of a thin strip of cloth, and I knew it was one he had woven himself, incorporating his magic into the fabric with every pass of the shuttlecock. We'd found through trial and error that if I held one end of the fabric and he kept hold of the other, he could see my vision when I tranced.

"Okay," I said, taking a deep breath and letting it out. "Let's see what's got him running scared."

I closed my hand around the statue and found that it was painted wood, not carved stone as I had thought. I could sense its age—at least a century or two. The figure had a warm glow in my inner sight, a mix of serenity and worship and forgiveness that stilled my churning thoughts with an otherworldly peace.

But I could feel Jason's anxiety overlaying all of that like a stain. His terror felt like a punch in the gut, and my heart sped up as my breathing grew shallow. Nightmares. Terror. Voices in the dark. And beneath it all, the whiff of something evil, maybe even infernal.

"Cassidy!" Teag's voice urged me to break contact with the statue, and immediately the vision vanished. I slumped in my chair as I tried to get myself under control. Teag pressed the glass of very sugary sweet tea into my hand. "Drink."

We've done this so often, Teag and I have the routine pretty well rehearsed. Sweet tea grounds me, and the sugar rush re-sets my inner gyroscope. After a minute or two, I was back to normal.

"You felt it?" Sometimes I get images, other times, just feelings. Tonight was less visual and more visceral.

"Jason's afraid something awful is waiting for him," Teag recapped, which was pretty much what I had gotten from the impressions. "But I didn't get the feeling it was a person, did you?"

"No. A ghost, maybe? Or a supernatural creature?" I took another long drink from the tea and set the glass aside. "Why don't we take a drive past his house and see what kind of vibes we pick up? Then we can figure out how to confront him."

"It might not just be confronting him," Teag pointed out. "We don't know if what he's afraid of is in his house or if he thinks it's going to come after him."

"Yeah," I agreed. "And we need to figure out why he stole the statues, so we don't accidentally let something bad loose."

"Plus, if we can do it without starting the apocalypse, we need to get him to release the Virgins so they can go back to the churches where they belong," Teag added.

Even with the seriousness of the vision, I couldn't help but chuckle at Teag's comment.

We locked up the shop and headed out to Teag's car. I sent a message to Father Anne about where we were going—safety precaution—since my boss, Sorren, was out of the country on business. Usually, he's our backup, since he's a nearly six-hundred-year-old vampire. Handy, that. But his work with the Alliance takes him all over the world, and tonight he was somewhere in Europe.

I wasn't familiar with the part of town where Jason lived. The houses were modest, and most looked in fairly good repair, although a few were boarded up or abandoned. As soon as we crossed into Jason's block, I felt a chill to the marrow despite a warm Charleston evening. Psychic ooze leaked like an oil spill from an unremarkable yellow one-story house.

"There," I said, pointing.

"Yeah, I feel it too," Teag agreed. Our gifts might take different forms, but dark, evil energy bled out from that little bungalow.

We kept on going, unwilling to let Jason or whatever entity he was hiding notice our interest or our abilities. "I think we need to bring Rowan in on this," I said, naming our favorite white magic witch. "Just in case it's more than Father Anne can handle alone."

"Agreed," Teag said as we drove back so I could pick up my car at the store. "You and I can be back-up, but whatever that was, it's not something we can fight outright."

Teag's martial arts training makes him pretty tough to beat, and I'm no slouch with my own set of magical weapons. We've both fought off enough ghoulies and ghosties and long-legged beasties to be able to throw down with the worst of them. But there's a difference between whacking the head off a zombie with a blessed machete and facing down something incorporeal—or possibly even infernal.

"Then let's call in the cavalry and figure out our next moves," I replied. "Because I got the sense Jason's protections are at their breaking point, and I don't want to see whatever that is get loose."

The next night, we closed in like a supernatural SWAT team. Rowan rocked a Buffy look-alike vibe, with her blonde hair up in a ponytail and wearing all black. Father Anne was her usual badass self, dark hair in a fade, clerical collar over a sleeveless black T-shirt that showed the colorful St. Expeditus tats on her shoulders and upper arms, jeans, and steel-toed Doc Martens.

Teag and I have both amassed a wardrobe of dark-colored clothing because it helps us blend in when we're somewhere in the line of duty we're not technically supposed to be, or because it hides the blood and monster guts. Always handy when you're running from a pile of creature corpses you've just torched.

Rowan set down a perimeter warding to keep the evil from getting out if something went wrong. It also carried a distraction spell, so unless we blew the place up—wouldn't be the first time—the spell would encourage the neighbors and the cops to look the other way.

Father Anne spoke a benediction, cleansing the area in her own way, making it naturally repellent to dark energies. Blessings and curses carry real power, more than most people give them credit for. I knew she also came prepared to do an exorcism, depending on what we found inside. While they did their thing, Teag and I set down a circle of salt and iron filings around the small yard, another layer of insurance.

We all wore protective charms—silver, onyx, agate—as well as religious medallions. Teag and I also carried gris-gris bags and jack balls from a friend who's a powerful Hoodoo root worker and some blessed Voudon *veves* on silver bracelets from another friend who's a kickass mambo. I'd found that protective energies tended to be more ecumenical than some of their ardent believers, and I knew the importance of taking good juju wherever I could find it.

As far as weapons—we were all carrying. I had my athame—my grandmother's old wooden spoon—that helped me channel my touch magic and concentrate it into a protective force. I'd brought an antique walking stick whose resonance enabled me to shoot fire. Teag and I both had silver and iron knives—good against ghosts and other supernatural creatures—as well as a sawed-off shotgun with salt rounds and a Glock with silver bullets. Rowan had her magic, and while Father Anne's faith was strong, her aim with a knife was downright wicked.

Time to roll. I felt a frisson of energy as I crossed the barriers, able to do so by the permission of their casters. Jason and the dark power would not be able to do the same. The closer I got to the house, the more I felt the taint of the entity or magic inside. Awful as it was, the power still felt muted, and I shuddered to think of what would happen if Jason hadn't stolen the blessed statues and called on their protection.

Rowan and I went for the front door; Teag and Father Anne circled around to the back. Rowan lifted a hand and blew it off the hinges, and I heard a crack from the other side of the house and figured our partners had kicked in the rear door.

"What the hell is that?" I recoiled at the sight of what lay before me. Where the living room should have been was a circle of saint's candles, most of them blackened and burned far down, as if they were lit 24/7. A row of unused candles sat to one side, and the soot-streaked empties supported my guess. In between the lit candles were the stolen statues of the Virgin Mary, facing inward, silent sentries to contain the evil Jason had loosed.

All around us, on every wall, someone had marked sigils and symbols of protection from every religion I could think of, and some I couldn't identify. They were spray painted, drawn with Sharpie, dug into the wallboard—and some looked to be written in blood. Little homemade shrines sat in each corner of the room, to Christ, Shiva, Buddha, and Papa Legba. The shrines held religious statues, candles, and offerings of food, coins, and liquor.

A thick haze of smoke drifted in the stale air—I couldn't tell immediately whether it was sage or weed—but it didn't completely cover the underlying stink of rot and sulfur. Because in the center of the candle circle, surrounded by a pentagram—good side up—and other protective symbols, was a small black hole that looked like it descended to the Abyss.

"It's a hell-mouth," Father Anne and Rowan said, nearly in unison.

Teag snorted. "Looks more like a hell-nostril to me." I knew he fell back on humor when he was scared, and his wide eyes told me he felt as terrified as the rest of us.

"Don't cross the circle!" Hoodie Guy—aka Jason Durant—lurched out from the hallway where he'd been hiding. "You don't understand—if that gets loose, we're all gonna die!"

"How did you open a hell-mouth?" Rowan turned her full attention on Jason, which made him wilt like the guilty teenager he was.

"I didn't mean to," he whined. "My grandmother was supposed to be some kind of witch, but my mama wouldn't let me study with her because Mama got religion and said magic was bad. Then Grandma died. Only I found out I could do things that weren't normal—magic things—and I didn't dare let Mama know. So I got some old books at a used bookstore and studied on my own. Except I screwed up, and that —" he pointed to the dark portal in the floor—"opened, and I don't know how to shut it. So I figured I'd put a fence around it and find out how to make it go away."

Jason didn't look like he'd been sleeping or eating, and he seemed contrite enough I believed his story about accidental magic. We run into that a lot in our business, along with cursed heirlooms and haunted antiques. People mess around with powers they underestimate and open up a highway to Hell.

"You're not going to turn me over to the police, are you?" Jason looked like he'd reached his breaking point. "I stole the statues, but I maybe saved the world a little. That counts, doesn't it?"

"If we all get out of this alive, we'll return the statues to the churches you took them from," Father Anne said sternly.

"And then you're going to apprentice with me, so this doesn't happen again," Rowan added with a glare that could curdle milk.

Jason nodded miserably. "Anything. I swear, I'll do anything. Just…make it go away. I hear it screaming in my dreams."

That was our cue. Father Anne moved to the right; Rowan walked to the left. Teag and I fell back, unable to help dispel the darkness Jason had conjured but ready to protect the two who could.

Father Anne began the exorcism rite, her voice strong and confident, rebuking the powers of evil. Rowan thrust out her right hand, palm forward, and blasted the hell-mouth with a torrent of white light that glared too bright to watch.

The portal shifted and writhed on its own like a living thing, trying to twist away from the all-consuming energy. But it didn't vanish.

A blob of black ooze bubbled up from the small hole and expanded into a horror of teeth and claws. Later, I'd find out we all saw it differently, that it played to our individual fears, but in that moment, I saw a creature somewhere between werewolf and demon. The stench of sulfur and rotting meat almost made me gag.

Teag didn't hesitate. He launched three silver throwing knives in quick succession seconds before I raised my athame and sent a streak of cold, blue-white energy to strike the monster in the chest. It roared, a noise I'd hear forever in my nightmares, but it did not break the circle of candles. Dark blood seeped from where Teag's knives embedded, hilt-deep, in its ribs, and charred skin hung in ribbons where my strike had ripped into the body. Yet the were-demon still stood, teeth bared and claws unsheathed, promising bloody death to all of us if it ever got free.

Rowan and Father Anne's chants rose and fell, reinforcing each other. The creature stalked within the circle, glaring at us with a malevolence that made me shiver, and then it threw itself at the warding. A bright yellow light flared, rising from the saints' candles, and the monster fell back, howling.

"Look," I whispered to Teag. The symbols on the walls around us glowed with inner fire, shining as brightly as the boundary of light that rose above the sacred candles. Father Anne and Rowan spoke with authority, their voices growing louder, commanding the creature to be gone. Inside its prison, the were-demon shrieked, its body arcing in agony. I watched, holding my breath, as its immense form was drawn back to the small black hole from where it came, vanishing inch by impossible inch as the chants and liturgy continued.

I felt the struggle as the monster fought with all its power and the borrowed energy of hell itself, and I knew that Father Anne and Rowan had to be tiring. Teag and I didn't have the right magic to send the creature packing, and I hated feeling helpless. Then I spotted the woven and knotted cords on Teag's belt that he uses to store magic.

"Your cords," I hissed. "We'll be their extra batteries."

Teag loosed a cord, and we each held an end. I put my hand on Father Anne's shoulder while Teag gripped Rowan tightly. I felt my gift flow through me and out to them, reinforcing and healing, renewing and energizing. Alone, the creature was too much for us to handle. Together, we were enough.

"*Benedictus Deus, Gloria Patri, Benedictus Dea, Matri Gloria!*" Father Anne shouted defiantly.

GAIL Z. MARTIN

"So mote it be!" Rowan cried, sending another flare of white light at the luminous boundary that made it flash so brightly I had to look away.

When my vision cleared, all that remained was a blackened streak in the middle of the pentagram on the floor. No monster. No hell gate. Just Jason, on his knees, sobbing, and the four of us, gobsmacked to still be alive.

I shook myself to clear my mind and loosened my hold on Father Anne's shoulder, fearing I'd gripped tightly enough to leave bruises. Teag let his hand fall as well. When we broke contact, both the priest and the witch staggered as if the infusion of our energy was all that was keeping them standing.

Father Anne rallied first and said an additional blessing to clear the space before she began to extinguish the candles and gather up the stolen Virgins. Rowan collected her wits a moment later and strode over to Jason.

She squatted down and pulled him into her arms until he quieted. "Get your things," she ordered. "I'm not letting you out of my sight. Tomorrow, you start your training program."

"The police—" he began in a ragged voice.

"The police are the least of your worries," Rowan said in a stern voice. "You're now in the custody of my Coven, within the jurisdiction of the Society. And you will not be rid of us until you're properly trained and no longer pose a threat." The chill in her tone suggested that Jason didn't want to find out the alternative.

Her expression softened, just a little. "You'll get the training you need and the answers you deserve—and a group to have your back." She followed him as he went to pack a bag. It was obvious Jason was badly shaken by his mistakes, but I was confident Rowan and her coven's tough love would get him back on track.

"What about all this?" I asked, waving a hand to indicate the now-darkened sigils painted on the walls and the pentagram on the floor. "It's not going to help resale value."

Father Anne looked grim. "I'll make a few calls. Between the

152

Alliance and the Society, we've got people for that. I think we're covered."

I suddenly felt all of the night's work in every muscle and sinew, down to the marrow of my bones. I was drained and empty, starved and thirsty, and utterly exhausted.

"What about the statues?" Teag asked.

Father Anne shrugged. "The less said, the better. If they come back via a few well-placed 'friends' in the diocese, no one will ask awkward questions."

Rowan and Jason came back into the room. Father Anne tucked the holy figures into the small duffel she'd left by the door.

"Go home," Father Anne said, giving me a weary smile. "And...thanks."

Teag and I walked back out to my RAV4 as the others got into Father Anne's truck. "I don't know about you, but I've had all the excitement I can handle for today," I told him. Once again, we'd saved the world, and no one would ever know except us. "Time to call it a night."

THE PIPER'S SONG

First appeared in the anthology:
Tales from the Old Black Ambulance

THE PIPER'S SONG

THE FIRST INKLING SOMETHING WAS WRONG CAME WHEN THE WHITE Ghost Bikes began to clang and buck against the chains that bound them to lamp posts and street signs, wheels spinning without a breeze to turn them. Those whitewashed bicycles, symbols of riders killed in traffic, dotted the streets in and around Charleston, somber and usually silent memorials.

The second warning came from the roadside markers, the home-made crosses and wreaths near the highways commemorating fatal accidents, the passing of loved ones. Calls surged to 911, reporting detailed accounts of car wrecks along the state routes and interstates, and all of them had two things in common. First, that the wreck details were completely correct, and second, that the fatalities had happened months, sometimes years, ago.

The last time those particular two sets of ghosts acted out, Charleston teetered on the edge of an apocalypse, beset by Nephilim raised by a long-dead hanging judge bent on fulfilling a vendetta. He and the Nephilim were gone—I knew because I'd been part of the fight to destroy them—and they weren't coming back.

What frightened the ghosts now, I didn't know but would make it my business to find out. Anything that terrifies the dead is more than enough reason to cause concern for the living.

"Can you read anything?" Teag Logan asked, standing next to me as I laid my hands on one of the Ghost Bikes that had started to rattle and clank on its own several hours earlier.

"I see a beautiful day, bright sun, music playing somewhere…the rider glanced to one side…then the crash, flying through the air, hitting the ground, darkness," I murmured, reading the strong emotions imprinted onto the bike by its dead rider. Not all of the Ghost Bike memorials are the actual cycles from an accident; some are purchased and painted as a tribute. The stand-in bikes weren't the ones causing problems, just the twisted and damaged ones that had been part of their riders' last moments.

"The memories of the crash are faded," I continued. "But the fear is new and strong." I strained to glean more from my connection with the bike's resonance and let myself open up to the memories that had sunk deep into the mangled steel.

The first vision had been of flowers and sky, sun and warmth, memories of life. Now, I saw through the eyes of the biker's ghost, the spirit that had remained attached to the place and vehicle that caused his death. The color and heat had faded from this view, leaving it cold and gray.

I had read the placard about the rider, George McMillan, a bicycle delivery messenger who had lost his life in a hit-and-run crash. Now, I saw through the eyes of George's ghost, surveying the landscape around me and feeling his fear. The ghost stood next to the ruined bike on a city side street, but all alone, separated from the living souls around him by the veil of death, present but unacknowledged. I got the feeling that George had made his peace with that and wasn't ready yet to find out what happened if he sought out the light and transitioned to the next stage of existence. He wasn't hurting anyone, but now, I knew that something had come looking to hurt George.

I heard the tune, a strange, mournful song that carried from a distance as if seeking an audience. George panicked, and I had to remind myself that I was seeing what had already happened, seeing the ghost of a ghost, so to speak, and that I could do nothing to calm the spirit or ease his fears.

The song grew louder, and George tried to run, but like most ghosts, he could only go so far beyond the object that anchored his spirit to this world, and the bike was chained to the light post. The bike shuddered and shook, wheels banging and chain rattling, but George could not flee. I tried to identify the tune and couldn't quite retain the melody, although it played over and over, a hypnotic, compelling score. Perhaps it wasn't meant to be heard by the living, but it certainly affected the dead.

George clapped his hands over his ears and shook his head. "No, no!" he shouted, as the song grew louder. I had just decided that the strange tune was being played on some kind of reed pipe when George began to scream.

The images flashed past me, jumbled and chaotic, infused with George's utter terror. I glimpsed a presence, some kind of being, but only as an indistinct outline of a hunched creature upright on two legs. The music reached a crescendo, and George's ghost began to disintegrate in front of me as if the song had the power to pull the ghost apart, bit by bit, until nothing remained.

The music stopped. George's ghost was gone.

"Cassidy!"

I followed my way back to Teag's urgent voice and woke from my trance, leaning against the light pole, and removed my hand from the bike's worn seat. "Something hunted him," I said, drawing in a deep, shaking breath and trying to collect my wits. My connection to George's memories had been visceral, and I had felt the last lurch of his terror and the instant his consciousness was extinguished. Witnessing his unmaking, the violence against his spirit, affected me to my core. I wanted to scream, to collapse, to throw up.

Instead, I managed a wan smile as Teag placed a warm, anchoring hand on my shoulder and pressed a bottle of orange juice into my hand.

"Don't try to tell me about it now," he soothed.

"Is she okay?" a woman asked, stopping her morning jog to check.

159

"Low blood sugar," I murmured, hating to lie but knowing she really didn't want to hear the truth. "I'll be fine, thanks."

The woman jogged off, and Teag glanced around to ensure that we were alone again, at least for the moment.

"I heard music in the dark and saw a…thing…and then something tore George's ghost apart," I said, still breathing hard.

"You got a lot. More than with any of the other bikes."

I drank the juice gratefully and shook my head. "Not enough to make sense of what's going on, unfortunately. The last time the ghosts got upset, things went bad in a hurry."

I'm Cassidy Kincaide, owner of Trifles and Folly, an antiques and curio shop in historic, haunted Charleston, South Carolina, that is a lot more than meets the eye. We get cursed and haunted objects out of the wrong hands, and we've saved the world on more than one occasion.

We also keep some important secrets, especially about magic. My magic is psychometry, the ability to read the memories and magic from objects by touching them. Teag has Weaver magic, and he can weave spells into cloth and data into information, making him one hell of a hacker. My business partner, Sorren, is a nearly six-hundred-year-old vampire who was once the best jewel thief in Antwerp. We're part of the Alliance, a coalition of mortals and immortals who protect the world from supernatural threats. When we win, no one notices. When we lose, the carnage gets blamed on natural disasters.

"Ready to head back to the store?" Teag asked. We had spent the morning checking out the Ghost Bikes and roadside memorials where disturbances had been reported. I'm not a medium, so I don't channel the ghosts, and I can't summon them, which means I have to rely on the spirits to make themselves seen and heard. Failing that, I can use my psychometry to pick up the resonance of their emotions before—and after—death and then piece the clues together. It's a tedious process.

"Sure," I said. "We can pick up lunch and bring something back for Maggie." Maggie is our fantastic part-time assistant. She doesn't have any magic of her own, although she knows all about ours, but she's got sass and an awesome sense of humor. Maggie retired from teaching, then retired from retirement to help out with the store. I'm pretty sure she can honestly say that it's never been boring.

We picked up pizza and took turns eating and watching the front of the store. That's when I noticed the large wrapped rectangle leaning against the wall in my office. "What's that?" I asked Maggie.

"You or Teag had it shipped from that estate sale you went to last week," she replied with a shrug. "We have the two other cartons of stuff from there you brought back yourselves."

I remembered as soon as she mentioned the sale. Teag and I keep an eye on auctions and estate sales because they're a way objects with harmful resonance can make their way from person to person. We not only buy items suitable for the store to re-sell, but we also cull out problem pieces before they have a chance to cause havoc.

The mirror hadn't struck me as dangerous, merely unsettling. We knew very little about the old woman who had died, only that her home was full of beautiful, expensive, and odd items, a curiosity seeker's paradise. The old house had been a solid brownstone in a nice part of town, and from the very sparse bio the auctioneer shared, Eliza Roberts had died at age ninety-five, never married, and was the last of her family line. What had intrigued me was that while I saw very few religious items in the house, a fair number of pieces had possible connections to spiritualism. I didn't know whether or not Eliza had been a medium, but I'd lay money on the possibility that she dabbled in speaking with the dead.

"You're thinking something." Teag jarred me out of my reverie. "Spill it." He's my assistant manager for the store, but he's also my best friend and on occasion, bodyguard.

"After we close up, I want to get a closer look at that mirror and some of the other things we brought from the Roberts house," I said. "If the spirits are restless, maybe they'll contact us."

"Or you could just call Alicia," he suggested. Alicia Peters, a powerful medium, was a friend and an ally who had helped us on a number of occasions.

"Alicia's canvassing her side of the city for Ghost Bikes and roadside shrines, remember? So we'll hear back from her when she's done," I replied.

"You don't know how the objects will react to your magic."

"Do we ever?"

Teag sighed. "No. All right. Go help Maggie up front, and I'll get everything ready."

Fortunately, the rest of the afternoon passed quietly, but as I wished Maggie a good evening and locked the door behind her, I felt my nervousness ratchet up, wondering what would come from Eliza's mirror.

The rectangular-looking glass had a dark mahogany frame. The silver backing showed none of the signs of age that too often marred a big piece, so the reflection showed clear and true. Teag had moved a more comfortable chair out of my office so I could have better support as I touched the mirror and opened up my magic. He's used to my psychometry by now, and more than once, he's had to help me off the floor when a vision landed me right on my ass. I noticed he also made a pitcher of fresh sweet tea, which helps me recover from the huge energy drain that a difficult psychic connection can cause.

"I wove some new strips," Teag said, nodding toward several hand-woven fabric runners, each several inches long and a few inches wide, like overgrown bookmarks, which lay on the table. "They'll help ground and protect you, and this way, I can see what you see."

Teag could weave his magic into the warp and woof of fabric, creating powerful protection spells, but he could also create a psychic bridge between us so that he didn't have to rely on me to recount what I saw. That had saved my butt more than once when a vision turned suddenly dangerous.

"All right," I said, settling into the chair facing the mirror. "Let's see what's through the looking glass." In my left hand, I held one end of the woven ribbon, and Teag held the other. I put my right hand on the cold pane, and like Alice, felt myself fall through the looking glass.

Everything around me was made of silver and shadows, like a moonlit night. I knew I wasn't alone but feared to call out, unsure of whose attention I might draw. This place beyond the mirror was far colder than our break room, and when I glanced behind me, I saw my own face staring back and the warm light of the real world setting it apart.

"Who are you?"

I startled and turned to face a woman whose somber black dress reminded me of the mourning clothes of a past era. I recognized the face. Eliza Roberts, the woman who had owned the mirror.

"My name's Cassidy. Are you Eliza?"

The woman nodded.

"We're not alone here, are we?" I could sense other presences all around us, just out of sight in the shadows. We stood in a pool of moonlight, distinct from the darkness all around. I did not want to leave the light or venture out of sight of the mirror and the way home.

"No. Mirrors harbor spirits. It's a safer place than many, especially now," Eliza replied.

"Do you know what's frightened the ghosts?" I turned slowly, scanning the darkness. I glimpsed eyes and pale skin, but no clear faces or forms.

"Not exactly," Eliza replied. "There's an old, strong power at work, one I don't recognize. I studied such things when I was alive. I've been able to see spirits in mirrors since I was a child, and since no one would teach me, I taught myself. But this new presence, it's dangerous and hungry."

"Hungry?"

"The entity is eating souls," Eliza said.

"So the ghosts it eats, what happens to them?" I felt the cold that surrounded me seep into my bones at the idea that even greater dangers existed after death.

"They cease to exist," Eliza answered. "At least, their consciousness is gone. They say energy never is destroyed. But they are no longer who they were, and they have not passed on to the next level, gone to the light. However you would phrase it."

Vanished, with a finality even greater than death. Many ghosts retained sentience and chose to stay behind to watch over loved ones, protect something important, or see justice done. I'd seen those spirits eventually find peace once their task was completed, moving on to whatever came next. To think of them being hunted, trapped, *consumed,* shook me on a visceral level.

"I offered sanctuary to those who sought it, here with me," Eliza said, gesturing to the shadows that surrounded us. "I couldn't save them all, but those who came, I protect."

No wonder the mirror gave off such a powerful resonance, disquieting but not evil. "I'll help you protect the mirror," I promised. "But please, tell me anything that might help us stop whatever is out there hurting the ghosts."

"The creature selects its victims," Eliza said, choosing her words carefully. "It preys on more recent spirits. The old haunts are rooted too deeply for it to disturb. It favors violent deaths. Few of those who took refuge here came from their sickbed. I believe creatures like this may have stalked battlefields, and now without that kind of carnage, it takes its pickings where it can."

Violent deaths—like the car crashes and bike accidents. I felt my anger rise. Those ghosts often stayed behind because it took time for them to process what happened to them in a single, traumatic instant. Even crime victims often had a few minutes before death to understand what was happening, but those from wrecks were alive one minute, dead the next, and wandered lost and confused until they finally figured out what had happened to them. The idea that a predator stalked them at their most vulnerable made me furious—and determined to do something about it.

"We'll find a way to stop this," I promised. "When we do, can the spirits leave here?"

Eliza nodded. "We are all free to move on from this place, whenever we choose. I consider it a halfway house for wayward spirits," she said with a faint smile. "Go back to your world," she told me. "It's cold here, and you have work to do."

With that, Eliza Roberts turned and walked into the shadows until she vanished, leaving me alone in the moonlight.

"Cassidy!" Teag's voice called. "Cassidy, can you hear me?"

I closed my eyes and let Teag lead me back to the warmth and light

164

of the mirror, and through it, back to myself. I shuddered and drew a harsh breath.

"You're cold as ice," he said, letting go of the fabric ribbon to fetch me a sweater from my office and a glass of sweet tea. "Here you go," he said, tucking the sweater around me and handing me the glass. I drank it down and snuggled into the soft wrap, waiting to warm up and feel the sugar rush. Teag sat quietly, patiently biding his time until I had recovered.

"What did you make of all that?" I asked, hoping that our connection through the spelled cloth had given him a front-row seat.

"It's not the weirdest thing we've ever run into," he said, sitting back once he was sure I wasn't about to pass out. "We've seen dark witches drain energy from ghosts before, like cosmic batteries."

"They weren't particularly easy to stop, as I recall," I replied and shivered. "But I don't think that's what we're up against this time. At least, not from what Eliza knew. She made it sound more like a creature, almost a psychic parasite, something that gravitates to natural disasters and wars where there's a lot of violent death."

Teag fetched me a hot cup of coffee with plenty of sugar, and I gripped the mug, warming myself from its contents. "Alicia should be back soon," I said, glancing at the time. "In the meantime, I've got a call to make."

My cousin Simon picked up on the first ring. In certain circles, he's better known as Dr. Sebastian Simon Kincaide, folklorist, author, former university professor, and now the owner of Grand Strand Ghost Tours.

"Hi Cassidy! Good to hear from you. Is this business or pleasure?"

"Business, unfortunately, although it's always great to hear from you," I replied, putting him on speaker so Teag could listen. "We've got a situation."

"Tell me."

I explained about the Ghost Bikes and the roadside shrines, the spirit refugees in the mirror, and the creature that tore apart George's ghost. Simon listened to it all with rapt attention. He knows about my gift and what we really do here at the shop, and his background with mythology and the occult—not to mention his own abilities as a clair-voyant and medium—have come in handy.

"I think it's a *maita*," Simon said when I finished. "I've read about them, but I've never run into one before."

"That's a creature I haven't heard about before," I admitted. "And I thought we'd seen everything."

Simon chuckled. "Probably not—although you do seem to see more than your share of cryptids and creepies. *Maita* come from African folklore, and there are varying tales depending on the tribal origin. Most agree that the *maita* begins as a cannibalistic witch and becomes a ravenous spirit after death—a soul eater."

Teag and I exchanged a look. "How the hell do we kill it?" Teag asked.

"That's the problem. There are ways to kill the living cannibal-witch to stop it from becoming a *maita*," Simon replied, and I was in awe of his encyclopedic knowledge. "Once it's become one, I'm not sure there's a way to destroy it—at least, for someone on this side of the divide."

"The divide?" I questioned

"The Veil," Simon replied. "Between the living and the dead."

That added a new wrinkle. "If someone were going to try to kill a *maita*, is there a type of weapon that might be better than others?"

"Cassidy, you can't be serious. Please tell me you're not thinking of going after one of these."

"It's kinda what we do, Simon," I replied. "And we have a pretty amazing group of friends. So, weapon?"

Simon hesitated and then sighed. "Iron works on most spirit ener-gies. Probably not salt, because it's more of a creature than a ghost. I don't think silver has any special protection either. The only thing the legends say about killing a *maita* is that its power is held in special stones in its stomach. Cut open the stomach, spill out the stones, and the *maita* is destroyed."

"Do we have to do anything to the stones?" Teag asked.

"It wouldn't hurt to scatter them, although I don't think the *maita* can re-gather its energy," Simon replied. "Just please, be careful. The lore is very spotty; don't risk your life on it."

We thanked him and hung up just as we heard a knock at the back door. Alicia Peters, a good friend, and a powerful spirit medium, stepped inside.

"What a day!" she and I both said in near unison and had to chuckle despite the dire circumstances. "You first," I said, as Teag pulled out a chair for Alicia and I went to get her some sweet tea. I filled my coffee cup as well since I figured it was going to be a long night.

Where my magic reads the memories and energy resonance of objects, Alicia is a true psychic medium, able to talk to ghosts. I wondered how much our experiences checking out the same types of memorials differed.

"The ghosts are terrified, and some of them have gone missing—been destroyed," Alicia said, sipping her tea. "They're aware that something is preying on ghosts, and no one knows when it might come for them. It doesn't feel like the power of a dark witch or a rogue necromancer. From what the ghosts could tell me—and it wasn't a lot of detail—it sounds like we have a creature out there feeding on spirits."

"Simon thinks it might be a *maita*," I told her and was ready to explain when Alicia frowned.

"That's really interesting. I'm surprised we haven't run into something like that before," she said.

"How's that?" Teag asked.

Alicia took another long drink of the heavily sugared sweet tea, letting it replenish her. "Charleston was one of the top ports for receiving enslaved individuals back before the Civil War. Some of those people came from the areas where belief in the *maita* originated. Just like with Voudon and Hoodoo, people brought their beliefs with them, and sometimes, they mingled with other influences to become something new and different."

"How do we fight it?" I asked. "Is this something Donnelly or Sorren could handle?" Archibald Donnelly is a mostly immortal necromancer, and Sorren, my boss, is a vampire. Their special abilities—and the fact that both are extremely difficult to destroy—have come in handy when we have to battle bad nasties.

Alicia shook her head. "I don't think so. Simon told you that the *maita* has to be fought in the realm of the dead. It's not a ghost, so Donnelly wouldn't have any special power over it, and we don't even know if he could cross over to that realm and get back, given what he is. Same with Sorren—he's undead, not dead. I wouldn't want to risk having him enter and not be able to come home. There are plenty of stories about living people being able to go across and get back if you're careful."

"We'll need iron knives," Teag said, "and I'll bring my silver whip, just in case. Protection charms, definitely. And something to guide us back, in case the path isn't clear."

"Us?" I questioned. I had figured I would go—if we could figure out how to get to the frickin' *realm of the dead* and that the others would stay behind to make sure I got home.

Teag and Alicia both glared at me. "Us," Teag repeated forcefully, and Alicia nodded. "We all go, or none of us goes."

"Okay," I relented. "But if this creature exists in the realm of the dead, we can't do anything until we know how to cross over—without doing it the usual way—so we can get back."

"I think I know just the place," Alicia said, giving me a grin I knew meant trouble.

"I know this road. There's no bar here," I said as Alicia drove us down Huguenin Road, the avenue of cemeteries where more than a dozen graveyards held centuries' worth of Charleston dead.

"It depends on who's looking," Alicia replied as she parked along the side of the road. "I *am* a medium, after all."

"Whoa," Teag murmured as we got out of the car and stared at what my mind knew should have been an empty lot with the remains of an old foundation. Instead, a long one-story brick building stretched the length of the lot, running alongside the stone wall that marked the edge of Magnolia Cemetery, windows alight, and smoke rising from the chimney. A wooden sign proclaimed it to be "Hearseman's."

"I don't understand," I said, stretching out with my gift. I felt a strange resonance I'd never encountered before, something solid and yet *not*, real and other.

"For two hundred years, Hearseman's bar stood where you see it, and while it served everyone, it was particularly known for taking care of the men who dug the graves at all the cemeteries on this road," Alicia said. "The gravediggers, the groundskeepers, the landscapers, and the hearse drivers, as well as the priests and ministers who held the services—they all came to the pub when their work was over."

"But it's not there anymore," Teag protested. "At least, it wasn't—"

"It burned down seventy years ago," Alicia replied. "The fire went up quick and took a lot of the regulars with it, as well as the bartender. Times had changed, and some of the community fathers didn't think it was fitting to have a tavern adjacent to a cemetery. So the bar wasn't rebuilt. But it never really went away."

"It's a gateway?" I asked.

Alicia nodded. "Among other things. When conditions are right and the ghosts are willing, Hearseman's is as real as you need it to be. It's a gathering place for spirits and for those of us who can see them. And if you walk out the back door, you walk into the nether realm."

"How long will it last?" Teag asked, eyeing the old building skeptically. "We don't know where this *maita* is or how to find it. What if we go through, and the tavern vanishes?"

"That would be bad," Alicia admitted. "We'd have to find another gateway, and while they're not uncommon, they're not on every corner. As for locating the *maita*, I suspect it's more likely that we'll find him sniffing around Hearseman's like a kid outside a candy store."

"If the creature is stealing souls, it's not going to be able to resist a big prize like Hearseman's," I said.

"I don't think the ghosts who anchor the tavern are at risk if the *maita* prefers to poach the newly dead, like trauma victims," Alicia replied. "But Hearseman's attracts ghosts, new and old, when it appears. And Reginald, the barkeeper, says some of the recent customers have wandered away and not been seen again."

"They're ghosts. Is that so strange?" I asked.

"Reginald sounded like he kept track of his regulars and that the core group doesn't change a lot. I got the impression he kept an eye out for the newcomers. But when he said that customers told him about hearing strange music that called to them, that's when I thought it might be our *maita* at work," Alicia replied.

Teag pulled out a small cloth bag from inside his jacket. "Before we go in," he said and emptied three amulets into his palm. "I worked on these last night. They're kinda like beacons to help us find our way home. Each of these has tendrils of energy that wind between the wearer and someone who serves as an anchor. The charm is woven using hair from both of you," he added.

Alicia and I had both given Teag a bit of our hair, something we would only do for a person we trusted implicitly because hair is such a powerful, personal connection in magic. Apparently, he'd made some house calls as well.

"Cassidy, yours is linked to Kell," he said, naming my serious boyfriend. "Mine, of course, is connected to Anthony," he added. No surprise there since he and Anthony were a long-time couple. "And Alicia's links to Megan," he said, mentioning the medium's wife. "They have all agreed to allow us to draw on their energy, woven together with ours, to give us a lifeline in case we get separated, or we can't find our way back to the gateway."

I slipped the amulet's leather strap over my head and wrapped my hand around the charm. I could feel the thrum of Kell's energy and my own and closed my eyes, appreciating that I had someone who cared so much about me.

"Hearseman's is a place for the dead, not the living, so all the standard warnings apply," Alicia said. "Don't eat or drink anything, either in the pub or beyond. Injuries that happen across the Veil are real back here, so be careful. Don't try to bring anything back with you that you didn't carry over."

Pretty simple, but myth and legend are full of people who couldn't follow the rules.

Alicia led the way. I concentrated on my touch magic as we headed for the phantom bar, since I can often sense a strong resonance through the soles of my shoes. One minute, the ground beneath my feet felt neutral, and the next, as I stepped over the transom, my gift went flooey for a moment, like a compass spinning without finding true north. The floor held my weight, the bar's patrons and furnishings looked solid, and the scent of pipe smoke, roasting meat, and beer seemed real enough. Yet my psychometry insisted that everything around me was not right, something other than it appeared. I just hoped I could tamp down the conflicting input from my gift before it gave me a splitting headache, or worse, distracted me in a moment of danger.

Hearseman's looked like a country tavern, the kind that welcomed working men and women with dirt under their fingernails and a sheen of sweat from a hard day's labor. Given the bar's true age, there was no TV and no recorded music. The buzz of conversation, punctuated by occasional guffaws, filled the space.

Photographs around the room showed proud drivers with their fancy hearses from the Civil War on up through the bar's lamentable demise in the 1940s. Those opulent hearses were quite probably the most dignified transportation the deceased would have ever known, and many a mutual aid society or beneficence organization took great pride in being able to send one of their own off in style.

Some long-time patrons were immortalized by the tools of their trade, shovels scrubbed clean enough to shine, fastened to the wall with a plaque commemorating those who wielded them. A few aged photographs showed dozens of men with dour expressions and somber black suits standing in rows for the camera, the proud gravediggers of the cemeteries of Huguenin Road.

I glanced at the ghostly patrons. Some were black men with arms of corded muscle, sitting next to beefy white fellows and Jews with yarmulkes and forelocks, sharing a bottle or a pack of cigarettes. A few hard-worn women gathered at their own table, their tanned faces and broad hands a testimony to a life of hard work. Despite what might have been common elsewhere when the tavern physically existed, Hearseman's was open to all those who helped the dead cross over, regardless of color or creed.

"Hello, Alicia," Reginald greeted the psychic from behind the bar. None of the regulars bothered to turn around. "You've brought friends."

"Just passing through," Alicia replied. She looked around at the patrons. "You've got a full house tonight."

"People gather when they're frightened," Reginald replied, raising one eyebrow with a knowing look. "I'll hold us here as long as I can, but best you be on your way and get back fast as you can, you hear?" He gestured toward a hallway that led into darkness.

Alicia thanked him, and we followed her down the shadowed corridor. The sounds of the tavern faded quickly behind us, making me wonder just how long the hallway extended. I thought we might pass the kitchen or some other rooms, but the passage was long, narrow, and unbroken until we came to a door at the end.

"Ready?" Alicia asked as we paused by the exit. When we nodded, she opened the door, and we entered the realm of the dead.

From the books and movies I'd consumed since I was a child, I expected something that looked like black and white photographs or perhaps a true underworld of caves and tunnels. Instead, I stepped into a blighted landscape of dead trees and withered plants.

"Is this the afterlife?" I asked, thinking that religion down through the ages had gotten the details terribly wrong if this was the endgame.

"No," Alicia replied. "It's an antechamber for souls that are too conflicted to move on. Spirits that want to leave our realm but don't feel ready to go to the next level, so to speak."

That made me feel marginally better since I didn't want to vacation in this bleak place, let alone spend eternity here. My psychometry found an uneasy truce with the strange land underfoot, registering it much the way it did a cemetery—unquiet ground.

"How do we know where to look?" Teag asked. We had all pulled out our iron knives and other weapons when we left the back door of Hearseman's, and now we stood back to back, surveying this strange, forbidding terrain. No birds sang, no leaves rustled, only the skeletal clicking of bare branches in the cold wind.

"There!" I whispered, afraid that if I spoke aloud, it would stop the music. "Can you hear it?" The notes of a flute carried through the air, beautiful and poignant, calling for me to follow. My spirit lurched at the sound as if it might be tempted to leave my body, and I clamped my hand around the amulet to ground myself.

"I hear it too," Teag echoed, and Alicia agreed a second later. They looked as uncomfortable as I felt, torn between wanting to follow the music and find the *maita* and the sense of self-preservation that insisted on running the other way.

"Look!" Alicia pointed, and I saw that we weren't the only ones to fall under the sway of the music. Two ghosts appeared ahead of us, too far to catch up with but still in sight. "Go back!" Alicia called out to them. "You're in danger!" But the ghosts kept on walking, managing to stay far ahead even when we picked up our pace.

Then we saw the piper. The creature had a distorted body, with arms and legs too long and gangly to be right, and a hairless head with bat-like ears. The face might have been human once, but now the features were contorted, the nose pushed in and wrinkled, eyes slitted, mouth protruding like a lamprey with rows of sharp teeth that were visible when the *maita* paused its playing. A distended belly hung down with the weight of the spelled rocks inside. The monster raised its flute, which looked like it was made from a hollowed human bone, and began once more to play its tune.

"The ghosts look like they're in a trance," Teag said quietly. "They're heading right to him."

"I wonder why it pulls some and not others," Alicia mused.

"Now's the time," I urged, "while he's focused on dinner."

We spread out and rushed forward, counting on the *maita* to be distracted by the ghosts, because the lifeless landscape offered us no cover. I veered right, Teag went left, and Alicia headed straight for him. Teag had his coiled metal whip, and while the silver might not do extra damage, the sharp edge of the thin blade was dangerous enough. Teag and I both had our iron blades ready, and I also had my athame, a wooden spoon with strong positive resonance from which I could pull power.

Alicia was our secret weapon, and while she also carried a knife, it was her ability to call spirits that might give us the advantage we needed. We closed in on the *maita* just as it reached for the first of the two mesmerized ghosts, sinking its claws through the insubstantial form and yet somehow snagging the wraith to draw it forward toward its maw.

Teag launched himself at the creature, striking with his iron dagger and landing a deep blow to the *maita's* side. I dove forward at nearly the same instant, driving my knife through the *maita's* tough hide and into its back. Neither of us could get a clear shot at the belly of the beast, where we needed to land the killing blow.

Realizing its danger, the *maita* let go of the ghosts it had snared and turned its attention to Teag and me. Its sharp teeth chattered, and its dark eyes watched us, and then it sprang at Teag, moving faster than its heavy belly suggested might be possible. It snapped at him with its teeth and grabbed for him with its clawed hands. Teag lashed out with his metal whip, cutting a deep gash across the *maita's* chest but not low enough to make a difference. Behind me, I could hear Alicia calling out to the ghosts, asking for their help to bring down a threat bigger than any spirit could evade on its own.

I lunged at the creature, slashing with my knife, managing to land a blow close to its stomach, but not close enough. Teag and I wove and dodged, trying to steer clear of those sharp claws and pointed teeth and still inflict the damage necessary to destroy the *maita* and save the ghosts.

That's when I realized it had grown much colder, and when I looked up, I saw that a host of spirits had answered Alicia's summons. They surrounded us, watching as Teag and I battled the monster, managing to wound but not yet kill the *maita*. The creature lunged for Teag, ignoring the slash of his knife and the slice of his whip, and took them both to the ground, its sharp talons raking across Teag's chest.

I leveled my athame, drew on its resonance, and sent a blast of cold energy at the *maita*, tearing him off Teag and sending him sprawling.

Teag staggered to his feet, bloody but alive, and we both went after the *maita* before it could regroup.

The ghosts surged forward, massing around the downed monster. Individually, the spirits were at the *maita's* mercy, but collectively, emboldened by Alicia, they were far too many for the creature to threaten all at once. The spirits swarmed over the *maita*, keeping it on the ground, and Teag and I approached warily, looking for our opportunity. I slipped my athame back beneath my sleeve and gripped my knife tighter, ready for the right moment.

The creature struck out against the ghosts, flailing with its sharp claws and kicking with its taloned feet, snapping its teeth and shrieking as the wraiths dodged its blows and fought back against the monster that stalked them. Teag circled around, coming in above the downed *maita* and then rushing forward to drop a loop of his sharp metal whip around its head as I mustered my nerve and dove for its bulging belly.

I plowed through the cloud of ghosts that were keeping the *maita* down, feeling as if I were sinking through ice-cold mist. The gray revenants were corpse cold, frigid as the tomb, and my whole body shuddered and shivered as I brought the iron knife down two-handed and sank it hilt-deep into the creature's distorted abdomen.

The *maita* let out a piercing shriek that felt like someone raked a scalpel along my bones, but I couldn't stop now. I had to trust that the ghost would keep the creature's hands and feet away from me and that if Teag's whip didn't decapitate the *maita*, it would at least give it something else to fight against. Using all my strength, I ripped downward with the blade, opening the monster from chest to groin. Black ichor spilled out and with it hundreds of smooth stones of all sizes, each with a faint, sickly glow.

The *maita* bellowed in pain and fury, and one of its feet caught me on the thigh, ripping into my leg and sending me sprawling. Alicia's voice rose, shouting for the ghosts to keep fighting, and their numbers grew, a surge tide that nearly hid the monster from my view.

Teag gave a final jerk on his whip and stumbled backward as the *maita's* head came free, rolling clear of the ghosts. I crawled back into the fray and steeled myself for the freezing cold as I came back to finish the job.

A heap of glowing stones lay slick with foul black goo, spilled out between the *maita's* legs. I swept them away with one arm, sending them out of the creature's reach, and then fell on its body, digging into the cavity with my hands to make sure all of the stones had been removed, no matter how tiny.

Alicia found the bone flute that had fallen in the struggle and crushed it underfoot.

Bleeding and freezing, I startled as Teag laid a hand on my shoulder. "Come on, Cassidy. It's done. We need to go home."

He helped me to my feet, and when I tried to put weight on my injured leg, I cried out. Teag leveraged his uninjured shoulder under mine.

"Quite a pair we make, huh?" he asked, and I could see he was as dead tired as I felt.

"Alicia?"

"Right here," she said and then held both hands up in blessing, murmuring something that I didn't catch but which made the ghosts pull back from the *maita's* corpse. They regarded us in a somber, gray line like spectral soldiers.

"Thank you," Alicia said to the spirits, and Teag and I added our gratitude. "The creature is gone. It can't hurt you anymore. Take what rest you can." She lowered her hands, and the spirits dispersed, some vanishing in a blink and others drifting away.

When they were gone, I could see the monster's body. The head lay several feet away, severed by Teag's sharp whip. The magic stones had been pushed far away from the corpse, and we scattered them even farther.

"I wish we could burn the body and those stones," I said.

"Not sure how you start a fire in the realm of the dead," Teag said with a pinched smile.

"Can something else find the stones and use them? What if there's another one of those things out there?" I asked as the reality of the fight finally caught up with me. I was covered in blood from my hands to my shoulders, spattered with gore everywhere, and bone-weary.

"Then we'll deal with it, when—if—it happens," Alicia replied.

We turned around in the direction I was certain we had come from and saw nothing but a gray, blighted horizon.

"Where's Hearseman's?" My voice sounded hollow.

"It's still there," Alicia said, "the ghosts are watching it for me. But we need to get back. Reginald can only hold the gateway open for so long."

"How—" I started to ask, and then I remembered the talismans, our very own ruby slippers to take us home.

I closed my hand around the amulet, and I felt the warmth of Kell's concern and the life energy of the tether Teag's magic had woven.

"Ready?" Teag asked.

"Very," Alicia replied, and I nodded fervently.

We made slow progress, me with a bum leg and the others on the brink of exhaustion from the fight. Without the amulet, I would have despaired, because the way back seemed to stretch much farther than when we had come. Whether that was true or just a trick of the strange realm, I didn't know, but when the lights of Hearseman's finally came into view, I nearly cried in relief.

"Is it done?" Reginald asked as we made our way out of the long corridor and back into the pub. Despite the fact that we looked like we had come from a war, none of the patrons paid us any heed.

"It's over," Alicia said. "The *maita* was destroyed."

"Thank you," Reginald said, taking in all of us with his gaze. "We owe you a debt." He inclined his head toward the door. "Now, you'd better get going. It's time for us to move along."

We hobbled out the door and into the night. I had no idea how long we had been in the realm of the dead, but I was hungry, tired, and thirsty and all I wanted was to go home.

To my surprise, we found three cars waiting on the darkened street. Anthony, Kell, and Megan stood huddled together and sent up a quiet cheer as we headed toward them. I looked over my shoulder and saw that the plot behind us was once again empty land. Hearseman's had gone to wherever good ghosts went to drink, and I hoped I didn't have reason to visit it again.

"We brought food, water, and first aid supplies, plus some whiskey —for medicinal purposes, of course," Kell said as he came to relieve Teag of helping me hobble. Anthony was a step behind him, heading for Teag like a guided missile. Megan rushed for Alicia and pulled her into a tight hug, murmuring into her hair. I felt like we were returning from deployment back to our waiting loved ones, and perhaps that wasn't too far off the mark.

The shadowed length of Huguenin Road held Charleston's dead in its many cemeteries. I hungered for light and warmth. "Let's get out of here," I said. "For the rest of the night, the world is going to have to look after itself. We're officially off duty."

CREWEL FATE

BY MORGAN BRICE

First appeared in the anthology:
Christmas at Caynham Castle

The Caynham Castle series of anthologies is a shared world set in a fictitious English castle and town. Several authors write stories that all occur at the same time in the castle and town (and a seasonal special event) which gives the reader multiple perspectives and a fun experience.

The anthologies are romance, so while there's a solid plot involving ghosts and magic, there's a lot more emphasis on Teag and Anthony's relationship—including on-page sex, which isn't usually part of the books written under my "Gail" name. So this story is for readers 18+ years old!

My story takes Teag and Anthony on vacation to Caynham Castle, per the birthday present Teag receives in Inheritance. Of course Teag's Weaver magic uncovers a haunted piece of needlework, which leads to discovering old secrets and a forgotten scandal.

Enjoy getting to see things from Teag's perspective for a change!

Ewe & Ply and The Eclectic Tearoom names are used with kind

CHAPTER 1

TEAG

"If I'd realized how cute you are when you're excited, I'd have started planning trips like this ages ago," Anthony Benton said, sliding his hand to give Teag's thigh a squeeze. The rumble of the train along the tracks jostled their seats as the English countryside flashed by outside the windows.

"It's my first international trip, and we're in the UK, and we're going to a castle," Teag Logan replied, grinning from ear to ear. "*And*, we're engaged." He couldn't help waggling the fingers on his left hand, where the platinum band with the embedded baguette diamond sparkled as it caught the light, just like the matching ring on Anthony's hand. "Best birthday presents *ever*."

Anthony chuckled, a deep, rich sound that made Teag happy inside. He and Anthony had been a couple for several years, but the proposal had happened just a few months ago, at the birthday party Anthony had thrown for Teag. The party itself—with all their close friends—and the trip to a castle for Christmas would have been amazing enough as a present, but having Anthony pop the question put Teag over the moon.

"I hope you like the castle. Friends of my parents stayed there, and when they talked about the place, I just knew it would be perfect for you," Anthony replied. "And the best part? It's not supposed to be very haunted. So you can really take time off from your *other* job."

Teag reached over and twined his fingers with Anthony's. Anthony was a lawyer in his family's law firm, and he had the blond, broad-shouldered, prep school boy-next-door looks to match. His family was old Charleston money, and Bentons had been living in the tony South of Broad neighborhood since before the Civil War. Teag, on the other hand, came from a solidly suburban middle-class background. His dark hair with its asymmetrical haircut gave him a bit of a skater boy vibe, although he had been close to finishing his Ph.D. in History before a summer job changed his life.

"I'm ready for a break from anything haunted or cursed," Teag swore. He leaned in and whispered confidentially, "And the only thing going bump in the night should be us."

Teag's day job was assistant store manager for Trifles and Folly, an antiques and curio shop in historic, haunted Charleston, South Carolina. The shop had been in business over three hundred years, almost from the founding of the city itself, and had a reputation for fine estate jewelry, silver tea sets, and vintage decorative items. But Trifles and Folly had a secret—and so did Teag. The store's real mission was to get cursed and haunted objects out of the wrong hands and save the world from supernatural threats. Teag's Weaver magic—being able to weave spells into cloth—earned him a place among a small group of allies who kept Charleston—and the world—safe from monsters, dark magic, vengeful ghosts, and much worse.

"I didn't think you'd mind that I skipped booking any ghost tours," Anthony replied. "You'd feel like you were working, and the tour guides would probably be miffed if you banished their source of income."

"I'm totally up for a ghost-free vacation," Teag swore. "Bring on the roasted chestnuts, figgy pudding, hot tea, and partridges in pear trees!"

Despite the overnight flight and early morning, Teag felt as bouncy as a kid on Christmas morning. Anthony had been to Europe several times with his family growing up, but Teag's family's idea of a big vacation involved Disney World or a national park. He'd used his passport for a couple of long weekends in the Caribbean and longed to see the places in person that he had studied in college and grad school, but the circumstances had never seemed right. Until now.

"I'm already thinking that vacations might make the best anniversary presents," Anthony teased. "If I'd have realized you had a touch of wanderlust, I'd have done this before now."

Teag shrugged. "It's not exactly wanderlust as much as I've read so much about certain places—like London—in novels or studied them with my classes that it's exciting to see them for real."

"It makes you happy. That's enough for me," Anthony replied, leaning over to brush a kiss against Teag's temple.

The three-hour train ride to Caynham-on-Ledwyche passed quickly. When he and Anthony weren't comparing thoughts about the things they wanted to see at the castle and in the nearby village, they were people-watching as their fellow travelers made their way to the commissary car for tea, snacks, or sandwiches. Teag could have sworn that even the cold box lunch tasted better because it was part of the adventure.

After the bustle of Heathrow, the clamor of the Tube, and the clatter of Paddington Station, the small platform at Caynham-on-Ledwyche felt quiet and unhurried. Teag hoped that was a sign for the rest of the vacation.

"As soon as we have the luggage, we'll get a cab to the castle," Anthony said, heading toward where the porters were unloading the suitcases. They each had a medium bag, a small roller one, and a backpack, and although Teag had gone on longer vacations with less luggage, the cold of a Shropshire winter meant packing heavier clothing as well as bringing a warm coat, hat, scarf, and gloves.

A cab pulled up to meet them as they came to the curb with their luggage. "Caynham Castle," Anthony replied to the driver's question as he loaded the bags into the back.

"You've come at a nice time of year," the man said. He wore a brown tweed cap and a tan canvas jacket, and Teag guessed the man was in his sixties. "Lots to do around here, especially now. You fellows going to stay for the Ball?"

"We're not sure yet," Teag replied. He and Anthony had talked about the Frost and Flame Ball, which would be just a few days before Christmas. While it sounded like it would be a wonderful event, neither of them were quite sure how open the rest of the guests might be to a same-sex couple joining in on the dance floor.

"Better make up your mind soon," the cabbie advised, stowing the last of their luggage.

Teag climbed into the backseat, and they took off with a rumble. He figured the vintage cab had to be at least forty years old.

"I hear they're almost sold out." He adjusted the visor against the angle of the sun. "My name's Henry, by the way."

"I'm Teag, and this is my fiancé, Anthony." Teag tried not to let a hint of challenge seep into his voice. He could have just stuck to names and left out their relationship. In some situations, that would be the wise thing to do, although both he and Anthony had been out and proud all their adult lives. But the new, shiny ring and the excitement of the proposal were too hard to resist. Teag found himself bracing for Henry's reaction.

"Well, congratulations," Henry replied without missing a beat. "If you decide to come back for your honeymoon, ask about one of those tower suites. I hear they're really fancy."

Teag had already pored over the castle's website and had decided to check out the suites if they enjoyed staying at the castle.

"What's your recommendation on things to do around here?" Anthony asked, clasping hands with Teag. Both men looked out the side windows as they drove through town. Teag decided he'd never get used to being on the "wrong" side of the road and tried to stop wincing every time a car passed.

"Well, now. There's the Boar and Knight Pub, which is as fine a place as any you'll find anywhere in Shropshire, I wager," Henry replied. "Good place for a pint or two, and their Shepherd's Pie is tasty. Although, mind your wallet if you decide to play a round of darts with the locals."

"I'll definitely steer clear," Anthony replied with a laugh. He elbowed Teag and shot him a look that Teag interpreted without a problem. *Just because I'm good at throwing knives doesn't mean I'd take on the town's hustlers at darts.*

"If you're looking for a nice bite at tea time, there's the tea shop up at the Castle. It's very good. But the Ewe & Ply—that's a wool shop—has a lovely tea room too. It's worth checking out both," Henry added with a wink. "Can't have too many scones, I always say."

"Oh, wow." Teag couldn't help himself as they drove past the half-timbered shops that looked like something out of a Dickens novel, interspersed with other stores built from brick and stone. The cut-stone parish church stood out, with its bell tower and stained glass windows, anchoring the village for over five hundred years.

"Back in Charleston, we think something's old if it's over three hundred years," Teag murmured. "But a lot of the 'new' stuff here is already older than that!"

"Aye, we often joke that we have furniture layin' about that's older than most of your cities," Henry teased. "All in good fun, of course."

"I can't help feeling like everything should have a velvet rope around it and 'do not touch' signs," Teag confided.

"Now where would be the fun in that?" Henry said with a laugh. "Over at the Boar and Knight, they've been serving up pints to thirsty folks since 1415. Yer lookin' at one of the last two thatch-roofed buildings in the town."

"Oh look, Teag," Anthony chimed in. "Right next to the pub is an antique shop. We can stop by tomorrow."

"I'm on holiday," Teag replied, shaking his head. "Not talking shop, remember?"

"If you like old stuff, we've got it," Henry said. "In fact, someone just discovered several needlepoint samplers tucked away in a closet that were done by one of the daughters of the family who owns the castle back in the day. Gave them back so they could be on display. You never know what might be lurking in a drawer or the back of a shelf!"

That was very true, Teag thought, but not in the way Henry

thought. In Teag's experience, those tucked away oddities tended to be bad luck.

The town square sat right in front of an old stone bridge across Ledwyche Brook. A tall fir tree adorned with electric lights and baubles stood proudly in the center of the square. Ribbons and ever-green cuttings graced the lampposts, and all the shops they had passed seemed to have gotten the holiday spirit because their windows were bedecked with electric candles or light strings, bunting in red, green, and white, dangling snowflakes and candy canes.

"Now look sharp, boys," Henry said as the car turned from the main road onto the driveway. "We're almost to the castle."

Teag caught his breath as the outer walls came into view. The tall buff-colored stone walls rose high, originally built for defense. Henry drove through the first gate, and both Teag and Anthony murmured when the main castle came into view.

"It's beautiful," Teag said, taking in the thick walls, mullioned windows, and stately towers. "Just like in all the stories."

"Wait 'til you get a chance to explore," Henry told them. "I've brought the missus up here a few times over the years, for birthdays and such. Down in the garden, there's what they call a 'folly'—it's a right nice place to sneak a snog," he advised with a wink. "Not to mention the conservatory, which might warm you up a bit with how hot they keep it for those exotic plants and all."

Henry pulled into the car park to the right of the castle. Up ahead, Teag saw where a bridge crossed a dry moat and led through a narrow gateway into the inner bailey.

"I can't go closer—not safe for cars," he told them. "But if you give the front desk a ring to let them know you're here, they'll send out a man with a golf cart to take you and your luggage in." Henry got out and helped pull their bags out of the back.

"Now this is real important," Henry said with a serious expression. "If you two want to make a proper go of things, you need to find the original gargoyle. The legend says that if you kiss in front of the orig-inal gargoyle—not just any old one, mind you—that you will find and keep your true love." He gave them a broad wink. "Me, I don't like to take chances, so I say, kiss in front of every gargoyle you see. Better safe than sorry!"

They waved goodbye as Henry drove off, and moments later, a white golf cart headed their way, driven by a teenager wearing a bell-man's jacket and hat.

"Welcome to the Castle," the boy said. Teag figured he was probably seventeen, eighteen at the most. "Let me get your bags."

Teag and Anthony helped, and before long, they were headed for the check-in office, with the two of them riding in the back seat.

"I'm Patrick," the young man said. "Bellman, cart driver, unplugger of drains, and stomper of spiders—not that we ever need that sort of thing," he added quickly. "But I'm sort of the jack-of-all-trades around here, so if you need something, just give a yell, and it'll probably be me they send."

"Are you from the village?" Teag asked, trying to remember how involved the Mortimer family—the owners of the castle—were with the actual day-to-day-operations.

"Aye. My mum's the manager of the gift shop, has been for thirty years," Patrick said proudly. "She got me a job here because she was afraid clearing tables down at the pub would be a bad influence to my impressionable youth," he said, turning so they could catch his dramatic eye roll.

"Your mom sounds like a smart woman," Teag said with a laugh.

"She does all right," Patrick agreed. "And Priscilla Donovan, at the front desk, will take good care of you. Keep your eyes sharp, and you might get a glimpse of the Earl, Sir Edward Mortimer. He's a busy bloke, what with the castle and a few other businesses and that new microbrewery of his in town. Here's a tip—if you go down to the brewery and you see a fellow behind the counter wearing an apron that says 'Earl,' he's the real deal. But you don't have to bow or nothin'. Not anymore."

"Microbrewery?" *Anthony's ears certainly pricked up at that*, Teag thought.

"They say it's pretty good. Not that I'd know myself or nothing, if my mom were to ask," Patrick added.

"I'll stay here with the cart while you gents check in," Patrick said, pointing toward the main lobby. "Then come back out, and I'll drive you to your room. We're a bit spread out if you didn't notice."

"I think the room I reserved is on the wall of the inner bailey," Anthony said, turning to try to orient himself from the map. "Dower apartment area. Second floor."

"Your second floor or our second floor?" Patrick asked. "There's a difference, you know. You count the ground floor as one, and we don't."

"Um, yours?" Anthony replied, sounding unsure.

"Go get your key, and I'll make sure you get to the right place," Patrick promised.

Teag and Anthony walked into the reception area, and Teag couldn't help swiveling his head from side to side to take in the Mortimer family coat of arms, several flags, and some crossed swords, as well as the rough stone walls and dark wooden check-in counter. Evergreen swags hung from the counter and adorned the doorways. Sparkling electric twinkle lights wrapped around the large fir wreath that hung over the mantle of a huge fireplace, and instrumental Christmas music played in the background.

Anthony stepped up to talk with the vivacious woman behind the desk, whose brown ponytail swished back and forth with every movement. Teag guessed she was Priscilla, and she looked like she could handle any complications that might arise. He really hoped that none did, but already Patrick, Henry, and Priscilla made him feel like they had friends here.

"Priscilla said we should try the tea room for lunch, and then we have a number of places to eat for dinner, including the pub and the microbrewery," Anthony told him.

"This place is wonderful," Teag said, leaning over to give Anthony a peck on the cheek. "Thank you so much for planning all this."

Anthony's big smile warmed Teag's heart. "I was hoping you'd love it."

"I love *you*. Everything else is icing on the cake."

Patrick took one look at the room number, and then they headed off in the golf cart toward the bridge. "Out here where the gift shop, tea room, and front desk is, that was the outer bailey," Patrick called over his shoulder like a tour guide. "Across the moat and through the gate is the inner bailey, and there's even a private garden, near the keep. When the castle got attacked, all the people would fall back to the walled yard, and if things got real bad, to the keep. Like in Lord of the Rings. Only, without orcs."

"And did it get attacked?" Anthony asked.

Patrick nodded vigorously. "Oh, yeah. Back during the War of the Roses and all. Lots more than just that. Goes all the way back to 1282, so you know it's seen some stories in its time."

Teag wondered what his best friend, Cassidy Kincaide, would make of that. She was a psychometric, which meant her magic could read the history of objects by touching them. Museums could give her the willies, and her abilities had unlocked the secrets of more than one historic home back in Charleston. For once, he was glad his gift was unlikely to trigger unless Caynham had haunted tapestries hanging around.

"You'll want to make sure you see the decorations in the Great Hall and the folly," Patrick told them as he trundled their bags into the elevator. "The chapel's nice, too. And of course, everything in town is done up. But if you're going to the Frost and Flame Ball, that's where it'll really be fancy. That big tent in the outer bailey is part of all that."

"We haven't made up our minds yet," Teag said. "But it sounds nice."

"If you decide to go, Priscilla can fix you up with tickets," Patrick assured him. "If there are any left."

Teag and Anthony thanked Patrick and watched him drive away in the cart. Their suite had a bedroom and a living room. The comfortable furnishings were an elegant melding of style and practicality. While Teag doubted that any of the guest rooms were outfitted with valuable antiques, he knew from his work at Trifles and Folly that the eclectic assembly of pieces in their suite spanned several eras. Some were good reproductions, while others were much older. It gave the suite a lived-in feel, with the continuity of pieces being re-used and added to over generations.

"What do you think?" Anthony asked, with an anxious glance, as if he were afraid Teag might be disappointed.

"I think it's perfect." Teag walked up to him and set his hands on Anthony's hips, pulling him in for a kiss. "You're perfect. Everything is perfect."

Just then, Anthony's stomach rumbled loudly. "*Lunch* would really be perfect," Anthony deadpanned.

Teag gave a wicked glance toward the plump, down comforter on the thick mattress of the four-poster bed. "And I'm thinking that bed is going to be perfect for all kinds of things once we go eat and find our way around."

"Mm. I like the sound of that." Anthony turned in for another kiss, but he couldn't deny his rumbling stomach.

"Come on," he said, tugging Teag by the wrist. "Let's go eat and do some exploring."

The castle's Lady Neville Tea Room was close by, and Teag followed Anthony inside. Monogrammed china cups and saucers sat ready atop white tablecloths. A front counter case held a delectable array of treats, and the chalkboard overhead listed enough varieties of tea to make Teag's head spin.

"Is it too late for high tea?" Teag asked.

"You're just in time," the efficient woman in a taupe twinset replied. "I'm Helen. Follow me." She led them to a table for two in the corner, where they had a good view of the rest of the tea room.

"I hope you're hungry because our high tea is more than a snack," she advised. "First, you pick your tea—one pot per person, so you can each have a different flavor." She placed a sheet of paper in front of them, listing all the teas Teag had seen on the chalkboard.

"First, there are four varieties of tea sandwiches—cucumber, egg salad, cheese and pickle, and smoked salmon. After that, there are the sweets—apricot scones with clotted cream, lemon tarts, macaroons, strawberry jam cake, and the like. Then if you're still hungry, there's a slice of layer cake. We have three varieties—changes each day. Today it's blackberry and coconut cake, chocolate biscuit cake, and a Battenberg cake. Can't really go wrong with any of them," she added.

"It all looks so good." Teag figured they would have to come back several times to try all the specialties. He and Anthony debated over the tea selection, finally choosing a Darjeeling and an Earl Gray.

"I always thought afternoon tea was a little nibble between meals—like a few cookies," Anthony confessed. "We may need to eat a later dinner."

Their early departure and the hours on the train made them more hungry than they had realized, and they made short work of the small sandwiches, slowing only as they came to the end of the sweets.

"I really want the blackberry and coconut cake, but I also want to see what a Battenberg cake tastes like," Teag said. "I've seen those people on the baking show make them, and I'm curious."

"Then let's get one of each," Anthony replied. "They're included, and we don't have to finish them."

"We can walk it all off when we go exploring," Teag agreed with a grin.

When they finally finished, Teag thought he might never need to eat again. They thanked the hostess, assured her they would return, and then headed out to walk the perimeter of the castle walls before checking out the Great Hall.

"Keep an eye out," the hostess said. "You might see our ghost, although she usually only re-enacts her tragic fall from the tower during the summer."

"I knew there had to be one," Anthony said with a chuckle. Teag just groaned.

The cool air helped to settle their food, and when the wind picked up, Teag felt it nip his nose and bite his cheeks. He was glad for the warm gloves, hat, and scarf, things he rarely needed back in Charleston.

"Look how thick the walls are," Anthony remarked. "The oldest buildings back home are like that too. Built to last."

Teag and Anthony chatted as they walked around the outer bailey and then crossed the bridge back to the inner bailey. Teag eyed the castle architecture and pointed out things he remembered studying when he had been working on his history degree.

"Keeping up with one of the old houses in Charleston is an expensive proposition," Anthony said. "I can't imagine what it's like trying to do the upkeep on a castle, but the Mortimers have done it up nicely."

Without warning, Teag pulled Anthony in for a kiss. He grinned at Anthony's surprise. "Technically, that's a grotesque," he said and pointed up toward the roof's edge, where a squat stone figure glowered down at them, so ugly it was cute. "If it's a waterspout, it's a gargoyle. If it's just decoration, it's a grotesque. I'm not taking any chances on which one is original," he said, tapping Anthony on the nose.

When they finally reached the Great Hall, Teag welcomed the warmth. Everything was done up for Christmas, with evergreen boughs, red ribbons, fairy lights, and gold bells. A huge fir tree nearly reached the ceiling, and Teag could only imagine how much more decorating would happen before the night of the ball.

"It said on the website that the mother of the current Earl took that hand-blown glass tree topper down into the air raid shelters during World War II," Teag added. "She said she wasn't going to let the Nazis ruin Christmas!"

"It's pretty fantastic," Anthony said, slipping an arm around Teag. "Look at that ceiling!"

Teag craned his neck. "It's called 'hammerbeam,' and it's an English Gothic style of open timber roof truss," he said. "See the kind of stuff I remember from my classes?"

Hand-cut beams arched downward at intervals, while still others formed arches along the flat of the timber ceiling, embellished at the corners with intricate woodcutting. It reminded Teag of the ceiling of the great hall in the Harry Potter movies.

"I wish they could really make candles float in the air," Teag said with a sigh. "But I guess twinkle lights are almost as good." He took in a deep breath. "I love the smell of a real Christmas tree."

"And the fireplace looks big enough to roast a boar—or maybe an ox," Anthony said, with a nod toward the huge opening in the stone wall with its carved firebox and ornate mantle. "I could stand up inside and not hit my head. And I bet that if I spread my arms wide, I still wouldn't touch on either side."

"Come on," Teag said. "There's more to see in the solar and conservatory." He led Anthony by the hand out of the Great Hall through an archway into two adjoining glass-enclosed rooms. Christmas lights twinkled in the now-dry central fountain and wrapped around the potted shrubs. Poinsettias, icicles, ribbons, and tinsel turned the greenhouse rooms into a wonderland.

Anthony hauled Teag in for a kiss under a ball of mistletoe tied with a red velvet ribbon. "Turnabout's fair play," he said.

"This is so beautiful," Teag gushed when they headed back through the main hall. "And there are a few of the other rooms open for display if we go this way." He led them toward Bride's Tower, where two sitting rooms on the third floor were decorated and furnished as the castle would have looked during the 1920s. From the colors, fabrics, and scale of the furniture, it was clear that one room was meant for women and the other for men.

"So this would have been the way it looked right around World War I," Anthony mused, reading a sign near the door. "Their *Downton Abbey* period."

"I love that show. So elegant. And the old miniseries we watched of *Brideshead Revisited*? If I could have tailored suits like those, I might not mind giving up my jeans," Teag gushed.

"Maybe we'll have to throw a Gatsby party for Halloween next year if the spooks give you the night off," Anthony teased. "Just thinking of you turned out like that is giving me all kinds of naughty ideas." He leaned against Teag, brushing his groin against Teag's leg to let him know exactly what kind of thoughts were going through his mind.

"I like the way you think," Teag purred.

The more masculine of the two rooms had dark wood wainscoting and upholstery in rich emerald and sapphire hues. Brass fittings and etched glass shades accentuated the wall sconces and table lamps. Leather-bound books filled the shelves, along with display cases of watches, silver cigar boxes, monogrammed flasks, and a taxidermied lion that was likely a trophy from safari in Africa. It was easy to imagine well-off men sitting down with cigars and good Scotch to discuss the news of the day or play a few hands of cards.

"This is so far beyond 'man cave' I'm not sure what to call it," Anthony remarked. "But I guess it's not that different from what some of the big plantation houses had. For as nice as this is, I'm glad things have changed. I like our friends, and I'd hate to have to split everyone up instead of being able to all hang out together."

The ladies' sitting room had high-backed upholstered couches and wing chairs arranged in conversation groupings, with side tables to hold drinks. The furniture was roped off for display only, and glass covered the bookshelves, protecting both the books and an assortment of family personal items and trinkets from around the world.

Teag felt a pull toward a framed piece of hand-embroidered fabric. It was a sampler, the kind done by young women learning to practice various stitching and designs common at the time. But as soon as Teag saw it, he felt traces of the maker's magic—old, faint, and still potent.

"What's wrong?" Anthony laid a hand on Teag's shoulder. "You've got that look."

Teag managed a smile. "Nothing bad. It's just that whoever did that embroidery had my kind of gift. Weaver magic."

"You can pick up on that, after all these years?" A note next to the frame said that the needlepoint had been done by Lillian Mortimer in 1916.

"Uh-huh," Teag replied, distracted as he read the rest of the note-card. "So Lillian was one of two daughters to the Mortimer family who lived in the castle around the time of the First World War. She and her older sister, Mabel, would have been in their late teens or early twenties when the war started. It ran longer over here—the war. In the States, we think of it as just 1918, but it started in 1914 in Europe." He couldn't help being a history nerd, and thankfully, Anthony shared his interest.

"From what we've watched on the History Channel, that war pretty much broke the aristocracy, didn't it?" Anthony replied. "The death toll was so high—wiped out most of an entire generation of men. I can't even begin to imagine what it must have been like."

Teag shivered, although the room was warm. Lillian's needlework held both power and emotions. Now that Teag's gift had tuned in, he could sense sadness, grief, loneliness, and anxiety that made his heart pound.

"Teag? Hey!"

Anthony's voice brought him out of his thoughts, and Teag stepped back. "I'm okay. I just could pick up some feelings from the magic Lillian used. I don't think she was very happy."

"It must have felt like the world had gone mad during the war. I don't imagine most people were happy," Anthony replied.

Lillian's magic had brought Teag's ability to the forefront, and as he walked around the room with Anthony, he gently probed other objects like a needlepoint pillow and a small tapestry near the fireplace. None of them held any magic of their own.

But when he came to the display case with a gold and pearl hair comb, an ivory fan, and a black, enameled cigarette holder, Teag recoiled as he glimpsed a gray, transparent figure near the case.

"More magic?" Anthony asked in a whisper, glancing around to make sure they were alone.

Teag shook his head. "No. There's a spirit attached to those pieces, I'm sure of it. Maybe not the one they told us about at the tea room, but it's definitely a ghost. And she's not friendly."

CHAPTER 2

ANTHONY

Anthony and Teag agreed to set the issue of the haunted hair comb aside for now, and walk down to the village while there was plenty of daylight left. Heading across the inner bailey from Bride's Tower, they had another look at the huge Christmas tree and all its gleaming decorations.

"I want to check out the chapel too," Teag said, pointing to a round structure a little farther away. "I've heard it has some very pretty decorations—and maybe the original gargoyle!"

"How do you know where all the gargoyles are?" Anthony asked, enjoying this playful side of Teag that he got to see all too rarely.

"Well, there's a cheat sheet on one of the travel sites," Teag admitted. "Although visitors are encouraged to hunt on their own first, and then use the sheet to find the carvings that are more challenging."

"But you already looked?"

"Of course! We don't want to miss any!" Teag replied, aghast.

Anthony gave his hand a squeeze. "Want to check out the gift shop? We can head into town from there."

"Welcome to the Castle Shop," a woman called out as Teag and Anthony entered the store. She had short blonde hair, and when she turned around, Anthony could see the resemblance between Patrick, their golf cart bellboy, and his mother. Her name tag read "*Marianne*."

"Patrick told us to stop in," Teag said. "He saved us from having to haul our luggage all the way from the parking lot."

Marianne laughed. "He loves that silly cart! I'm glad he helped you get settled. Please, have a look around. And if you're heading into town, I can hold your purchases until you get back."

The small shop smelled of locally-made goat milk soaps, the castle's own brand of tea, and a clove and orange potpourri that simmered near the register. Most of the items either had the likeness of Caynham Castle or the monogram of the Mortimer family. Teag picked out an ornament of the castle and a few other small gifts for friends back home.

"I'll just put these behind the register with your name on them until you get back," Marianne said after she rang them up. "If we're closed, no worries. Just stop by in the morning."

They thanked her and headed out. Anthony pulled his cap down over his ears. "It must be true what they say about Southerners having thin blood. I don't know how anyone lives with the cold here!"

"You know we aren't to the worst of the winter yet," Teag joked. "And I heard we're supposed to get a dusting of snow for Christmas."

Anthony glared. "That stuff is pretty on Christmas cards and in holiday movies, but not for real."

"Grinch."

"Scrooge."

They both laughed, and Anthony took Teag's hand as they headed out of the castle area and down toward the village square. It had been a long time since he'd felt this light-hearted, and he decided they needed to make vacationing a priority.

"The whole place looks like a movie set," Teag said in awe. Between the half-timbered buildings—what Americans often called "Tudor" style—and the old brick or stone buildings, the village seemed too picturesque to be real.

"You know, most people think that about Charleston," Anthony pointed out. "Or did you forget about the busloads of tourists who come to oooh and ahh over our architecture and all the 'old' buildings?"

"I guess you're right—this is just home for the people who are from here," Teag conceded. The square was in fine holiday form with another big tree, twinkle lights wrapped around lampposts, and ribbon-bedecked evergreen swags everywhere they looked.

Knights Road was the main street in Caynham-on-Ledwyche, and Anthony couldn't wait to check out the shops they had seen on their way in. "It's really great that all the stores are local," he said. "No big chains. Helps keep the feel of a place. Once the chains come in, everything's all the same."

"From what I saw in the comments on the tourist rating sites, the Mortimers—at least the more recent ones—have done a lot to support the local economy," Teag replied. "A lot of the items in the castle gift shop were by local companies or artists. And I'm sure the castle itself is a huge draw."

"There's the antique shop," Anthony said. "Do you want to go in?" He left that up to Teag, not only because the store might seem too much like the shop he worked in back home, but because he didn't know if Teag wanted to risk finding more items with a hint of haunt.

"Yeah, actually. If you don't mind. I'd like to find out more about Mabel Mortimer and why her ghost is so pissed off," Teag replied. "Just in case there's trouble."

"*Curiouser and Curiouser Antiques*" was the name emblazoned in gold lettering on the store window. A bell tinkled as they opened the door. Anthony and Teag stepped into a shop filled nearly to the rafters with dark wooden shelves laden with curios and antiques. Bone china, porcelain figurines, mantle clocks, and silver tea sets vied for space beside Wedgewood vases, cut crystal bowls, and vintage kitchenware.

"Hello there! Come on in and have yourselves a look around." An older man with a fringe of white hair waved at them from behind the counter, setting aside his cup of coffee and newspaper.

"Are you the owner?" Teag asked.

"Oh, no. I'm Mr. Porter, one of the staff," the man replied, chuck-ling. "What can I help you find?"

Anthony couldn't help looking at the fascinating mishmash of items. A large, taxidermied bear stood next to a tall mahogany coat rack. Behind that were several pieces of furniture that looked like they came from India's Colonial period, next to a brass telescope and an ornate Victorian floor lamp with a fringed shade.

"I couldn't resist coming in," Teag confided. "I work in an antique shop in Charleston, back in the States."

"Ah. Busman's holiday, is it? Can't quite get away from the job," Mr. Porter said with a laugh. "I know the feeling. Antiques get in your blood, they certainly do." He shook his head. "It's a wonder, really, how you can feel like you've seen into the past when you handle an old object. These pieces have seen a lot of living."

From the way Teag's eyes narrowed in thought, Anthony guessed his fiancé was thinking Mr. Porter might have a bit of psychic sensi-tivity himself.

"I heard someone say that a few pieces of needlework were found that were done by Lillian Mortimer and given back to the Castle," Teag said. "I'm always fascinated when things find their way home. Do you know the story of how that happened?"

"Well, now. That's quite a tale. Both Lillian and her sister, Mabel, were born just before the turn of the last century. Mabel, the older sister, was the serious one. Lillian, from what I've heard, was more of a free spirit. They clashed, as sisters do. Or maybe a bit more."

Mr. Porter perched on the stool behind the counter as Teag and Anthony drew closer. No one else was in the shop, and Anthony wondered if the older man welcomed a chance for conversation. Passing gossip about people long dead seemed harmless enough.

"When the Great War broke out, the Earl and Countess volunteered to help with the war effort, so they were gone for long periods. That left Mabel in charge of the castle, and—at least to her mind, Lillian." He laughed. "I don't think Lillian saw it that way. Anyhow, right before the war, Lillian had taken up with a young man from a wealthy family, Bertram Granville."

Mr. Porter peered over his spectacles at Teag and Anthony and clarified since they were clearly not local. "The Granvilles are landed gentry, with a country house a distance from town. The Earl's family, the Mortimers that own Caynham Castle, are titled nobility. It's been Granvilles and Mortimers in these parts since long, long ago. Anyhow, Bertram Granville went away to the war, and like many of the young men, didn't come back."

"What happened?" Teag asked, leaning forward.

"Lillian didn't take the news well, as you can imagine. I guess today, they'd call it a nervous breakdown," Mr. Porter replied. "She turned to her needlepoint—it became something of an obsession—and didn't often leave the castle. Unfortunately, she died young, of Consumption—Tuberculosis. Mabel eventually married and produced an heir. But…"

"What?" Anthony couldn't help being drawn into the story.

Mr. Porter shook his head. "Somewhere along the line, Mabel and Lillian had a big falling out. Mabel stayed bitter, even after Lillian's death. While she was alive, none of Lillian's needlework was permitted to be on display—a pity, because Lillian did fine work. No one knows what came between the sisters—or at least, if they knew, they didn't tell." He shrugged. "That's all I know of the tale."

"It's very interesting," Teag said. "Thank you for sharing it with us." He purchased a few vintage photographs and postcards of the castle and the village. Anthony avoided touching anything, wary from all the tales he'd heard from Teag and Cassidy of objects that carried bad mojo.

"Make sure you grab a pint at the Earl's brewery," Mr. Porter said. "It's very good."

They promised to do so, which to Anthony's mind was no hardship. Next, they wandered into the Ewe & Ply yarn shop, which also carried some lovely scarves, shawls, capes, and other pieces made by the owner. Anthony felt Teag relax almost as soon as they stepped in the door.

"Can you feel that?" Teag asked quietly.

"Feel what?"

"Whoever's done the knitting definitely has my kind of magic—whether they know it or not. It's very comforting. Serene. I can't imagine how they can keep pieces in stock. I just want to wrap myself in them like a giant hug."

"Then pick a scarf or whatever you'd like," Anthony said. "Consider it a late birthday present."

Teag chose a blue scarf for himself and insisted on buying a green one for Anthony. The owner wasn't in, so Teag passed along his compliments. They stuck their heads into the tea room. It was as cottage kitchen comfy as Lady Neville's Tea Room back at the castle was formal, with mismatched china, tablecloths, and chairs. The walls were covered with a mix of old photos of the area, vintage prints of sheep and spinning wheels, and work by local artists.

"We're definitely coming back here," Teag said. "Those cakes look delicious."

Anthony groaned. "How can you even look at food? I'm still stuffed!"

Teag shot him a look. "It's always good to have a plan. That way, I can look forward to my meal, and then I can enjoy it twice."

Seeing Teag so relaxed warmed Anthony's heart. Back in Charleston, they often kept a hectic pace between Anthony's responsibilities at the law firm and Teag's job, not just with Trifles and Folly, but his *other* job with the Alliance, helping keep the world safe from supernatural threats. It had been too long since they had just taken a day to wander and see the sights.

Back outside, Teag slipped his arm through Anthony's. Anthony tensed, but only for a second. Caynham-on-Ledwyche seemed tolerant enough, but old habits died hard. Charleston had gotten a lot better than it used to be, but two men hand-in-hand on a busy street would still draw unwanted attention. As if he sensed Anthony's discomfort, Teag withdrew his arm, and Anthony immediately felt a loss.

"It's okay," Anthony told him. "I like walking arm in arm. I'm proud of us."

Teag gave him a hug and instead snagged Anthony's pinkie finger with his own. "I know. I am too. But it's a small town. And we're a long way from home."

Anthony let it go, and Teag walked close beside him, shoulders bumping. He felt chagrined at his reaction. Their coming out experiences had been very different, and sometimes, it showed. Teag had come out in middle school, and his family had been supportive. Anthony hadn't come out until law school, and while it hadn't cost him his position with the family firm, he was well aware there had been family members and clients who hadn't been happy about it.

"Hey, quit thinking so hard," Teag said, jostling his elbow. "Vacation, remember? And we're *engaged*! I'm going to keep saying that over and over to myself until it really sinks in," he added with a grin, waggling his fingers on the left hand.

"Sorry. You're right. And look—there's a book store!"

Caynham-on-Ledwyche was picture-perfect, Anthony thought. Decked out for the holidays, every store glistened with tinsel, lights, red bows, and accents of gold and silver.

"Oh, and there's a hotel in town, as well as the rooms at the castle," Teag pointed out.

Anthony nodded. "I saw that when I made reservations. It's a lovely place, and the restaurant is very good. But I thought you'd rather be in a real castle."

"You totally understand my inner geek," Teag replied, but the look in his eyes was worth every penny of the cost of the room.

"And I love your inner geek, as well as your outer one," Anthony assured him. "Just remember when you're in the bookstore—we have to be able to fly home, so whatever you buy needs to fit in the luggage."

Cadwell's was a charmingly old-world bookstore with bookshelves packed full from floor to ceiling and extra volumes spilling over onto tables and into corners. New books were in the front of the store, and the used books stretched in a warren of connected rooms and repurposed closets.

"I could get lost in here and stay for a year," Teag whispered in awe. "And there's an upstairs and a downstairs!"

"Can I help you find anything?"

Both Teag and Anthony jumped at the voice. They turned to find a short, bald fellow in a plaid shirt, sweater vest, and corduroy pants.

"You're—" Teag started.

"Ptolemy Cadwell, proprietor. At your service," the man replied. "Now, what kind of books are you looking for?"

"Weaving," Anthony said.

"Magic," Teag answered at the same instant.

Cadwell's eyebrows rose. "Well. That's an interesting mixture. I happen to have both. Follow me."

"I thought you were on vacation," Anthony whispered as they hurried to keep up with Cadwell. The stacks seemed to go on forever, and Anthony marveled that the store managed to pack so much into the space.

"I am. But you never know what you'll find in a place like this," Teag replied.

Anthony had to agree. There was something fanciful about Cadwell's and its odd proprietor that made him think anything might be possible—like meeting a troll or a unicorn around the corner or walking through an armoire or a grandfather clock into another world.

"Here you go," Cadwell said. "Weaving is here," he added, thrusting out his left arm to indicate a section of shelves. "And magic would be over here." He bustled away, leaving Anthony to hope he could find his way back.

"Just let me know if you need anything else," Cadwell said when he had led Teag to the books on magic. "I'll be up front."

"What are you looking for?" Anthony asked, keeping his voice low.

"Nothing in particular," Teag replied. "Mostly making sure there isn't anything dangerous. Habit," he said with a shrug.

In the end, Teag selected a slim volume on the history of the Pendle Hill witch trials and a thin book on needlework. If Cadwell thought it a strange combination, he didn't say so, packing them up with a smile and adding a flyer to come back after Christmas for the January book sale.

"So no cursed grimoires, I presume?" Anthony asked as they strolled back toward the pub.

"Fortunately, not," Teag replied. "But I am interested now in finding out a little more about needlework. I think there's something still going on between the Mortimer sisters, and Lillian's embroidery is the key."

Anthony couldn't bring himself to be put out at Teag finding a potential ghost problem. It was too much a part of who Teag was, and Anthony wouldn't change that for anything. "All right. I'll be your sidekick," Anthony said once they got settled at a table at the Boar and Knight. "Just tell me what to do, and try not to get us thrown in the dungeon."

Teag peered over his menu. "I really don't think they do that anymore. Wait. Does the castle *have* a dungeon? Is it on the tour?"

Anthony smacked his palm to his forehead. "Me and my big mouth," he grumbled, but he grinned as he did it. "There's no dungeon on the castle map, but if you ask Priscilla at the desk real nicely, maybe she'll tell you whether there's one on the tour."

Teag leaned in. "Maybe we could pretend our room is a dungeon. The *other* kind."

"You're incorrigible," Anthony sighed, but he couldn't deny that his face reddened, and his pants tented at the mental imagery. Neither of them were really into that scene, but a little fantasy role play certainly added spice.

The Boar and Knight was one of the oldest buildings other than the castle, and Anthony marveled that it had been in continual use as a pub since the early Middle Ages. A sign with the names of every proprietor going back over six hundred years graced one wall. The pub looked its age. A fireplace across from the bar was blackened with the soot of ages. The dark wood of the tables, chair rail, and bar was worn from use, and the plank floor showed the toll of centuries of foot traffic.

"The food must be good if they've been around since the

Crusades," Teag said, as he looked in one direction and then the next to see everything in the pub's cozy rooms.

"I suspect the ale is good too," Anthony replied. Teag went for Shepherd's Pie, while Anthony chose Bangers and Mash, and they each got a pint of the pub's signature brew.

Anthony loved the way Teag's eyes lit up at the old pub and how excited he was to dig into his food and sample the ale. Anthony had been over to the UK several times, both for business and with his family, but seeing everything fresh through Teag's eyes made all the difference, and he felt himself fall, impossibly, even more in love than before.

The pub was fairly small, and the tables were closer together than in modern restaurants, so it was difficult not to overhear conversations.

"...when Old Man Granville dies, that's the last of the lot," a man at the next table said to his companion. Both were men who looked to be in their late sixties. The speaker had a shock of white hair that poked out at all angles, while the other man had a monk's fringe of gray hair around a bald pate. "There's no one to inherit his country house or the land with it."

"How'd he manage to end up without heirs?" the other man replied.

"Dunno. Guess it wouldn't be too hard with a run of bad luck. All you'd need is a generation or two without many kids, and then toss in accidents or sickness. It's a shame. There've been Granvilles in these parts since the War of the Roses. I always heard tell that's when the Granville family got their land from the king. Same time as the Mortimers got the castle."

"So, what now? Everything Old Man Granville owns reverts to the Crown? Next thing you know, the land'll get sold off, and we'll have flats going up, you mark my word."

Anthony couldn't help listening, caught up in the mini-drama of a stranger's tale. Other patrons argued about soccer scores or cricket or the latest political news. When Teag tapped him on the arm, Anthony realized he had been lost in thought.

"Tuppence for your thoughts," Teag asked with a grin. "I'd have offered a penny, but when in Rome…"

"I'll tell you later," Anthony replied, well aware that others could hear them as clearly as he heard the people at the next tables.

By the time they finished their food, polished off the ale, and paid their tab, night had fallen. Twinkle lights festooned the trees near the walkways, wrapped around light posts, and sparkled in shop windows. The big fir tree in the town square glowed.

"It's so pretty," Teag said with a sigh as they strolled back toward the castle. "Now, what was the big secret back in the pub?"

Anthony shook his head. "No secret. I just didn't want the old men at the next table to know I'd been eavesdropping. They were talking about a local family—the Granvilles, well-to-do, I'm sure—who might lose their lands because there aren't any heirs after the patriarch dies."

"That happened to a lot of landed gentry over the years," Teag replied. "It's really more of a surprise that a family like the Mortimers were able to hang onto their castle and make a go of it. The upkeep alone has bankrupted plenty of nobles, and two World Wars went hard on descendants. It's a shame—that's the way history gets lost."

When they reached the inner bailey of Caynham Castle, Anthony looked to Teag. "So do we go up to the room and call it a night, or did you want to go back to the sitting rooms?"

Teag took his hand and gave it a squeeze. "I have all kinds of ideas for when we go back to the room, none of which involve calling it a night," he said with a lascivious smile. "But I'm worried about the ghost I thought I sensed. It might be a good time to catch Priscilla and see if she knows anything if she's not busy."

They headed to the front desk. Anthony figured Priscilla would be gone by now, but she was still there, albeit looking a bit less perky than she had earlier.

"Hello, gentlemen. Problem with your room?" she asked.

"Oh no," Teag assured her. "Everything with the room is great. But I had an odd question I was hoping you could answer. Has anyone reported anything strange happening in the ladies' salon, over in Bride's Tower?"

"Strange, like…"

"Odd cold spots, things suddenly falling off shelves, people feeling a push when no one's around, that sort of strange," Teag replied, with his most winning smile.

Anthony loved watching his boy work. *He'd have been a natural at swaying a jury if he'd gone into law,* Anthony thought. Teag had a way of setting people at ease and getting them to talk to him, regardless of age or status.

"A ghost, you mean. One that isn't Lady Alice's daughter."

"More like Mabel Mortimer," Teag said. "And very unhappy."

Priscilla gave Teag a measured glance and then looked at Anthony. He thought they might be about to get tossed out on their ear for wasting her time.

"You're Teag Logan, from Charleston? Mr. Sorren said you'd be coming here. And that if you asked for help with something, to do whatever we could."

"You know Sorren?" Anthony's eyes widened.

Teag's best friend and boss, Cassidy Kincaide, owned Trifles and Folly. Sorren was her business partner—and a nearly six-hundred-year-old vampire who had founded the store back when Charleston was first chartered. Anthony knew Sorren had dealings in Europe with the Alliance—the coalition of mortals and immortals who used Trifles and Folly—and other stores like it—as a cover for dealing with haunted and cursed objects and occasionally saving the world. He just hadn't expected to stumble over a connection on their trip.

"He's an old friend of the Earl, and the Earl's family, the Mortimers," Patricia said. "I'm a Mortimer cousin. The castle is really a family affair. And as for ghosts, I'm not sure we'd want the other guests to overhear, but yes, there have been some…disturbances… lately in the ladies' salon. That's kind of what you folks do, isn't it? Handle that sort of thing?"

"Actually, I'm a lawyer," Anthony said. "But that's totally Teag's area."

"I might be able to help, so no one gets hurt," Teag said. The registration area was empty, and Teag figured everyone was at dinner or the castle restaurant's bar.

Priscilla glanced around again and relaxed when she didn't see anyone nearby. "We never had any problems in there before," she said. "Family items like Mabel's hair comb rotate on and off display. But we'd never had anything from Lillian before. She died young and tragically, poor thing," Priscilla confided.

"So this is the first time you've had something from both sisters on display together?" Teag asked. Anthony could practically see the wheels turning in his fiancé's head as Teag formed a theory.

"Yes. There are a number of items belonging to Mabel in our archive storage," Priscilla said. "She lived into her nineties, so it's been less than thirty years since she passed away, and she was born and died in the castle."

"What about Lillian's personal belongings? What happened to them?" Teag asked.

Priscilla shook her head and shrugged. "No idea. She died in 1920. A century is a long time to keep track. And since she had Tuberculosis, the family might have gotten rid of her things for fear of catching it."

"But the needlepoint pieces, they just found their way back to the family, right?" Teag was definitely on the trail of something, but Anthony wasn't sure yet exactly what.

Priscilla nodded. "Yes. She'd given some as gifts, and the families gave or loaned them back to the castle for display. They're scattered about in several of the rooms."

"And the salon is the only place where there are pieces from both sisters together?"

"Yes, but there are other items Mabel owned elsewhere." Priscilla hesitated. "I'm glad you said something. Odd things have happened to me in that sitting room, but I'd convinced myself it was my imagination. We'd heard a few guests mention that they thought it was very cold in the room, or that they had the feeling someone was watching them. And then the day before yesterday, a guest was walking through and tripped, right by Mabel's display case. The guest thought she caught her foot on something, and she wasn't hurt, thank goodness, but now I wonder what really happened."

Teag chewed on his lip, Anthony knew it was a sure sign he was working out a puzzle.

"If Mabel's strong enough to hurt people, then we need to do something. Just putting her items back into storage won't be enough, because her spirit is attached to them, and she's riled up now. It might be as simple as saying a banishment ritual over Mabel's grave," Teag suggested. "Do you know where she's buried?"

Priscilla nodded. "Yes. In the family crypt. I can make arrangements to give you a private tour tomorrow if you'd like. And if, during the tour, you happen to recite some strange poems or prayers, I won't tell anyone," she added with a broad wink.

Teag grinned. "I think that tour would be a lovely addition. Thank you very much."

They agreed to meet Priscilla at ten the next morning and said goodnight. As they walked back to the inner bailey where the dower apartments were located, Teag reached out and took Anthony's arm. This time, Anthony didn't flinch.

"Look at those stars," Teag marveled, staring into the sky. The cold, clear night made for good viewing, even if their breath misted in the chill. "This is absolutely perfect. And so are you."

"Even if the castle does have a ghost problem after all?" Anthony asked.

Teag ducked in to press a quick kiss to his lips. "You know, that makes it even better, somehow. Thank you for being so patient about me finding a 'job' on vacation."

Anthony shrugged. "If Mabel is hurting people, something needs to be done, and you know what to do. We'll go to the crypt tomorrow, you'll say the banishment, and we can go on with our vacation. It's like doing a good deed."

"Hmm...since I've done a good deed, does that mean I can do some naughty deeds now?" Teag teased in a voice that went right to Anthony's groin. The heat in Teag's eyes left absolutely no room for misinterpretation.

"I think that could be arranged," Anthony replied, in a tone made husky by more than just the cold air.

Once they were in the elevator, Teag pushed Anthony against the wall, slipping a hand between them to cup his package. "You're filling out your briefs, Counselor."

"I plead totally guilty," Anthony replied. "But since I'm sure there are cameras in these elevators, let's save the rest for our room, and then maybe I can make you plead—I mean, beg."

Teag gave him a quick kiss on the lips and turned to wink at the camera in the corner. "Sounds like my kind of plea bargain."

CHAPTER 3

TEAG

THE NEXT MORNING, PRISCILLA MET THEM AFTER BREAKFAST, AND they headed outside the castle walls to the Mortimer family crypt.

"This isn't all of the family," she told them as they trekked along a gravel path. "Some of the older burials are in the crypt beneath St. Peter's church in the village. But Mabel and Lillian are recent enough, relatively speaking, to be in the 'new' crypt."

The crypt looked like a small church without a steeple, made from the same Silurian limestone as the castle's walls. *Mortimer* was engraved on the lintel.

"The crypt is only for the Earl's direct descendants," Priscilla told them. "The rest of the newer folks would be laid to rest in the churchyard."

"Do you know where Mabel was placed in here?" Teag asked as they entered the family mausoleum. The stone held a chill. Light filtered down from windows around the eaves. A stained glass rose window over the engraved bronze front doors bathed the interior in warm shades of blue, crimson, and gold, the colors of the Mortimer family crest.

Priscilla nodded. "I looked it up before we came. She should be over here." Her heels clicked on the marble floor as she led them toward the corner and pointed to a square stone marking Mabel's niche, engraved with her name and dates.

Teag pulled out a bundle of sage and an abalone shell. "I'm going to burn some sage to purify and say the banishment rite Father Anne taught me. Sometimes, that's enough."

What he didn't say was that often, it wasn't. Teag hated dragging Anthony into a ghost problem on their vacation, but if Mabel's spirit had turned vengeful, having her loose in the castle with a holiday ball just days away could lead to catastrophe.

"I'm just going to stroll around outside," Priscilla replied as if she hadn't heard him. "When you've paid your respects, just come to the door." With that, she headed outside.

"Score one for plausible deniability," Anthony said. "What can I do to help?"

Teag used a lighter to catch the tip of the bundle on fire and let the flames settle to a glow as the smoke rose. "Watch my back. If I'm concentrating on the words of the rite, I'm not paying attention to what's around me."

"You've got it." Anthony palmed the iron fireplace poker they had borrowed from their room in case Mabel showed up, and he had a salt shaker in his coat pocket from breakfast. Salt and iron disrupted ghosts and made them vanish—at least, temporarily. That meant Anthony could buy time for Teag if Mabel decided to throw a hissy fit.

Teag laid down a thin line of salt in front of Mabel's drawer—more insurance, in case she showed up. Then he walked clockwise around the small open area in the center of the crypt with the sage, letting the smoke fill the air.

"Mabel Mortimer. You have departed this life, and it is time to move on. By all that you hold holy, by the saints and apostles, and in the name of the Father, Son, and Holy Ghost, leave this place and trouble their house no more."

Teag's voice echoed in the stone room. He tensed, waiting for a cold gust of wind, or the grip of invisible dead hands, or maybe a glowing orb diving for his head. Nothing happened.

"Do you think she heard you?" Anthony asked.

"Dunno. The banishment isn't like an exorcism, and I'm not a priest."

"Obviously," Anthony smirked.

"What I meant," Teag replied, rolling his eyes, "is that it's more like a sternly worded request to leave, but it's not the same as picking her up by the scruff of the neck and throwing her out."

"Have you ever seen it work?"

"Sometimes. Mostly when spirits don't realize they're dead and that they've become a nuisance. If Mabel has more of an agenda or some serious unfinished business, she might not take the hint." He blew out the sage, closed the abalone shell around it, and tucked the shell and the salt shaker back in his pocket.

"I guess we'll find out," Anthony said. He stepped closer and ran a hand down Teag's spine, ending at the small of his back. "Have I ever told you how sexy you are when you do your ghostbuster thing?"

"Really?" A grin tugged at the corner of Teag's mouth. "Sort of like how sexy you are all dressed up for court when you do your Atticus Finch thing?"

"Yeah," Anthony replied. "The day's still young. Why don't we head back to the room before lunch? We have plenty of time."

"I like the way you think," Teag replied with a saucy wink.

They headed to the door and found Priscilla on the steps of the crypt with her phone against her ear. Her expression was distraught. She ended the call as they reached her and looked up.

"We've got to go back. A guest was injured in the ladies' sitting room by something that 'seemed to fly off the shelf,'" Priscilla said. "I don't think Mabel is ready to give up."

Teag swore under his breath. A glance at Anthony told him his fiancé was on the same page without needing to confer. "All right. Lock up here, and we'll go back with you. I'm sorry this didn't work. Thank you for giving it a try."

An old ring of keys jangled in Priscilla's hand. Teag and Anthony helped close the heavy doors, and the lock *clunked* into place. "I appreciate you taking time out of your vacation to help. I feel guilty asking."

"We couldn't just ignore the problem when people are getting hurt," Anthony said, and Teag's heart warmed. It had taken a lot for Anthony to fully embrace his "side gig," and at one time, Teag had feared that Anthony might leave him if he ever discovered the truth. Instead, Anthony had held on tighter than ever, and Teag felt so thankful.

"Let's go find out more about what happened. Then I think the next step is to go see the rooms that used to be Mabel's and Lillian's," Teag replied.

Priscilla pocketed the keys, and they walked back at a brisk pace. "We know where Mabel's room was, but we've never been sure about Lillian's. Mabel's is on the fifth floor of Bride's Tower. She moved there during the First World War because it seemed safer and never left."

"Maybe Lillian's room was somewhere nearby," Anthony suggested.

"I just wish you had more of Lillian's possessions than just the few needlework pieces," Teag said, thinking out loud. "There's something driving this, and I don't think we'll get rid of the ghosts until we figure it out."

Teag was relieved not to see an ambulance when they reached the tower. Still, he could see several castle employees hovering around a woman seated on a chair who was holding an ice pack to her head.

"I'm going to have to deal with this and fill out paperwork," Priscilla said, turning to Teag and Anthony. "How about you two go over to the tea room and have a bite, and I'll catch up to you when I'm done here. On me," she said, pulling two vouchers out of her pocket.

Teag thanked her and watched her walk toward the injured woman, not envying the clean up she was going to need to do. Fortunately, the guest didn't look badly hurt, but Teag knew that for vengeful ghosts, it was only a matter of time before problems escalated. They stopped by their room just long enough to return the fireplace poker, then headed to the tea shop.

"Back again?" Helen, the lady in the tea shop, greeted them. "You're early for lunch."

"We just stopped by for tea," Teag replied. "And maybe two of those scones…with the apricot preserves and clotted cream?"

"We've got those fresh right out of the oven," Helen said. "Let me get you seated."

She led them to a different table, affording them a slightly new perspective on the tea room. "Have you had a chance to explore the village?" Helen asked as they got settled.

"We've walked up and down Knight Street," Anthony replied. "But I'm sure there's more to see."

"Not really," Helen replied with a laugh. "Well, a little. You'll want to go to the Earl's brewery because it's very nice, and the beer is good. I'd say that even if he wasn't the Earl or my boss. If you haven't walked to the folly, down by the river, it's worth the hike, especially the way it's done up now for the holidays. The gardens aren't blooming, of course, but the trees and shrubs give it good bones. And there's a second pub, over by the grocery store, if you feel the need."

She bustled off to get their order. Teag unfolded his linen napkin and set it in his lap. "Well—there's still lots to do, apparently."

"I'd like to go to the folly," Anthony replied. "It looked interesting on the website, and I bet it looks great with the Christmas decorations." He paused. "Have you thought any more about whether you want to go to the ball?"

"If I lose my shoe, will you chase after me at the stroke of twelve and carry me off?"

"I already know your name and where you're staying. I can find you and bring you your shoe."

"That's it. Ruin all the romance," Teag fake-pouted. Something about Caynham Castle brought out a whimsical side he hadn't indulged in a long time. Grad school had taken a toll, and it seemed like he and Cassidy often went from one supernatural crisis to another. But here at the castle, they could play. Teag knew he didn't have to prove anything to Anthony. His fiancé was well aware of Teag's martial arts ability, and he'd seen Teag in a fight. That sense of security made Teag feel safe being flirty and silly, and he appreciated that Anthony was willing to play along.

"Come back to the room with me, and I'll romance you." Anthony bumped his knee against Teag's under the table, and the look in his eyes made Teag's cock fill and his stomach do a little flip. They had broken in the new room very enthusiastically the previous night, and Teag was hoping for a repeat tonight.

"I'll hold you to that," Teag teased.

"Oh, there'll be a lot of holding. Count on it." Anthony's sexy wink meant Teag needed to surreptitiously adjust himself.

"Here you go!" Helen interrupted, bearing a tray with tea, scones, and all the fixings. "Enjoy!"

The scent of the English Breakfast tea filled the air, mixing with the smell of the scones. Teag realized he was more hungry than he had thought. Still, he couldn't resist teasing Anthony a bit more as he took a bite of his scone and very obviously licked the remnants of the clotted cream off his lips.

"You're killing me," Anthony whispered.

"You know how much I love cream," Teag replied, not even trying to look innocent.

Anthony groaned. "You're going to be like this all day, aren't you?"

"Uh-huh. And you love it."

They took their time, knowing Priscilla would need a chance to deal with the guest situation. She arrived just as they finished their pot of tea, looking frazzled.

"You look like you need the tea more than we do," Teag said. "Do you have time for a cup?"

Priscilla shook her head. "I'm afraid not. Did you give Helen the vouchers? I can get you into the fifth floor of Bride's Tower if we go now."

Teag handed over the vouchers and thanked Helen, promising they would be back. Then he and Anthony followed Priscilla back to the inner bailey. She had walked over in just a tweed jacket and scarf, without a coat. Looking at her made Teag shiver and burrow down into his heavy jacket.

"The upper levels of Bride's Tower aren't usually open to guests,"

216

Priscilla said. "It's where we keep items that aren't on display. The family had apartments there, during both World Wars, but they haven't stayed in the Tower in years."

"What about Mabel?" Teag asked.

"She was the last to leave Bride's Tower," Priscilla said. "I guess she was just comfortable there. Or maybe she felt like the manor house wasn't really her home. She died in her room, in her sleep. I was just a kid, but I remember thinking it would have been creepy to be all alone in Bride's Tower at night."

Priscilla unlocked the door at the base of the thick-walled tower and flipped on the lights. They followed her inside. "The stairs are this way," she said. "That's another reason why we didn't use this for guests for a long time. It only had an elevator put in after Mabel's death."

"Mabel navigated the stairs all those years?" Anthony asked.

Priscilla shrugged. "She was pretty spry for her age, until the very end."

The stone stairs were in good condition, but Teag wouldn't have wanted to run them, certainly not when he was in his eighties.

"We use the first floor for the brides' and grooms' rooms and other wedding preparations," Priscilla said as they climbed. "The second floor is the Honeymoon Suite. You've been to the sitting rooms on the third floor. The fourth floor houses the archives and storage for off-rotation items. Those floors are climate-controlled. The fifth floor is exactly as it was when Mabel died. We haven't needed the space, so nothing's been done with it."

When they reached the fifth floor, Priscilla turned on the hall light. The scuffed paint and old light fixtures made it clear that the area hadn't been modernized. Framed prints hung on the walls to the right. A large tapestry hung against the left wall, starting midway down the corridor.

"This was Mabel's room," Priscilla said, opening the first door on the left. Dust motes floated in the air as she turned on the light. Sheets covered the remaining pieces of furniture, but everything personal had been removed, including anything on the walls. The space had a cold, impersonal feel to Teag, more like a dormitory than a home.

"What was Mable like?" Teag asked.

"I never met her," Priscilla replied. "But even her picture frightened me when I was a kid. I remember family members talking about her. They didn't really like Mabel. Not that she did anything mean to them. She just wasn't a warm person. I remember this picture of her in a black dress, with a severe look on her face. People didn't talk about her much, and what they said was polite...but I don't think anyone was comfortable around her. I got the impression she was very judgmental and more strict than necessary."

That squared with what they had learned from Mr. Porter at the antique shop. "Can we look in the other rooms? One of them probably belonged to Lillian, if the sisters came to the tower during the war."

"Sure," Priscilla agreed. "But anything that belonged to her would be long gone."

They walked back into the hallway, and Teag turned his attention to the tapestry. "It's a scene from Mallory's *Le Morte d'Arthur*," he said, recognizing the depiction. "Interesting choice. Arthur's betrayal by Mordred. If it's not a reproduction...and I don't think it is...the piece probably dates to the late sixteen hundreds."

He looked to Priscilla. "Rather odd that it's just been left in an abandoned hallway, isn't it?"

"It's how Mabel wanted it," Priscilla replied. "She was rather odd herself. Other than wanting to be buried in the family crypt, the only other stipulation of her will was that she wanted the tapestry to remain where it was. I honestly think that people just forgot about it after she passed."

Teag moved closer to the tapestry. The workmanship of the piece was excellent, and given its age and the fact that it had been hanging in a dusty hallway, it remained in relatively good shape. But as he drew nearer, the Weaver magic danced in his mind's eye like threads of flame.

"What are you seeing?" Anthony asked.

"Someone stitched magic into the tapestry," Teag said, moving slowly from one side of the piece to the other, close but not touching. "The stitches are much, much newer. Less than a century, I'd guess. And it's not just magic…" he concentrated, focusing his gift on the places where he envisioned the bespelled threads.

"Whoever added the threads to this didn't just work their magic into the stitches. They left behind a piece of their soul," he said, turning to face Anthony and Priscilla, wide-eyed.

"How is that even possible?" Priscilla asked.

"I don't know," Teag admitted. "I imagine there are ways to do that, but I'm not sure why anyone would want to." He turned back to the tapestry and frowned, then reached out and grabbed hold of one side, lifting it away from the wall. The Weaver magic of the added threads tingled through his arm.

"There's a door under here," he said to the others. "I think we just found Lillian's room."

They left the tapestry hanging, so as not to damage it, and slipped behind. Teag tried the door. "Locked."

"Let me," Priscilla said, shuffling to change places. She withdrew a bulging keyring from her pocket and found the key she was looking for. "This is supposed to be the master key."

Teag held his breath while she tried the key and exhaled when the knob turned, and the door opened.

"Wow," Anthony said, summing up what they all felt from their gobsmacked expressions.

Other than a thick coating of dust, the room looked like its owner had walked out and never returned. Enough light came from the window for them to see. The faded bedspread was pulled up neatly on the bed, with a book propped open on the nightstand. On the desk lay paper and writing pens. A partially open armoire revealed clothing on hangers. But what caught Teag's attention was the full-sized loom in one corner and the many embroidery hoops with half-finished pieces of needlework scattered on every surface.

"Everything looks like Lillian just wandered off," Anthony said. "So why is there a big trunk in the middle of the room? She was very sick at the end, wasn't she? She wouldn't have been packing for a trip."

Priscilla walked over to the trunk and opened it. Inside were piles of needlework pieces of all sizes—tablecloths and runners, doilies and antimacassars, handkerchiefs, and scarves. Nothing was neatly folded; instead, it looked as if someone had just dumped the pieces in and shut the lid.

In the corridor, a door slammed, then another, and another, but not the door to Lillian's room.

"Uh-oh," Teag murmured. "Someone just woke up."

The air in the bedroom grew suddenly cold. Teag reached for the salt shaker in his pocket, wishing he had his iron knife. Anthony and Priscilla took a step back, away from the trunk.

Gray mist rose and took the form of a young woman. She had long dark hair and a heart-shaped face. Her long nightdress hung from a thin body.

"Help me."

As quickly as the ghost appeared, she vanished, and so did the sudden chill. Teag, Anthony, and Priscilla exchanged wide-eyed looks.

"Did you see that?" Priscilla whispered.

"Yeah. I think we all did," Anthony replied.

"I'm betting that's Lillian," Teag said. "And the temper tantrum in the hallway might be Mabel."

"She wanted the tapestry left in place," Anthony said. "Why would she want to hide Lillian's room? It's almost like she wanted to—"

"Erase her from history," Priscilla finished. "I think that's exactly what she wanted. But why?"

Teag ran a hand through his hair. "I know you don't know us very well, other than Sorren vouching for us. And I know it's a lot to ask. But I think if we could stay in the room for a while, go through what's here, we might find out what happened and why Mabel's ghost suddenly got violent."

"What are you thinking?" Anthony asked.

Teag gestured toward the loom, and the unfinished needlework scattered about. "I think I might be able to read Lillian's Weaver magic from her pieces. There's so much—it's almost like it became an obsession. Did Mabel lock her up? Why would she do that? Maybe there's a journal or something…" He turned to meet Priscilla's gaze. "I think this is the heart of the haunting. If we can solve this, we might be able to make the sitting rooms safe again."

Priscilla swallowed hard, then nodded. "Okay. Seems like you're our best shot. What do you need from me?"

"Salt," Teag replied. "A canister from the kitchen. I'll put a line of it down by the door. It'll keep Mabel from bothering us. An iron fireplace poker, just in case. We took ours back to the room," he said. "And please let your security guards know not to arrest us if anyone notices we're up here."

"I'll do all that and bring you some cold drinks and wet wipes as well," Priscilla said. "Thank you. I really appreciate all you're doing."

"We're happy to help," Anthony replied, and the genuine smile assuaged some of Teag's guilt for dragging them into a case. "Teag's good with this kind of thing. He'll get to the bottom of it."

Priscilla left, and Bride's Tower seemed eerily quiet. "You could go do something fun," Teag said as he walked around the room, mentally cataloging all the needlepoint pieces and trying to figure out where to start.

"I came here to be with my fiancé. Which is exactly what I'm going to do," Anthony said. "How about this? Since I can't pick up any clues from the embroidery, why don't you focus on that, and I'll search the room for anything else—diaries, journals, letters, that kind of thing."

"I love you so much," Teag replied.

"Because I'm going to help you search the room?"

"Because you're taking this in stride and not making me feel awful about it."

Anthony moved closer and turned Teag's chin so their eyes met. "We're helping people, making sure no one gets hurt, and solving a mystery. Some people pay extra to get a mystery package at a hotel, you know. So think of it as a bonus."

Teag decided to start with the least complete embroidery, on the assumption they might be the last pieces Lillian created. The needlework was finely crafted, with careful, regular stitches. Teag could feel traces of Lillian's native Weaver magic—untrained but still strong. In the pieces where she had stitched in a nearly invisible set of symbols with white thread, Teag could sense the presence of a wisp of something more powerful and feared it was a breath of Lillian's soul.

The echoes of power were fainter in the least finished works. Those were also the pieces that were flecked with rust-colored stains Teag feared were blood. He remembered how Lillian died, and wondered if she had stitched until the very end.

"It's odd," Teag remarked, as Anthony started at one corner and devoted himself to thoroughly searching the room. "The pieces that Lillian did before the war were all kinds of designs—samplers, flowers, still lifes. But all her later pieces have an archery theme. Arrows, bows, quivers, bowmen, targets. There must be a reason she chose those images, but I don't understand."

"How about the pieces in the trunk?" Anthony asked as he moved slowly from searching in, around, behind, and under one piece of furniture to the next.

"I'm working on those now," Teag replied. "I can almost feel Lillian fading from one piece to another. She must have worked obsessively to create all these."

"If she was shut away in her room, there might not have been many other distractions," Anthony replied. "Poor woman. First she gets her heart broken, then she dies young from TB. And it doesn't sound like her sister was very supportive."

"I don't get it. What was Mabel's deal? Lillian got dealt a shitty hand, and Mabel stood to inherit everything. Why all the drama?" Teag handled the pieces in the trunk carefully, pausing with each one to take in the design, type of stitches used, and the expertise, as well as sensing the magic.

"None of the pieces in the trunk have the soul-threads," Teag said after a while. "Just the ones laying about in the room—and the tapestry. I was right about the variety in the designs—but there aren't any arrows or archers. There's so much life and energy in her early pieces. The colors are bright, and I think a lot of the designs were original. And then it all changes."

"Is there any way to put a date to the shift?" Anthony leaned into the armoire, carefully going through pockets, drawers, and nooks. Dust lay like snow flurries across his shoulders and in his hair.

"Not all of her pieces have a date stitched in, but I haven't found anything with soul-threads or the archer theme before 1917," Teag replied.

"Then we need to figure out what happened in 1917 that changed everything."

Priscilla returned with the salt, a bag full of bottled water, and the fireplace poker. "If you find anything you need to examine closely, there's a small meeting room you can use near the front desk. Just bring whatever it is down, and I'll get you set up," she offered.

Once Teag had gone through the needlework, he felt exhausted and knew he needed to set the stitchery aside for a while, so he joined Anthony in searching the room. As Anthony moved to check the desk, Teag went to the bookshelves.

"I haven't found anything odd so far," Anthony said. "Let's hope there's more on this side of the room."

Lillian's taste ran to mystery and romance, with a mix of classics, some yellowed with age. Several of the books were accounts by botanists and explorers, and Teag wondered whether Lillian used their descriptions for inspiration in creating her designs. He was all the way down to the bottom row when a dark leather book caught his eye. Teag pulled it from the shelf and let out a low whistle.

"Well look at that. I found a grimoire, after all," he said, holding the book up for Anthony to see.

"Seriously?" Anthony looked puzzled. "What would Lillian want with a book on magic?"

Teag sat down and started to page through the old book carefully. "It doesn't actually come right out and say that it's a grimoire—or about magic. It's almost written in language like a prayer book. Not unusual, back in the day, to try to protect the owners of such dangerous books."

"Do you think she knew what it was?"

Teag frowned as he found some of the symbols Lillian had used in her hidden stitching. "Maybe not," he mused. "She was young and rather sheltered. Magic wasn't exactly a common topic, and there was no internet to look things up easily. Maybe she really did think it was a prayer book, and, I don't know—she was trying to ask for divine help?"

He noted the symbols that looked familiar. "She used several of the same markings. According to this, they were for protection, memory, finding lost things. That's a rather unusual focus, don't you think?"

Nothing else on the bookshelves looked out of the ordinary. Teag even pulled a few volumes at random to see if Lillian had put false covers over more controversial books, but to no avail. The desk, likewise, held no secrets. But when Anthony checked under the bed, he found a locked suitcase, and when he shook it, the sounds from inside were definitely more paper than clothing.

"I doubt anyone has the key," Anthony observed.

"If you didn't find it in Lillian's things, then I doubt it too." Teag found a bobby pin, straightened it out, and jimmied open the lock.

"Should I be worried that you know how to pick a lock?" Anthony asked.

"Can I plead the Fifth?"

"Only on TV. That's not how it actually works."

Teag shrugged. "We get a lot of old locked boxes at Trifles and Folly. Someone needed to know how to open them."

"Uh-huh," Anthony responded skeptically but didn't push. Teag figured his fiancé could figure out that handling haunts and monsters sometimes required a bit of breaking and entering.

Teag opened the suitcase reverently as if they were entering a tomb. He and Anthony both let out a breath when the contents were revealed. Inside were yellowed envelopes with faded postmarks, thin leather-bound notebooks, sketchpads, and small keepsakes that must have been dear to Lillian's heart.

Outside in the hallway, doors opened, then slammed shut. "I don't think Mabel wanted us to find this," Anthony observed, gripping the fireplace poker

The temperature dropped, and Teag felt the hair rise on the back of his neck. They turned to see Lillian's ghost take shape once more. A ghostly finger traced letters in the thick dust on the dresser. *Save Archer*, it read.

"Who is Archer?" Teag asked the spirit. "What do the arrows and bows mean?"

Lillian's ghost had the pale, fragile appearance that went with Consumption, but determination blazed in her eyes. She pointed toward the writing in the dust and then vanished.

A woman's furious shriek echoed in the empty hallway, and a tremor passed through Bride's Tower, rattling glass and making the cobwebs sway.

"I think we'd better get out of here," Teag said. "I can come back later and remove the soul threads to let Lillian rest in peace. For now, let's figure out what was so important in this suitcase."

"How are we going to get out? There's a pissed off ghost in the hallway!" Anthony's eyes were wide. He'd been up against vengeful ghosts before, and Anthony was right to be cautious, Teag knew. But he was determined that Mabel Mortimer was not going to keep them trapped like she did Lillian.

"We stay close together. I'll take the suitcase, and I'll fan the salt out ahead of us. You come right behind me with the poker, so you can jab and slash if Mabel gets handsy," Teag told him. He grabbed the case and made sure the salt canister was open, then moved to the door.

"Ready?" he asked.

"Not really, but we're going anyhow," Anthony replied.

Teag sloshed salt into the corridor ahead of them, spreading it wide across the hallway. He stepped out and heard the grains crunch beneath his feet. "Go!" he yelled to Anthony, who was right behind him.

The temperature in the hall was colder than outside, enough that they could see their breath. The doors opened and shut, the overhead lights flickered wildly, and Mabel screamed in fury as a ghostly shadow chased them toward the stairs, clawed hands grasping to catch hold.

Anthony swung the iron poker, keeping the ghost at bay, as Teag kept up the spray of salt. The salt limited where Mabel could go, and if they kept to the center of the hallway, they could elude her grasp.

"Do you think she'll go down the steps?" Anthony yelled, jabbing at the ghost when she slipped along the wall, at the very edge of the salt. She vanished, only to reappear in another location.

"No idea. I just want to get out of here."

They thundered down the stairs, and Mabel's shrieks reverberated in the stairwell, but she did not follow. Neither man felt like taking chances, and they ran as fast as they could down the steps and then outside, where they gasped for breath until their lungs ached from the cold.

"Look!" Anthony said, pointing to a window at the top of Bride's Tower. Just for a moment, Teag thought he saw the shadowy form of a woman with upswept hair, and then the apparition vanished.

"Let's go find Priscilla," Teag huffed. "And set up in that meeting room. Maybe we can also get some lunch. I think we've earned it."

CHAPTER 4

ANTHONY

WHEN THEY DRAGGED THEMSELVES INTO THE RECEPTION AREA covered in dust and flushed from outrunning Mabel's ghost, Anthony knew they probably looked like madmen. Teag clutched the old suit-case like a drowning man with a life preserver, and he had a white-knuckled grip on the salt canister. Anthony had the presence of mind to lower the fireplace poker before heading into public areas to avoid scaring anyone.

Priscilla ushered them into a meeting room before their appearance could raise eyebrows in the lobby and promised to be back with hot tea and sandwiches. When she returned, Teag and Anthony had spread the contents of Lillian's suitcase across one half of the large table.

"What's all this?" Priscilla asked, setting down the tray of food at the other end.

"Something Mable really didn't want us to see," Teag replied. He brushed dust out of his hair, but Anthony knew they would never be rid of it until they showered. "If it's all right with you, I figured we'd hole up in here and read."

"Did you figure out any more about her needlework and the... magic?" Priscilla looked curious, not fearful.

Teag nodded. "Yes. I found the book she took the spells from, and

I'm sure I can undo them and set her soul free. But first, I think we need to figure out what's got Mabel riled up before someone else gets hurt."

"All right," Priscilla replied. "I have to be up front, but if you need anything, just let me know. Lunch and dinner are on me. You're doing us a great service." She cleared her throat. "When you've got every-thing figured out, at some point, we need to brief the Earl."

"Understood. Do you have any idea how he'll take it?" Teag asked.

She shrugged. "He knows Mr. Sorren, doesn't he? I imagine he'll deal with it just fine." With that, she headed back to her post.

They settled down to eat and found a pot of hot Earl Gray tea, a variety of tea sandwiches, a box of scones and tarts, and a slab of cake for each of them. "I'm going to be so spoiled by the time we get home," Teag said, polishing off the last of his cake. "Is there a tea room in Charleston? If not, we should start one. This food is too good to give up!"

"I'm sure we can find one," Anthony replied. "But I agree—aside from being chased by screaming ghosts, this is all a pretty great adventure."

Teag smiled at him, and Anthony felt his insides turn to jelly with the emotions in Teag's eyes. Love, gratitude, and acceptance. Figuring out a century-old mystery wasn't the worst way to spend part of their vacation, and Anthony had plenty of plans for their time after they stopped the ghost problem.

"Divide and conquer," Teag said once they had finished their lunch and washed their hands to avoid leaving marks on any of the old docu-ments. "Do you want letters or journals?"

"Letters," Anthony replied. "And if I get finished first, I can help with the journals that are left."

"I've got a hunch that what we want is from 1916 forward," Teag said. "Let's start with that."

They each took a stack of papers and sat across the table from each other, engrossed in their reading. Anthony squinted to make out the neat cursive script in faded ink.

"I feel like a peeping Tom," Anthony said. "These are love letters, written to Lillian from Bertram—Bertie Granville. Why is that name familiar?"

Teag looked up from the journal he was reading. "It's the name that guy in the pub mentioned and Mr. Porter in the bookstore. Landed gentry, country manor outside of town."

Anthony nodded. "Okay. I knew I'd heard it from somewhere. It looks like Mr. Porter had the story right. Bertie and Lillian were very much in love. He even wrote out a proposal and signed it." He couldn't help tearing up a bit. "But I guess he never came home from the war."

Teag went back to reading through Lillian's journals, and the squinch between his eyebrows told Anthony his fiancé was fully immersed in what he was doing. Anthony hadn't been completely kidding about feeling like a voyeur reading the old love letters. He knew that people in past generations were just regular folks who loved and laughed and cried, but it was one thing to try to imagine an elderly couple as being young and in love, and entirely another to read the intimate endearments between two lovers from a prior generation.

An hour passed in silence as they worked their way through the letters and diaries. Teag's sudden outburst made Anthony startle.

"Holy shit!"

Anthony looked up. Teag was staring at the journal as if it had bit him. "What?"

"It's all here. In TMI detail," he added, his cheeks coloring a bit. "Bertie didn't just propose to Lillian. They had a 'last night on earth' lovemaking session before he got sent off to war. She, uh, noted all the details," he added, looking adorably flustered.

"And?" Anthony nudged, having a feeling where this might be going.

"The war was going full tilt, and not well for the Triple Entente—Great Britain, France, and Russia," Teag said. "So Bertie got rushed through training and sent off to the front in short order. He died almost as soon as he was deployed, in the Battle of the Somme," Teag said. "Of course, there was a lag between when Bertie died and when his family was notified and a few days more before Lillian heard. A couple of months. Long enough for Lillian to realize she was pregnant. She sent Bertie a letter, but it sounds like it didn't reach him until it was too late."

"That poor woman couldn't catch a break," Anthony said, feeling fresh grief for a loss suffered more than a century ago.

"Mabel was furious," Teag said, flipping journal pages to keep up with the story. "The Earl and Countess were off helping the war effort, so Mabel was in charge, like the man at the antique store told us. And Mabel couldn't stand the thought of the family reputation being sullied by an out-of-wedlock pregnancy."

"But they were engaged," Anthony protested. "Didn't Lillian tell her that?"

"Lillian says in her journal that Bertie got a hero's funeral, and she didn't want to 'besmirch' his name," Teag replied, sighing. "So she kept quiet."

"So what about the baby?"

"Here's where I think Lillian has more of a reason to haunt Mabel than the other way around. Lillian had a difficult birth. By the time she was really coherent, Mabel had given the baby to a cousin who had suffered a miscarriage, to raise as their own."

"But the baby wasn't really a Mortimer," Anthony protested. "He's a Granville. Oh, shit."

Teag and Anthony's gazes locked. "He's the heir to the Granville estate—or at least, his descendant is," Teag breathed. "That's what the men at the pub were talking about, how Old Man Granville was the last of his family and when he died, the estate would revert to the Crown. Remember?"

"Wow. What else does it say?" Anthony prompted.

"Obviously, Lillian didn't take it well, that Mabel gave away her baby, which was all she had left of Bertie. She had a 'bout of hysteria'—a nervous breakdown. That just made Mabel more angry, because she didn't want anyone saying the Mortimers were 'weak minded.' So she locked Lillian up."

"She sounds like a real peach," Anthony growled.

"But Lillian wasn't as weak as Mable thought," Teag went on, and Anthony felt like he'd been dropped into a soap opera. "Before she gave birth, she'd begged the midwife to have the child baptized and make sure there was a certificate. And there is—for Archer Mortimer Granville," he said, with a gleam of triumph in his eyes. "Mabel never found out."

"But the cousins still took him, right?"

Teag nodded. "Yeah. Lillian never saw him again. Her later journals are really bleak. She got depressed—no big surprise. She said her loom and her needle were her only companions, and she wove or sewed until she was too exhausted to sit up."

"All those 'archer' designs," Anthony supplied.

"Yeah. That strain probably broke her health, and then when a TB epidemic came through, she was vulnerable. She was twenty-two when she died."

"Jesus," Anthony murmured. "While Mabel lived into her nineties, inherited everything, and had a husband and family. That's just all kinds of wrong." He thought for a moment. "But no one's reported seeing either of the sisters' ghosts until now."

"I think that somehow, Lilian knows about the Granville estate. And she wants her son's descendants to have their rightful inheritance."

Anthony drummed his fingers on the table. "I'm a lawyer, not a barrister. All I know about English law I learned from watching BBC crime dramas. So how do we do right by Lillian and Archer?"

Teag's eyes were alight, and it was clear he enjoyed playing ghost detective. "First, I think we need to figure out which 'cousins' took Archer and then try to find out who his direct descendants are."

"I think there was a Mortimer family tree on the website," Anthony said.

"Let me run back for my tablet, and we can look it up—assuming we've got Wi-Fi in here," Teag replied. He left and came back quickly, flushed from running in the cold air.

"I kept the tablet inside my coat, so it shouldn't be too cold to boot up," he said. Anthony pulled his chair closer, and Teag turned on the tablet, crossing his fingers until they found a signal. A few clicks got them to the right page on the website.

"So we have to go back to who would have been the Earl during World War I—Mabel and Lillian's father," Anthony murmured, thinking aloud.

"Okay. That's here," Teag pointed to the family tree. "Earl Charles Mortimer is the grandfather of the current Earl. Charles had a brother and a sister. The brother had three children. The sister had four."

"All right," Anthony replied. "Charles's brother and sister would have been Mabel and Lillian's uncle and aunt. So baby Archer was given to one of their children—someone who would have been Mabel and Lillian's cousins. So which of those cousins had a male child in 1917?"

Teag did his best to enlarge the small writing. "Charles's sister's son, Elliott, had three children. A daughter, Elizabeth; a son, Reginald who died as a baby. And look—there's a third 'son' named Archibald."

"Archibald. Archer," Anthony said quietly, meeting Teag's gaze. "Do you think it's the same child?"

Teag squinted to see the birth and death dates. "Let me do a little math. We know when Lillian and Bertie spent their night of passion together. So nine months from then should have been…yeah. It's gotta be Archibald. The similarity in the names might be a coincidence."

"Or perhaps Mabel mentioned the Archer name, and they did their own twist on it."

"Maybe." Teag leaned closer, trying to see better. "The type gets fuzzy when you blow it up too much. If Archer was born in 1917, he's probably dead by now. So let's look at his descendants. Okay, he would have been just the right age to end up serving in WWII. So that explains why his kids weren't born until after 1945. And he's got three —a son in 1945, a daughter in 1946, and another son in 1947. The oldest son died four years ago, and the daughter died in her forties. But the youngest son…" He trailed off, then raised his head, triumphant.

"Shit. He could still be alive," Teag said, with a look on his face as if he'd just discovered King Tut's tomb. "The youngest one, Theodore, would be seventy-two. This says he had two children, Ben and Helena, who are probably in their late forties, and they had children whose names aren't listed, probably for privacy reasons."

"Want to bet Priscilla could fill in the blanks?" Anthony asked with a grin.

"I bet she could!" Teag headed toward the lobby, where Priscilla was just finishing up with a guest. She saw him in the doorway to the meeting room, and he gestured for her to come over.

"We need to pick your brain for a moment," Teag said, bringing her over to the tablet. "You said you were a Mortimer cousin. How much do you know about the family tree?"

Priscilla grinned. "I'm a total genealogy nerd."

Anthony held out a chair for her. "Sit down. We've got a story to tell you."

"And that, my lord, is how you ended up with a ghost in the sitting room and the lost heir to the Granville estate as your extended cousin," Teag recapped, sitting back in his chair and waiting for the Earl's reaction. Priscilla stood nearby and seemed to be making a real effort to keep from bouncing on her toes in excitement.

"That's quite a tale," the Earl said. "And please, call me Ward."

"All the documents are right here," Teag replied. "The signed proposal from Bertie Granville to Lillian, his letters to her, her diaries —and the baptismal certificate."

"And these were all under a bed in a room people forgot about up in Bride's Tower?" the Earl said, looking a bit gobsmacked at the revelation.

"Yes, my lord, er, Ward," Teag replied. "We just found the room and the suitcase earlier today and brought them here to read through."

"Well, that's a very interesting turn of events," the Earl replied. "I've known Hollister Granville all my life—he was a friend of my father's—and he's been most distressed about the lack of an heir. It wasn't for lack of trying—he had three children and outlived them all. No grandchildren. I think he'll be relieved, finding there is a blood heir to his estate. And if he accepts the evidence you've found—and I think he will—he can acknowledge Theodore Mortimer as actually being

Theodore Granville," the Earl said, shaking his head as if it was all too much to take in.

"Hollister doesn't just dislike the idea of having his manor and estate all revert to the Crown; he hates to see the family name disappear and all its history with it," he added.

"Now it doesn't have to," Anthony responded, and part of him couldn't believe he was talking to a real, live Earl.

"I'll have to ring up my barrister, and he'll need to look everything over, authenticate it, of course," the Earl said, "so that when Hollister Granville turns in documents to acknowledge Theodore and leave him the Granville estate, there's no trouble. And I guess that means I'd better call 'cousin' Theodore as well and let him know he's the descendant of Lillian's love child." He shook his head. "Theodore never did care much for Mabel. There'll be no living with him if he ends up foxing her plans to keep Lillian's child a secret." His tone was resigned, but his smile suggested otherwise.

"Is there time?" Teag asked, then looked chagrined. "I mean, we overheard some of the locals down at the Boar and Knight talking, and they sounded like Mr. Granville wasn't long for this world."

The Earl let out a roar of laughter. "Oh, I'll have to tell Hollister. He'll get a kick out of that. Hollister Granville might be close to one hundred years old, but I assure you—the reports of his death are greatly exaggerated."

"What about the ghosts?" Priscilla asked. "And why did Mabel fuss at both of you in the bedroom and not at me when I was in the hallway?"

Anthony shrugged. "You're a Mortimer. She might have respected the family connection. We were strangers, about to reveal what she thought was a shameful secret."

The Earl cleared his throat. "Yes, well. About that. A good bit has changed since those days. It sounds to me like Lillian and Bertie were very much in love and married in all but technicality." He leaned forward conspiratorially. "Not to speak ill of the dead, but just between us—I never liked Mabel, either."

"It might be as simple as having you go up to the fifth floor of

Bride's Tower and telling Mabel that the jig is up," Teag replied. "That you know the secret and don't care—and that Lillian's son will get his due."

"You think it could be that easy?" the Earl asked.

Teag nodded. "Sometimes, it is. These ghosts are aware. They've been here all this time without causing problems. Lillian 'woke up' because, in her mind, Archer was about to lose his inheritance. And Mabel became active to protect the family name. Unfinished business is a powerful tether for spirits. But now that the matter is settled, they can both move on—and hopefully, find peace."

"I do hope, when it's all said and done, that more of Lillian's handi-work can be displayed somehow," Anthony said wistfully. "The pieces are beautiful, and it's a shame they've been hidden away for so long."

"I think that can be arranged," the Earl replied.

"You know, Uncle, when the dust settles, and everything is official with Theodore and the Granvilles, this would make for marvelous publicity," Priscilla said. "Interest is still high in the Great War, with the centennial so recent. And the story has it all—a tragic love affair, a secret baby, all set against the backdrop of world war, and then redemption. The BBC might even want to make it into a miniseries," she added with a wink.

"Saints preserve us," the Earl said with a shudder, but Anthony didn't get the feeling he really objected to the idea.

CHAPTER 5

TEAG

"I still can't believe you already had tickets to the ball—and shipped our tuxes!" Teag sipped from a flute of Champagne as the music played. He and Anthony had stepped off to the side after dancing to several of their favorite songs.

The Great Hall looked even more spectacular than when they had seen it earlier in the week. Acrylic sculptures around the edge of the room had the look of ice and the glow of flames. Icicles and silver tinsel hung from the ceiling, evergreen boughs with crimson ribbon and gold bells adorned every window, and the tables all had matching artisan-created centerpieces. The lights and decorations on the huge fir tree just made the whole scene even more festive.

"I loved the Christmas Market-style stalls under the grand marquee in the outer bailey," Anthony replied. "And the hot chocolate!" The big event tent offered a variety of local crafts for last-minute shoppers, as well as delicious "small plate" servings of holiday fare. The serving tables in the Great Hall matched the look of the market stalls.

"I was blown away by the ice rink in the moat! I guess it's too cold for alligators here, right?" Teag remarked, taking in the whole glistening scene. Mistletoe balls hung everywhere, and he and Anthony had discretely kissed more than once as they danced. They were both pleasantly surprised when no one seemed to think that two men dancing together was anything out of the ordinary.

"At this point, I think anything is possible," Anthony replied. "Especially after you dragged me on a find-the-gargoyle kissing tour."

"We've done all of them but one," Teag said. "I think it's the real one. We couldn't get into where it is today, but we can later on. I am not going to miss out!"

"The folly was just as pretty as you promised. Even if I did freeze my…nether parts…off getting there." The open-air folly, located close to the river, stood exposed to the sharp winds, but the visit was completely worth it for the opulent and fanciful lights and decorations, and the chance to see the castle's famous statue.

"The folly gave the solarium and conservatory a run for their money with decorations," Teag agreed. "That's where the desserts will be served, so we'll get another look. Whoever handled the decor did a fantastic job."

"You clean up well, did I ever mention that?" Anthony reached out to adjust Teag's bow tie and ran a proprietary hand down his arm.

"You're not too shabby yourself, Counselor," Teag said with a grin.

Anthony leaned closer. "I've wanted to peel you out of that tux since you put it on. That's going to be the highlight of the evening."

"Mm," Teag murmured. "I totally agree."

They finished their drinks and headed back to the dance floor. The slow song was one of Teag's favorites, and he leaned into his fiancé, enjoying the scent of his cologne and shampoo and something else that was uniquely Anthony. He loved the way they fit together and how close Anthony held him.

Anthony rested his cheek against Teag's head and tightened his grip on Teag's hand. "What are you thinking?"

Teag nestled closer. Anthony was just enough larger and more solid that Teag always felt sheltered in his arms. "Just that this has been the best vacation ever."

"We still have a few days left, plus Christmas—and no more ghosts," Anthony pointed out. The Earl had gone up to have a chat with Mabel and Lillian, and since then, no trace of ghostly activity had been reported. Just in case, Priscilla didn't plan to re-open the sitting rooms until after the holiday.

"I'm glad I could set Lillian free. It wasn't as hard to neutralize the soul-threads as I'd been afraid it might be," Teag replied, quietly enough no one else would hear. "And I'm sure she's happy that her son —or at least his descendant—looks likely to get his due."

It would take a while for the Earl and Hollister Granville to have the letters and birth certificate authenticated, but Priscilla had given Teag and Anthony an update, saying that Hollister was very willing to accept Theodore Mortimer as the long-lost son of Bertie and Lillian and make him the Granville heir.

"I'd think it certainly helped that Hollister had saved that box full of Bertie's correspondence from the war. Finding an unopened letter from Lillian telling Bertie she was expecting a baby kind of ties it up with a bow when you put it together with what we found," Anthony said.

They swayed to the music, and Teag swore the Champagne bubbles had gone to his head because the feelings in his heart made him giddy. He was here, in a beautiful castle, with the love of his life, dancing the night away. Teag couldn't imagine being any happier.

When they finally slipped away from the ball, not long before midnight, the crisp air felt good after the warmth of the ballroom, and the clear winter night had a velvet canopy of stars.

"The perfect end to a perfect evening," Teag sighed.

Anthony laughed. "Not yet. Or did you forget about the naked part?"

Teag gave him a wink. "Of course not. That's what makes it perfect!"

They hurried, hand-in-hand, across the open space to the wing where their room was located, happy for the relative warmth of the elevator. Inside, Teag pushed Anthony against the back of the car, fitting against him like on the dance floor, stealing a heated kiss.

"That's just to get you warm," Teag teased, stepping back with a grin.

"Oh, I'm plenty warm." Anthony reached down and discreetly

shifted himself in his tuxedo pants. "I've been 'warm' all night watching the way that tux fits your shoulders, and those pants cling to your ass. I'm glad you clean up, but now I'm ready to get you dirty."

"I like the sound of that."

Anthony led the way to their room, and Teag enjoyed the view. The modern cut of the tux pants accentuated Anthony's muscular ass and strong thighs, in the same way the jacket showed off his shoulders and V-shape to its best advantage. He was glad the room wasn't farther away, because walking was becoming difficult with a raging hard-on.

Anthony opened the door and yanked Teag inside, then closed and locked the door and pinned Teag against the wall. He cupped Teag's face, leaning in for a kiss that was hungry and hot. His tongue slipped across Teag's lips, and Teag opened to him with a breathy moan. Teag grabbed Anthony's jacket and pulled him even closer, then straddled Anthony's thigh and ground against him, making it clear just how ready he was.

"Too many clothes," Anthony gasped when he came up for air. His blue eyes were dark with lust, and his lips already kiss swollen from Teag's stubble.

"Then let me fix that," Teag replied, never losing eye contact. He reached forward and untied Anthony's bow tie, tossing it onto a nearby chair. He eased off the jacket, which quickly joined the tie, then rucked up Anthony's starched shirt, pulling it loose from his pants. Anthony's belt disappeared with a flourish, and Teag opened his fly, sinking to his knees, fully clothed.

"God, you're beautiful."

Teag didn't reply. He wrapped one hand around the base of Anthony's hard cock and licked the head, tasting the salty pre-come, then took him deep, bobbing and licking until he felt the quiver in Anthony's legs and heard him moan. Anthony's fingers combed through Teag's hair, tugging gently.

Teag pulled off with a wet *pop* and looked up through his lashes, well aware of what the sight did to Anthony. "I don't think we're naked enough yet."

"Not by half," Anthony agreed. He pulled Teag to his feet and made short work of his bow tie, then took his time unbuttoning the stiff shirt, letting his fingers slide down Teag's chest with every movement.

"Cuff links," Teag managed to remember when the front was unbuttoned. The onyx and silver set had been a Christmas gift from Anthony the previous year. Teag worked them off quickly, setting them in a bowl on a table by the door. Anthony was already stripping off his shirt, and his cuff links clinked into the bowl with Teag's.

They toed off their shoes and sent their socks flying. Anthony stepped out of his pants and boxer-briefs as Teag hurried to shuck off his pants and underwear. Finally, they were both naked, and Anthony pulled Teag to him, wrapping his arms around him and reaching down to grab his ass. The hair on Anthony's chest scraped against Teag's smooth skin, making Teag's breath hitch and his cock leak.

"What do you want?" Anthony's voice was a husky drawl that went right to Teag's dick.

Teag moved to rub their erections together. "Obvious, isn't it?"

Anthony nipped his way down Teag's neck. "I meant, *how* do you want it?"

They liked to switch, although Anthony probably bottomed a little more often. In the years they'd been together, there had been plenty of time to try new things, but sometimes, basic was better.

"Long and slow. You, in me. Please."

"Anything you want, baby."

Teag gave Anthony a kiss, lightly nipping his lower lip. He slipped out of Anthony's arms and arranged himself on the bed, laying back, legs bent at the knee and spread wide, giving his lover a good view. Teag reached down and gave himself a tug, fully aware that Anthony's gaze followed his every move.

"I want to eat you up." Anthony's growl made Teag shiver. Anthony crawled onto the bed, stalking toward him, the look in his eyes predatory. He grabbed the lube from the nightstand and tossed it onto the bed, then he leaned down to kiss Teag's mouth, slowly working his way down Teag's throat, to his collar bone, then lower.

Anthony licked and sucked first on one dark nipple and then the other until they pebbled, and he blew lightly over them, making Teag shiver.

"Yes. This. Want you so much," Teag groaned. He could feel the sticky trail of Anthony's leaking cock on his belly, teasing him as it bobbed with every movement.

Teag slid his hands into Anthony's blond hair. It wasn't as long as his own, but there was enough to get a good grip, and he loved to see his usually-impeccable lover looking disheveled and knowing it was because of him.

Anthony was as good as his word, leave each nipple with a kiss and a gentle tug of teeth, and then moving on, licking, kissing, and nipping his way down Teag's belly to the trail of dark hair that led to his groin.

"Please." Teag's voice hid none of his raw emotions. He loved their openness with each other, with no posturing, no pretending. He'd never let himself be vulnerable with a lover before Anthony, not like this, with no secrets between them.

"I'll take care of you, sweetheart. We're just getting started." Anthony moved to trace the tip of his tongue down the crease where leg met thigh, first on the right, then the left. He left Teag's rigid cock untouched and nosed lower, taking Teag's sac into his mouth, rolling it on his tongue. Teag arched up, and Anthony's broad hands took firm hold of his hips, lifting him so he could lick down the taint to the tight furl below.

"Jesus. Anthony, please."

Anthony drew a swipe across the sensitive skin with the flat of his tongue, then came back with the tip to tease at the rim. Teag shuddered and jerked at the sensation as Anthony lapped and poked with his tongue, alternating strokes until Teag could feel his balls draw up.

"I want to come with you in me," Teag begged. "Please."

Anthony reached for the lube and slicked up his fingers, then pressed one against Teag's pucker and pushed it slowly inside. "Taking my time, like you asked me to. Gonna make this good for you."

"I'm not going to last."

"Then I'll have to keep it up until you're ready to go again."

"Fuck."

"We'll get to that part." Anthony worked a second finger inside, turned them to hit Teag's sweet spot, and took Teag's cock in his mouth, down to the root, burying his nose in the tangle of dark hair at the base.

"God, Anthony!" Teag arched, throwing his head back and tightening his hands in Anthony's hair as his release tore through him. Anthony swallowed it all, and the movement of his throat and tongue against Teag's sensitive cock drew a whimper.

Anthony pulled back, then swirled his tongue around the head of Teag's cock and drew the tip through his slit, getting every drop. Teag's heart hammered, and a light sheen of sweat covered his body as he lay panting and sated.

Anthony leaned over him and bent down for a kiss. Teag could taste himself on Anthony's lips, and damn if that wasn't hot enough to make his spent cock twitch.

"Let me in," he murmured against Teag's lips.

"Christ, yes!"

Anthony slid his hands to get a good hold on Teag's hips and lifted him to get the angle just right, then pressed the head of his stiff cock against Teag's hole and slid inside, one slow inch at a time. Teag tried to push forward, but Anthony held him off, chuckling.

"You wanted slow."

"You're gonna kill me!"

"You'll die happy."

When Anthony was fully seated, he hesitated, letting Teag adjust to the fullness, and then began a long, slow slide all the way out and a fast rush back in.

"More," Teag begged.

"Gonna give you what you need. Hush." He kept up the slow, deep thrusts until Teag was panting and clutching at the sheets, and his dick had begun to fill again. Anthony shifted to make sure he hit Teag's spot, and Teag cried out, lost in the sensation. He reached between them to wrap his hand around Teag's stiffening cock and give it a few pulls, still keeping up the rhythm with his hips.

Just when Teag didn't think he could take the slow pleasuring any longer, Anthony slipped his hands behind Teag's shoulders and sat back on his heels, drawing Teag up to face him, straddling his lap.

Teag groaned as the position drove Anthony's cock deeper inside. Anthony leaned forward to kiss his throat and chest.

"Move for me, baby. Make it feel good for you, and I'm damn sure it'll feel fine for me."

Teag knew how much Anthony liked to watch him get lost in the sensation, fully admitting to his voyeuristic streak. Still buzzed from the intensity of his first orgasm, Teag draped his arms over Anthony's shoulders, getting his legs under him so he could lift enough to fuck himself on Anthony's cock.

"That's it. So damn sexy. So hot. I love to watch you," Anthony urged in a low, deep voice that went right to Teag's balls. "Ride me. Get yourself off. Take all of me." He slid his hand between them and gripped Teag's cock, making a channel for him to fuck.

Teag rolled his hips, satisfied when that drew a moan from Anthony. He rose and plunged down, and Anthony bucked up to meet him, again and again. Teag loved that he could put that look on Anthony's face, pupils blown, face flushed, hair sweaty and askew—in short, utterly fucked out.

One last undulation, which drove Anthony's cock against his spot and threatened to send Teag over the edge. Anthony was close, and he grabbed Teag's hips again, taking charge and chasing his release. He thrust hard once, twice, and then cried out Teag's name as he spent, filling Teag's channel as it tightened around him, and Teag came, shaking and gasping for air.

Teag fell onto him, resting his head on Anthony's shoulder. They were both a sticky mess. Teag could still pick up a hint of Anthony's cologne, mingled with the smell of sweat and come. He fluttered his tongue over the throbbing pulse in Anthony's neck and relished the shiver it sent through his lover's body.

"I love you," Anthony murmured with his face buried in Teag's hair. "Will you marry me?"

"Pretty sure you already asked, and I already said yes," Teag said, blowing in his ear.

"Good. 'Cuz I'm never letting you go."

"If we don't get a shower, we're going to stick like this, and you won't be able to."

Anthony responded with a smack to Teag's ass, just enough to sting. "Come on. Let's get cleaned up." Teag reluctantly crawled off of Anthony's lap and took his hand as they walked to the bathroom. The hot shower felt amazing, and Teag thought he might fall asleep standing up.

"Let me." Anthony worked up a lather between his palms and then slid his soapy hands all over Teag's body, washing away the remnants of their lovemaking. He slid a slick hand over Teag's cock and balls and then down his crack, managing to get a twitch of acknowledgment. Then he washed Teag's hair and turned him gently to rinse, making sure none of the soap got in his eyes.

"Your turn." Teag offered, though he could barely keep his eyes open.

"Next time," Anthony said. "Let me wash up quickly, and let's go to sleep. We can start again in the morning if you want."

Teag slipped his hand down Anthony's chest. "Oh, I want. I definitely want."

They toweled off and practically fell into bed. Teag retrieved the lube and put it back on the nightstand, then snuggled against Anthony, front to back. Teag wrapped an arm around Anthony, drawing him close.

"How about tomorrow we go to that tea shop in town and then try out the Earl's brewery for dinner?" Anthony murmured. "And in between, we can come back here and *relax*." His emphasis left no doubt as to the type of relaxation he had in mind.

"Mm. Sounds like a plan. And I saw some comfy couches in the main lobby, near that huge fireplace. Looked like the perfect place to curl up with a sexy man, a hot drink, and a good book."

"We can do that too. Anything you want. Always." Anthony sounded barely awake.

Teag leaned forward and kissed Anthony's bare shoulder. "I love you too."

~

"Shouldn't we be waiting with the luggage for our driver?" Anthony protested as Teag dragged him by the wrist toward the castle's chapel.

"Shh. We have time. And with all the holiday events, this is the first chance we've had to get inside."

Teag opened the door to the Caynham family chapel. It was still decorated for the holidays since today, the day after Christmas, was Boxing Day and part of the holiday festivities.

They had spent the last few days exploring the town, sprawled on the comfortable lobby couches in front of a roaring fire or attending the Christmas Eve service at St. Peter's in the village, and then the bell-ringing event at the castle. Christmas Day had been perfect, with just a dusting of snow. Teag and Anthony had agreed to leave their presents back home and traded small wrapped boxes with pictures of the gifts inside instead.

Anthony gave Teag a custom-designed, protective silver amulet with the help of some of their Charleston friends who were in the know about such things. Teag gave Anthony a vintage watch, knowing it was a kind Anthony really liked to collect. Of course, he had made sure it had no negative juju or bad magic attached.

"Up here." Teag tugged Anthony toward a stairway in the back of the chapel.

"Where are you taking me?"

"You'll see."

They emerged in a room with a dark wooden bench around the walls and heavy ropes that hung from holes in the ceiling, each ending in a loop.

"What the hell? Are those…nooses?" Anthony asked, wide-eyed.

"Of course not. They're bell ropes. This is the ringing room," Teag explained. "The bell ringers hang onto those loops, because the bells are very heavy, and when they start swinging back and forth, it can lift the ringers off their feet." He glanced up. "That's why there's a ceiling, so they don't get pulled up into the bell tower."

"I hope they have earplugs," Anthony replied. Teag agreed, remembering how loud the peal of the bells had been at a distance.

"That's not why we're here. Look!" Teag pointed upward, toward the stone molding around the top of the room, just below the ceiling. Carved gargoyles, ugly little faces that looked like gnomes or imps, looked down from every corner.

"I'm certain that's the original one," Teag said excitedly. "I brought you up here to kiss where he can see us. "If you kiss where the gargoyle can see, your true love you've found and will forever be."

Anthony reached out and drew Teag into his arms. "I like the sound of 'forever.'"

"So do I. I'm all in, you know that, don't you?"

Anthony nodded. "I know. And so am I. You're it for me."

Teag reached up to cup Anthony's face and drew them together in a long, satisfying kiss. When they finally stepped apart, they were both breathing hard.

"Did it work?" Anthony asked.

Teag looked up at the gargoyle, but the carving looked unchanged. "I'm going to believe it did," Teag said, giving the squat imp a wink. "That's my story, and I'm sticking to it."

Anthony pulled him close and kissed him again. "Just in case he wasn't looking the first time," he told Teag with a grin.

They headed downstairs and back to the front desk. Patrick and his golf cart had already brought down their luggage, and they had enjoyed a final full English breakfast at the castle restaurant earlier that morning. Now it was time to catch the cab to Heathrow and the flight back home. Teag knew he was going to miss Caynham Castle.

"We can reserve the honeymoon suite once we pick a wedding date, right?" he asked Anthony, suddenly needing to know that they weren't taking leave of this very special place forever.

"Absolutely," Anthony promised. "And if it isn't available exactly on the date we want, I'm all for planning a trip around when it is." He leaned down to whisper in Teag's ear. "I think you might just have an in with the Earl for un-haunting his castle."

To their surprise, Priscilla was waiting for them. "Sorry to see you go. I hope you enjoyed your stay." Both men hurried to assure her that they loved the castle, the ball, and the village.

"Just let me know when you decide on your honeymoon dates," she told them. "We'll take good care of you." Priscilla held out a small, wrapped box. "This is from the Earl, a token of his thanks for figuring out the haunting and doing right by Lillian."

"I'm just glad Mabel and Lillian's ghosts were willing to listen when he went to talk to them," Teag replied. The Earl had taken Teag's advice and gone up to the fifth floor to tell Mabel it was time to move on and assure Lillian that her son's descendants were acknowledged and restored to the Granville family.

"I think he was sort of hoping he'd catch a glimpse of the ghosts," Priscilla confided. "But I guess they didn't want to show themselves. Anyhow—there hasn't been a hint of anything strange happening in the sitting room since then. Although we did move Mabel's hair comb to another location, just to put more distance between it and any of Lillian's needlework."

"Probably a good idea," Teag replied.

Teag and Anthony worked together to open the box while Priscilla watched them with a smile. Inside was an embroidered handkerchief, and Teag recognized it immediately as one of Lillian's early pieces when she was happy and in love.

"Wow. This is really amazing," Teag said, completely surprised by the gift. Anthony nodded, slipping an arm around him. "Please let the Earl know how much this means to us." He silently vowed to write a thank-you note on the best stationery he could find once they returned to Charleston.

"He thought it was a fitting reminder of your visit," Priscilla said with an impish grin, and Teag wondered if she'd had something to do with that. "And you can tell him yourself, when you return to Caynham Castle."

They thanked Priscilla again, both for the gift and for all her help. Teag and Anthony headed out to the parking lot, where their cab was waiting with their luggage already loaded. To their delight, Henry was once again their driver.

"Did your holiday go well?" Henry asked.

Teag turned in his seat so he could see the castle as they drove away. "Very well," he assured their driver.

"It was full of surprises," Anthony added. "But they were all wonderful."

"I hope that means you'll be coming back," Henry replied. "A place like that can get under your skin, you know, if it calls to you."

"Oh, we'll be back, that's for sure," Teag told him. He met Anthony's gaze and took his hand, giving it a squeeze. "The sooner, the better."

HEAP OF TROUBLE

First appeared in the anthology;
Witches, Warriors, and Wise Women

HEAP OF TROUBLE

"MORE GLOWING ORBS." TEAG LOGAN SAT BACK FROM HIS LAPTOP computer. "I haven't seen this many reports of spirit lights outside of the Old Jail in...come to think of it, never." His dark hair, cut skater-boy long in front, hid his face as he stared at his screen.

"Can you find any connections?" I asked, leaning against the counter and sipping a cup of coffee.

Teag shook his head. "Aside from them all happening in Charleston and in the older sections of the city? No. At least, not yet," he amended. "I'm working on it."

I came back to the kitchen table, where my laptop was open, displaying a search screen. Teag had stopped by my house after work, and we'd ordered a pizza for dinner. "The appearances are getting more aggressive," I replied. "At least, according to what the tourists are posting on the rating sites. People are getting chased by bobbing lights, tour groups scattered by dive-bombing orbs, and more than one driver claims that 'glowing balls of lights' caused accidents. We've got to figure out what's going on before someone gets hurt."

I'm Cassidy Kincaide, owner of Trifles and Folly, an antiques and curios shop in historic, haunted Charleston, South Carolina. Teag Logan is my assistant store manager, best friend, and sometimes bodyguard. Taking responsibility for stopping ghostly harassment might seem strange for people who run an antiques store, but Trifles and Folly isn't your average shop. I'm a psychometric, meaning I can read the history or magic of objects by touching them. Teag has Weaver magic, so he can weave magic into fabric and data into information, making him a hell of a hacker. My business partner, Sorren, is a nearly six-hundred-year-old vampire who co-founded the store with my ancestor 350 years ago. We're part of the Alliance, a secret coalition of mortals and immortals who get cursed and haunted objects off the market and protect the world from supernatural threats. When we succeed, no one notices. When we fail, the destruction usually gets chalked up to a natural disaster.

Tonight, Teag and I were holed up at my house, trying to figure out what had Charleston's ghosts in an uproar. "Have we missed a practitioner moving into the area?" I asked.

Teag shrugged. "I would have thought that Rowan or Donnelly would notice a powerful new witch in town." He referenced two of our friends who frequently brought their talents in magic and necromancy to help with the threats we fought against—the forces of darkness and things that go bump in the night.

"Someone could have brought in a powerful relic," Teag said.

"Maybe. But again, if it were just someone mucking around with magic or powerful objects, Rowan and Donnelly would have also picked up on it."

"What I don't get is why it started all of a sudden." Teag reached for his half-empty glass of sweet tea. "Like someone flipped a switch."

"And it's not just at one location." I looked at the map where we had already marked all of the reported incidents we could find with red dots. Other than covering the Historic District and the antebellum houses South of Broad, the marks included museums, private homes, public parks, restaurants, shops, tourist attractions, members-only clubs, and—frequently enough to be dangerous—the middle of streets.

"Nothing about this looks like a normal haunting," Teag said, shaking his head. And that right there summed up my life. We could use the term "normal haunting," and it made perfect sense.

"We'd know if there'd been some sort of massacre," I said, only partly in jest.

Charleston is a beautiful city built on a bloody history. The Spanish, French, English, and Americans all fought over the land and its harbor, and before the Civil War, the port was the busiest slave market in the United States. Back in the day, sailors and soldiers brawled, pirates raised hell, cutpurses stalked the dark alleys, and spoiled young rich boys challenged each other to duels. Yellow fever epidemics claimed tens of thousands of lives. Add a jail that in its day housed everything from serial killers to prisoners of war, often under abysmal conditions, and it's easy to see why Charleston is one of the most haunted cities in North America. But nothing in the history—published or secret—suggested that there had ever been a mass killing in the area where the orbs were terrorizing people.

"Some of the newest reports talk about ghostly faces in windows or candles that move from window to window in empty buildings," Teag said. Restaurants, hotels, and shops may thrive on rating sites to drive customers to their businesses, but the comments are a gold mine for tracking paranormal activity. Tourists either think they've seen a clever show or get scared out of their wits, and either way, they can't wait to tell everyone on the internet.

"So whatever's causing it is getting stronger or affecting more spirits." I looked back at my computer, wishing it would just spit out the answer.

"What worries me are the reports of seeing people who look solid, and then they just vanish into thin air." Teag ran a hand through his dark hair. "Or the ones who report a 'feeling of dread' that made them turn around and leave. It takes a lot of juice for a ghost to manifest that strongly. They weren't doing it a month ago, so what changed?"

"I asked Kell what he and his team have run into." My boyfriend, Kell Winston, heads up SPOOK, Southern Paranormal Outlook and Outreach Klub. They're experienced ghost hunters and legit when it comes to documenting haunts. "He confirmed an uptick in activity that seemed to come out of nowhere."

"Looks like we need to go for a walk again," Teag said.

I glanced at the time. "It's already eight. Don't you want to spend the evening with Anthony?" I asked, mentioning Teag's long-time partner.

"Yes, I'd like to spend the evening with him, but his firm's been tied up with that big case that's been in the news, so he's been working all hours." Anthony is a lawyer at his family's law firm, a powerhouse in the Southeast.

"Kell's busy with a project, so he won't be stopping by either," I said in commiseration. Kell is a freelance video producer when he's not busy with SPOOK, and work is usually feast or famine.

"You know, the track record for big increases in spectral activity is pretty grim," Teag said. "It's never been for a good reason."

We had fended off several rather dire situations that all caught our attention because of ghosts behaving badly. It takes a lot of power to upset spirits over a large area, and often there's malicious intent behind it. So we knew to tread carefully.

"No time like the present," I said, standing and gathering what we would need to stay safe while we did some recon. I grabbed the back-pack I kept stocked and ready to go and double-checked the supplies. Plenty of salt, a large bottle of holy water, a coil of rope infused with colloidal silver, and several iron knives would provide a good baseline of protection against ghosts, along with the silver, agate, and onyx jewelry both Teag and I wore. Since we weren't sure what we might be going up against, we made sure to conceal both silver and steel knives in sheathes beneath our jackets. I had a few more tricks up my sleeve, and I knew Teag would be equally well prepared.

I patted my little Maltese, Baxter, and told him we'd be back soon. He gave me a skeptical glare, then trotted off to finish his kibble. Teag and I headed out to my car and drove down to the Historic District, with both of us keeping an eye out for anything strange.

"Shit!" I jammed on the brakes as a flash of light bobbed in front of the windshield, then braced myself in case anyone behind me couldn't stop. Fortunately, no crash came. "Did you see that orb?" I asked Teag breathlessly. He looked a little pale and wide-eyed himself.

"Yeah. When we get back, I'll look to see if there've been more accidents than usual in this area. I bet there have been, even if the drivers didn't tell the cops about the orbs."

I could just imagine trying to explain to a police officer that a ghostly light made me wreck my car. Even if a driver had reacted to a spooky glowing ball, most people wouldn't mention it.

We found a parking space—a minor miracle given how quickly the curb spots fill up in the residential areas—and went for a stroll. Normally, walking in Charleston's historic neighborhoods is one of my favorite things. There are so many beautiful homes and gorgeous gardens. Tonight, I felt on edge, waiting for an attack.

I could see the tension in the way Teag moved. He's an experienced mixed martial arts competitor, and it shows in the way he carries himself. Teag is tall and lanky, but although he looks lean, I've been in enough fights beside him to know it's all whipcord strong muscle. While I can hold my own in a fight, I'm more likely to rely on magic than clever footwork.

The hot, humid evening felt sultry even for Charleston. I pushed a strand of strawberry blonde hair behind my ear, sure that with my pale coloring, I was already flushed from the temperature. We had walked a block before I realized what seemed strange.

"There should be more people out walking."

Teag nodded. "Yeah. Usually, you're dodging people out with their dogs or just stretching their legs after dinner." Charleston is a walking town, both for tourists and for those of us lucky enough to live here. So the lack of pedestrians seemed odd, maybe even ominous.

I'd driven us to the edge of the area where the sightings were concentrated. We wouldn't be able to cover all the territory tonight, but we could certainly walk toward the center of the disturbances and see what happened.

"I'm pretty sure we're being watched," Teag said, dropping his voice.

My intuition told me the same thing, although I didn't see anyone on the sidewalk or peering out through the windows. The night felt too quiet, the air too still.

As we walked, the temperature grew colder, although in Charleston's sub-tropical climate, it was far too early in the year for the weather to cool off. The back of my neck prickled, and the hair on my arms stood up as if the air was charged with static electricity. I let my wand fall from inside my sleeve into my hand, the handle of an old wooden spoon from which my touch magic could pull deep emotional resonance to harness power. Teag shifted, and I saw him palm an iron knife in one hand and a silver blade in the other.

"There!" I hissed, pointing toward the shadows where a live oak tree hung over a wrought iron fence. The gray form of a woman in an old-fashioned dress was clearly visible, looking solid enough that someone might not have taken her to be a ghost at first glance if they weren't expecting haunts. Off to the left, a blue-white spirit orb materialized out of nowhere, bobbing at chest level near the door to a home on the other side of the street. I felt gooseflesh rise, although moments before, I'd been sweating.

"Look!" Teag pointed toward a historic home with darkened windows. I could make out a ghostly image framed by one of the casements, something that should have vanished in the blink of an eye but didn't.

"Over there."

Teag followed my nod toward a home on the opposite side of the street where a candle flame inexplicably hovered inside a dark upstairs window.

The sense of being watched grew even stronger, an oppressive weight that carried with it a sense of dread. I'm not a medium, and I have no special ability to speak with the dead. Yet my touch magic can often pick up on the emotional resonance a spirit leaves behind on objects, giving me a second-hand insight into the temper of the ghosts.

"I don't think they mean to hurt anyone, not directly," I said slowly as I tried to make sense of the impressions my gift gave me. "They're disoriented, frightened, and angry, but not with us. It's like they're frustrated, and that's making them lash out the only way they can."

"How do we find out who's calling them?" Teag asked as smaller orbs danced around us like fireflies. If the residents in the nearby homes saw the dancing lights, they chose not to show themselves.

Maybe they were hiding behind drawn curtains and closed shutters, hoping that whatever roused the spirits of the dead would soon send them to their final rest.

"I think we need to pull Alicia into this." Alicia Peters, another ally of ours, is a gifted medium. "I can sense the ghosts' mood, but I'm not getting images that are clear enough to get an idea of what's going on."

"It would help to know what got them riled up all of a sudden," Teag said. "Something changed, and until we figure out what, we're all in danger."

Teag and I stood back to back on the sidewalk as the orbs dove and rose, and a fog of spirits gathered all around us. I didn't want to antagonize the ghosts since they hadn't yet done anything truly hostile. They had shown themselves, perhaps their only way to communicate.

"We aren't here to hurt you," I said in a low, steady voice like I was talking to a spooked horse. "We might be able to help. Please don't harm anyone. We'll figure this out."

For an instant, the lights grew brighter, the wind picked up, and the ghosts looked nearly solid. In the next breath, they vanished, leaving us alone on a balmy summer evening.

"I think they might have heard you," Teag said. "Now let's hope we can keep our side of the bargain."

The next morning, Alicia called me before I had a chance to call her.

"Cassidy, something weird is up with the ghosts. I keep hearing 'let us go,' and then I get images of some really weird glowing bottles and an old-fashioned Victrola record player. Does that mean anything to you?"

I was out walking Baxter around the little garden in back of my house, and my stomach growled because I hadn't eaten breakfast yet. "No. At least, not yet. Was there any other context? Do you get anything out of it?"

"Except for a feeling of being trapped and an overwhelming sense of anger, no," Alicia replied. "Except—"

"Yeah?"

"I had a few other impressions, but nothing to back them up. I don't think that the ghosts I sensed are the ones causing the freaky haunted stuff people are talking about. The regular ghosts feel... disturbed. Upset. They might be warning us. I also think that the ghosts that went with the bottle vision had been dead for a long while. And they weren't nice spirits. We need to be careful. There may be a reason someone felt they had to keep these ghosts locked up, and setting them free might not be a good idea."

"Unfortunately, if they're causing problems, they're not as locked up as they used to be," I said. "So whatever's kept them in check this long is failing, and we need to find out where they are and how to keep them from hurting anyone."

"I'll keep listening for what I hear from any of the spirits who feel like communicating," Alicia assured me. "And I'll let you know what I find out. Yell if you need me."

I went back inside, finished my breakfast and coffee, and got Baxter settled for the day. Before I had even pulled out into traffic, my phone rang again. This time it was Valerie, a local tour guide who is also a good friend.

"Hey, Cassidy, what's going on with the ghosts? My customers like to be mildly spooked, not scared out of their wits." Valerie was one of the best ghost-tour guides in the city. The normal ghosts didn't make her bat an eye, so this was more confirmation that what we had going on was something that was anything but "normal," even for Charleston.

"I don't know yet, but I'm planning to find out. What have you seen?"

"Zippy orbs all over the place, ghosts sightings where we don't usually see any, and so many cold spots, I started expecting snow."

I told her what Teag and I saw on our walk and what Alicia had reported. "I'll let you know if I hear what's causing it," I said. "And if anything changes, call me."

Teag and our assistant, Maggie, were already at the shop when I got there. Teag greeted me with an official-looking envelope in hand.

"I figured you'd want to see this. No idea what it is, but it looks important."

I frowned as I read the return address, a local law firm. When I tore the envelope open and read the contents, I had to re-read the letter to make sure I hadn't imagined it.

"What?" Teag asked.

"Trouble?" Maggie echoed.

I looked up at them, utterly confused. "Someone I've never heard of just willed their house and all the contents to Trifles and Folly."

While Maggie and I handled customers in the front of the store, Teag went to the break room to research our mysterious benefactor. I also texted Sorren, my vampire boss, because this was the kind of thing he'd want to know about. After that, we were busy enough with customers that I didn't come up for air until the pizza delivery guy arrived, and I realized Teag had called in an order. Maggie and I took turns going back to the kitchen to take a break and eat.

"Find anything?" I asked as I took a bite of pizza.

"Irene Sacripant, the person whose name is on the deed and the will, lived in the house for thirty years." Teag leaned back in his chair. "The problem is, there's no record at all of her existing before then. No birth or marriage certificates, no hits on the genealogy websites, nothing."

Teag is a super hacker, so if he can't find someone, there's nothing to find. I glanced toward the door to the front to make sure no one was close enough to hear.

"Think she's one of 'our' kind?" Meaning witch, vampire, shifter, or some other supernatural creature.

"Yeah, I think it's likely. And thirty years ago, it was easier to disappear and invent a new identity than it is today. I've got a call in to Rowan and Donnelly and a few others to see if they know her. But there has to be a reason she left the house to Trifles and Folly."

"That's a first. I've never had anyone bring the estate sale to us before."

"I'm really curious," Teag said. "When can we get access to the house?"

"According to the letter, I need to go in and sign some papers. Maybe I can see if I can do that this afternoon, but the letter sounded like it was all wrapped up with a bow." I tossed my paper plate in the trash. "We need to be smart about this. I have a feeling Irene didn't pick us out of all the antique shops in Charleston because she wanted to sell off the family silver."

"You think she's got something supernatural in there?"

"Don't you?"

Teag pushed his hair behind one ear. "Well, yeah. I just wanted to see if you thought the same thing." He stretched his arms and cracked his knuckles. "If you're okay with running the front a while longer, I'd like to keep digging. I've got a feeling that Irene was hiding her real identity, maybe hiding from someone. The house is up on the Ashley River, kinda remote."

"Maggie and I can cover the store," I told him. "It could be that Irene didn't have any heirs and knew we'd take good care of her belongings. But my gut tells me that she picked us because of our 'special skills.' I think we just inherited a heap of trouble."

Teag researched for a while, then came up front to cover for me while I went to see the lawyer, and a late afternoon surge of customers kept us from any meaningful conversation until after we closed. Maggie—who knows the scoop about what we really do—made us promise to call her if we needed anything and headed home.

"Did everything go okay?" Teag asked as we locked up.

I nodded. "It's all signed, sealed, and official. Although, there was one thing that was a little off. The lawyer said that Irene's will was adamant that I be given a detailed floor plan of the house."

"Sounds to me like there's something she wanted you to find."

"Sorren said he'll stop by my place after dark. Is Anthony still working late?"

"Yeah. He's been dragging in around ten, so as long as I'm home before then, he'll never notice. At least, not until the case is over."

"I've got stuff in the fridge for dinner, and we can see if we can dig out any of Irene's secrets while we wait for Sorren," I said. Teag agreed and followed me in his car back to my place. Baxter yipped and danced when we came in, then chased me into the kitchen for his dinner after he got his snuggles. Teag and I chatted about the customers and local gossip while we made supper and ate, waiting to get back to the Irene problem until after the dishes were done.

"She wasn't much of a joiner," Teag said. "Which is unusual for Charleston. Especially thirty years ago. But I think I've turned up a photo."

I leaned over his shoulder. The grainy picture was from a newspaper article, and from Irene's expression, she wasn't pleased to be captured on film. "If that's really Irene, at least the photograph rules out her being one of the kinds of creatures who won't show up on camera."

"Well, that's something," Teag said grudgingly. "I'm going to try to run it through facial recognition software. The resolution isn't great, and we'd be trying to match to a photo from before 'Irene' showed up here, which assumes those pictures would have been digitized, but I'll give it a go."

I spread the floor plan out on the table, and both Teag and I bent closer for a better look. "It's a big house, but I don't see anything unusual in the drawings," I said, trying to figure out what had been so important to Irene. "And given where it's located, there's definitely no basement."

"No hidden rooms, secret passageways—at least nothing marked."

"Maybe that's the point," I replied, straightening. "Maybe she wanted us to find where the house has been altered."

Teag raised an eyebrow. "Clever. The plans alone don't give anything away, but she's counting on us going through the house."

I nodded. "The more I think about it, the more I doubt what Irene wanted us to deal with is going to be out in the open. Or at least, I don't think the big problem will be just sitting in plain view."

As soon as the sun set, I heard a knock on the door. I'd been expecting Sorren, but the way Baxter immediately sat with a goofy grin on his face confirmed it. Apparently, vampire glamor works on dogs, and my dog was utterly bespelled.

"Hello, Cassidy. I take it Teag is here too?" Sorren asked as he stepped into the hallway. Sorren looks like he's in his late twenties, although he's centuries older. With his blond hair in a trendy cut, gray eyes the color of a storm at sea, and dressed in a concert T-shirt and artfully ripped jeans, he looked like a grad student. Back in the day, he was the best jewel thief in Antwerp—before he was turned. Now he spends his time hunting down dangerous magical objects, moving among the many stores like ours he's established all over the world.

"In here!" Teag called from the kitchen.

Sorren followed me back to where Teag was still at work on his computer. Sorren listened intently as I filled him in, both on the odd inheritance and everything we had learned about Irene Sacripant.

"I don't recognize that name," Sorren said, frowning. I can't imagine sifting through six centuries of memories when I sometimes can't recall the name of someone I met last week. "But the photograph seems familiar, though I don't think from Charleston. Interesting."

"We don't know where she was before she moved here—or who she was," Teag said. "The facial identification software is still looking, but it's a slog when it comes to old photos."

"I'd like to send Rowan and Alicia over to the house to get a feel for it—from the outside," I said. "Nice to know what might be waiting for us." I'd run into magical traps and aggressive ghosts too many times to walk in blind.

"I'll go with you when you enter the house," Sorren said, not making it a choice. "I agree that whoever this Irene was, she sought out Trifles and Folly because she expected there to be supernatural problems with her legacy. It would have been nice if she had given us a clue."

It's not uncommon for us to run into haunted objects and cursed heirlooms. A few real estate agents know to call me if they run into spooky problems with houses that come on the market after an owner's death. And more than once, we've had to deal with collectors who acquired problem objects that had some seriously bad mojo attached to them. I shuddered to think what kind of trouble might be waiting for us in that old house.

"Do you know if Donnelly has noticed any issues with the local ghosts?" I asked. "Because I'm hearing things from Alicia and Valerie."

"Archibald has been away handling an issue," Sorren replied. "He's only just returned. I'll check in with him and meet you at the Sacripant house."

Teag and I drove out to the property we'd inherited. "Rowan said she didn't pick up any magical traps around the outside of the house. She couldn't guarantee that the inside was safe, but she said that the power she sensed didn't feel like a threat, even though it was very strong," I said.

"And Alicia picked up on ghosts, around the house and in it, and she was worried about them being dangerous," Teag added. "So... maybe magic, definitely angry spooks. Totally our kind of thing."

I had Rowan on speed dial in case something went wrong, but she would have offered to go with us if she was worried about magic. In Alicia's case, if there were dangerous ghosts around, I wanted the medium as far away as possible because her gift could make her vulnerable. Teag and I came prepared, although I hoped that tonight's trip wouldn't turn into a fight.

We pulled up to the house at twilight. The Sacripant place was probably at least a hundred years old, a two-story white clapboard house with deep porches on both levels. It must have been grand once, but it had fallen into disrepair, with peeling paint, an overgrown lawn, and missing shingles.

Large live oak trees formed a corridor along the driveway, old enough that their gnarled limbs dipped to the ground and rose back up again, and their upper branches hung heavy with Spanish moss. This close to the river at dusk, fireflies rose like fairy lights from the grass, and bullfrogs croaked. I could smell the salt marsh and beneath that, the wet-leaf smell of mold and decay.

"You're sure we haven't been pranked?" Teag wondered aloud. "Because that looks like something right out of a horror movie."

"Perfect place to meet a vampire then, isn't it?" I replied. Despite my attempt at humor, I agreed the place looked creepy, exactly like Hollywood's idea of a haunted house.

"It's a big place for her to live all alone," Teag said as we got out of the car. Neither of us wanted to go closer until Sorren was with us. Teag glanced from side to side. "And there aren't any neighbors close."

"The obituary said she was in her eighties." I wondered about the woman who had lived here. None of Teag's picture-matching programs had worked, but I figured that was due to how bad Irene's single photo had been. That didn't give us much to work from. Maybe we'd find a better one in the house, or with luck, the answers to Irene's mysterious past.

"I trust you came prepared." Sorren came up from behind us soundlessly, and I managed to merely flinch instead of jump. Moving quietly is one of the perks of his Dark Gift, along with enhanced strength, healing, heightened senses, and of course, near immortality.

"Of course," I replied as Teag nodded, and I hefted my backpack full of salt, holy water, and silver, in addition to the weapons and protective charms we wore. Sorren didn't look heavily armed, but his abilities were lethal on their own, and I saw two iron blades in sheaths on his belt.

I hadn't needed my wand when we had confronted the ghosts downtown, but I felt better feeling its comforting weight in my hand as we walked toward the house. I jangled the old dog collar I wore wrapped around my left wrist, and the ghost of Bo, my old golden retriever, appeared next to me, my spirit animal and protector. Silver bracelets and an agate necklace helped to ward off supernatural threats.

Teag carried an iron blade in his right hand and had a second blade ready in a sheath on his hip. A hand-loomed belt woven with protective magic wrapped around his waist, and I knew that the knots dangling from it stored extra power, like batteries for him to draw on. He wore amulets of his own, a hamsa and an *agimat*, and an earring of black onyx. We both had loose salt and iron shavings in our pockets. We knew the drill. It was showtime.

"I've called Archibald. He'll meet us here as soon as he can,"

Sorren told us. It says something about my life that I take comfort in having a powerful necromancer along for the ride.

The night felt darker as we reached the steps to the porch. Although the place was badly in need of maintenance and minor repairs, for its age, it didn't look at risk for collapsing on our heads. That was a plus. I hesitated on the steps, listening to my magic. When there's a strong resonance, I can pick up on it through the soles of my shoes, and the impressions already beginning to creep into my consciousness were disquieting.

"Cassidy?" Teag asked, hanging back.

I nodded to let him know I was okay. "There's bad stuff in there. Nothing we didn't already know." As Teag opened the door and invited Sorren inside—it's a vampire thing—I concentrated on the input from my psychometry, hoping for something more helpful than just "trouble."

"There's a lot of negative psychic energy," I said, trying to put feelings into words. "It's seeped into the house itself, so whatever's causing it isn't new. But I think that losing Irene made it worse." I shook myself out of concentrating so hard, so I could pay attention to my surroundings.

"Can it contaminate us?" Sorren asked.

I shook my head. "It's not a sickness. More of a deep rot."

"How did we not notice this place with that kind of energy?" Teag asked.

"If Cassidy's right, it hasn't always been…transmitting…like this," Sorren said. "Perhaps Irene was the key to keeping the energy in check, and now that she's gone, whatever was bound is working its way free."

That thought chilled me, but I felt certain Sorren was correct. I stood in the old house's entranceway and looked around. Teag had turned on the lights, but they barely made a dent in the gloom. Either Irene had used very weak lightbulbs, or the house had a darkness that light itself couldn't dispel.

Long ago, the house had been grand. Now, the inside looked as worn and shabby as the exterior. A layer of dust lay over everything, and heavy cobwebs in the corners and on the chandeliers made me suspect they predated Irene's death. I had feared that she might be a hoarder—one more reason to leave everything to the store to sort through—but as we moved slowly from room to room, I realized that given her age, the house was surprisingly uncluttered.

"No mirrors," Teag noted as we moved from the parlor to the dining room. "That's odd."

A surge of vertigo hit me so hard I stumbled. Teag swayed on his feet as well. Only Sorren seemed unaffected. "Did you feel that?" I asked, a little breathless.

"Yeah, but I don't know where it came from," Teag said. "It felt... weird...like getting a head rush on a roller coaster."

"I felt nothing," Sorren said, frowning. "Interesting."

I walked into the library. High bookshelves filled with leather-bound tomes and a worn, comfortable chair beneath a floor lamp gave me an idea of how Irene spent her evenings. On the far side of the room sat a leather couch that looked comfortable and well-used. A writing desk with tidy stationery and pens sat against one wall.

Tucked into the corner on a mahogany stand was a very fancy, old-fashioned Victrola, albeit one that appeared to be custom-made. I hadn't noticed any portraits or pictures in the more public rooms, but here I spotted several framed black and white photographs and yellowed newspaper clippings.

I looked at the shelves, noting that each one held a variety of silver-plated knick-knacks nestled among the books. Fine white dust covered everything, even thicker on the shelves than elsewhere. I saw chunks of onyx and agate, minerals known for their protective properties, used as bookends.

Bundles of dried plants tied with ribbon were nestled on shelves, on the mantle, and on the windowsills. The room held the faint odor of sage, and I saw an abalone shell filled with ashes that I guessed was used for frequent smudging. Sigils that I recognized as wardings against evil had been drawn on the windows with soap.

"Irene must have been afraid something was going to get in," I said, noting the abundance of precautions.

"But we haven't seen any markings or protective objects in the other rooms," Teag pointed out. "Maybe she made the library her fortress."

My attention went back to the photographs. "I think I've got something," I called out. I leaned over for a better look, hesitant to touch anything and activate my magic unless I had to. More than once, a strong reading has knocked me flat on my ass, and we still didn't know what we were up against.

The woman in the photograph was a much younger version of the matron in the picture Teag found online. Irene sat primly in a long black gown at a table surrounded by six other people, all of whom were holding hands. The newspaper clipping's headline read, *Chicago Welcomes Famed Medium.*

"She was a medium," I reported as Teag and Sorren joined me. Teag lifted the framed article to read it in better light.

"That's Irene," he said, "but this says her name is Catherine Jenkins." He set the frame back on the bookshelf and reached for his phone, doing a quick search.

"That's interesting…Catherine Jenkins shows up quite a bit. She was a medium who appeared to have real talent, and she traveled all over, often hosted by the rich and famous. Even some of the infamous —a few reputed mobsters were big fans of her Vegas appearances. Oh…"

"What?" I prompted.

"According to this article, she vanished without a trace thirty years ago. She wasn't married and didn't have children. Some of the theories said that the Mob put out a hit on her for knowing too much, and others said she might have committed suicide."

But we knew better. Catherine—Irene—had pulled a disappearing act worthy of Houdini and lived out the rest of her life in seclusion. "Why would a medium choose to live in a haunted house?" I asked. I didn't have any special talent to see ghosts, but my psychometry picked up on plenty of ghostly energy. Even if I didn't see them, I knew they were all around us, some stronger than others, watching and waiting. And as Alicia warned, I had the distinct impression that not all the ghosts were friendly.

Sorren had moved to the desk and withdrew a folder, wiping off a layer of dust. The vibrant red of the cardstock seemed out of place among the faded memorabilia of Irene's exile. "I have the feeling Irene wanted us to find this," he said. "Since it's quite a bit newer than anything else here." He flipped open the cover, revealing more articles and a slim journal. Sorren set the journal aside and leafed quickly through the clippings.

"It would appear that Catherine Jenkins attracted a questionable clientele in the years just before her vanishing act," Sorren said. "Mobsters, politicians of ill repute, and very rich men with sordid reputations apparently wanted her to plumb the secrets of the afterlife for them. She was investigated for her connections, especially when some of her clients disappeared. None of the charges stuck, but that's not very forgiving company."

I looked at the photograph of Catherine at the séance table. "Do you think she was coerced into doing readings for crooks and wanted out?"

"Maybe," Teag said, moving to stand beside Sorren. He picked up the journal and turned the pages. I looked over his shoulder, but at this distance, I couldn't make out the cursive script in faded ink.

"If I'm reading this right, I think Catherine took notes on the sessions she had with her more infamous clients," Teag said. "Just from the ones I've read, it looks like they wanted her to contact other dead criminals to find out where they hid their stash or get information that they could use for their own benefit."

"Let me see what I can pick up," I said. Teag pulled out the desk chair, and I sat since I didn't want to find myself suddenly on the floor from a particularly strong reading. Teag and Sorren stayed close, protecting me since I was vulnerable in a trance.

I laid my hand flat on the journal, and immediately, I saw the room through Irene's eyes. Everything looked fresher, newer. Opened curtains let the sunshine in, and the dust and cobwebs were gone. The library looked comfortable and lived-in, but I could feel the uneasiness of the woman who had made it her hermitage.

Irene was afraid. I picked up on the fear clearly, though the reason was less clear. She felt guilt over the way she had been forced to use her gift, and she loathed the men who had coerced her into being a part of their crimes. And yet, I had the oddest feeling she wasn't afraid of being found or that she feared arrest. No, her fear ran deeper than that. She didn't fear death. Irene Sacripant feared the dead.

I came back to myself with a gasp, and Teag gently took the journal from me. He pulled a sports drink from his backpack and pressed it into my hand. I gulped it down, needing the sugar and wanting a moment to compose myself and order my thoughts. Bo's ghost, my spectral protector, bumped against me, reminding me of his presence and protection.

"She was afraid of the spirits doing…something," I told them. "But I'm not sure whose ghost she was worried about or what she thought they'd do. Maybe she thought that the ghosts the mobsters made her contact were angry at being disturbed."

"I'd like to read that journal more closely," Teag said. "There were some odd phrases about 'preserving souls' and 'cheating the scales' that don't make a lot of sense."

Sorren shook his head. "I think we're missing something here. The story doesn't add up. Let's have a look upstairs, and then see if we can find anywhere that the blueprints you talked about don't match the current rooms."

The second floor held bedrooms and bathrooms. All but one appeared to have been long disused. Some of the rooms weren't even furnished, and the bedchamber that had been Irene's was oddly devoid of personal possessions beyond clothing.

"It looks like she spent most of her time downstairs," I said. "In the library, I'd guess."

"That room does appear to have been her focus," Sorren replied, in a tone that made me wonder what he was thinking.

Another wave of vertigo almost dropped me to my knees. For a few seconds, everything around me looked blurry, and I had the oddest sense that it was reality itself and not my eyesight that was affected. This time, I swore that the house shook beneath my feet like we were having a private earthquake. Beside me, Bo's ghost growled and bared his teeth.

"Did you—" I asked Teag, who nodded with a sick expression as if he wanted to puke. My stomach was fine, but my head had started pounding. Once again, Sorren missed out on the excitement, and I figured it was no accident that the undead guy wasn't being affected.

"Let's finish what we came to do so we can leave," Sorren said, and I knew his response was from worry for our safety.

Teag unfurled the blueprints, and Sorren paced off each room upstairs, comparing the dimensions to those on the drawing. All of them matched exactly. Sorren found the access to the unfinished attic, but a quick examination revealed nothing hidden or even stored among the rafters.

He repeated the process downstairs, starting in the parlor. The front room, dining room, and kitchen all matched the blueprints. But in the library, Sorren's measurements didn't add up. He paced the walls again, and once more, the numbers were off.

"We're missing a couple of feet along that wall," Teag said, pointing to the back of the library.

We all walked over to take a closer look. I squatted to look at the floor. "I think there's a salt line here."

Teag and Sorren ran their hands along the shelves and the supports, pressing their fingers into crevices, checking to see if any decorative carvings might activate a hidden latch.

I hung back, readying salt and holy water in case we were attacked. "It's gotten colder in here," I noted. "And it feels like we're being watched."

"I think...yes. There," Sorren murmured, and we heard the snick of a hidden latch. Part of the bookshelves swung forward like a door.

Inside the secret compartment were more shelves, but instead of books, these held rows of glass jars and odd wax cylinders. The jars were each topped with a strange collection of copper wires which both fastened the stopper securely and extended down into the containers themselves. More disturbing were the odd flashes of green and blue that flickered intermittently like a slow heartbeat.

"What the hell?" Teag said.

I moved closer, still keeping weapons at the ready. Inside the hidden room, a thick layer of salt lay on the floor, which Sorren and Teag were careful not to disturb. Suddenly, the abundance of silver, onyx, and agate decorations on the shelves made a lot more sense.

"Those are Leyden jars," Sorren said. "Bastardized, to be sure, but the spiritualists of the eighteen-hundreds thought the soul to be mostly electrical, and the jars could store electricity somewhat like a battery."

"Those rolls. They're Edison cylinders," I said in a hushed voice. "That Victrola wasn't created as a music player; it was originally meant to record the voices of the dead."

"So you're saying that Irene recorded the confessions of the dead and trapped their souls?" Teag asked, aghast.

It all clicked into place. Catherine's hatred of her criminal patrons, their unexplained deaths, and her dramatic disappearance, as well as Irene's voluntary exile and the numerous warnings. Hell, it even gave me a good idea about what was up with all the ghosts downtown, if they were afraid Catherine's bottled criminals might stage a jailbreak and descend on the city. All the orbs and manifestations were good spirits trying to warn us in the only way they knew how.

"She got her revenge," I replied. "Whether or not she killed the men who forced her to work for them, I think she stole their souls. Maybe she wanted to punish them or thought they might cause harm from beyond the grave. But that's why she went into hiding. She was their prison guard."

"And once she died, without her magic to help keep the souls contained, they've started to 'leak,'" Teag added, taking a step back reflexively.

"I'm not entirely certain about her motives, but I think we have discovered why Irene left the house—and its contents—to the shop," Sorren said in agreement.

"No mirrors," I said, suddenly making the connections. "Stories say ghosts can hide in reflective surfaces or travel between mirrors. That's why there aren't any."

"So we've basically got a toxic waste dump of damned souls," Teag said. "And we get to be the supernatural hazmat crew."

I felt a chill against the back of my neck, but not from the ghosts in the hidden chamber. The air behind me stirred, and I had the overwhelming sense that someone stood behind me. "Where did Irene die?"

"No idea," Teag replied. "Why?"

"I'm betting she passed away right here," I said. "And I don't think she ever left."

The door to the hallway slammed behind us, and the wooden slatted shutters closed by themselves as the lights flickered wildly. The temperature plummeted as if we were in a walk-in freezer, so cold I could see my breath. The house shuddered, hard enough this time to rattle the objects on the bookshelves and make the chandelier swing.

Vertigo hit me hard, making me reel, and I caught myself with a hand on the edge of the writing table. The room...wavered. It shimmered like heat rising off asphalt, its dimensions skewing until it looked as if it were trying to fold in on itself.

Teag had gone pale, looking as if his knees might buckle. Sorren drew both his iron blades, alert for an attack.

"Look!" As my vision cleared, I could see what had caught his attention. A red pinprick of light glowed almost too brightly to look at, right in the center of the wall behind the Leyden soul jars.

Irene's ghost took shape, standing between us and the shelves, and I could not tell whether her intent was to protect us from the trapped souls or to keep the glowing jars safe from our interference. Bo lowered his head and growled, baring his teeth.

Gooseflesh rose on my arms. The air felt charged with twisted energy; perhaps the tainted magic used to imprison the souls or force their unwilling confessions. Irene did not attack, but she did nothing to lessen the assault to our senses. Behind her, the red light grew from a speck to a larger dot.

"You willed the house to us." I thought perhaps Irene didn't recognize us and thought that we were come to steal or harm her unholy collection. "We're here because you summoned us."

Teag moved behind me and grabbed the journal. He paged to the end and then looked up at Irene's determined ghost. "It's not just the evil spirits you trapped, is it?" he asked. "There's something else here we need to figure out before we try to deal with the jars, and you want us to figure it out." Irene nodded.

The house shuddered again, sending a fine white cascade down the bookshelves. *Salt,* I thought. *Not all dust. She lined the shelves with salt. But did she mean to keep the souls inside, or keep something else out?*

Another tremor, this one hard enough to rattle the glass dangles on the chandelier. Behind Irene's ghost, the *pop-pop-pop* of shattering bottles sounded like gunfire as three of the Leyden jars exploded, freeing the spirits housed inside. I didn't need to be a medium to feel the shift in the room and know that the ghosts who had freed themselves were malevolent and hungry.

Three glowing red orbs from the broken jars dove at us as Bo snarled and jumped to intercept. I didn't know what would happen if those orbs hit us, but I doubted it would be good. Teag deflected one with a slash of an iron blade, which made it veer and dimmed its light for a second.

Sorren's quick reflexes kept him out of the way of the dive-bombing balls of energy, and he struck again and again with his iron knives, forcing the spirit lights to draw back or lose some of their glow. I couldn't spare much attention for Irene, but I wasn't sure whether her ghost was trying to block the orbs or us. The orbs blinked in and out as we tried to hold off the attack, and Bo continued to lunge and snap at them.

My martial arts experience wasn't as extensive as Teag's, and I didn't have Sorren's speed. I leveled my athame at those that came my way and pulled on its strong emotional resonance, sending a blast of cold power that swept the balls of light out of its path and rattled the bookshelf behind them. I angled my shot so I didn't break any more of the bottles, and after I hit the orbs a few times, they drew back, giving me space.

The orbs obviously disliked contact with iron as much as they reacted to the force of my magic, and whether being struck hurt them or drained energy, it didn't matter so long as it kept them clear of us. Our defense hadn't gotten rid of them, but they were considerably dimmer than when we started, and I wondered if they could recharge or if we might win if we could outlast them.

"Cassidy, the light!" Teag said, and I saw that the fiery red light had grown to at least the size of a quarter. "What is that?"

"Nothing good," Sorren replied.

The room shuddered, but this time it felt different. Even Sorren jolted with the tremor, and in the next heartbeat, the door to the hallway crashed open, splintering with the force that broke through the power holding it shut.

Archibald Donnelly framed in the doorway, and behind him, Father Anne Burgett. Donnelly was a big man with a shock of white hair and the kind of bushy sideburns and mustache that went out of style with the Civil War. Put a pith helmet on him, and he'd look like one of those English colonels from the height of the British Empire. Father Anne, a highly unorthodox Episcopalian priest, couldn't be overlooked with her short, spiked black hair, clerical collar over a black T-shirt, and steel-toed Doc Marten boots.

"Watch out!" I shouted to warn them. "Irene trapped souls, and they're getting loose!"

Donnelly gestured and spoke a word of power. A golden glow sprang up between where we stood and the wall of jars, keeping the orbs—for now—on the other side along with the slowly growing red light.

"She's not their jailer. She was helping them cheat death," Donnelly replied, anger sparking in his eyes. His gaze fell slightly behind me, where a cloud of mist coalesced into the figure of the woman in the photographs. "Aren't you, Catherine?"

He didn't wait for the spirit to answer. "The criminals were afraid of having to pay the consequences for their actions. They feared eternal judgment, going to hell. And so they bribed Catherine to 'bank' their souls, putting off the inevitable. She *was* their guardian—and their protector."

"So you can just send them on, right?" I asked. I'd seen Donnelly go up against some scary-powerful entities. A few bottled ghosts seemed tame in comparison.

"Unfortunately, these aren't just any souls. They've grown stronger and even more vengeful by being contained," Donnelly replied, glowering at Irene's ghost. "For a medium to use the gift to do such a thing is forbidden in every tradition. The reckoning they've cheated has grown impatient."

"You mean hell's coming to get them?" Teag asked, horror making his voice sharp.

"That's exactly what I mean. Without Irene's magic to hold the wardings in place, the containment spells are weakened. They've been degrading since her death. And when they fail, a hell-mouth is going to open to lay claim to the souls that belong to it."

Holy shit. We were on the brink of a supernatural Chernobyl.

"So she willed the house to us to clean up her mess?" I asked, feeling a lot less charitable toward Catherine/Irene's ghost.

"That's my guess," Sorren said. "It wouldn't be the first time we've ended up picking up the pieces after someone else made an unholy bargain."

"We've got one chance," Father Anne said, stepping up to stand beside Donnelly. "When Archibald drops the barrier, I'm going to chant Last Rites while he keeps the hell-mouth from opening completely. All of you need to keep the spirits off us—they're going to fight as hard as they can to keep from being destroyed. But be careful —you don't want to get sucked into the maw yourselves."

No indeed.

"Ready?" Donnelly rumbled. "Now!"

The scrim of glowing power vanished. The orbs had regained their energy, and they launched a furious attack, ignoring us to dive at Donnelly and Father Anne, recognizing that they had the magic to send them on.

The glowing red hell-mouth had grown larger, at least the size of a baseball, and blindingly bright. How much larger did it have to get, I wondered before it could pull us all into its infernal blaze?

I didn't want to find out, so I gathered my magic and used the cold force of power that blasted from my wand to sweep the orbs away from the priest and the necromancer. Bo dodged and lunged, planting himself squarely in front of Father Anne and Donnelly. I was on their right, with Teag on their left. Sorren moved fast enough to blur wherever he was needed.

The room shuddered once more, knocking the silver statues from the shelves and sending picture frames crashing to the floor. The crystal chandelier overhead vibrated hard enough that its pendants clattered like wind chimes. The rest of the Leyden bottles exploded, sending shards of glass flying as the terrified souls imprisoned inside fled the judgment seeking them.

The air smelled of sulfur and ash but was still freezing cold. Maybe my imagination got the best of me, but I could swear I heard distant screams coming from the direction of that infernal, blood-red light. Father Anne shouted the Last Rites defiantly while Donnelly wove magic to recapture the dozens of soul-orbs that careened through the room. Irene's ghost had grown stronger, gray but looking almost solid, and I realized that she had gained enough energy from our magic to call to her power.

"Push when I say," I heard an unfamiliar woman's voice whisper in my ear as a chill ran down my spine.

The ghost orbs dimmed, whether because of necromancy or the Last Rites, and Irene raised her arms, standing only a few feet from the hell-mouth. She threw back her head and shouted something I could not hear, but the ghosts took heed, gathering around her.

Now.

I mustered my courage, reached for my magic, and *pushed* with all my power, sending a blast from my wand with all the energy I could summon.

The blast shoved Irene and the orbs that clustered all around her directly at the glowing hell-mouth. Donnelly shouted and threw up his glistening barrier as soon as my burst ended, as Father Anne called out the final words of the Last Rites at the top of her voice. Bo huddled next to me, his spirit safe on this side of the energy curtain.

The hell-mouth widened, and I had to look away because it was like gazing into the sun. But I glimpsed Irene, silhouetted against the crimson fire, shoving the orbs into the inferno, and then, with a scream, being drawn inside herself. The maw flared, and I threw up my arm to shield my eyes. Wails and shrieks filled the air, deafeningly loud.

Then, suddenly, all went dark and quiet.

I lowered my arm and opened my eyes. The far wall held no glowing bottles, wax cylinders, or pulsing orbs. Everything was gone, and in its place was a blackened scorch mark where the hell-mouth had been. Irene and the souls she had helped to cheat fate were gone.

"Was that really…Hell?" Teag asked in a voice just above a whisper.

Donnelly shrugged. "It was what they expected, feared, and thought they deserved. It is real enough for them." His unruly white hair looked like it had stood on end, and the outlay of power showed in his eyes.

"Expectations are powerful things," Father Anne replied, her voice raw from shouting. "But where they've gone, they won't trouble anyone, ever again."

"What would have happened if you and Irene hadn't forced the souls through?" I asked, not sure I wanted to know the answer.

"The hell-mouth would have taken them, and everything else it could pull into itself," Donnelly answered. "And without my magic and Father Anne's litany, there's no saying whether it would have sealed back shut."

"Thank you all," Sorren said. Donnelly inclined his head in acknowledgment, while Father Anne just shrugged as if it were all in a day's work. Sorren looked to Teag and me. "I believe we've removed the danger that caused Irene to will us the house. But tomorrow, I'll meet you here at dusk, and we'll check everything over again to make sure. If there are any other tainted objects, we'll handle them, and the rest can be appraised."

I looked around the room. Other than the disarray near the book-shelves and the burn on the wall, you'd never know we faced down a soul-fueled nuclear meltdown. No one outside the house would ever know how close the world had come to catastrophe. But we knew, and even if that knowledge didn't change the world, it changed us.

We saw things we couldn't un-see, knew things we couldn't forget, and would dream of what could never be expunged. It wasn't the magic that kept us sane and functioning, it was each other, and the small network of allies and loved ones who believed in us. In what we did, anything could happen, and every day could be the last, so I'd learned to find comfort in the small things that grounded me.

"I'd really like dinner and a drink," I said. "Anyone care to join me?"

ACKNOWLEDGMENTS

Thank you to everyone who believed in the stories and in me. Thanks to my wonderful husband Larry N. Martin, and to my editors, beta & ARC teams, cover artists, and especially my readers and the Shadow Alliance. My virtual assistants and marketing partners also have my eternal gratitude. Thanks to the anthology organizers/editors who pulled the original collections together, and thanks to Leslie for the sensitivity read. Because you read, I write.

ABOUT THE AUTHOR

Gail Z. Martin writes urban fantasy, epic fantasy, and steampunk for Solaris Books, Orbit Books, Falstaff Books, SOL Publishing, and Darkwind Press. Urban fantasy series include *Deadly Curiosities* and the *Night Vigil* (Sons of Darkness). Epic fantasy series include *Darkhurst, The Chronicles Of The Necromancer, The Fallen Kings Cycle, The Ascendant Kingdoms Saga, and The Assassins of Landria*. Under her urban fantasy MM paranormal romance pen name of Morgan Brice, she has five series (*Witchbane, Badlands, Kings of the Mountain, Fox Hollow,* and *Treasure Trail*) with more books and series to come.

Co-authored with Larry N. Martin are *Iron and Blood*, the first novel in the Jake Desmet Adventures series and the *Storm and Fury* collection; and the *Spells, Salt, & Steel*: New Templars series (Mark Wojcik, monster hunter), as well as *Wasteland Marshals* and *Cauldron: The Joe Mack Adventures*.

Gail's work has appeared in more than forty US/UK anthologies. Newest anthologies include: *The Weird Wild West, Gaslight and Grimm, Baker Street Irregulars, Across the Universe, Release the Virgins, Witches, Warriors,& Wise Women, The Four ???? Of the Apocalypse, Nevermore, Three Time Travelers, Christmas at Caynham Castle, Trick or Treat at Caynham Castle, and Ring in the New at Caynham Castle*.

Join the Shadow Alliance street team so you never miss a new release! Get the scoop first + giveaways + fun stuff! Also where Gail and Larry get their beta readers and Launch Team! http://www.facebook.com/groups/MartinShadowAlliance

Join the newsletter and get free excerpts at http://eepurl.com/dd5XLj Gail is also a con-runner for ConTinual, the online, ongoing multi-genre convention that never ends. www.Facebook.com/Groups/ConTinual

Support Indie Authors

When you support independent authors, you help influence what kind of books you'll see more of and what types of stories will be available because the authors themselves decide which books to write, not a big publishing conglomerate. Independent authors are local creators, supporting their families with the books they produce. Thank you for supporting independent authors and small press fiction!

ALSO BY GAIL Z. MARTIN

Darkhurst

Scourge

Vengeance

Reckoning

Ascendant Kingdoms

Ice Forged

Reign of Ash

War of Shadows

Shadow and Flame

Convicts and Exiles: Collection

Chronicles of the Necromancer / Fallen Kings Cycle

The Shadowed Path: Jonmarc Vahanian Collection

The Dark Road: Jonmarc Vahanian Collection

The Summoner

The Blood King

Dark Haven

Dark Lady's Chosen

The Sworn

The Dread

Watch for the new Legacy of the Necromancer series, which picks up 17 years after the end of The Dread.

Deadly Curiosities

Deadly Curiosities

Vendetta

Tangled Web

Inheritance

Legacy

Trifles and Folly: Collection

Trifles and Folly 2: Collection

Trifles and Folly 3: Collection

Assassins of Landria

Assassin's Honor

Sellsword's Oath

Fugitive's Vow

Exile's Quest

Night Vigil

Sons of Darkness

C.H.A.R.O.N.

Other books by Gail Z. Martin and Larry N. Martin

Jake Desmet Adventures

Iron & Blood

Storm & Fury: Collection

Spells, Salt, & Steel: New Templars

Spells, Salt, & Steel: Season One

Night Moves

Monster Mash

Creature Feature

Wasteland Marshals

Wasteland Marshals Volume One

Joe Mack: Shadow Council Archives

Cauldron

Black Sun

Chicagoland